BY
LIGHTALONE

BY LIGHT ALONE

ADAM ROBERTS

GOLLANCZ

LONDON

Copyright © Adam Roberts 2011

The right of Adam Roberts to be identified as the author
of this work has been asserted by him in accordance with the
Copyright, Designs and Patents Act 1988.

First published in Great Britain in 2011 by Gollancz
An imprint of the Orion Publishing Group
Orion House, 5 Upper St Martin's Lane,
London WC2H 9EA
An Hachette UK Company

A CIP catalogue record for this book
is available from the British Library

ISBN 978 0 575 08364 6 (Cased)
ISBN 978 0 575 08365 3 (Trade Paperback)

1 3 5 7 9 10 8 6 4 2

Typeset at the Spartan Press Ltd,
Lymington, Hants

Printed and bound in the UK by CPI Mackays,
Chatham, Kent

The Orion Publishing Group's policy is to use papers that
are natural, renewable and recyclable products and
made from wood grown in sustainable forests. The logging
and manufacturing processes are expected to conform to
the environmental regulations of the country of origin.

www.adamroberts.com
www.orionbooks.co.uk

'The masses are lovable; they are kind, decent, tolerant, practical and not stupid. The tragedy is that there are too many of them, and that they are aimless, having outgrown the service for which they were encouraged to multiply. One day these huge crowds will have to seize power because there will be nothing else for them to do, and yet they neither demand power nor are ready to make use of it: they will only learn to be bored in a new way.'

Palinurus, The Unquiet Grave

ONE

THE ICE-CREAM MOUNTAIN

1

Some of them wore their skis like clown-shoes. They tripped and tumbled and then they struggled, with comic laboriousness, to get back on their feet. But *some* wore their skis like the fins of fish or the wings of birds in the white medium, and made fizzing, sinusoidal passage down the mountainside. They were the effortless ones. There are, after all, two sorts of people in the world. 'It's like the moon,' somebody said, and George, eavesdropping (fiddling with the buckles on his boot), knew what they meant. Not the actual moon, of course, which is tarmac-coloured and desolate. But the ideal moon, that shining platinum shield in the sky. That *white* place.

He had a vantage. A spaghetti of ski-trails leading down the mountain. These were braids of hair: they were Rapunzel paths. George looked around and around, amazed.

Strands of his soul were escaping out of his mouth.

The landscape was a purified ideal of white, and the sky put down a kind of swallowing brightness. The trees lost their trunks in amongst all the radiance, becoming floating piles of dark green. Behind them the hotel, and its many balconies, looked like a chest with all its drawers pulled out. Plus a white witch's hat of snow on its sloping roof. That tune kept going through George's mind.

Superfast, superfast, superfast.

You know the one. He tried to get himself into a good launch position, rotating his skis with myriad little crunching steps, and orienting himself with respect to the downwardness of the mountain. Whilst he laboured, Marie swooped by with insulting ease, stopping dead with a shimmy and a little flume of snow.

'I think I've blistered my heel,' he said.

'You *do* look bothered,' she replied.

So he tried to move on, but the tips of his skies crossed and he tumbled. A draught of scalding snow went in under his collar and down his neck. Writhed, he writhed, like an up-ended beetle.

'You handle your skis like chopsticks,' crowed Marie, neatly reorienting her body downhill with one hop. 'Like big fat *chopsticks.*' And then she was off, leaning perilously far forward – or so it seemed to her husband – but somehow *not* falling, instead vanishing with a blissfully fluid rapidity. Her legs were tucked into a double bend, like a corporal's stripes. She went up a prominence, stood for a moment on empty air and then shot down out of view.

George Denoone levered himself upright. He leant on his poles for a moment. Sweating inside his suit. There were little beads and crusts of ice on his eyelashes, like sleep. His breath produced a spectral foam in the clear air. Away on the right others were being dragged up-piste by their various drones – mostly resort machines, although a few swankier individuals had their own personal floaters. Everywhere else myriad people in their harlequin-coloured suits swerved and twisted their way down towards the big double-haven McDonald's M in the white valley. Shocking pinks and olives; bright purples and lime greens; any colour contrast so long as it jarred, and all laid against the amazing extent and brightness of the white ground.

'Come on George,' he told himself, gasping. 'Come along and *down* we go.'

In the sky above, high in the zenith, a blimp was trundling. Seeding the high air with whatever it was they used to get the snow to settle in the night. 'Off we go,' George said again. He didn't move.

Somebody swooped and crunched to a halt beside him, with that little spray of white powder from the flank of her ski. 'Hulloa George,' she boomed. It was Ysabella, the Canadian woman. She was the one married to what's-his-name, tall man with the pudding-y face. The one with the jug ears and the green eyes. Green as old dollar bills, Marie said.

'Why, it's Y,' said George, glad of the distraction. That was his little joke, that 'why' and then her name; on account of her spelling it with 'Y' like that. They had only recently met, but already they were at the stage of shared little jokes.

'We were watching you from up there,' she said, skewering the air near George's shoulder with her pole. 'Peter said you should positively join the *circus*.' She laughed like a car alarm.

Peter. That's his name.

'It's this design of skis,' George said. 'This antique design. They're hard to *line up*. When Marie and I stayed at Saint Moritz last month, the skis were Zephir brand, that—'

But Ys was away, with an expert swank of her muscular rear-end. She plunged ferociously in a straight line, straight down. Her mauve, blob-shaped shadow rushed after her across the snow, like a faithful dog eager to catch her, but doomed to disappointment.

George shuffled himself further closer towards position.

Snow was adhering to his suit all down the left side; powdery but clumping like overcooked rice. 'Now or never,' he told himself.

Trying to remember all the things needful, he pushed off. Lean forward. Tuck your arms *in*. Legs, so. The skis won't straighten themselves, like modern boards do: you need to keep them parallel by effort of mighty will, and by the clenching of sore leg muscles. He moved slowly, with an audible crunching sound. And then – abruptly, it seemed – he was *flying* down-slope, hurtling with insane and dangerous abandon. He howled. He really howled out loud. He couldn't stop himself. As he strained to put his body through those ineffectual resistances against gravity's hostile intent, the possibility of all the harm that could befall him gushed into his mind: colliding with some obstacle; disappearing into a cartwheel of limbs and a breaking wave of exploding snow; snapping an armbone, a legbone – or a spine, or a neck. Swerving uncontrollably towards the jagged-looking trees on the left-hand side; col-liding with a fat coniferous trunk with enough vehemence to stave-in his ribs, or punch out his chin. Or else simply to die of fright as he hurtled – faster and faster, he was going. When the railways first came, people thought that travelling faster than a horse's canter would flat kill the passengers. Lungs can't suck in the air from the whoosh of the slipstream; the heart can't cope with the adrenalin overload as the world warp-drives around you. The trees seemed to lean under the pressure of his enormous velocity. The frozen air lashed his face. His uncovered mouth, his goggleless eyes. *Warp* drive.

Superfast, superfast, superfast.

And then the fastest portion was behind him. The slope gentled. The padded barrier, the left-hand arch of the terminal

∩∩, loomed up. The snow whistled contentedly under his blades. He leant to the left and tucked his knees in, more by instinct than anything. A satisfying skirt of ice-dust rose glitteringly from his ski-edge. And then it was all over, and all the terror had been magically alchemized into exhilaration. Marie was waiting for him, her skis over her shoulders like a soldier's rifle. Oh he was *hyper*, like a little kid, and stomping towards her. 'Did you see me?' he boomed. 'Did you see me *fly?*'

2

They took lunch with Ysabella and Peter, and also with a couple from England called the Horner-Kings. She was Emma Horner-King, and she was as quietly hesitant as her name implied; but *he* was called, of all things, Ergaste. They made him say it, and spell it, and explain that it wasn't an Anglo-Saxon king, or some fairy tale giant (very good, not heard that one before), that, he said, 'it had some obscure literary significance to my parents'. Ergaste took all the ribbing in good spirit, and the mood of the sixsome waxed jolly. Good to hit it off with people; spontaneity its own reward. They all drank Chianti, and it was as cold and bright and elevating as the mountain itself. They ate blue grapes, and little spears of compressed caviar dripped in a creamed-chilli sauce. Peter liked to roll a grape around the inside of his mouth, push it with his tongue such that his upholstered cheeks bulged alarmingly.

There was a good deal of laughter.

They dined on a balcony, shielded from the full glare of the glitter-freeze by an awning. There was something indulgently *parental* about the peak of the mountain itself, watching over them from its distance.

'Tomorrow,' said Marie, leaning back in her chair, 'I shall try the ice-cream slopes.'

'Mobbed,' said Ergaste, with his ridiculously fruity accent. 'Always. Not worth it.'

'Oh,' his wife added, 'except to say you've *done* it, you know. Ski it, and have a nibble too.'

'Not good *skiing* snow,' said Ergaste, drawing a thumbnail through his close-cropped red hair. 'Is my point. And nor is the mix very *tasty*. They have to mix it, jewsee, to make it skiable at all. One of those horrible *compromise* plays.'

'You'll excuse my husband's Shrek-y mood,' said Emma.

'The *problem* I have with the ice-cream slopes,' said Peter, loudly, 'is the machinery.'

'At the top, you mean?'

'*Loud!*' said Peter, loud himself. 'I mean, let's appreciate they've to generate the stuff somehow. I can appreciate ice cream's not going to *fall from the clouds by itself*. But still.'

'Agree,' boomed Ergaste. 'Surely, this dayn*age*, they could make the stuff less *noisily*.'

A waitress came to clear their table. She bent to gather the plates, almost as if presenting her centre-parting to George's scrutiny. Ink-black hair, a strip of pale brown scalp.

'I really *flew* down the slopes today,' George announced to the whole group, apropos of nothing. '*Positively* flew.'

'I don't believe they're allowed to wear their hair like that.' Ysabella said. As she leant forward to retrieve her wine glass a Y-shaped vein blued and swelled slightly beneath the plaster-white skin of her brow. 'I mean, when they're *working*? Aren't there any rules against it? It's disgusting, really.'

'Fucking leafheads,' said Ergaste without violence.

'Sunny day,' said George, absently.

'But I mean – when they're working? I'd say they might tie it decently away when they come to—' She searched for the right word, before alighting, in a way that seemed almost to surprise her, on: 'us.'

'Oh, *plenty* of sunlight in these latitudes,' said Ergaste, sarcastically.

'Oh I'm sure they're *fed*,' said Marie. 'Oh I don't doubt they take actual food as part of their wages. Don't you think?'

7

'We could ask, I suppose,' said George, without the least intention of doing anything of the sort. He found himself wondering why, when he could clearly see his own shades reflected in Emma's shades, he couldn't see *her* shades reflected in the reflection of *his* shades in her shades. It seemed to him that he ought to be able to do that.

'It's a *little* indecent,' Ysabelle said, vaguely.

'Not that you're *prejudiced*,' boomed Peter.

'I'm sure they're fed,' said Marie again, as if this point were important to her.

'I'm sure food is the height and length and breadth *of* their wages,' said Ergaste. 'That and a shared dorm room in which to sleep. I'm sure no actual *money* changes hands.' He seemed to find this richly amusing.

'I know it's a shocking thing to say,' Ysabella went on. 'But I find it wasteful for them to eat *actual* food. It's not as if they *need* to. Perhaps they may crave the . . .' But here her conversational powers really did fail her, and she fell silent.

'Women,' said Ergaste. 'The men are too lazy to do it. The women work, to build up bodyfat. *Greedy* little leafheads.' He looked about. 'Not greedy for food, ysee,' he clarified. 'Greedy for *babbies*.'

But nobody was really very interested in this. George drained his drink. Wherever he placed his wine glass on the polished table it fitted neatly onto the base of its reflected self. There was something satisfying about that. It said something about the innate harmony of the cosmos. The day's skiing had left a distant ache in his thighs. Intensely satisfying. Real work, real hard physical work – and actual danger too. And it *had* been dangerous, for all that MediDrones floated nannyishly over every bulge.

The conversation had moved on to food production. Ergaste was expatiating, in his clipped style, on the role of the gentleman farmer these days. His main point was, staples were right out. Right out. No margin in them any longer. Pretty much all food production geared to the luxury market now; which had had the strange consequence that staples had *become* luxury foods – for faddists, or religious cultists, or people who had mad reasons for needing it. Wheatgrain weight-for-weight was caviar-expensive. He knew people groused about this, but it was an inevitability. Get with the programme, or get out of the game altogether. No margins in staples any longer. Not now that the world had the hair.

'It's a blessing,' said Emma.

'Certainly it's the way the world is, now. For good or ill,' said Ergaste.

The early afternoon sun was splendorous. Away at the far end of the balcony, two waitresses stood with their backs to the sun. One swivelled her face towards the other and whispered something into her ear. The other, holding her tray like a chivalric shield before her torso, clapped a hand to cover her mouth: shocked, or perhaps amused, by what she had heard. George wondered what the gossip was. Had they been looking in his direction? Probably not. Plenty of other busy tables on the balcony.

At this point Marie decided abruptly that she *must see* Ezra. She had her Fwn out and had called up to his room before George could intervene. 'It's his naptime, darling,' he said. But it was too late. 'I haven't seen him since yesterday,' she told him – or rather, she told Peter, pushing George's shoulder with her free hand. 'A mother has emotional needs and instincts. Only a monster would stifle the free expression of my maternal instincts.'

'Since there are instincts,' said Emma, cheerfully, 'then why aren't there *out*stincts?'

They all chuckled at this, because it actually was rather

amusing, and clever, at least coming from somebody as mousy as Emma. Ergaste laughed loudest, boomingly even, and Emma slapped his lapel with the back of her hand. But it was all terribly jolly, it really was.

The sunlight was as sparkly as a *white firework*, and gemstones of brilliance twinkled across the entire snowfall.

And here was Arsinée, carrying a *very* grumpy-looking Ezra across the balcony towards their table. 'Here's my little package of loveliness,' cried Marie. Arsinée presented the baby to its mother rather after the manner of a wine-waiter offering an unusually expensive bottle to a diner, and for a minute or so Marie cooed and poked a finger into the dimples of the thing's little face. Miraculously Ezra did not bawl. Which is to say: he *did* screw up his little eyes against the brightness of the day, and he did ready his hands for an imaginary munchkin boxing match, but no sound accompanied the opening and closing of his mouth. Marie redirected her attention back to Ergaste, and Arsinée hovered for a moment, uncertain whether she was required to stay or to go.

'I want to see mine too,' Emma declared, pulling a Fwn from her sleeve.

'Oh for fucking out loud,' groaned Ergaste.

'Language!' his wife chirruped.

'We *had* her for *breakfast*.'

Emma pulled out her Fwn and briskly instructed somebody called *Shirusho* to bring Charlie down to the balcony restaurant, darling, right *now*?

'We had her *all through* breakfast,' said Ergaste

'Is Leah your one and only?' Ysabelle asked George.

'Don't listen to my ogre husband,' said Emma. 'It wasn't even five minutes at breakfast.'

'She kicked my chococross right off the plate,' boomed Ergaste.

'It was an accident and it was *delightful* actually, really, it was spontaneous physical comedy.'

George turned his face from Emma and Ergaste's little squabble. 'Two,' he replied, meeting Ysabelle's eye. 'Ezra, there. We've a daughter as well.'

'Two!' repeated Ys, as if this number were one of those mind-stunning statistics you hear on documentaries about the vastness of interstellar space.

'Physical comedy *bollocks*,' announced Ergaste, in a slightly too-loud voice.

'Language!'

'A man's entitled to breakfast!'

'Who's for some after-lunch skiing?' Marie put in, brightly, her attempt to break this unseemly display of discord. Arsinée, looking from person to person for further cues, wrapped Ezra up and slipped away off the balcony.

'I *simply* don't see it's too much to ask,' said Ergaste, sitting back in his chair as a bearish lump, 'that a fellow be allowed to break his *fast* in peace.'

'I'll have another go skiing,' said Peter, loudly. 'That Chianti has set me up nicely.' His sticky-out-ears had changed colour, chameleon-like, to match the pink of the awning.

'Not me,' said Ysabella. 'That Chianti has set *me* up for a little nap.' She trailed her gaze languidly around the little group, and, just for a moment, her eye met George's. There was a little electro-something, a spark. 'A little *lie down*,' she repeated.

'Why, Ysabella,' he said, testing the instinct. 'Surely you haven't overindulged, winily speaking?'

Ysballe looked him straight in the eye. 'It was too tempting,' she said, with a slight, voluptuous slur in her words.

'Alcohol,' he agreed.

George had met her for the first time only days earlier. But this – this was the inward vertigo, that exciting and alarming sense of hurtling into something new. Everything was all about exciting possibilities. 'What about you, darling?' he said to Marie.

'I've not come all this way to *lie down*,' she replied, sharply. 'I can lie down at home. *I'm* giving the slopes another bash.'

'You could try the ice-cream slope,' he prompted – because, after all, that was a whole hill away, more distant from the hotel, which would give him that much more time alone. To cover the obviousness of this gambit, he added: 'It's the big feature, after all. People come from all over the world to, and so on, and so forth.'

'Maybe tomorrow. Regular piste will suit me for now. Will you?'

'No, I've done my death-dicing today,' he announced. 'I'll go and see what's happening in the games room. Or maybe just catch up on the news.'

News was a dirty word, and the group flapped their hands disapprovingly. Life was too short for *news*. But news was one of George's little eccentricities, and he was perfectly aware of the mild distinctiveness it gave his otherwise blandly unmemorable character. And now Marie was on her feet, so Peter scrabbled to his legs too, with just too much eagerness. And Ysabella bade them all good afternoon and wandered over towards the lifts. So George got up and sauntered away, carefully picking a trajectory across the balcony that made it look like he wasn't simply following Ys. That was all part of the game, of course. And it was a splendid game. The Horner-Kings' carer was emerging into the light carrying a wriggling bundle of tiny Horner-King – superfluously now, of course; for the point in having her brought down in the first place was to show off to the others.

3

He caught up with Ysabella by the lift. They ascended to-gether. Not a word was spoken. This feature of the tryst was something that George found almost more thrilling than the prospect of actual sex. It was the thought that it was possible to arrange these things without ever having to spell out the awkward specifics in words. That an understanding could be arrived at spontaneously, as it were; like leaves coming voice-lessly to the branches of trees, or like whisky-coloured sunlight laying itself down intimately upon the white snow.

He kissed her in the corridor outside her room, and then they tumbled through the door like teenagers. Down they went, onto the crisply made bed. He grasped at Ysabelle's splendidly ample flesh, dug his fingers in to the contours of thigh and buttock. She pushed him away for a moment, dialled down the glass balcony-doors' glass, and then was straight back at him, pulling off his clothes with an efficient series of yanks and hoiks. In moments he was naked, and the fact that she was still fully clothed was – well, alarming, really. Perhaps there *was* simply something subliminally intimidating about her muscular confidence. Not that this did anything to diminish the visible solidity of his desire. He wouldn't be the first man to be drawn precisely by the desire to be alarmed.

'Well,' she said. 'Shall we?'

He went to her, fitted his arms around her broad torso and began kissing her neck, and kissing her face, rubbing his fingers over her bristly scalp. She undid the catch and shook herself free of her trousers. Her knickers fell to silky pieces with a twitch of her thumb. George's heart was hammering. And in the moment the foreplay was a process of postponing the inevitable, terrifying exhilaration. It was getting the top half of her clothing off, running his mouth and hands over her dark skin, the small, low breasts, the nipples like black olives. It was all that. But it couldn't be postponed for ever – and *down we go*.

Superfast, superfast, superfast.

He pumped away, despite the tiredness of his thigh muscles, for the longest time, all the while fumbling as best he could at Ysabelle's cleft with his right hand. But it seemed to take her a long time to get where she was going. She lifted her long, mannish legs and brought the soles of her two feet together somewhere behind George's head. This neither thrilled him, nor put him off. On and on he plugged, to a rising sound-effect of squelching that made him think, randomly, of jelly-fish. The undersea kingdom. Bubbles, and bubbles, and bub-bles. Then – finally! – a mist of opal crept over the oily surface of her eyes, and she was gone.

Afterwards he got up for a piss, and loitered a little in the enormous bathroom. With a fine feeling of superiority, he poked a finger in amongst all of Peter's myriad grooming products on the mirror-shelf. Coming back through he helped himself to a glass of wine from the minibar, and lolled on the bed, watching the screen.

For quarter of an hour Ysabelle lay on her side. She snored with the noise of a fly trapped behind a windowpane. But then she awoke, with a shudder, and stretched out all her limbs enormously, and got off the bed, and took herself off to the shower.

On the news, a stare-eyed US official, his widow's-peak

shaven into a cruciform shape, was being interviewed by a Japanese chat anchor. 'Repetitive raiding heavily leverages our core capability to break states,' the US wallah said. The screen ran his words along the bottom: *repetitive raiding heavily leverages capability to break states.*

'But if Triunion government retains its oppositional—' the interviewer tried to say.

'Triunion needs to understand the investment the US Government has *already* made in military intervention.' He rolled the phrase 'US Government' into a single word: five syllables compressed to three. 'The *financial* investment,' he added, as if there were any other kind.

George scratched an itch on his kneecap with a circular motion. To the right, the darkened glass of the balcony door had turned the bright sky to a shadowy gentian colour. We are the immortal offspring of the heaven and the earth. The interviewer said, 'Everything remains just as it was.' The screen cut to a montage from Triunion. It was the usual thing: crowds surging like fans at a music concert, up and down dingy-looking low-rise streets. All with their crazy trailing hair. Another shot of a courtyard, or a town square, or something, filled with angry-looking longhairs. There was a shot of a military Quadpod pulling its metal legs up and hoofing them down again with almost comical fastidiousness, stepping over the tin roofs, striding up and down the dirt alleys. The guns under its belly looked like ski-poles. People surged, washed up and down the alleyways. The guns spat and sputtered. Here was a shot of a crowd tugging down street-lamps and rushing at the Pods like pedestrian Sir Lancelots. Here was another shot: the fat tiling of a wall of army riot-shields.

Ysabelle came out of the shower with a towel draped over

her shoulders, but otherwise superbly, enormously, statuesquely naked. 'What's this?'

'Riots in Triunion.'

'I don't want the *specifics*,' she said, bending all the way down to the minibar to pluck herself a drink. Holding one of the miniature little wine bottles she looked for all the world like a giant, a *vrai* giant, something splendidly and erotically Brobdingnagian. 'What I mean: you're watching the *news*?'

'I like the news,' he said.

She sat herself back on the bed, beside him. 'I thought we sorted out Triunion last year,' she said, shortly, perhaps so as to show George that she wasn't entirely a news philistine.

But, for some reason, George wasn't in the mood to be placated. Something vaguely unsatisfying about the encounter was niggling at him. The sex, or the wine, or the anticlimax, or *something*. 'I don't believe the Republic of Canada had anything to do *with* it,' he said.

'By *we* I mean,' she drawled, looking through the half-darkened glass at the flank of the mountain. But instead of finishing the sentiment she took a swig of yellow-white wine.

They were silent for a while. The interview continued onscreen for a minute or more: the US guy explaining the scaled punitive tariff that would be applied to Triunion if hostilities continued. A barchart sprang up in front of him to illustrate his words; this many native deaths for this much resistance, this larger number if the unrest continued into next week, this much larger number if—

'I thought *you Americans* sorted out Triunion last year,' Ysabelle said, shortly.

'You're right,' said George, changing the channel. 'It's boring.'

They watched some sport; then a musical stab-match

16

between two hard-pop superstars. Then they watched a book for a few minutes.

'Did you say you had two children?' Ysabelle asked.

'Ezra you saw,' said George. 'There's also Leah.'

'And how old is Leah?'

'Ten.'

They sat in silence and watched a whole book. Belatedly, George grasped that Ysabelle had been prompting him. So he asked: 'You?'

Her posture on the bed relaxed marginally. 'What do you *think*?' she asked.

'How's that?'

'Do you think I have any kids?'

'I've no idea,' he drawled. 'How would I know, one way or another?'

She moved herself a little closer to him. 'Come along Sher*loon*. Would you say my pussy is the pussy of a woman who has had a child?'

'Sherlock,' he said.

'Sherlock, whatever. Use your little grey cells.'

'No,' he said. 'Would be my answer. I'd say that pussy is too pristine.'

The way she wriggled with self-consciously girly deliciousness really was not suited to her powerful frame. 'I have,' she purred. 'I gave *vag*inal birth too – my lovely Ernesto!'

'You'd never guess,' he said, trying half-heartedly for gallantry. 'Not by the state of – uh, state of your pussy.'

'Oh and Ernie was *enormous*, too! One of the largest they'd seen at the clinic. It's a good thing, for the health of the infant, but *hard work* for me, and for my pussy. But I had a genius surgeon called Mowat, called *Lev* Mowat, a graduate of the Moscow school. He did *amazing* micro-work up there. *Amazing* muscular work.'

'Amazing,' agreed George.

'It's tighter than it was before! It really is.'

'I could,' George began, starting to say *I could tell*. But this would be a ridiculous thing to say, for to say *I could tell* surely implied prior experience against which he was judging it. Instead he said, 'I can imagine.'

'He did something with the nerve-endings too. It's much more pleasurably sensitive in there than it was before.'

'Excellent,' said George, feeling uncomfortable. 'That is excellent.'

Afterwards they strolled down together and had a coffee in the hotel's Costa. The circular logo circumferenced the company name around the stylized representation of three coffee beans. George's eye kept drifting to the logo, and its beans, like three torn-out brown tongues. He was in a morbid sort of mood, really. Caffeine wrestled with alcohol in his streaming blood. Ys chattered on. The encounter seemed to have perked her up.

Eventually they parted, and George hung vaguely about the games room for a bit. His Fwn murmured, and it was Marie – breathless and strawberry-cheeked from her exertions. They agreed to supper *à deux*. After the call, George dawdled through the basement-level mall, and bought himself a complete new suit of clothes, all the while thinking that he ought to feel perkier than he did. It was not that he felt *bad*, exactly; but there was an insubstantial sense of apprehension somewhere in his sensorium. He couldn't pin it down. From the basement he travelled up to the penthouse bar. He ordered a Poppy. He pulled a leaf of the hotel's viewsheet from the dispenser, but found he couldn't concentrate on the images, flicking through the channels until he ended up, almost perversely, back at the news.

On a whim he took the elevator down again to the kids'

suite. He stepped in without knocking to find Leah almost upside down in an easy chair – her legs hooked over the back, her head dangling down, a gamescard in her hand. Those fantastically precise fluttery fingers going over the screen, like a Renaissance concert pianist, or something. Or an artist working the canvas – or something. He didn't know what game she was playing. 'Hel*low* Leah,' he said with mock ponderousness, as if he were a fairy tale giant and she a princess to be rescued, or menaced, or however it was those sorts of stories went. She ignored him, of course. Pixels outrank parents in a child's order of priorities. Ezra was in the next room on the playmat with his toys parading about him in a circle; and Arsinée was on the balcony, her long black hair spread wide and dangling.

'Mr Denoone!'

'Arsinée!' he snapped at her, suddenly very cross. 'But what are you *doing*?'

What she was doing was hurriedly gathering up her queue, and tucking it away down the back of her shirt; and then she ran blushing through into the room to sweep Ezra into her arms.

'Arsinée,' said George, wagging a finger. 'Are you not eating your regular meals? Is that why you're sunning behind our backs? What do you do – sell the food on?' He had only the vaguest notions how that sort of black economy worked, or, indeed, why it existed at all. But of course he had heard the stories.

'No, Mr Denoone, no! Only, the children were so placid, and the sunlight is warm, and—'

'I *can't* talk to you,' he said, feeling absolutely *superb* in the way he turned his shoulder to her and put emphatic dismissal into his voice. 'I have a rendezvous with Mrs Lewinski.' It was an ancient pleasure, this *de-haut-en-bas* play acting. The thing with master-and-servant, as with other games, was to cause the maximum emotional distress and insecurity in the underling with the least possible exertion on your part. 'I will discuss this with you later. You should consider your position!'

He swept out, past his upended and absorbed daughter. A flash of Arsinée's aghast face. And, in the elevator going back up to the penthouse bar, he *did* feel a little better. These footling little humps of up-and-down emotion. Demeaning really. Not for the first time in his life he was aware of the sense that he needed some project. It didn't really matter what, of course; only to find something purposeful to help elevate him, keep him on a more noble emotional level.

4

He and Marie spent an hour together in the shops; and then played a game of echo-ball in the holographic suite. It was perfectly pleasant. Then they made their way to the Arabian Eatery, and sat at a little table on the balcony. They had a very nice view. The angling sun played splendidly over the pyramidal southern flank of the mountain: conjuring not only light-effects of gold and plum and grape-pink and cherry-red on the planes of snow itself, but creating the most extraordinary shadows too. The shadows were perhaps even more beautiful than the lit areas, George thought: lines and wedges of the most extraordinary deep-sea blues and purples, bruise-greys, darknesses tinted green and ochre, slotted intricately into kaleidoscope tessellations.

Marie had lately taken up the California habit of ordering a container alongside the table for her evening meal, so that she could, after chewing and tasting the various morsels, spit them out. Lunch for nutrition, supper for the taste. The fashionable mantra. George didn't mind this, not really; although perhaps he was a *tad* annoyed by the way Marie pretended that this had *always been* her habit – he would have testified in court that she had started it no more than a week earlier. Of course these little quirks and petty fictions are part of the tapestry of marriage. Of course they are. We wouldn't love our partners so much without their little eccentricities and peculiarities.

They finished the last of the Hormoz White with a clink of glasses.

'Your health Mr Denoone,' said Marie.

'Your health, Mrs Lewinski,' he replied.

The waiter brought a second bottle of wine, an Indonesian vintage; and the shrimp-and-pomegranate purée arrived, two murex-coloured lumps. A memory passed through George's mind of Ysabelle's dark little breasts set firmly upon her powerful ribcage. And Marie, as if she were reading his thoughts – as perhaps she was, for long-married couples do acquire that quasi-telepathic ability – Marie asked him:

'So did you boink Ysabelle?'

'I did,' he said. 'This Indonesian stuff is rather nice, don't you think?'

She squished a mouthful through her teeth, like mouth-wash, and spat it into the bucket. 'Not bad at all.' Then she stuck out the tip of her tongue, and drew it back in again. 'A little bit rhubarb, maybe. Do I mean rhubarb? The green one.'

'The long, tubular green one?'

'No. Round.'

'Apple.'

'Yes, that's what I mean.'

They both tasted the purée, and Marie spat hers into the bucket with a retching noise.

'Took her a long time,' said George, shortly.

'What?' said Marie. 'Ysabelle, you mean?'

'Mmm.'

'Really?'

'My legs were achy anyway, from the skiing. It was hard work, really.'

'I'm somehow surprised it took her a long time to come,' said Marie, absently. 'She's so athletic. She does everything so quickly – she skis like the devil is after her. She's one of life's sprinters.'

'She told me she had work done on her hoo-haa,' he said, taking another slurp of wine. 'After the birth of her, eh, son.'

He couldn't recall the boy's name. A boy, though, for certain. Was it? George thought so. 'Talked about it as if she was super-pleased, but I reckon it mucked up her responsiveness.'

'No matter what they say,' Marie declared, 'they can't guarantee they won't snafu the nerve endings. That's why,' she added, a little smugly, 'why I'd never let a surgeon poke a laser *anywhere* down there.' She had had both her children by perineal caesarian precisely to obviate the necessity for too much subsequent surgery.

The waiter had swept up her bucket, and was about to shimmer off, when Marie raised her voice. 'What do you *think* you're doing?'

He bowed towards her, murmuring something, inter-spersing it with several *Madam*s and begged pardons. But Marie was unspooling one of her shriller tirades. George took his attention away from this, and instead poked the two-tine fork in amongst his food: shredded swan in yoghurt. The fibres of the meat were surprisingly thin for so large a bird. George separated several, and then combed them into parallel lines on his plate, like hair.

He wasn't really very hungry.

The waiter had gone. 'Off with a flea in his ear,' George noted.

'He didn't even ask me!' said Marie. 'Just made to steal my bucket without so much as an excu-u-use me.'

George peered into the mouth of the bucket: a vomitous swill of chewed food in the thin medium of spat-out wine. There *was* a bit of a smell. Maybe the other diners had told the fellow to remove it. He thought about saying so to his wife, but, really, it wasn't worth the grief.

A different waiter was approaching their table. 'Either you scared the other one off,' George noted with a chuckle, 'or they've sacked him.'

'It would be nothing more than he deserved,' said Marie. 'His hair all down the back of his jacket like that.'

'It *was* in a queue, I thought?'

'It was. But dangling *outside* the jacket. Like a horse's tail. Couldn't he tuck it *in*?' She turned to take in the view again: the now dark flank of mountain drew a jagged upward graph-line of charcoal against the tomato-and-gold sunset sky behind. 'It's not as if there's any sunlight left,' using the fork as a baton to indicate the scene, 'for him to feed upon.'

The new waiter was at the table, bowing. 'Mrs Denoone? Mr Denoone?'

'Mrs *Lewinski*,' said Marie. She had a this-is-the-last-straw expression on her face. You know how she can be when she's pushed too far by some careless insolence or other. George fancied a touch of something chocolaty to sweeten his mouth, and looked the waiter up and down to see what he had brought. But he didn't appear to be carrying anything.

'My apologies, Madam,' he said, bowing again. 'I must ask: you are the mother of Leah Denoone, Mrs Loving-ski?'

'Le*win*ski, for crying out loud,' snapped Marie, making fists out of her tiny hands and holding them a few inches above the table. 'It is not *hard* to get *right*.'

George, though, had picked up on the fellow's tone of voice. 'We are her parents, yes,' he said. 'What's the matter?'

'Again my apologies Sir, Madam. I regret that I must interrupt your meal.'

'Oh, what *now*?' wailed Marie. 'Evening's been a complete disaster from start to *finish*!'

'Would you be so gracious as to follow me?' The man had a very narrow, prominent L-shaped nose. It stood out all the more startlingly against the die-cast cheekbones of his sucked-in face. His queue was at least decently tucked into the back of his shirt. Guinness-black eyes flitted from George to Marie, from Marie to George.

'What's the matter?' said George.

'Please, Sir, Madam.'

George's chair sang the tuneless, mournful squeaking note chairs make when they're pushed back over a polished floor. Like minor spirits in torment. None of the other diners gave them a second glance.

5

Leah had disappeared. *Disappeared* was the word they used. Marie insisted on precision in a loud voice – 'What do you mean disappeared, exactly? What, *exactly*, does disappeared *mean?*' – but they were unforthcoming. George and Marie were escorted to a huge office and a desk the size of a car. The head of security, a scrawny-framed woman with a large head and protuberant lips that looked, somehow, untucked, came round to the front of the desk as soon as they were ushered in. Arsinée was in a chair in the corner, clutching a sleeping Ezra to her body and weeping silently. 'Mr and Mrs Denoone,' the head of security said, bowing to each of them in turn, and then shaking their hands, one after the other. 'My name is Captain Samira Afkhami, and I am head of hotel security.'

'What?' said George, meaning *what's going on?* and meaning *what's happened to my daughter?* The truth was he felt so discombobulated by the wine and the day's dissipations that none of this felt real enough to pierce his bubble. 'What?' he said again, as if whatishness was the only concept his head could hold.

'Please to sit down.'

'I will *not* sit down!' Marie cried, striking a blow against tyranny with her words. 'You *must* tell me what has happened.'

'Your daughter has disappeared.'

The phrase, already uttered several times, still made no real impact upon George's consciousness. He flicked the touch-screen of his memory, and a variety of possible responses scrolled past. What he said was: 'When?'

Captain Afkhami looked at the large-nosed man. '*Saat kaç?*'

The man gawped at her, and said something rapidly. The captain then apologized on his behalf. 'This man thinks he is Irani, but he is Turk, and cannot understand me correctly if I speak Farsi to him.'

'What?' said George, again.

'He insists on Farsi, but it is a sham,' said the captain.

'I don't understand,' said Marie. 'I don't know what you're saying.'

'There is no need for you to alarm yourself, Madam,' the captain said. And to the other man, she spoke rapidly: '*Az un khosh am nemiyad, agha. Sa'at chand e?*' When he did not reply, she turned to George, 'I am asking him the time your daughter disappeared. He claims to understand Farsi, but you see the result. This shows that he is a sham. Rest assured, al*though* there remain many Turks in this area. Nevertheless Ararat province is *firmly* under the legal authority of the Iranian Judicial system.'

The other man began to say something but the captain cut him off. '*Gom sho! Gom sho!*' This seemed to mean 'get out', for the fellow drooped his head and left the office. 'We do not need *him*,' said the captain, to nobody in particular.

The horrible, yawning sense that something genuinely bad was awry in his life was percolating into George's numb sensorium. The fear of something that money and influence could not simply undo. He directed his fuzzy gaze towards Arsinée, in the corner. 'Arsinée,' he said. 'Where's Leah?'

'I don't know, sir,' she said, sob-tremulously.

'What do you *mean* you don't know?'

Arsinée responded with two deep, shuddery breaths and a fresh outflow of tears. The captain, slapping the palm of her hand upon the surface of her desk, said: 'It is a deeply regrettable situation! It *is*! Beyond all, and at the beginning, permit me to express the hotel management's deep regrets.' She stopped, felt her own chin as if reassuring herself that it was still there, and added: 'I must also, for legal reasons, say: regrets is not an admission of liability or apology. I trust you understand what I mean.'

'I *don't* understand what you mean,' said Marie, fiercely. 'I don't at all.' In response to the ferocity in her mistress's voice, Arsinée's sobbing grew louder.

'Why do you go on after that manner?' asked George, with a sort of stupefied slowness. 'Why don't you just tell us where our daughter is?'

'I answer your two questions from last to first,' said the captain. 'I do not tell you where you daughter is, and it is because I do not know. I stress the nature of the legal authority because you must know this, in terms of your possible legal redress, and such is complicated.'

'How can it be complicated?' flashed Marie. 'You either know where she is or you don't.'

'It is complicated because of the region,' said a new voice. Away in the far corner of the long room a heavy-looking man was wedged in an elegant chair. They hadn't even realized he was there; but there he was, sunk in that chair. His face was grimly hairy; a black moustache possessing almost structural solidity and density, and little wiry hairs sparking in several directions from his long eyebrows. He was dressed in a nondescript suit, and his head – ostentatiously – was shaved down to a raincloud-purple oval of stubble.

Turning to face this man Marie asked: 'Do *you* know where my daughter is?' The stranger nodded slowly, as if in affirmation, but then spoke in a sepulchral voice from the chair to deny it: 'No, Madam, no. Perhaps it seems callous, but this is the information you will need to master. Your daughter is no longer in the hotel. This means she is somewhere in the district.'

'No longer in the hotel,' said George, stupidly.

'What do you mean?' Marie said again.

'We have, of course, sent out officers of hotel security to search,' put in Captain Afkhami. 'And alerted local police, and bosses.'

'Bosses?'

'Indeed. Bosses run the villages, police keep them in line. But,' the deep-throated man in the chair continued, and his thrum appeared to fill the room, 'we *must* alas, alas, face the possibility that such inquiries will be fruitless. Accordingly, you will need to know that this part of the world has a – *complicated* political history. This history has been complicated since Noah's time, it *has been* so. It is one of the portions of the globe that humankind has *squabbled* over.' There was a particular inflection, or accent, about the way the man spoke English, but George couldn't quite place it. It sounded almost Irish, or perhaps Scottish. Not Scottish, no. That wasn't it. 'I am talking,' the man said, 'about Iranians, and Turks, and Kurds, and Armenians, and Russians too – we must not forget the Russians. Since Noah's times. Since the time of *Noah*, but also more recently.' There was some extra twist or flavour to the man's Iranian- or Turkish-accented English. But it. George couldn't focus his thoughts. But. 'Since two decades now,' the man said, 'a form of Protectorate has operated.'

'I don't see,' said Marie, in a high, loud voice, 'what this has to do with *anything*.'

'Only, Madam, that you may instruct your lawyer to hire Iranian experts,' said the man, ducking his large, vaguely cubic, head so that his chin touched his chest. 'And I shall say nothing more to intrude upon you at this difficult time. It is very sad that this has happened, but – *mashallah*.'

At this word Captain Afkhami looked sharply round at the man. George was still trying to find a way of understanding what he was being told; which is to say, of understanding on a more than merely semantic level. Something momentous had happened. This was a day, like any day, except that as this day slid innocuously past something shadowy and monstrous had risen from between the flower-dotted green hills in the background. What had come up was a head the size of the moon, and it had flashed sword-long teeth and bitten down into the tender flesh of George's being-in-the-world. He didn't really feel it; but, he reflected, sometimes people lost limbs, or suffered terrible gunshots, and felt nothing. Perhaps the numbness was actually an index to the enormousness of what had happened to his life. Prompted, possibly, by an obscure sense that he ought at the very least to *act out* the requirements of shocked bereavement, he said. 'Marie, would you like to sit down?'

'I do not want to sit down,' his wife replied.

'I think *I* need to sit down, at any rate,' he said. A servant – another individual George had not even realized was in the room – was immediately at his side with a chair, and George settled his weight into it.

'Of course it is a shock,' said Captain Afkhami, blandly.

'I want to go to her room,' said Marie. George could hear in her voice – a voice whose emotional tenor he had, of course, become adept at decoding – that she had come down on the side of furious action, rather than furious melancholy. 'I want to go *straight* to her room,' she said.

'Of course Madam,' said the captain. 'And anywhere else in the hotel you wish to look. But I assure you we have looked everywhere, and every room—'

'I want to *go* to her room,' said Marie.

'—is covered by surveillance technology,' the captain rolled on smoothly. 'And regretfully your daughter is no longer in the hotel.'

Arsinée's sobbing had the irritating regularity of an unoiled wheel. As if it had just occurred to her that she had another child, Marie suddenly strode to where the girl was sitting, hauled Ezra from her grip and clutched him tightly. The baby did not wake.

'I suppose,' said George, from his seated position, and speaking tentatively – since this was to articulate the ultimate surety of his peace of mind, the ground of his reality, and to articulate it was to risk having that surety, and ground, contradicted. 'I suppose it is a matter of *ransom*?'

The captain looked round to the large man in the room's far corner, and he in turn stirred in his chair, as if about to rise from it. He cleared his throat, and his corpulent torso quivered, and then he spoke, still seated. 'I regret to say, not so, Mr Denoone.'

'You regret to say,' repeated George, dully.

'Alas, no. If it were a matter of ransom then – well, then it would not be complicated. But I am afraid it *is* complicated.'

'Somebody has *kidnapped* my child,' said George, and as he spoke these words, for the first time that evening, it came home to his soul that this had really happened, that Leah had really been stolen from him. A trembling stirred the inert mass of muscle in his lower torso. 'Somebody has kidnapped Leah, but they don't want money?'

'No, Mr Denoone. I fear they do not.'

'I am a wealthy individual, quite wealthy,' said George. 'My wife is also wealthy.' He felt he might be sick. He felt a horrible shudder in his stomach.

Both the captain and the man in the chair dipped their heads at this, in mute recognition of this brute fact of individual existence.

31

'That *must* be why they've taken her,' George repeated. 'How much will they ask? What are the usual levels of ransom.'

'I regret to say,' the man in the corner repeated, 'I do not believe that they will demand ransom.'

'What then?' asked Marie. 'Political, is it? Is it *political*?'

At this thorny and non-specific signifier the captain and the man swapped glances. 'To be plain,' said this latter, across the room. 'I should say: if whoever kidnapped your daughter wanted something *for* her, money or publicity or anything like that, then our job would be infinitely easier. But I fear the kidnapper wants nothing more than to disappear without trace forever into the wide districts of Anatolian anonymity.'

'Are they *personal* enemies?' George asked, his heart alternately thuddishly convulsing and lying still. 'Do they have some *personal* grudge against us?'

'With a certainty approaching the absolute,' said the lady captain, 'whoever took your daughter knows nothing whatsoever about you. They probably do not even know your nationality.'

'All they knew,' said the man in the corner, 'was that you had a daughter. It was enough. They saw her, and they took her, and that is all.'

6

After this awkward, stilted interview, a period of several hours passed in a debatable and limbo-like state. First, still clutching Ezra, Marie stormed off to Leah's room, with George, Arsinée and the captain in train behind her. But there was nothing to see. Then there was a ten-minute period of angry interrogation (or reinterrogation, for the girl had already told her story over and over to the authorities) of Arsinée herself. She curled herself up as if expecting blows, and reworked the same narrative in various different handfuls of grief-shaky words. She had put Ezra down for his night's sleep; she had eaten a little something with Leah whilst watching children's dramas; she had put Leah to bed – still awake, playing on one of her games, and then she had gone through to her own cot to watch her own screen. She had dozed a little, but woken at nine with an uncanny sensation that something was wrong. Leah was not in her room. Discovering this, she had searched the suite, for sometimes the little girl liked to tease her carer by hiding. When it was clear she was in none of these rooms, and after Arsinée had (she said) made her throat sore with calling her name (but not too loudly, for she did not wish to wake Ezra), she had picked up the baby – for he could hardly be left by himself – and ventured out into the corridor. Up and down, calling Leah's name, calling for the darling child, over and over. Meeting guests coming and going and asking if they had seen a small girl, in her pyjamas, to be met with incomprehension, or the brush-off, or hostility. She had been by her own admission 'in a state' at this stage, weeping and disordered and not knowing where to go. So she had gone barefoot all the way down to the Kidarium, because she knew Lah-Lah liked to play there sometimes. But it was all closed, and switched off, and the bubblepit looked sinister and enveloping in the dark; and the furry robots, some taller than she was herself, loomed alarmingly as if they were liable to come to life at a motion. So she had fled to the ice-cream café, on the same floor, and walked amongst the booths and through the crowds of people, crying Leah's name and weeping; and the bright lights and the noise had woken Ezra and set him off wailing too, and still Arsinée had wandered, calling the name, until security had come over to see what the commotion was. The guards called their superiors, and when they realized that a guest's child was missing they called their superiors. Pretty soon after this, the surveillance net was programmed with Leah's details, guards worked systematically from basement to roof, and then back down again. By the time George and Marie had been approached in the penthouse restaurant, the grounds had been searched, and teams sent out along the most likely exit roads.

Eventually, under the continued pressure interrogation, Arsinée just crumpled, and nothing more could be got out of her except tears. What game had Leah been playing? I don't know. Which show did you watch, in your cot? I can't remember. What time *precisely* did you last see Leah, before you went through? I'm not sure, I don't know, not *precisely*. They stuck a tab on her wrist, and this showed Arsinée to have consumed perhaps half a glass of wine that evening. This revelation increased the flood of tears prodigiously. 'It's true! It's true! I'm a terrible person!' She had, she sobbingly confessed, sometimes carried away the leftovers from her employers' discarded bottles, and drunk them in secret, in private, when the kids were abed, never very much, never enough to make her lose control, but just a taste. Beautiful wine, and the lovely confusion it made in the thoughts. This was exactly the sort of thing she had never had the chance to experience before Mr and Mrs took her on. And then more tears. It was amazing, in fact, that she was able to weep as copiously as she did without simply drying up like a raisin. Tears, tears, tears.

It was gruelling, extracting this testimony from the sobbing girl; and at the end Captain Afkhami smiled and patted her on the shoulder, before saying 'And now I must arrest you.' For George this was yet another mentally indigestible twist in the evening's events. Marie had more presence of mind. 'But who is to care for Ezra?' she said, the baby still asleep on her shoulder.

The lady captain faced her. If the thought occurred to her *you are the child's mother, and must care for him*, then she at least had the good sense not to say it aloud. Instead she said: 'What arrangements did you have in place should your carer fall sick?'

'Arsinée fall sick?' Marie said. 'The very idea.'

Once again, the captain had the look of a woman choosing not to say aloud something she was thinking. She said: 'One of the hotel's employees might be assigned, on a temporary basis. Perhaps from the crèche?'

'Why must you arrest Arsinée?' pressed Marie.

'It is our experience that when a kidnap has been, uh,' said Captain Afkhami, straightening herself, 'performed. That when a kidnap has, has occurred, an insider is often involved.'

'Nonsense,' said Marie, although the iron certainty had gone from her voice. She looked at Arsinée. The girl had hidden her face completely in her hands.

'Sometimes servants are bribed, or otherwise seduced by the kidnappers. We cannot be sure.'

And so, without another word from the girl, a uniformed security *pesar* led her out of the room and away. The shock of the arrest stemmed her sobs; or else she had simply run out of steam as far as crying was concerned. 'Did you see the way she stopped crying when they arrested her?' said Marie.

'I'm sure it doesn't mean anything,' said George.

'No? She cried and cried, and as soon as they clapped her in irons she stopped.'

'You have had a hard piece of news,' said Captain Afkhami, waving her one remaining security *pesar* to the door and nodding her head sagely to the two Westerners. 'I shall leave you tonight, and, with your permission, meet with you again in the morning.'

And that was that. The hotel sent a bleary-eyed teenage girl up to look after Ezra, but it took Marie a very long time to surrender the baby. She handed him across, but took instant exception to the way the kid was holding him – 'Have you never held one before? No, *support* his head' – snatching him back. Although he had slept through everything else that had happened that evening, this pass-the-parcel finally woke him up. He hid his eyes in a tangle of fleshy creases, opened his mouth and cried with the immense volume of which babies are capable. This howling took the form of a drawn-out iambic pattern, short inbreath, long yell, short inbreath long yell, and each syllable darkened and reddened the colour of his little scrumpled face. Marie tried jabbing a pacifier in the mouth, and snapped at the girl to make up some milk, and when that didn't work, she walked him very briskly round and round the room. And when *that* didn't work, she ordered George to call for a doctor, since the baby was clearly ill. Finally, in a state of expressive, tearful misery herself (and you know Marie! – she's not one for tears, she *never* cries), she handed the baby back to the teenager, who with a little judicious cooing, and cuddling, and the application of the milk-teat, got him to stop crying. Marie, looking more drained than George had ever seen her before, went through and lay down.

At the end of this prolonged interlude, George's nerves were scraped raw. On some pretext he slipped out of the room and made his way to the Deluge Bar. There he found Ergaste drinking brandy out of what looked like a one-legged fishbowl. Peter was there too, fiddling with his own ears, drinking from a regular glass some liquor so bright green it looked radioactive.

'Dear fellow,' said Ergaste. 'The rumours! You wouldn't credit them.'

George filled the two of them in. A waiter brought him a glass of Hyderabad Red wine. The servant was a silent fellow with a young, grave face and hands so much larger than was proportionate to his slender frame that George, for a moment, thought he was wearing some kind of prosthetic giant-hands, like a Freak showman or comedy performer.

'Good grief,' said Peter, when George had finished.

'Fuck my nostril,' said Ergaste, with less refinement but with more force. 'Ransom, I suppose?'

'Apparently not,' said George, and sighed. He sighed loudly, and lifted his glass. 'Security people say not,' said George, fitting his snout into the wine glass, and tipping it until the wine overran his lower lip.

'Not?' boomed Ergaste.

'But if not *ransom*,' asked Peter, 'then for what?'

'They didn't say,' said George. 'They didn't tell me. They didn't say.'

'It must be money, it boils down to money, always, with these people,' said Ergaste. 'I'm not a racist, indeed not. I don't mean *these people* racially, you comprehend.'

'Of course not,' said George, vaguely.

'Hhh!' sniffed Peter, in perfect agreement, or perhaps in pointed disagreement.

'I'm as free from race-hate as the snow itself,' insisted Ergaste.

'Of course you are, I believe in you,' said George, uncertain as to what he might be committing himself.

'By *these people* I don't mean Iranians, or Turks, or Armenians, or Kurds, or Arabs, or Parsee, or fucking Russians, or moon-men, or, or,' he lifted the glass balloon of his cognac slowly before him, as if acting a dumb-show lift-off to orbit. 'Or *any* racial category. I mean poor. I mean the poor.'

'The poor,' repeated George, tentatively, as if the concept were being introduced into his consciousness for the first time in his life.

'It's the poor,' said Ergaste, banging his glass back down on the table between them. 'We're an island of Enough in an ocean of Poverty. I mean, here, on this mountain, this Ararat. But I mean – you know. In life, generally. And the poor, you mark my words, young George, the poor *only ever want one thing*. Money.' The cognac had made him unusually talkative.

'Assuming it is poverty, behind this?' put in Peter. He patted George's arm, companionably. 'Maybe it's political? Maybe it's a news-grab? Either way it ought to be possible to get the little lady back. Which is to say, it *will* be possible. Of course it will. And it goes without saying,' he added (whilst Ergaste nodded his massy nose, and grunted 'goes without saying'), 'that anything we can do to help, we will do. Anything at all.'

George stared with, in the first instance, frank non-comprehension at this offer of assistance. He ought to have been able to process the conventional companionship on offer. It should have been a supportive and readily graspable thing: manly society at a time of crisis, friendship. But for some reason, looking into Peter's moist eye, George felt a blurting urge to burst into tears. It was on the end of his tongue to say: *I fucked your wife this afternoon*. Naturally he didn't say this. But there was something painfully absurd in the man's ignorance –

about George, and about his own wife – that gave an oppressively poignant quality to his ingenuousness.

It was out of the question to cry.

George turned away to hide the new reflecting brightness of his eyeballs, and looked through the bar's main window at the floodlit snow field outside. Some brave souls were larking about in the night-time. At the wall, a few feet behind their table, the screen was on. What was on? Some show about dancing, a twinkling blur of colours. Most of the wall was taken up with a huge mirror, crusted about its rim with a light-brown crimped and scalloped frame, like a pizza's edge. The mirror itself, lit from within, reflected the narrow bar, its oval tables, its almost exclusively male clientele.

A moth, very hostile when faced with the sight of moth-ish rivalry, repeatedly and vehemently headbutted its own reflection in the bright glass. The moth made a noise like a rag pennant fluttering in the wind.

'I'm in hell,' said George, not loudly; but as the thought occurred to him – as a sudden realization, a novel insight into his new condition of existence.

The others either did not hear or chose to ignore him.

'Wine,' boomed Ergaste. 'Did I ever tell you I'm a Roman Catholic? Oldest religion in the world! Wine is part of our worship – did you know that? We drink wine to worship our God.'

'Wine,' said George. 'Wine.' It was night. And after night comes day, or more night, depending on the particular time-frame you choose to apply to your perspective.

7

The morning started with a Clear, to purge George of an irksome, leaden headache. He wore shades in the shower, and omitted breakfast. Marie, who had woken repeatedly in the night and who had angrily rejected his suggestion that she take a Doze, was now lying on her front like a corpse. Out of a vague sense of duty, rather than because he had any pressing reason, he went down to Leah's old room and found the teenager – Rana, she was called – feeding Ezra, and tickling his tender, dark-brown cranial fuzz with her free hand. He had no instructions to pass on to her, and nothing to say, so he left her and walked along the hotel corridors for a while with no particular destination in mind. Portraits came to life as he passed them, offering purchases that could be immediately delivered anywhere in the world, and freezing into lifelessness behind him as he passed.

Leah was gone.

Mid-morning he had a very unsatisfactory meeting with Captain Afkhami. There had been no progress, she said, despite unceasing efforts by her people. She promised she would arrange a flitter to take them to Doğubayazit, later that day, to liaise with the local law enforcement. They have opened a wiki on the case, she said. But there were certain adminis-trative trivialities to be cleared up prior to that journey. She unrolled a screen and typed some phrases into it. He and his wife were married, despite the disparity of surnames? Yes, hardly unusual, in this day and age. But it is difficult for our database to process! It keeps throwing up flags. It does not like it. Denoone is not a Jewish name? What did that have to do with anything? Nothing. Of course, nothing. But *her* name was down in the hotel database as both Marie and Miriam, and the House AI disliked this duplication very much. Very much. The House AI liked one person to have one name. Inflexible, perhaps, but who amongst us does not understand the preference for clarity? So: was it Miriam Marie, or Marie Miriam? George started to explain that the one was an affectionate idiom for the other, when the complete pointlessness of the interaction popped up in his head like a diary reminder. He got to his feet without saying another word, and went out of the little office. He faced Afkhami the whole way out, walking backwards to the door. 'Mr Denoone,' said the captain, passionlessly, as he went. 'It is important that our data records do not contain apparent contradictions. It is important for legal reasons.'

Out.

He walked on the terrace. The various hilarities and goofinesses of people larking in the snow seemed as alien as *The Pirate Moon of Co-RoT 9*. It occurred to George, with some force, that human enjoyment was a fragile skin drawn over a great depth of potential misery. A layer of moonlight slicking the surface of the ocean silver. More than that, there was more. For the moonlight's beauty was a lie, for no amount of shine changed the fact that the waters extended straight down black as oil for kilometres and kilometres into crushing, airless, oblivious depths.

A ramjet passed over the sky – impossibly high, no bigger than a rice-grain, yet drawing after it, like a monarch's weighty cloak and train, the aftermath of its profound bass-tone roar. A scratch and scuff in the blue. A tower in the sky, a needle, a triangle.

He went back to his room. Marie was awake now, sitting on

the bed. She was holding a mug of coffee: her left hand underneath the base and her right hand cupping its flank. Rana was playing with Ezra on the floor beside her. When George came through the door, his wife looked at him with eyes like loaded guns.

'I've had another meeting with the captain,' he said.

Marie considered this. 'Her English isn't very good,' she said.

'You think so? I'd say she was pretty fluent.'

'No,' said Marie, with enormous vehemence. '*Her.*'

George looked at Rana with a sort of helpless vagueness.

'I can't get her to understand,' repeated Marie.

'Understand?'

'That she must come back to the States with me.'

'Must she?' said George.

Marie's shellac-hard gaze. Her lower jaw moved incrementally forward. 'Of course she must.' These four English monosyllables did not literally include the phrase 'you moron', and yet Marie conveyed the extra sentiment.

'Madam, Sir, I may not,' said Rana, in a mild, fluty voice. Ezra threw out a giggle-gurgle that had the neat little rhythm of a drum-fill.

'I'm sure we can find somebody native in NY,' George offered.

'I am going back to the States,' said Marie. 'You, George – stay here until they find Leah. And when they find her, I want you to bring her back with *you* when you have her, and we have her back again.'

George's eyelids flickered, down-up, down-up. He experienced these sorts of lid fibrillations from time to time. Presumably it was related to stress. Brightness flickered in his head, like a fan spinning in front of the light.

What could he say?

He said: 'Yes.'

'You understand that I cannot stay in this place,' said Marie.

'Place,' said George.

'You understand that *one* of us has to stay. And you understand that it won't be me.'

George thought about saying *but actually I don't understand that*. The problem, though, wasn't at the level of comprehension. What was the problem? I suppose the problem was habit. A relationship may become habituated to the dynamic of one party being more decisive and the other less – to one individual taking predominant control and the other cheerfully acquiescing. In such circumstances, whilst the play may be a sustaining and refreshing aspect of life, the intrusion of reality upon the playacting will be all the more unsettling. In other words, George's lack of understanding did not have to do with the content of his wife's communication so much as with the tectonic grumble of the ground shunting beneath his stance. He had always been the one comfortable with the fiction that she was in charge. Evidence that circumstances had overwhelmed her – evidence, in other words, of her very overwhelmability – constituted a sort of anti-Copernican revolution. For the rich, few things are as disabling as *uncertainty*.

'And I *can't* get her to understand and she needs to understand.'

'It is unpossible,' said Rana, speaking to the carpet.

'What is it that she must understand?' asked George.

'That she is to come back to the States with me.'

'Oh,' said George, ingenuously. 'We'll easily find somebody native in NY. We can use the agency Dench recommended.'

The quality of Marie's silence quietened him. She sat there, cross-legged on the bed, holding her mug of coffee in front of her. She raised it up like a chalice and tipped it over. The oval of blackness in its mouth elongated and broke over the lip. One, two, three seconds of micturating sound-effect. Then Marie swung the mug (still half-full) to the side to fall to the carpet.

George and Rana were looking intently at her now. Even Ezra seemed to sense that something significant was happening. He stopped on all fours, mid-crawl, and looked up to his mother.

'Are you suggesting,' said Marie, in a level voice, 'that I tend Ezra myself, the whole journey, from here to home?'

Silence. Mossy-edged, flanked by dark green shadows. Sunlight on the pond. A single fin slicing the water like a paper-knife.

Silence.

George opened his mouth to speak without knowing what he was going to say. And indeed, when the words came, they came from somewhere other than his conscious mind. Possibly from somewhere quite other than him, at all. 'Nothing about your life is *you must*, my love,' he said. 'Nobody can say that.'

She eyed him. She was, presumably, trying to determine whether he was being sarcastic or not. But, then again; wasn't this a simple statement of the truth of things? Wasn't this a nutshell definition of what it means to be rich? She kept her eyeline on him, and said nothing, and nodded, once.

'I will, I will,' said George. His eye was momentarily snagged by the view through the window. The view was of unscarred ground. Bleached sheets; the snowfreeze. White.

Silence was never far away. Silence was always there. It falls, as snow falls, and covers us all. George summoned his will-power and put a footprint in it.

'I'll *call* the agency,' he said, pulling out his Fwn. As he did so he felt something shift in his breast, like a tide hauling itself over and round. Some grand, hidden, gravitational reorientation of the world focused on his heart. 'Better, better than that, I'll call the agency we got what's-her-name from. You remember, the Ecuadorian girl. I'll call them, and I – will – have them fly a new carer over *here*—' as he typed the search into the Fwn-screen with his thumb, laboriously, one character at a time. 'It's an hour and a half to Tabriz. She can be here early afternoon, and—' and the more he spoke, the more a momentum gathered in his speaking, '—of course assuming she passes muster, assuming you like her, my dear, you, she and Ez can be on an evening flight back home before the sun sets.' And in the spurious assertion of action, the logic of connection between this human being and this other human being altered. Marriage is a very old manuscript, and there are always gaps in the text. Two people may choose to be linked when what there is between them is *something*; and that something may be practical or sexual or habitual, a shared sense of humour, a shared disinclination to holiday alone. What*effer*. Whatehva. Choice is intoxicating enough at the best of times, and it fair makes the head spin when it tangles with such a linkage. But more potent than something is *nothing*, for that dissolves choice as salt dissolves a slug. And this is what George now understood, or rather (at any rate) what he now had some inkling of. Their marriage had once been a voluntary contract, but now they were joined by something much stronger than the will of either of them. Prison is a perdition, and perdition means something lost. That he and Marie, having previously been lightly connected by various *somethings*, were now, abruptly, terrifyingly welded much more solidly together by an absence, the *nothing* where their daughter had been.

8

That evening George saw wife and son off at the flitter park. Ezra was in the care of a new young woman called Janet Devault, and Marie stared past George and past the hotel and stared into the distance with unthawed eyes. Then the flitter did its salmon-leap thing and shrank away in the sky, heading east.

George stayed for a while, unsure what to do with himself. He scanned the sky. The sun like a neon coin. The moon its own ghost. As he made his way back to the hotel, he became conscious for the first time of a weird, dark dignity in himself. Of course he was sad his daughter had been taken – for ransom, of course, whatever the police captain lady said. It must be that. He *was* sad. How could he not be sad? But it was not a demeaning sadness. This thought occurred to him as he walked. For circumstances had gifted him with a type of tragic dignity. It was entirely new to him, this hollow grandeur. He liked it. He imagined the hotel staff looking at him with a new respect. It was sad, but sadly serious. It was a painful absence in his life naturally; but it was an absence like a zero added to a number: it turned him from inconsequential 1 to notable 10. He was conscious of that unnerving tingle, like an itch inside the web of his nerves. It felt like the great wall was about to crumble, the dam was about to give way, and just behind the barrier was something huge, and important, and sublime, balanced on the threshold of flooding down into the cosmos.

But even the most transcendent sensations of tragic dignity don't excuse us from the need to fill our hours with something.

For lack of anything better to do, George went to the Fitzgerald Bar and started drinking. His new friends did not abandon him: Peter and Ysabella both found him there, and Ergaste too – even Emma put in a brief appearance, drank a single pomegranate-vodka and went off to bed, squeezing George's shoulder as she passed him. 'They'll find her,' Peter kept saying. Iteration robbed the words of weight. 'They'll find her, old man. Don't worry. They'll find her.' George pondered that to say a word once is communicative, and to say it twice is emphatic, but to say it twenty times turns it into a trippy floating nothing. Utterance was strange like that. Was there something corroding his sense of dark eminence, his new tragic significance? Was something eating away at it from the inside? He knew what that was, intuitively. It was the true misery of the situation. But he didn't want to experience *that*. This dignified centre-of-attention role-playing was much more agreeable. Keep *that* at arm's length. The more Peter said 'they'll find her, boyo' and 'they'll find her' the more the fear was actualized that *he would never see his Leah again.* That sentiment was not the stuff of dignified tragedy. That sentiment was demeaning, red-eyed, wailing, snotty, unbearable loss of everything, and tears flowing, and choking, and intolerable, intolerable. 'They'll find her,' said Peter.

Peter was a little drunk.

George kept drinking, but the booze all vanished into some inner void. It went into his inner cavities without so much as touching the sides. He sat straight up and stiffly. Misery-as-dignity, to keep a lid on his panicking soul.

After a while they all went through to the Jazz Bar. A musician typed frantically at his piano keyboard. Tinkle tinkle tonk. This chappie wore a look of almost unhinged concentration on his face, the point of his tongue visible in the corner of his lips. George couldn't decide whether or not he liked the *fiddliness* of it all. The open whale-mouth of the piano lid emitted filigree, unpredictable structures of sound. So big a mouth deserved a grander song. Ergaste was drinking Cognac. Peter and Ysabella both had glasses of Afghani fruit beer. Lights shimmered in waves across the ceiling, the fabric of the room imitating – what? – the pelt of a deep-sea squid. Two tables along a pokemon card game was in progress. Barks and whistles of surprise or pleasure erupted at irregular intervals from the players.

George levered his right shoe off, and pushed his bare toes through the pile of the carpet. It was soft as sand. The pattern was one of those fat-pixel Persian carpet sorts: stepped tri-angles, blocky swirls, like images from the very dawn of the computer age.

'Put your shoe on, man,' boomed Ergaste, indulgently.

George tucked his foot back in his shoe. He muttered the word 'never'. He did this as though trying it for size on his tongue. 'Never.' Sour. 'Never never never.' It was a pulse. 'Never never never.' Say it enough and it flipped about: ver-nev, ver-nev, ver-nev. Repetition really did drain the word of all its bitterness. Here was the very cornerstone of magic.

His wine tasted of jam.

'I *don't* blame Marie for pushing off,' said Ergaste. 'Trau-matic environment for her.' He fiddled a c:snuff dispenser up a nostril large as an eye-socket, and sniffed.

'You're bearing up, George. More power to you, though,' said Peter, in his horrid Canadian voice, with its whining, ski-jump inflection. I could take this wine glass, George thought. I could take the glass and crenellate its rim to jags with my teeth, and I could grind it into your eye. But of course he did no such thing. Of course he smiled wearily and mumbled his thank yous. 'No seriously,' said Peter. 'I know it's not easy. But you're doing the right thing. By staying behind, I mean.

48

Something as important as this, you don't want to leave it to underlings.'

The blood would leap out of the wound in a cascade of fire-red droplets.

'Quite,' agreed Ysabelle. She was acting rather weirdly; spending a period of time in intense scrutiny of George's face – an unnervingly close attentiveness – and then spending a longer period in embarrassed looking-away and a refusal to meet his eye.

Pull himself together. He sat up in his seat, or tried to.

'It's awfully good of you all,' George said, in a crumpled voice. Away in the corner the card-players began a three-part braying laughter-fugue. What could possibly be so horribly hilarious? No sane human being could be provoked to laughter of such profanity. And George had the sudden comprehension that nobody here was sane, that they were all mad, and the world itself mad to the core. It was one of those crystalline insights that come to us, suddenly, all of a bundle, when we are adolescent; but which, of course, become less and less frequent the older we get. But here's the thing: an absence is a harder thing to hold in one's head than a presence. Leah was less to him than this mouthful of gluey red wine, because the latter was inside his mouth right now; the fluid washing between his teeth and staining his striated tongue Persian-carpet-colours. The wine was actually there. Leah was – notion-ally – somewhere else. And feeling this disparity, on some level – although, to give him credit, without being fully consciously aware of it – George was prompted to stress the magnitude of his loss. Talk it up from its nothingness. Put a figure on it.

'Ten years,' he said, to the others. 'Ten years is a long time. Little Leah, my,' and he had to rummage mentally for an appropriate word, 'princess, for ten years. It's an investment of *time*, ten years.'

49

'Mmm,' grunted Ergaste, from his belly. *Investment* was vocabulary he understood.

'I mean an investment of the heart,' George clarified, although, of course, he didn't. 'Ah! My lovely Leah! She had—' and, still, moved by impulses of which he was consciously unaware, he proceeded to itemize his daughter as a physical being. 'The brown eyes. Such lovely *dark* brown hair – she wanted to grow it long, though Marie wouldn't let her.' With an unpleasant jolt in his breast, he realized that he was talking about her in the past tense. There is a horror barely concealed in the past tense. We all feel it. We treat that tense with wary respect, it and its myriad complicated grammatical variants. That tense is where all the misery of the universe is cached.

George began to weep. The tears surprised him, dribbling from his eyes.

'They'll find her,' said Peter, looking away. 'They'll find her, for sure.'

You're thinking: but when a person cries it is a ticklish calculation as to what proportion of tears are for the putative object of grief, and what is simply drawn from the infinite well of self-pity we all carry within us. Alcohol facilitates the emission of tears. That's right.

Ach! Ach! Ach!

Afterwards Ergaste, with hitherto-unsuspected tenderness, linked arms with George and walked him up and down the balcony outside. As they strolled, the Englishman gave him – for some reason – a detailed account of the rituals of the Catholic Church. George didn't understand why, but he listened as attentively as his drunkenness permitted, and found a strange comfort in the older man's chatter. The eating of little coins made of bread, the drinking of wine, which is after all only a sort of investment of grapes over time from which the compound interest of alcohol has been earned.

Prayers that are said. The priest in his expensive robes. George breathed the chill air, and watched the various artificial lights blur and smear as his gummy eyelids opened and closed. An unoccupied row of chair lined the space, pretzel-seats and double-∩ logo-shaped backs.

A snowbike roared and sped over the snow beneath them, from left to right. It carried before itself, jutting from its headlamp, a jouster's lance of light.

9

Day succeeded night. The following morning, waking alone in his room, George lay in bed, ill as ill could be. Not virus-ill, of course; hangover ill. For a while all he did was let his eyes rest on the large, planed flank of sunlight that fell through his wide window. The brightness shook colour from the carpet. Everything shimmered. He was alone. Everything trembled. He got himself to the shower room somehow, and stood for a long time inside the teepee-shaped zone of falling water. What he felt, he thought, was not depression. Because depression was something that had always seemed to him to be a mind-state of enormous complexity, compounded of anger and repression and ornate tourbillons of soured self- and other-relations. Despite superficial similarities, what he felt right now was something much simpler, purer almost. It was a kind of default inertia. A body at rest resisting the efforts of the outside universe to dislodge it. After a while he sat down on the ceramic pimples of the shower floor. He leaned his back against the tiled wall and let the water fall noisily into his lap.

What did the day hold?

Today he was to go to Doğubayazit, the nearest sizeable town, and meet some bigwig policeman to receive a report on the investigation into Leah's disappearance. George shut his eyes. He imagined stepping into a broad, cool room with shutters on the window, and a perfectly rectangular desk in the middle. He imagined a moustached policeman saying, 'We have found your daughter – here she is.' Then – what? Turning to see a door being opened by a functionary, and there Leah would be standing, with a beaming smile on her face (but Leah *never* smiled!), tripping and trotting across the floor to – but this was no good, he couldn't remember what she looked like. He closed his eyelids tighter, as if the memory could be physically squeezed out of his eyes. He remembered Marie's serene face.

George opened his eyes.

Captain Afkhami accompanied him in a hotel flitter. Flying twenty metres or so above the ground, they swept down the mountainside and passed from the white clarity of the snow-fields to a dusty, grubby-looking scrub. The beige was occasionally intersected by dark-water canals, or roads running straight as ruled lines. It was easy to make out the giant rectangles that had once been farmers' fields, each one now a mass of scribbly weed and low bushes scattered upon mustard dust. Occasionally a tractor, rusted to the colour of dark chocolate, stood up to its hips in undergrowth. Barns stood roofless.

Occasionally, George saw people, of course: sitting mostly, occasionally loping slowly along the side of the overgrown road, their long black hair marking them as have-nothings.

The sun sparkled upon the curved window of the flitter. The sun pressed the landscape flat.

Soon enough the low rise sprawl of Doğubayazit emerged over the horizon; and almost at once George began to see sunbathers in proper numbers. A week at the hotel, insulated from the baseline fact of existence, you might have thought they were a rare breed. But, no, here they were: the life of the ordinary man and woman in the raw. People lay in recliners, or on their backs on the ground, long arcs of black hair fanned out. George began to count them in rough tens, but soon – as the flitter passed over a wide municipal park – there were too many to process numerically. Every roof contained a number of

53

indolent human beings, lying perfectly still, hair carefully spread like lizard cowls.

'Lots of Ra-worshipping,' he said to the captain.

'Sunny day,' she replied.

Moments later they landed in a parkyard and George climbed out of the flit into a pliable wall of heat. 'This way,' said Afkhami. 'Here we are.'

They were parked alongside a three-storey block building, with *Doğubayazit Polis* upon its plate-glass frontage. There were four other flitters in the park, none of them in very good condition.

Antique traffic thundered along the nearby road.

'Shall we go in?' The captain smiled, and the sunlight burst in little stars upon her dark lenses, and that was the moment George understood that her confidence had deserted her. Her distraction during the flight here, the various little hints of her body language, and her tone of voice as she said *shall we go in?* – it passed a tipping point in George's mind. It occurred to him that, beyond the borders of her specific domain, she was as out of her depth as he was himself.

They made their way round to the main building entrance. Reflected cars and vans hurtled left–right and right–left within the glass of the Police Station frontage. There was such violence in the wheeled rush of their passage it seemed amazing they didn't shake the glass to shivers. When George pushed the swing-door open this frenzy of motorized movement tipped, alarmingly, as if to pour itself inside with them. But inside was quiet, and cool: a marble lobby, and the clacking of their shoes over the cold floor. They announced themselves to the man behind the desk, and then they waited in leather chairs for a quarter of an hour. George found he had no conversation at all; nothing to say to Afkhami. He ought to have been able to conjure some pleasantry, or benign question, or bland observation, but he literally could think of nothing. Finally a functionary led them through to a spacious marble office, and they sat down opposite the police chief.

Police chief. He was a canny-faced man of fifty or so: two earth-brown eyes, a neat grey moustache the shape of an orange segment on his top lip. There were lines running vertically, fanning across both cheeks, perhaps up-down knife-scars from some youthful criminal investigation, perhaps simply the creases where his flesh folded as he pressed it into the pillow as he slept.

'I am Commissioner Mehmet Sahim,' he said. His accent was more noticeable than Afkhami's.

'My name is George Denoone,' George said. 'I am the man whose daughter has been kidnapped.' It felt strange stating this fact so baldly, for it had not previously struck George that this would now, in all likelihood, be the horizon of people's know-ledge of him from this point on: *Oh, he's the man whose daughter was kidnapped at Ararat.* But Commissioner Sahim's reaction surprised him.

'You are one of very many,' he said.

George's eyes clicked wide open. 'Many?'

'I deal with dozens every week.'

'Dozens of kidnappings?'

'Dozens of children taken.'

'Dozens?'

'Of course, rarely from the tourist resorts, such as your hotel. But dozens, weekly.'

'Oh.' George said. Dozens? He pondered how this piece of news made him feel; but the truth was that it made him feel *resentful*. Losing his daughter was bad enough; must he now lose his sense of the *uniqueness* of his loss? Nobody likes to discover that they're not as special as they thought; even if their specialness was of a tragic cast. 'Dozens? That's a lot.'

55

'The number,' said the commissioner, 'is perhaps larger.'

The best George could do with this information was to look at Afkhami, and then back at the commissioner, and then back at Afkhami. 'I had no idea,' he said, uncertainly.

'Mr Denoone,' said the commissioner. 'Child theft is the main business of the police. The bosses control most other crime effectively enough, in their villages I mean. But they close their eyes to child theft – for obvious reasons.'

'The bosses?'

'The village bosses.'

'They close their eyes to child theft for reasons that are – obvious?' George said, meaning it as a question. But the commissioner took it as agreement.

'Indeed. You can understand why. Naturally it makes my job very difficult, for without the partnership of the bosses the investigation of crime is almost impossible.' He pronounced this last word the French way. 'I do not mean to discourage your heart, Mr Denoone,' he went on, smoothing his hand across the immaculate and polished desktop. 'You *are* an un- usual case.'

George perked up to here himself so described. 'Really?'

'Of course – you are a wealthy Westerner. This is not usual. Usually it is Turkish and Irani children who are stolen. Some- times Kurds and Armenians, but they more rarely.'

From this sentence it was the word *wealthy* that popped up and rat-tatted George's consciousness. He leant forward in his chair and said, in something of a gabble: 'Money is not an object. If there is a ransom to be paid, we'll gladly pay a ransom. If they want ransom, you will please tell them that—'

The commissioner employed a placidly forceful manner of interrupting this flow, saying, without raising his voice: 'They will not contact me, Mr Denoone. There will be no demand for ransom. These kidnappings are never about *ransom*. Of course I will speak to the local bosses. I will speak, and we will see.'

'I don't understand,' said George. 'How can it not be about money?'

'Money,' said Captain Afkhami, '*may* be required.'

The commissioner opened his eyes wide, and then narrowed them again. 'Oh money *will* be required,' he confirmed, in an *I took this to be understood* tone of voice. 'We will need to grease the bosses' wheels.'

'Money is not a problem,' said George. It was, in truth, the one sure thing on which he could draw, his sole possible contribution to the situation. He could be forgiven for stressing it. 'We can transfer any sums required – to whichever chips are needful.'

'This money will not be to pay any *ransom*, though,' said the commissioner.

Unable to comprehend this, George only repeated. 'Money is no object.'

'I must banish you now,' said the commissioner, mildly; although perhaps his command of English led him into a more alarming utterance than he intended, for he shook hands with both the captain and George, and promised to contact them as soon as he had information.

Back outside, they made their way back to the flitter and clambered inside. 'What did he mean, no ransom?'

'The money will be used to bribe the village bosses,' said the captain, tapping the drivescreen as the belt snaked itself round her waist.

'I see,' said George, although he did not. 'But *why* are so many children being – stolen? The commissioner said that so many children were being stolen.'

'There are many bad people in the world,' was Afkhami's

explanation. She spoke in a distant voice, feeding the hotel's location to the drivescreen. And the flitter lifted creakingly into the sky, and it soom-soomed north, and wild birds scattered before its passage.

10

George settled into a physically comfortable but existentially deracinated mode of life. He continued staying at the hotel, doing all the things guests did. He had daily meetings with Captain Afkhami, in her office — although there was never any progress to report — and spent several long sessions on either his own Fwn or the hotel's Lance, talking to Marie. He skied, sometimes once and sometimes twice a day. He ate and drank, and on three further occasions he had sexual relations with Ysabelle. But she soon came to the end of their stay, and left for Toronto with her husband. After that George spent more time with Ergaste, drinking, or playing idle games. But mostly he simply drifted in a state of existential nullity, day leaching into day. He watched whole strings of books. He sat for hours in one bar or another, sipping all the many vintages on offer. The sunset hour would ripen the snow from pale to pink and then to a sugary red. The lights would come alive up and down the resort. The hotel interior would shift its mode from being darker than the rest of the world to being brighter. 'It's a scandal,' Ergaste boomed, at his elbow. 'They could shake the whole province up, if only they wanted the bother. Oh, *they* don't want the bother.'

Another blurry, wobbly walk along the corridor to his room. Another morning's dose of Clear, and the shower-room's always welcoming cone of hot water.

The one unanticipated benefit to all this was that George's skiing improved. He passed smoothly down the piste, hooked himself to a drone and ascended to try again. Down and up, the recirculation of matter in a surprisingly satisfying cycle: fort, and the world rushes past; da, and it hauls itself back up again. New guests came, and inexperienced skiers essayed the slopes, and these folk gave George the opportunity to feel superior to their clowning – the way they'd hit a hump of the slope just wrong, and make mid-air Xs of their arms and legs before their head-down insertion into the snow; or the way they'd simply *stand* wrong and fall backwards, or fall forwards, without ever getting going. The more George skied, the more irritated he became at company. Growing bolder, he skied off piste; avoiding the famous ice-cream slope – which was always crammed with people – and instead exploring areas of unscarred snow, where man-high mounds of the stuff had been left untouched so long they had acquired pores all over, like patches of giant skin. He skied over to where the trees began, with their white-frosted boughs, dreadlocky strands of ever-green foliage weighed down with the previous night's snowfall. In at the edge of this forest George felt, not quite free but at least experienced a compelling intimation of what freedom might be like. Here, the air was only distantly touched by the noise of the blimps; or scraped vaguely by the distant passage of a ramjet heading to Tabriz. For long moments the woods even achieved a perfect, enamelled silence. Silence, and then the cello-thrum of the overhead jet, and then silence. The sky is made out of silence.

The leaves here do not rustle.

A hotel safety agent skied over to check he was all right. He took off his glasses to meet George's eye, nodding and smiling, and then had to put them back on to access the translation protocol. Hotel insurance liability does not include. Legal responsibility to inform esteemed sir. Some things cannot be translated. The silence cannot be translated.

But he couldn't stay in the trees for ever.

Back at the hotel he took lunch with Ergaste and Emma. The couple – either tenderly, or else out of plain insensitivity, George couldn't decide – insisted their baby be brought to the table to be cooed over. Five minutes of that, and the baby was waved away back to its room.

'I tell you something,' Ergaste instructed him, expansively. 'When we're in London, I'm speaking to some Media Stars I happen to know.'

At this, Emma grew hotly cross, for reasons that weren't quite clear to George. 'Those people!' she snarled.

'No need for that,' warned Ergaste, not looking at her. ''d be *tremendously* useful for George! Dozens a week, children kidnapped – George says the police told him that directly.'

'That *is* what the Doğubayazit Police Commissioner said,' George confirmed, speaking mildly and looking not at his interlocutors but at the liquid chalk of the sky, the bright, cold sun. He shifted the angle of his gaze and examined the hip and flank of the mountain, the dark shagpile of its distant forestation.

'Dozens!' said Ergaste. 'People should be warned. It *should* be on the Media.'

'I told Shiroko,' Emma said, confidentially, to George, 'that she's not to let Algy *out of her sight*. Not for a minute, I told her.' Then, perhaps belatedly thinking this undiplomatic, she cleared her throat, rolled her lower lip between her thumb and forefinger and added: ' Not that there's really anything we can do as parents. That's what's so alarming!' There was a lengthy silence. 'So,' she said, shortly. 'Anyway, whatever *happened* to your – dear – um, girl's carer? I can't remember her name, the carer's name I mean.'

'The captain says she's still in custody.'

'Ysee, these *media* people I know might make a book of it,' said Ergaste, abruptly. 'The world should know this is going on!'

'News,' hissed Emma at him, like an expletive.

'And I'll say something *else*,' boomed Ergaste, apparently addressing the bright sky. 'This holiday hasn't done an iota to unstring *you*.'

'But how could it?' she retorted. ' How *could* I unwind, given what happened to poor George and Marina?'

'Marie,' George said.

'*That's* not it,' opined Ergaste, loudly.

'Oh? Is it not? What is it then? Is it that you're using any excuse to get together with those – prostitutes and pole-dancers from ZYZ?'

'Oh for fucking out loud!' groaned Ergaste, with such volume that several other diners turned to look at them.

'Don't swear, so! George and Marina have suffered *such* agonies, and all you do is swear!' hissed Emma. 'And you can't *wait* to hot-tail it back to—'

'Please don't fall out on my behalf,' said George weakly.

'Oh George, if I told you *half* the things that happened in that ZYZ Media Palace,' said Emma.

'They might be able to help the man!' boomed Ergaste.

'—your ears would burn blue! They really would!'

'She's like this,' Ergaste appealed to George, 'dayn, dayout!'

The Horner-Kings left later that day, cutting their holiday short, and with apologies for leaving George in the lurch. But he could tell them perfectly truthfully that he didn't mind. He was looking forward to spending some time alone. He actually was. 'They'll find her,' Ergaste asserted. 'It'll be a ransom, that's what. What else could it be?'

'I'm sure you're right.' And the two Horner-Kings and their kid and their kid's carer got into a flitter and in moments they had all vanished into the wide sky.

After that George took some little care (and, in truth, it was not hard) to avoid picking up any new friends. He drifted through the days. He drank.

One day, a week or so after the departure of the Horner-Kings, he went back to Doğubayazit to meet the commissioner again; accompanied this time not by the captain but by one of her subordinates. The news was not positive. He was told that there was nothing to report. None of the local bosses could help. This was either because they were obfuscating, or else because they really did not know. The commissioner considered the former unlikely, given the generous amounts of money that were on offer. 'It's possible your daughter was taken outside the district. I am liaising with other districts.'

'But *why* did they steal her away?' George asked, in an anguished tone.

The commissioner dipped his head.

As he was being flittered back to the hotel, George tried to work out in his own mind whether it was better that the exact possibilities of Leah's fate remained unspecified, or whether the vagueness only intensified his dread. She was beyond his care, now. But whoever had stolen her, and for whatever wicked purpose, surely could not be tormenting her *every single hour* of the twenty-four. Could they? There must be times when the misery stopped and she knew relief, or possibly even enjoyed herself? Perhaps she was being kept in a room, somewhere, alone and afraid – but even then there must be moments when the sunlight would crop a section of the opposite wall with brightness. There must be toys for her to play with. Or other children – surely there would be other children. But, you see. But of course you see that the scope of *possible* sufferings a vanished child could be enduring is so vast, so much larger than interstellar, that it is quite literally inconceivable. It would collapse the mind to own the knowledge. The shadows of dread, rolled across the white landscape of George's inner world by vast clouds in stately motion. Even to think of the possibility of it made his ribs all clench together around his heart.

In practice, though, mostly he was able not to think about it. Sometimes, when talking with Marie in New York via Fwn, the unavoidable unmentionable *would* insert itself into what they said. But it was so sharply painful to them both, separated now by the whole globe, that they would hurriedly spin a floss of unrelated words around it, bundle it away. Every time somebody in authority mentioned 'the bosses', George felt a racing thrill of horror in his breast, sickeningly akin to excitement. To be boss; to have another human absolutely in your power. It made him nauseous.

At some point, he began the process of considering that he would never see Leah again. He couldn't say when this bleak possibility first consciously occurred to him. It insinuated itself into his thoughts, until before he was fully aware of it, it had become an old dread. It was almost as if this was a dread that predated the abduction itself – but how could *that* be? That made no sense at all. Let us stick with the rational, at all costs.

At the beginning he spent a period of each day watching images of his daughter at play in the snow, on their first day; or else mooning about her room playing her various games. The latter he could watch easily enough, but there were moments that made the former too painful: moments when Leah would look up at the lens and smile, breath steaming from her mouth, her teeth flashing in the sun. After a few days he stopped this belated voyeurism altogether.

One week became two. George sensed that he was, in small increments, being deprioritized by the hotel. Although he still had his daily briefings with Captain Afkhami, they became more and more perfunctory. There was nothing for her to say, and nothing for him to ask. The other demands of running a hotel intruded on the security staff.

This is what he now thought: there is something *grim* in the rhythm of ordinary existence. This is because the alterations from day to night, from moment to moment, are not the actual idiom of things. The idiom of things is a vast monotony. Existence belongs to the unyielding, not the yielding; and the most unyielding thing of all is the eternal changelessness of being. There are no stories to tell about it. Everything is always and everywhere boring. It must be, or we wouldn't need so many distractions.

George sank into it. The torpor possessed his soul.

Then, from nowhere, came news of a breakthrough. A breakthrough! It made the heart like a fish pulled out of the water and cast upon the dry pier timbers. George realized, if he hadn't already known it, that *things happening* is a more painful and less bearable state of affairs than *nothing happening*.

It was a fortnight into George's solitary stay, when the captain met him over breakfast. Something had come up. It was a breakthrough. They had broken through. He was flittered to a town east of Ararat, and once there he was told they must transfer to a groundcar. Commissioner Sahim attended in person. 'We are going to a town called Khoduz,' he said. 'We must go within a car, on the ground. It is a drive of half hour from here.'

'Why can't we go by flitter?' George asked. His heart was thundering.

'It is not so safe, where we are going, to fly' said Captain Afkhani.

'Have you found her? Are you taking me to her?'

'It is more safe to go within a car,' said the commissioner. 'We have this iCar Armoured, it is plated, it is very safe.'

'Flitters are more vulnerable to small weapon fire,' said

Afkhami, smilingly, as she walked briskly alongside him. 'They cannot fly high enough to evade evil people and their weapons.'

'Is it a war zone?' barked George, his chest tinkling with excitement, or fear (as if there is really any difference between *those* two emotions!). He no longer knew what he was saying, exactly. Standing in the direct sunlight. The iCar Armoured pulled up in front of him and the nearside passenger door clicked open and swung wide. Sweat was needling his face and torso. 'Is that why she was kidnapped? Is it something to do with war?'

'It is nothing to do with war,' said the commissioner, climbing into the iCar. 'There is no war here, although there are some bad people, and some of them have guns.'

'Leah is in Khoduz?'

'Let us get into the Car please,' said the Captain.

George stood looking at the cavernous cavemouth of the open passenger door. The whole machine was twice the length of a flitter, massy and ponderous, more like a house than a vehicle, from its broad domed snout to its room-sized trunk. Its paintwork was white as snow. It hurt the eyes to look directly at it, even through shades. George got in. The inside was cool, and the seat adjusted itself beneath him.

'Away!' said the commissioner.

They rolled for ten minutes along a rod-straight road of spongy tarmac; and then turned off onto a road of compressed dirt. An angled plume of pale dust shot from the back of the vehicle, like a rocket exhaust. George stared through the tinted glass. Where the canals ran, the land was scrubby with weeds. In between the zones of irrigation, sun and dryness had extirpated all life. The mountain dominated the distance, one big peak and an eastward downward slope to another, smaller peak. It looked like the profile of a mighty crocodile basking on the horizon. Objects near-to – parched trees, solitary buildings, discarded tractors – bulleted by, but the mountain was too huge and solid to move so much as a centimetre.

George peered through his window. He pressed his face to it, to look ahead. The road was taking them towards a small hill, scaled all over with single-storey buildings. They were in the outskirts already. People lounged on the ground, or sat on the roofs, with their hair out.

At a bend in the road just outside this village the car slowed to take the turn, and George saw two women in a dusty field, digging a trench, their arms glisteningly bare, their long black hair swaying with the motion of the spades.

Supine on the ground, a few metres from them, was a line of half a dozen shop-front dummies: every brown head bald as an egg, and far too skinny to be actual human bodies. George might have speculated on what these manikins were doing in this remote village, or why the women were burying them, but his mind was too agitated by the thought that Leah was in one of these very houses! That he was only moments from being reunited!

'This is Khoduz?' he asked.

They rolled through the place. The car pulled up in a narrow town square, with a central drinking fountain the shape of a rocket, and a couple of bang-haired palm trees. Men and children sat on the unshaded side of the square, letting the sunlight get to their hair.

The commissioner climbed out of the car, telling everybody else to stay where they were. George watched proceedings through the tinted window. The commissioner was standing in the sunlight, talking to two bulky men, one long-haired, one fuzz-headed. The conversation went on for many minutes. That *insectile* look of a human head wearing dark glasses. Abruptly the exchange became more heated. The commissioner threw both his arms in the air, and strode back to the iCar. When he opened the door, a palpable wash of heat poured inside.

The door closed with the thud of a guillotine blade hitting its stock.

'My apologies,' he said, calmly, to George, meeting his eye. 'This has proved to be – the English, I think, is *wild-goose chase*. We have chased the wild goose.'

From where he was sitting, in the back of the iCar, George could see the flicker of text upon the inside of the commissioner's dark glasses, as his AI fed him appropriate English idioms.

Nobody said anything as they backed out of Khoduz, and drove the half-hour back to the flitter.

11

George stuck it at the hotel for one more week. Time had rusted. The week took a month to pass. The final day stretched and stretched.

It was all about the waiting. Everything becomes boring in time: happiness does, but so does unhappiness. The glamour of his tragic eminence had rubbed away, and now he was only conscious of how horrible and demeaning and unrelenting his misery was. From time to time thoughts of actual self-harm would pop into his head, but he made no effort to act upon them. The making no effort, in fact, was his way of countering the temptation of suicide. The essence of suicide is impatience: for after all, if you want to die, all you need do is *wait*. But insofar as suicide is the purest form of depression – depression compressed to its logical extreme, as it were – then clearly depression is a function of impatience too. George held his drink in front of him such that the sunlight made white bobbles on the surface of the fluid, like suds. The sunlight passed incompletely through the body of the liquid, to cast a trembling oval of shadow on the white tablecloth.

Finally George took the schedule flitter to Tabriz, and there he boarded a scruffy-looking gelderm plane. There was a ramjet at noon, but he chose not to wait for it. Now that he was going back to the States he felt a kindling of urgency: not to see Marie again, not even to hold Ezra in his arms, but simply to *get out of that place*.

He watched the news the whole flight. He had gotten into the habit, during his sojourn at the hotel, of watching several hours of news every day. He found something queerly reassuring about it: the open-endedness of the situation in Triunion, or the latest upheavals in the Eastern Indian Federation, or the riots at the Sahara Games. Great mobs of the disaffected, the machinic efficiency of the modes of security containment. So much hurly-burly in the service of stasis. Everything constantly changing to stay the same.

As the plane descended, and did that horrid vibration-thing gelderms do, George looked down at the hoar-grey glints that sunlight spread over the Atlantic. He saw the ripple the plane's descent approach caused in the surface of the waters, a thin, almost spectral parabola line that chased after them until it splashed against the bulk of the Hough Wall. On the other side the Hudson lagoon was dotted with pleasure craft, and then the cogteeth towers of Old New York rose up to greet him. And finally he was back in the cool of a New York fall, and he was walking from the taxi up his own ramp, and walking through the lobby of his own building, and finally stepping into the familiar odour and ambience of his home, rendered strange by a two months' absence.

He waved the bagman away, tipless, and closed the front door behind him. Marie came out of her study. All she did, for a while, was stand at the far end of the hall with her arms hung loosely from her side. As he stepped over towards her she bestirred herself and came to meet him halfway, such that they embraced and held one another. And yet, for long marriage brings with it a telepathic form of incipient communication that is as much curse as blessing, George knew, as his arms snaked around his wife like a seatbelt finding its way to its socket, that she considered him to blame. He knew that she understood this to be irrational, but that she didn't care. Of course she was not about to rebuke him openly, or accuse him, or bring her resentment into any arena where it might be rationally disproved. She found a perverse source of emotional sustenance from her blame. But it was there, and it would not go away.

'I did miss you,' he told her.

Let's say tragedy is about death, so that we can ask ourselves: what dies? Or to put it another way: what *can* die? The first answer to come to mind, of course, is − people. And it is the death of people that most often informs tragedy. But other things can die too: hope, for instance. A marriage can die. A community can die. Then again: does it seem odd to you that we never use that idiom to describe recovery? 'My depression died, I am happy to say.' 'My cancer died, leaving me healthy again.' Why not? Fall, because that's what the leaves do. Or because that's what the whole year is doing. And down we go.

12

New York fall mutated incrementally into winter, and snow fell without the ordered restraint of Ararat, where clouds were seeded at night and cleared away during the day, so as not to interfere with the enjoyment of guests. The snow here did not lie pristine. It was veined with grime. The cubist imitations of mountain gorges echoed more dully than Araratian valleys.

George and Marie continued in their usual round. But isn't 'round' a strange way of putting it? Their lives, though in every respect metaphorically upholstered, lacked precisely the three-dimensionality implied by that idiom. Day replaced day, each sliding along to knock the night off its perch; and in turn dark crept up on day, approaching from exactly the same direction every evening, and with the same surreptitious intent, upon a day sky that never seemed to learn from the unbroken string of previous assaults. And with one sharp knock, the light went out, and post-concussive pin-prickle stars filled the darkness.

What sort of thing did they do, George and Marie? They did what the affluent did. Once, George and Marie went to a smoke-sculpture opening night; but Marie insisted their new carer (her name was Wharton, and she was a liquorice-skinned nineteen-year-old from Missouri) also came, and sat in an adjacent room with the sleeping Ezra in a portacot. George didn't want to say 'this is America', because, as he discovered by prowling online, it turned out children were stolen almost as frequently in the US as elsewhere in the world. He'd had no idea. But why *should* he have had an idea, before this terrible thing happened to him? At any rate, he didn't rebuke his wife's over-protectiveness. In fact he was grateful for it, since it excused him from voicing his own persistent anxiety.

At the exhibition he got into conversation with a nicely plump woman called Stephanie: a round face white as marshmallow and two large green eyes. Her short hair had been treated with some genagent to give it a *very* striking gold-metallic texture. The news was playing, silently, across the fabric of her wraparound dress: quadpods stomping deliberately in amongst swarming crowds. George felt some click, some subliminal pseudoelectric spark between them as they chatted. For the first time in months – for, in fact, the first time since Ysabelle, on the mountain – it was the old excitement stirring. She chattered at his jokes; he leant in towards her. 'So, you like the news? I do too!' 'How marvellous!' At one point in the evening, whilst the artist expatiated about the precision required in nudging magnetized particulates in the holding field into exactly the right position, Marie caught George's eye. He was standing next to this new woman, this Stephanie, and he smiled at his wife with a little flick of the head in his new friend's direction. But Marie only scowled. After the artist had finished yapping, when people were circulating again, she came over to him.

'That dumpy creature?' she said, in a boiled-hard voice. 'Better to bleach the thought *completely* out of your thoughts.'

He couldn't think of a response to this. All he said was: 'What?' He opened and closed his mouth with fishlike idiocy. His desire had shrivelled to a flaccid stump in the teeth of her hostility.

'You have heard me.'

He might have said: *But why is it a problem now?* Except that, of course, he knew straight away why it was a problem now. Which is to say, he knew that things had changed. He could have said: *I won't mind if you do* or *but it's just play! It's our game!* In Marie's head, the time for games was over. Out of the swirl of this complex intuition, the only phrase that came out was: 'I don't understand.' His tone of voice, unpremeditated though it was, seemed to irritate her further.

'You don't understand,' she repeated. She walked away from him. This might have been meant as simple sarcasm, or scornful reiteration of his ignorance, or conceivably as a statement of solidarity in his anchorlessness. He didn't know. In the days that followed the phrase came back to him at odd moments. He didn't like the sour scent it wafted over his thoughts. It was really very simple, actually; he had lived a childishly spoilt existence in which every whim was indulged and which no actual hardship had interrupted until *this* had happened. Marie had misunderstood. His *I don't understand* was his response to a deep change in his world. It was the largest of questions. It was the question that defined humans.

Winter deepened. The overhang of their building entrance sported two, and only two, icicles, large as sabre-teeth: one on either side – presumably the others had been snapped off by the building staff. Municipal drones trundled about the slippery sidewalks carving interlocking grooves into the ice. You could tell which pigeons had been genengineered to withstand the cold, because they bullied the unmodified pigeons, pecking them, harassing them, and in some cases cannibalizing them.

Some days George did nothing more with his day than watch the winter sun slide a tray of light over the bedroom carpet, and angle it up the wall.

From time to time they spoke to Ergaste and Emma, by Lance; or, less frequently, to Ysabelle and Peter. Ergaste said that he'd talked to ZeeYZee, but that it seemed child-theft was a ten-a-cent occurrence, and there wasn't any media publishing interest. 'Even when it happens to a person of means, such as yourself! On the other hand,' he went on, as sunspots, or ramjets, or whatever it was that causes those occasional flickers of interference, sent random barcodes of black lines through his image, 'on the *other* hand, I have the details of the *best lawyer in Europe*. When the time comes to sue the hotel – not now, too painful, too soon, yah-yah . . . but when the *time comes* . . .'

At the beginning of December George flew back to the mountain. Marie did not come. 'I will never again go to that God-cursed place,' she said. 'I vow never again to go there.' What could George do but agree?

Back in the hotel, feeling as if he had never really left it, George had a three-quarter-hour meeting with Captain Afkhani. She detailed the lines of enquiry pursued by the hotel security, and the separate lines undertaken by the police at Doğubayazit, and explained in many superfluous words, and with much hedging about, that they had all been fruitless. Of Arsinée she said, with an inflection that suggested she expected George to be happy at the news: 'She has been sentenced to a prison term.' There were no prisons locally, and the women's prison at Tehran had refused to take her (Why? George asked. Oh, because there was no actual evidence against her; although her guilt had been established to the necessary legal tolerances.) This meant that she was doing time at Ankara. 'It is by way of a strategy,' said the captain. 'It applies pressure. When she gives up details of her accomplices, we shall shorten the sentence.'

'And you're sure she's involved?' George asked, wondering if the little lump nestling visibly between Afkhani's pelvis and ribcage was pregnancy, or just weight gain, unable to think of a polite way of asking.

'It is our experience that such child theft almost always employs an insider,' the captain replied blandly.

So George came home again. There was nothing to stay for.

Boarding the ramjet at Tabriz it suddenly occurred to George, like a knifeblade being abruptly sheathed in his heart, that he would never see Leah again. She was dead; it was not a kidnapping but a murder trial. Or if she was not dead, then she had been taken so far from the usual routes of life as for it to amount to the same thing. He sat in his seat, trying to visualize his daughter's face, unable to do it.

13

Back in NY, George started going again to his assertiveness therapist. He had attended sporadically for a number of years, but let it slide after the birth of Ezra. Now he signed on again, and the thrice-weekly sessions gave a structure to his days. Part of the process was dream-reading. What this entailed was not interpretation, according to the assertiveness orthodoxy: it consisted of *strategies of reappropriation of dream narratives*. The theory was that dreaming was the chaos of the mind; and that assertiveness, as a holistic life philosophy, was about the seizure of agency in all aspects of the self. Dreams were related in such a way as to make the mulch and mess of symbols and surrealism part of a coherent story at the control of the dreamer. To put the orts and scraps of daytime experience back into the grid of narrative.

He and Marie and (of course) Ezra, with Wharton, went to a new seafood place called McAlmont's. George amused the boy by dangling squid tentacles from his mouth like fangs, and from his nostrils like boogers, and pretending to whip the table with them. Naughty table!

The recalcitrance of the inanimate.

There was a fire in the building. Municipal fireblimps bumped their noses against the side of the building as they sprayed the relevant portion of the structure with smartfoam.

The year turned.

There was a week in January during which George and Marie exchanged literally no conversational words whatsoever.

The clouds are icebergs, and the day repeatedly crashes

77

against them and eventually it goes down in flame-coloured splendour.

At the beginning of February Ergaste called on the Lance. 'Can you come to London?'

'London,' said George, in a watery voice.

'Just so. Right now – today?'

He was a shove-ball, and the universe kept firing bullet-pegs at him. With a click and a roll. A taxi brought him to the mid-morning ramjet, and by noon he was sitting in a central London eatery, with views of the swollen Thames, that ancient river. But all rivers are ancient, he thought. Flowing like bands of hair from the cranium of the land. Ergaste came, even more boisterously *present* here, in his homeland, than he had been on Ararat. With him came a slim woman of indeterminate age, dressed in dark blue and wearing a bulky headdress. 'This is Dot Mennel,' said Ergaste, as they all took their seats.

'Dorothy?' George tried.

'Dot,' she said.

They drank high-proof beer from tubular glasses, and ate little pots of creamed eel, with neat, origami-like structures made of folded slices of ham balanced on the top. 'Dot knows all about your situation,' Ergaste said. 'I took the liberty of retaining her services. Consider it my gift to you.'

George was past the stage when the events of the world surprised him. 'Kind.'

'Not at all.'

'And what *are* your services?' he asked her.

'I can help you find your daughter,' she said. Those seven words might as well have been Sanskrit for the impact they had on George's comprehension. Nominative, accusative, dative. Some notional sense could be derived from them, of course; but translated out of their uttered alternate-reality idiom they acquired the quality of words spoken long, long ago. 'OK,'

George said, and took another sip of the strange, yeasty, sour little drink. *OK* covered most things, he thought.

'Can you come with me?' she asked.

'Come with you?' Something wriggled inside George's soul at this offer, as if to show that it wasn't entirely dead. But she didn't mean it in that way.

'We can be at Ararat by three,' she said.

George, distantly, considered this possibility. He tried to conjure reasons to say no, but couldn't produce any. He did not remember if he had mentioned to Marie that he was coming to London that morning. He did not remember, indeed, if he'd spoken to her for days.

'OK,' he said.

'Let's finish lunch, though, eh?' said Ergaste.

'OK.'

So, buoyed by the alcohol, he sat through the rest of the meal. Ergaste kept talking, in his absurd high-volume voice. George took in perhaps a third of what he said; the rest was just English-accented babble and bluster. Dot, whoever she was, mostly kept her own counsel. The flesh on Ergaste's face, George thought, looked like a layer of something painted thickly on. His jowls wobbled asynchronously as he spoke. His neck, though tightened by the usual treatments, trembled as if with a life of its own. He was a large man; a swollen man. He was a man with something fierce exerting pressure from within, and pushing his skin out in all directions. He was talking now about his business – about the need to engineer quicker and quicker growing cycles for certain food plants so as to keep up with the rapidly oscillating fashions for luxury eating. 'Staples are all gone now; no market for them. But the rich *do* like their tidbits, so I'll always have a business. They're flibbertigibbet though!'

George didn't know this word. 'What?' he asked.

'The *rich* are,' said Ergaste, boomingly. 'No point in me spending six months growing and processing – let's say – lamb smoothie, if by the *time* I bring it to market the fashion's shifted to red snapper chocolate!'

'Lamb smoothie was very last season,' George agreed, vaguely. He couldn't decide if the salt odour he could smell was the beer or the river. He moved his glass away from him. The salt smell did not diminish. Presumably it was the river, then. He looked out over the waterway. The old riverside roads were visible under the tinted waters. Big fish, trout maybe, swam windingly around lampposts.

'George,' Ergaste said, changing the subject abruptly and fixing him with his fierce eye. 'It's time to light a fire underneath them. Not been properly *trying* to recover your girl, have they. Not *incentivized.*'

'I've visited the area,' said Dot, coming to life like a robot. 'It's an area I know. They're following the official lines, with an eye on the lawsuit they know is coming – everything they do is so that they have a case for court. But actually finding your daughter is not part of that strategy.' She had one of those opaque, matt, whiny London accents.

George gave voice to his new catchphrase. 'I don't understand.' Oh, but it's *always* sincerely meant. It always is.

'Dot knows the zone,' boomed Ergaste. 'She'll sort it, if anyone will. Her help is *my gift* to you.'

'You are very,' said George, staring dreamily at Ergaste's large face. 'Fat,' he said.

Ergaste cleared his throat. There was a pause. Then, visibly, he decided that George had just said *kind*. 'Don't mention it,' he said. 'You've been to hell. *Least* I couldoo.'

'There's a flitter on the roof,' said Dot, standing up.

They flew over west London; grey black roofs and the myriad glints of many pools. Standing water, mostly. At

Heathrow they boarded a ramjet to Tbilisi. Dot sat with ninja stillness in the seat opposite George the whole way. 'Have you,' he asked, alternately licking and sucking an orange-vodka lolly, 'worked kidnapping cases often?'

'Crime paradigms have changed,' she said. 'The New Hair changed the nature of crime.'

'Well,' said George, watching the clouds bob past. 'The New Hair changed everything, I suppose.'

Dot seemed not to blink as she watched his face. There was something discomfiting about her gaze. George tried meeting it, but he ended up looking away. He knew what that gaze meant. It meant: *nothing changed for you.* It meant: *that's a definition of rich. Wealth is mankind's oldest buffer against change.* It meant: *you have no idea.* But that's not true! He thought those words to himself. I do have an idea. I have several ideas. They're just not my ideas. I have acquired them from others, as is the case for all my possessions.

Shortly they were swinging low over Tbilisi. A giant's causeway of dwellings hemmed by dust-yellow hills; a sprawl of industry: basket-shaped commercial hangars and the myriad upended lampshades of iDishes. Over the outskirts of town a half a dozen sunkites trailed their shadow over the surface of the earth: drawing them up over the heights, dropping them down into the valleys. 'Why not Tabriz?'

'Tabriz is for tourists,' she said, as the plane nudged the ground and settled. 'Besides, I have an account at Tbilisi.'

She meant, it transpired, a flitter account; and she flew George expertly over the hills southwest and towards the slowly uprising prospect of Ararat. 'Do you understand why your daughter was taken?' Dot asked.

'I don't understand anything about the world,' George replied. 'I mean, about the world outside my Rapunzel tower.'

'Your what?'

The thing is, George hadn't particularly meant to say any-thing in reply to her question. The words had just, as it were, fallen from him. He thought back over them, registering them, and their meaning, for the first time. 'You know the fairy tale?'

'You'll have to enlighten.'

'It's just a story – there was a book last year, quite well known. Minnie Keuren starred.'

'I don't watch books,' Dot said, angling the flitter in the air and beginning a wide turn.

'No? I watch a lot of books. It was a Christmas book. That's why I watched it. And because I watch everything with Minnie in it. I love her.' And he thought: that's a three-word-phrase that pops out of me with remarkable facility! 'A story about a girl who's locked in a luxurious room at the top of a very tall tower.'

'And that's you, is it?' Dot prompted.

But George had not considered it from that perspective before. He was going to say: no! I'm the rescuer, not the princess! But he didn't say that. 'I suppose,' he said.

'It's not just you. In that position, I mean. There—'

'What?'

'Look there.'

The flitter's angle of flight gave George a clearer view of the ground. A road branched in two. Little dark rectangles scat-tered along it, like schematic leaves along the branch and boughs of a tree. 'What am I looking for?' he asked.

'There,' she said again.

The roads, the roofs, the open spaces were filled with human bodies. Many of them were lying horizontally, or slouching back. Presumably they were observing the bluebottle passage of George and Dot in this flitter, perhaps with detachment. A few were in motion, foreshortened to nothing but heads from which scilla-like legs poked and withdrew. 'People,' he said.

'The absolutely poor,' she said. 'People with no money.'

'Money,' he said.

'I don't mean, people with limited funds. I don't mean people with *too little* money. I mean people with literally not a cent of money. I mean, people who have never owned and will never own one red cent.'

George looked at her. He heard the words and understood them, but only on what you might call a semantic level. 'OK,' he said, tentatively.

'The ones walking around, the ones doing the work – do you know *what* they are?'

'Driven?' he tried. 'The get-up-and-goers.' He pondered. 'The ones making something of their lives?

She shook her head. 'They're women.'

'Women?'

'That's right. And you know *why* they're – look—'

It was a dark line scratched in the soil, with a long row of sunbathers lying beside it. In the trench were several miniature coffee-bean-sized figures, and little puffs of dirt being thrown out: diggers. 'A trench,' he said.

'The ones digging it are women.'

'How can you tell at this altitude?'

'Trust me.'

She righted the car, gunning the motor and sped past the village. For several minutes George was silent. There was a slumberous sense of the world's wrongness stirring in his soul. But what could he do about it, anyway? An existential indigestion, uncomfortable and pointless and best dispensed with. What could one person, or any one person, or any person who was him, do? 'I was going to ask,' he said, shortly, 'why are those women digging that trench?'

'You *were going to ask*?' prompted Dot.

'But I suppose I know the answer already.'

'And?'

'Those people lying alongside weren't recharging their Hair.'

'I'd wager you a dollar to a Degas they didn't *have* hair. Not any more,' said Dot.

'Corpses.'

'They were.'

'Those women were burying them.'

'That's right.'

'Why did they die?'

'Pissed off the bosses,' said Dot. 'Probably. It hardly matters. Cut off their hair and leave them to starve. But it's the women who dig the grave.'

The lower slopes of the mountain were underneath them now. Over the ridge, like a great page turning beneath them, and the piste came into view – the same coffee-bean-sized individuals, all scurrying and sliding and hurrying. Dot brought the flitter down in the visitors parkyard, and George stepped out, still dressed in the shirt and trousers he'd put on that morning, when he'd expected to spend the day in New York. The chilly fresh air woke him a little. 'The head of hotel security,' Dot was saying, 'has gone on maternity leave. I've arranged to meet with Colonel Jamshidiyeh.'

'OK,' said George, giving his naked hands alternately a rub and a squeeze.

'Let me explain the purpose of this meeting,' said Dot, briskly, as they walked. 'You will be there in person to explain to the colonel that you are deputizing me. He must be in no doubt that your trust resides in me, and that you will back any tactic I employ.'

'OK,' said George.

'By *back* I mean, mostly, money. Yeah?'

'OK.'

They came in at the main entrance, and were taken straight up to Afkhani's old office. George recognized the colonel as soon as laying eyes on him.

A functionary brought in coffee, and for a long period everybody sat in silence, toying with the thimblish cups. Dot introduced herself, and explained that she had been retained by Mr Denoone and Mrs Lewinski. Colonel Jamshidiyeh nodded briskly and said 'I see.' 'I have no relationship with the legal side of things,' Dot said. 'I am not gathering evidence for any lawsuit. Do you understand?'

'I comprehend you very well,' said the colonel.

Then Dot said something lengthy in what sounded to George like very fluent local lingo. The expression on the colonel's face did not change. '*Faghat negah mikonam,*' she concluded. '*Faghat negah mikonam.* My only interest is to locate the girl.'

Jamshidiyeh looked at her. Then he looked at George, and back at Dot. 'I wish you very good luck,' he said. Then he said something in Arab-speak, talking very rapidly in a low voice. Then he stood up. 'I of course offer you any and all assistance.'

Dot said: 'Thank you.' The interview was over. On the way back to the flitter, George asked: 'What did you say to him, when you spoke Arab?'

'It was Farsi. I explained that of course he knew a lawsuit was likely, but that I had no interest in that, one way or another. I told him I genuinely wanted to find the girl. I explained that I had complete powers of proxy. He said their attempt to locate the girl had been strenuous, and far-reaching, but if I wanted to press my own enquiries then good luck. He was glad, I think.'

'Glad?'

'No, not glad. That suggests he cares either way. He doesn't.

But he's content for somebody else to come and shake the tree, see if anything falls out.'

They got back in the car. '*Will* you find her?'

'I can't promise I will, Mr Denoone. But I *can* promise I'll try harder than they did.'

The car bounced upwards. George's stomach pressed into the cradle of his pelvis. Cloud hurried down to embrace them. A few moments of fog, and then up into bright sky again. The sun shone. They passed a few dozen metres from a seeding blimp, fat as a European socialite, or a New York supermodel. Then they were sweeping away through the enormous, compliant air of the third world.

14

Awaiting his ride home to New York, Dot and George had a conversation in a bar at Tbilisi air-station. Used to travelling in the company of affluent tourists George found the surrounding press of beaky, harsh-eyed businessmen and -women unsettling. With only a very few exceptions, himself amongst them, everybody was *thin*. It looked shabby. Seedy, in fact. The predominant dress was advertising pinafores and ponchos. Which is to say: these people were so strapped for cash it was worth their while generating this trickle of cents, even though the garb was deeply unfashionable.

George drank fruit whisky through a straw. Dot had a sherbet. 'Let's talk about why your daughter was stolen,' she said, without preliminaries.

'OK,' said George.

'No,' said Dot. 'Wait. A better way of coming at this would be: why, despite the earnest desire of the authorities to recover her, and despite all your money – which we can agree ought to lubricate things nicely – *why* has she not been found?'

This last phrase was closer to George's own language. He repeated it, with a Georgesque inflection: 'Why *has* she not been found?'

'So, Nic Neocles changed the world with his invention,' Dot said, airily, 'and nothing changed. That's the thing, actually. Understanding that nothing changes changes everything. There's no such thing as *revolution*. Revolution is just another way for things to stay the same. So, there were a few years of violence, but quick enough things settled down into a new pattern – a variation of a very old pattern. The oldest pattern, I suppose.'

'You're a little,' he observed, 'digressive.' Was that the right word? But she wagged a finger at him and went on talking.

'The situation in Ararat – which is to say, practically speaking, in Iran – is the same as the situation all round the whole *band* of the tropics. Wherever it is sunny, it is the same.'

'OK,' he said, assenting to he-knew-not.

'At village level – or at city-block level in the cities – the bosses run the world. They give out the orders, and dole out the punishments. If a crime is committed in an area, you shake down the bosses, make things either uncomfortable enough, or provide them with inducement enough, to sort out your problem. Otherwise you leave them alone. So, if there's trouble, lean on the bosses. They lean on the peasants. That works for almost any crime. Indeed, it works so well for most crime that we, higher-up, I mean, never even get to hear anything about it.'

'Higher-up.'

'I mean people who have some money, like me. Or people who have lots of money, like you. By lower-down I mean people who have *no money at all*. Once upon a time, even the lowest of the low had a *little* bit of money, because in the old days peasants had to eat. Had to eat or die. A dead peasant isn't any good to a village boss. You can't get any work out of a dead peasant. So village bosses had to make sure the peasants got subsistence monies – in cash or kind. Enough to eat, enough to live.'

'The New Hair freed people from that,' observed George.

'Just so. Now, you might think it would have freed up the peasants to spend their small money on something else, to better themselves, whatever. All that utopian jibberjabber. But it didn't. Instead it freed up the *bosses* to stop giving peasants any money at all. You drink water from the canal; you soak up sunlight from the ever-generous air, and you never need to eat. You may get odd cravings for insects or dirt, but you can scratch around in the mud for that. Otherwise you're pretty much self-sufficient.'

'Sure,' said George.

'And if you're a *monk*, or something like that, then sure, it makes you free – free to sit stylites for decades and commune with God. If you want. But if you're an honest-to-goodness peasant, all it does is free the bosses to squeeze more money for themselves from your labour. I know what you're thinking.'

If George had had more gumption he might have riposted: 'Even *I* don't know what I'm thinking.' But instead he sat silently, and peered at the little glistening circle of fluid in his cup. By tapping the side of the shot-glass he could make a transient circle appear in the middle of the circle.

'The bosses still need people to do the work, of course,' Dot was saying. 'So, you're thinking: why would any peasant work for any boss? Right? Why don't they just go off together and start a new village – or rise up and throw the oppressors in the canal? What's stopping them? They don't need the bosses for anything, after all – not for money, I mean. They can live by light alone.'

'Sure,' said George.

'It's the question. It's *the* question, actually. And there are three answers. And the third of those three answers is really germane to your unhappy situation, Mr Denoone. I'll come to that. But let's do it in order. The first answer has to do with the inertia of the peasants, especially the men. I mean, a deep-dyed ontological inertia. But that sounds a bit racist. Peasantist. I know it does. So people don't like talking about it. Not like that.'

George knew as much about peasant life as he did about life on the moons of Jupiter, so he held his peace.

'Another answer, more practical, has to do with the bosses' power. They can shave your head in a minute. How long would you last with a bald head?'

'How long?' George asked. 'I don't know.'

'Hair grows at half-an-inch a month'

'Half a what?'

'A little over a centimetre a month,' Dot said. 'Less if you're not well-nourished. So how long until you had enough hair to generate enough energy to keep yourself alive, from a bald standing-start?'

'I've no idea.'

Something like a smile, or at least a half-inclination of the corner of her mouth, touched Dot's expression. George hadn't seen *that* before. 'Well, the answer is,' she said, 'it depends. But it's a long time; half a year, nine months, something like that. And, of course, if you're getting your energy from your hair, then you want that hair to be as long as possible – really you need a three- or four-year growth of New Hair to give you enough energy to work properly. So, if the boss's men hold you down and shave your head, well – then you'll die. You'll die unless somebody supplies you with nutrients – milk say – for the whole course of the intervening period. Do you know anybody who'd be prepared to supply *you* with milk and meal for half a year? Imagine the cost of it! Remember you don't have a single cent. Remember you don't have *any* means of obtaining money. No one will gift you or loan you a penny. Half a year's supply of real food – you'd need to be rich as a banker to even contemplate it. So, mostly, you'll die.'

George thought of the bald-headed corpses he had seen lying by the trench on the trip he'd made to that village. He couldn't remember the name of the village. He remembered the commissioner describing the whole trip as *wild-goose chase*. He'd eaten goose in a Tokyo restaurant once. Or gosling, which amounted to the same thing.

'OK,' he said.

'But there's a third reason,' Dot said, 'why people don't just opt out of the whole village system, go live in the hills or wander the highways. It's the reason why your daughter got stolen.'

Just at that moment the call shrilled through the bar, and Dot and George shoe-shuffled through to the flexible corridor and onto the ramjet. A minute and a half of settling themselves in their seats. The plane eased into motion on the slipway. It and the ground parted company with a little sigh. George and Dot sat through several minutes of chest-squeezing accelera-tion at a steep angle, before the belts snaked away and the seats swung round in their floor grooves.

An R2 trundled along dispensing drinks.

'Mad Nic Neocles,' Dot said, as if they had never been interrupted. 'He thought he was giving the world a great new gift. And it's true that you can live a long life with his New Hair, provided you get water to drink, and don't mind nibbling the odd creepy-crawly from time to time. But here's what you *can't* really do, if the New Hair is your only source of blood sugar. You can't carry a pregnancy to term.'

'Really?' said George. 'I never knew that.'

'Often you can't even get pregnant in the first place. If you do then you'll almost certainly spontaneously abort long before term. With only hair to generate blood sugars, a woman's body doesn't have the level of nutrient to keep the foetus viable.'

There was something revolting about the clinical way this woman used such language. 'When I got out of bed this morning,' George said, 'I had no idea you even existed. Now you're discussing these very unpleasant things with me like—'

He was going to say: *like we were lovers*, but that seemed too forward. So instead he said: 'Like we've known each other for years.'

'You need to know this stuff, Mr Denoone. Growing a baby in your uterus is a huge drain on a human body. It's touch-and-go even in wealthy women with all the food-calories in the world to draw on. But if peasant women can't have babies, then how do new generations of peasants come into the world for the bosses to exploit? That's the question.'

'You're language is very,' George said, crinkling up his brow and waving his right hand. He couldn't think of the word.

'Because obviously new generations of peasants do arise, for the bosses to exploit.'

'—very *loaded*,' he said. 'Very *ideological*.' He pulled both his earlobes with two hands simultaneously. 'And "exploit" is a loaded term, isn't it, though?'

'This is what makes the world work,' said Dot, blandly. 'Because naturally the women want to have babies, so they don't die childless; and naturally bosses want them to have babies, so the source of their wealth and power doesn't vanish with the passing generation. So people find ways of making it happen. Some women do it by working: digging trenches for corpses, for instance, or any job that pays – they do it by working to earn money, so as to buy *food* to tide them over through their pregnancy. This is important.'

'Important,' said George. He had distracted himself with the fleeting thought of his unspoken *as if we were lovers*. He wondered what it would be like to go to bed with this slight, intense woman. The thought was exciting, though distant.

'It's important because it means women are prepared to work, indeed *eager* to work, in a way the men aren't. Plenty of peasant men are content simply to loll in the sun. If a boss wants a ditch dug, he goes to a woman. There's little point in going to a man. He lacks the motivation to do strenuous physical labour for you. But a woman *needs* to scrimp and to save.'

'I see.'

'Do you? Good. Because it's the most important of Mad Nic's unintended consequences. His invention made men idle and made sure that all the heavy lifting passed to women. Not,' she added, looking darkly at George, 'that that wasn't pretty much the case before.'

'I don't know why you keep looking at me as if,' said George, peevishly, 'as if it is *my* fault.'

'Bosses leverage their women's desire to have babies into many years of grunt-hard work; the women do it to stockpile enough protein powder to see them through pregnancy and breast feeding. And when that kid grows its hair and can loll about in the sunshine like its fathers and uncles, it's back to work *she* goes, to save up powdered milk or milled grain for the next one. Thus turneth the wheel.'

'Wheel?'

'The wheel of work. In the villages, the bosses pay *just enough* to allow this to happen. That's called capitalism. It used to be that the bosses paid peasants just enough to stop them starving; now they pay peasants considerably less – just enough to keep one fraction of a family in milk-powder for a year or two. That way the bosses make more money and keep more money. Which means that people like you or I, higher up the pyramid, have more money.'

'It's hard,' said George, haughtily, 'to feel a *personal* responsibility. I'd never treat another person so cruelly.'

Dot ignored this. 'Carrot, paying the women's pittance. Stick, shaving delinquent heads. Not everybody shaved dies, but most do. If *your* husband got his head shaved, would *you* give up your baby powder to keep him alive until the hair grew back? You can always get another husband – the village is full of idle men. They are *literally* lying about.'

'To talk of human lives in so cavalier a manner,' George began but vaguely, unable to inject any actual outrage into his voice.

Dot nodded, as if this were fair comment. 'Now, the bosses aren't stupid,' she went on. 'And women aren't stupid. Easier to grab a child than carry it two thirds of a year in your womb. The women get a kid; the bosses get their population of serfs renewed. That's why they're so reluctant to intervene. If a Turk or Iranian had stolen your gold-plated Fwn, then the police would've run the news round the local villages, a boss would have shaved a couple of heads, pocketed the reward and the trinket would have come back to you. But the bosses make a point of not getting involved where child theft is concerned.'

George was discomfited, though in a distant sort of way. It was some small thing that gnawed at his thoughts. Or else it was an ocean pivoting about on the hinge of its tide deep in his soul. He wanted to ignore it. He knew the way his world worked, which meant he knew the way the world worked. Surely. 'It's,' he said, searching for the right word, 'monstrous.'

'It's what makes the world go around. Usually children get grabbed from the moderate-poor in the cities. Pretty much, rural life is too closed and known to get away with stealing from a neighbouring village. But kids disappear from cities all the time. It is rarer to steal from the wealthy, such as yourself. Though the kids they get that way tend to be stronger – good long bones from years of actual nutrition. Have you seen how stunted kids arms and legs get when they're raised on pure sunshine?' Of course George had not seen this, and of course Dot knew he had not. So she pressed the point. 'Kids raised on nothing but sunshine and a little clean chewed mud? Small.

Height is an index of beauty, in this day and age. Just like body fat. A hundred years ago beauty was thin. Not any more.'

'Leah was in the ninetieth percentile for height,' George said, not really focusing on what he was saying.'

'There you go. That's why she was nicked.'

'What do you mean, *nicked*?'

'Stolen, I mean. Nicked means stolen.'

'Is that a Britishism? I thought you mean she had been cut,' said George, blinking.

'It's the hidden economy. But knowing all that doesn't make it any easier to locate her. Bosses won't talk, and of course the peasants won't. If she really stood out from the other kids – if she were Chinese, or black. But she's Jewish – yeah?'

'Her mother.'

'Semitic, right, so I daresay she'll look more or less like all the other kids in her village. Taller, sure. But the girls are usually taller than the boys anyway – they're fed for longer, nurtured more. They're more valuable, of course. Beyond that they'll have fed her the New Hair bug, the Neocles seed, and then weaned her off actual food for a few months. By now she'll be living like all the other kids; soaking the sun, scratching in the vegetation for worms.'

'Oh God,' said George. But he couldn't seem to get the word to come out with the appropriate force and heft. He couldn't, somehow, insert enough grandeur and woe into the syllable. He tried again, launching it from deeper in his chest. 'God.' Still no good. He tried bending the 'o' around his mouth, with a quavery thrum. 'God.' No.

'You need to understand the reality of the situation,' Dot drawled. 'Is why I'm telling you. I *will* look hard for your girl. Believe I will. But it won't be easy. I can't promise I'll find her. But – and you can allow yourself to hope – I *may* do.'

'Leah,' said George, more quietly this time. He felt as if he ought to be crying, now. He felt, that is to say, that tears would be an appropriate reaction. But his face wasn't putting out any tears. He wasn't skilled in forcing them out.

'I'll need data on your girl,' Dot said,

'What data?'

'Pictures, flash, physical details, medical details.'

George brought out his Fwn. 'I'll send you everything,' he said.

15

Marie received the news that 'a professional' (which was what George decided to call Dot) was searching for Leah and offered no reaction, neither good nor bad. She called up Wharton, took Ezra from her and, despite his wriggling protest, clutched him close to her. 'I don't care what you do,' she said. 'Only I'm never going back to that place. Do you understand?'

'Surely.'

'Never going back to that beastly place.'

'She said not to get our hopes up. But she knows what – she *knows* what's she's doing, I think.'

It was hard, though. For two days, the thought that this woman was 'out there', shaking things up and actually *looking* for Leah blimped up George's spirits. He felt as if he had woken from a slumber, felt energy fizzing within him. By the third, his spirits had sunk again. And for a time it was worse than it had been before. He knew he was skirting around the truth of things – that his daughter was gone, and he would never see her again. But it was too terrible to confront that fact. So he busied himself, and ignored it, or tried to.

He moved up to level 7 of his assertiveness therapy. His therapist was a completely bald woman with a chessboard pattern inscribed on her scalp, and a cleverly parsimonious manner with her smile. She lost no opportunity in touching him – laying a dry palm on his shoulder, or even his neck; letting her fingers touch the back of his hand as it lay on the table. George wondered if she were playing some complex therapeutic game, encouraging him to make a pass at her so that she could demonstrate her healthily assertive mode of turning him down. And in turn he wasn't sure if he were supposed assertively to own his randiness and make the pass, or whether he were supposed assertively to deny his urges. Still, he was pleased to make level 7. It felt like a real achievement.

Life had to go on, didn't it?

Ezra picked up an infection from somewhere – from where precisely, George had no idea; because his preschool was all virtual, and Wharton rarely took him further afield than Central Park. It wasn't a problem in itself, of course; except that the machine the doctor put in the lad's bloodstream to tag the infection and boost his immune kickback produced a pseudoallergic reaction. This, the doctor told them, was similar to a *traditional* allergic reaction in every external respect, but followed some arcane internal pathological route that meant standard treatments were not appropriate. Poor little Ezra's lips became swollen and hard as mug handles, and his eyes went so dark red it was hard to see where the 'whites' ended and the pupils began. He whimpered continually, and writhed pitiably, so that Marie couldn't bear to be with him, and gave up her usual breakfast and evening sessions with him entirely. Indeed, Marie took this development extremely hard, retiring to her bed and watching whole series-runs of bright-coloured storybooks over and over. But, with the help of some expensive neutral machines, the original batch was purged, and older medical antivirals cleared away the infection, and within a week Ezra was back to his old self.

Dot submitted weekly reports on her progress. George read them without too much attention, for they were full of detail that added up to very little, and he found his attention wandering. Marie avoided them altogether.

They all took an Easter holiday in Tokyo, their first since

Leah's evanishment. They didn't do very much more than stay in the Superhotel Suzuki: playing in the forty-storey flotation cube, citywatching from the rooftop observation platforms. Wharton brought Ezra everywhere George and Marie went, without exception. Some of Marie's anxiety about Ezra seeped into George's sleeping mind, such that he found himself waking at odd moments in the dead night. But generally they agreed it was a success. Life had to go on. Life went on, at any rate. Even Marie understood that, at some subterranean level of her grief.

Then it was spring in New York, and the trees were pushing cottony blossom out at the end of stiff tentacular branches. The chill faded from the outside air. Ergaste called through on the Lance to propose a spring party – which was, George presumed, an English tradition. 'Em and I, but also Ysabelle and Peter. Let's get together. You've been through *hell*,' he said with enormous emphasis on this last word. 'You and Marie both. We want to show you we're *right there* with you – solidarity, yeah?' Despite his new level 7 status, he couldn't think of a way of saying no to this offer; of, that is, communicating his fear that Marie would detest such a get-together. But after he had agreed he equivocated with himself, maybe it would do her good to be confronted with it? Didn't she need to take properly assertive ownership of her trauma? Not to carry on fleeing it. At any rate, it was agreed that the other four would fly to New York, and that the six of them would have a meal together.

To his surprise, Marie seemed pleased at the news; and took the opportunity to have a complete vanity workover. They met at Frye's, and the meal went well. For one thing, although Marie insisted that Ezra (and Wharton) stay in the car parked directly outside the restaurant, she did not, as George had thought she might, repeatedly interrupt the eating in order to run out and check that things were OK. They ate granules of beef in tequila sauce, and carrot tips threaded on strings of noodle. Then they had thimbles of gin-broth, little saucers of flavoured salt, and finally tubes of choco-rich. George drank plain red wine, congratulating himself, inwardly, on his monkish restraint. The others drank sugar cocktails mixed so that the colours shifted according to ad-sense kaleidoscopic. Ergaste was on surprisingly diplomatic form. He hardly boomed, or bullied, at all. Instead, producing an unexpected tenderness out of his manner like a conjurer, he prompted Marie to general conversation, and from time to time squeezed her hand. Ysabelle, after some bland pleasantries with George, focused all her attention on Ergaste, breaking into a weird brakepad-friction laugh from time to time, in an exaggerated way. It was as if she had never had sexual intercourse with George. George, for his part, was happy to go along with that. Peter kept checking in on some sporting fixture or other on his Fwn, but seemed generally in good humour. Emma, it turned out, was also in assertiveness therapy.

'I *knew* you were in the therapy!' she told George, in her singsong voice. 'I could sense it.'

'Really?' he said, rather pleased.

'Oh yes. You have a *splendidly* assertive manner.'

'I do.'

'It *shines* from you.'

'Do you really think so?' he replied. He was milking it, he knew. But the cactus craves the tiniest moisture drops. It was hard to believe that Emma, this timid woman, was also undergoing the therapy. How did she possibly get by? The way she sucked the left portion of her lower lip into her mouth, or folded it outwards into a little crease between her fingers. The way her eyes would never settle, darting continually from sinister to dexter and back to sinister. She was the least healthily assertive individual he knew. But of course courtesy required he repay in kind. 'And, ah! You too, of course,' he said, in an unconvincing voice.

'I've been going for years,' she told the tabletop.

'Really?'

'It's so obvious to me now that *true* mental health is a superstructure built upon the base of a properly assertive being-in-the-world,' she said, lifting her mouse-grey eyes to look at George. She dropped them again.

'Just so,' said George. He wondered if it was polite to ask her what level she was at, aware that he'd be doing do only to brag about his own recent ascent. But just as he decided that he couldn't raise the subject, she volunteered the information. 'I'm level seven,' she said.

'Oh,' he said, feeling a shock of disappointment.

'Er thinks it's a waste of time,' she added, gesturing twitch-ily with her head. George heard this as 'her thinks', assumed it was a British idiom. 'Who does?' he asked, following the direction of her gesture. 'Ysabelle?'

'Ergaste,' she said, in a low voice. 'He says I'm no more assertive than a clod. But I explained to him – *you* understand this, I know – that it's not about turning yourself into a bully, into a blustering oaf – like – like *some* people I could mention. It's inner assertiveness. It's spiritual, really.' She put her atten-tion into an intimate examination of the streaks of choco-rich still adhering to the side of her little half-sphere bowl.

For George, who assumed that assertiveness therapy did indeed translate into more forceful external behaviour, held his peace. 'I'm sure,' Emma said, after a while, 'that it's been a help.'

'Help?'

'Dealing with your horrid, your foul, your *tragic*, rather, thing. Your *tragedy*.'

'Oh,' he said. 'I guess. Sure.'

'You're certainly dealing with it really well!'

At this point the six of them went up to the building's roof. Frye's had installed diffraction projectors all round the rim, to block out the city lights and create a sort of funnel of darkness – the point, of course, was to make the stars visible mid-city. So they all stood for ten minutes with their heads cricked backwards like pez-dispensers, gazing upwards. 'Never fails,' boomed Ergaste. 'Never fails to amaze!'

Ergaste, Peter, Ys and Marie wandered to the far corner. But Emma crept up close to George, she said: 'Oh, look at the stars! Aren't those stars simply *splendid*?'

'There's rather more of them,' George said, 'than is absolutely necessary, I've always thought.'

'Oh, but the beauty is *in* the profusion!'

'The untidiness certainly is.'

She laughed at this, a series of little, piping sounds. 'You are funny.'

'Hey! Really? Well *that's* not something generally remarked upon.'

'You are funny,' she insisted. 'You're *wry*.' Then, glancing nervously over her shoulder, she stretched up and kissed him. George could not have been more astonished had she punched him on the nose – kissed him on the front of his face, not quite connecting with his mouth, her upper lip pressing against his lower and the rest of her mouth squelching against his chin. At the same time she put her left hand on his right arm, her right hand on his left arm, and squeezed with an almost mannish grip, as if fearful he'd bolt and run away.

George disengaged as best he could. 'Emma.'

She began gabbling a good deal of stuff in a low voice, several times looking over her shoulder at the others: 'You're so *sensitive*, your carriage and bearing is so sensitive. You have such a beautiful *face*. I'm crushed by Ergaste. He's crushing me. *You* understand me – *you* have a beautiful soul.'

'Emma, look, really . . .'

'I *love* you, I feel this tremendous *passion* for you, I confess it, how rare it is to feel a *connection* with a person in this hothouse of life. The *stars* have determined our meeting.'

It was all very tiresome indeed.

'You've got the wrong link, Emma,' he said. 'I'm – no – I'm a no. I'm sorry.'

But she wasn't to be deterred. She tried a different angle, hissing quickly in a hoarse voice: 'I'm a woman living in a hellish prison. Er doesn't care about me, he doesn't love me, he never shows me any affection. He's shown no more decent husbandly interest in me than if I were a piece of furniture.'

'He has shown,' George said, removing the grip she had reasserted on his right arm, and trying to keep his voice on the civilized side of anger, 'enough interest in you to father your child.'

She flinched away at this, as if at a slap. And just in time, too; for the other four were strolling back, discussing which of the several rapidly sliding lights belonged to the Orbital, and which were L8 burners. Ergaste, blithely unaware of his wife's mood, putting a tampon-shaped c:snuff dispenser into his left nostril. 'Shall we go back down?' he boomed. 'A snifter before we call it a night?'

All down the sliding walkway Emma kept peering over at George. She looked distressed. Or perhaps she looked angry. Either way, George was relieved to get to the bar, I'll not lie to you, and to top up his blood-alcohol level with some Red Whisky.

Marie conducted a long conversation on her Fwn with Wharton about Ezra, even though only five metres and one wall separated them. Peter and Ergaste had a bantering disagreement on the proper way to cook jellyfish. 'Point the Fwn at him again,' Marie was saying. 'No – at his face. Is his mouth open? Is that an open mouth? Is his nose blocked?'

Then Emma, turned her back on all of them with an actor's command of the space, and began sobbing loudly. Ergaste swept her up in his right arm and whisked her away. '*Splendid* to see you all,' he said. 'George, Marie, we're *with* you. You're doing *tremendously* well.' He was at the door, and his car was drawing up outside, but he turned once more, cradling his sobbing wife into his armpit, and called back to them: 'Look how *well* you're doing!'

Later, in their own car, with Ezra snoring like a mosquito in his cot, and Wharton's eyelids slipping down and perking open over and over, Marie said suddenly: 'Did Emma make a play?'

'Oh,' he exclaimed, genuinely. 'Horrid woman!'

'I thought I saw her all over you. On the roof, wasn't it?'

'It came from *nowhere*,' he complained.

'I thought I saw her make a play,' she said, in an unreadable tone of voice.

16

Something invisible in the city was releasing, or relaxing, and it was the seasons changing. Spring was increasingly filled the city's vacuum. Spring. Dot called through, on the Lance. Her usual weekly progress reports usually came as ordinary messages on the Fwn, so it was startling – portentous, almost – to see her actually there in the room. 'I have found her,' said Dot.

George drew a long breath into his lungs from the exhaustless reservoir of the world's air. He held it and blew it out again. There was no tingle in his skin at these words; and no apprehension in his stomach. Isn't that strange? Shouldn't there have been? 'You've found her,' he said. The inflection of that last word was exactly halfway between the upward slope of a question and the horizontal tonality of a statement.

Dot waited, perhaps for some specific prompt from her employer; but when George said nothing she said: 'She's all right. You and your wife must get the next ramjet – I can meet you at Tbilisi. Right away; I'll meet you at noon.'

'Now?' said George, dully.

'That's right. Straight away.'

George thought of his daily routine: the gym session; his therapy at twelve; the café for lunch; a chess game. For some reason, the thought of abandoning it all to go shooting off to the other side of the planet distressed him. Dot's words: *I have found her*. The *her*, of course, meant Leah. George shifted the weight from his left to his right leg. He had no mental picture of Leah at all. 'Marie won't come,' he heard himself say. 'She's vowed never to go back there.'

'Then *you* come, George,' said Dot, displaying – un-characteristically enough – an impatience amounting almost to ill-temper. 'Come on!'

'Of course,' said George feeling not elation or anticipation but, weirdly, a kind of profound sleepiness. He slouched though into the wardrobe to put suitable gear on. He put on a smart overcoat. He sat on the carpet fitting a shoe onto his left foot and then fitting a shoe onto his right foot. And yawning. Big jaw-creaky yawns. 'Marie,' he cried, syncopating little right hand/right cheek, left hand/cheek slaps, trying to haul himself into full consciousness by sheer willpower. 'Marie!'

He had to go from room to room before he found her.

'Marie! Leah has been found!'

She received this news with inscrutable placidity. George explained that he had to catch a ramjet, and said that he'd Fwn her as soon as he arrived at Tblisi. But she scowled at this. It took him a sluggish moment to realize that she *did* want to come with him after all; and George, in a kind of foggy stupor, reminded her of her vow. 'You want to *stop* me from coming?' she snapped.

'Of course not. No!'

'I'm coming.'

So they caught a ramjet together from Ronald Reagan, and as the windows darkened to deep-space black George at last felt something like excitement swelling in his belly. Leah had been found. He repeated the phrase, inwardly, to himself. To make it realer to himself. He was going to get his daughter back.

'What's that you're saying?' Marie asked him. 'What are you muttering?'

'I just can't believe it,' he told her. 'It's a dream.'

'You gave up hope,' said Marie.

'I never gave up hope!' he returned.

'*I* never gave up hope,' she snapped. But this claim that she alone had kept the flame alight infuriated him; and out of his annoyance he felt the kindling of excitement in his bowels. The catalyst of strong emotion. Outside, the air was breaking into yellow and white sparks. Luminous dashes and hyphens were flowing past the window. The tug in his gut of descent; the thrill of incipient reunion with his lost child.

George and Marie disembarked like zombies.

Dot was there in the landing lounge. Standing beside her was a tall, bearded man wearing combat-style trousers. 'This is Ivan Indrikov,' said Dot. 'He has been working with me.'

'To *meet* you,' said Ivan, shaking both Marie and George by the hand, in turn, with a stiff politeness. He had a wide face, tanned skin and a spread of untanned lines converging on the outer edge of each eye. A pale mole was tucked in by his right nostril, like a reset button. 'Great! So pleased!'

'He knows the area,' Dot explained. 'I could not have located your daughter without him.'

'We're very grateful,' said Marie, uncharacteristic nervousness tingeing her voice. 'Is Leah here? Have you brought her?'

'Not here,' said Dot.

Marie said 'Can I see her?' at exactly the same time that George explosively cleared his throat.

'We must go to village,' said Ivan.

'*We* could not claim her,' Dot added. 'We're not her parents. But we can be at the village in an hour and then you will have her.'

So they passed through the terminal and out into the parkyard. In moments the four of them were squeezed into a flitter and were zipping through the bright sky. George cleared his throat again, coughed, and thrummed his tonsils noisily. His previous numbness had somehow transformed itself into an agitation of the uvula. Cough, cough. He rehearsed the thought that he was about to be reunited with his daughter, after eleven months of cruel separation. It did not feel real. Cough. He thought about it, and it occurred to him that it did not feel real because the separation itself did not feel real. With a mild, notional panic he wondered if anything felt real to him. But it was all right; because looking through the flitter's passenger window he saw the sky, a purer and more enduring blue than even the sapphire of his Fwn-screen. And he saw the tawny ground beneath, creased like a dirty sheet into little humps and hillocks. Khaki stretches of barrenness, and then a rectangle of crow-coloured weeds running wild over what had once been cultivated land.

Cough.

They came in a little lower, on the outskirts of a town. A huge crowd of people had gathered, like the crowd at a football match; but there was no game being played, and no purpose to the gathering. So many hairy heads, all crowded together, had the appearance of a great expanse of black seaweed at low tide – and then they were over a huge wire fence and into a commercial compound.

'We must continue the journey in an iCar Armoured,' said Dot.

'We cannot,' Indrikov elaborated, 'be safe in the air over the territory.'

Marie stared at him as if he had spoken in Russian.

So they landed, and stepped out into a stone heat so fierce it made both George and Marie shudder. Walking five metres to the hefty iCar was enough for both of them to start sweating incontinently; but then they were inside, and sitting upon the cool, bed-broad seats of the vehicle. The driver, looking over his left shoulder, grinned at them, and then held up a Versace chain-pistol – perhaps to reassure them, although in truth it was an intimidating gesture. Indrikov, clambering in to sit beside George, spoke sharply to the fellow and he put the gun away.

'Should we be worried?' asked Marie, in an eerie voice.

'No ma'am,' said Dot, firmly, climbing in to the front seat. She pulled the weighty passenger door closed with an enormous clunk. 'We will go to a village, and collect your daughter.'

The car grumbled into life and pulled away. Cumbrous but well engineered.

'Some money is paid,' said Indrikov, leaning forward. His jacket gaped open to show – like a girl at a party inadvertently displaying her cleavage – a glimpse of his own holstered handgun. 'More money must be paid. I know these people.'

'What is the name of this village?' George asked.

'It is,' replied Dot, looking to Indrikov for confirmation. 'Orc—'

'Öcalan,' said the Russian.

Everybody in the car fell silent. The minutes passed, as minutes invariably do. The landscape, darkened by the tinted windows, rolled monotonous variations out of brown, yellow and cream. They drove through a smallish town. When the iCar slowed to go through the narrower, built-up streets George saw Indrikov slide his hand inside his jacket.

George directed his attention outside. This frazzled, desert place. He was still trying to come to terms with being here and with the imminence of seeing Leah again. Or would it be another goose-chase? Through the window he saw an empty dust-field between buildings, and in it a long trench being dug by women, and a tangle of skin-sheathed skeletons, heads bald as footballs, lying beside it. A man in a cowboy hat stood watching this excavation, cradling a shotgun to his breast as if it were a baby. On the other side of the road a score of long-haired men were sitting or standing, observing the proceedings with dispassion.

Round a corner, and up a slope, and here were many more long-haired men at the roadside, standing or walking or sitting. Several had gathered round a precarious-looking tin table, on which a game of cards was being played. They turned a corner. George had a brief glimpse in through an open doorway as the iCar rolled by. As they passed, the view down a narrow hallway swung on its perspectival hinge. At the end was a bright room in which a woman stood rubbing at the unclothed torso of a muscular man with – George thought (he only saw it for a moment) – a sponge. There was something about this brief glimpse, about the unsought *intimacy* of it, that startled George. That there were such things as rooms, and private lives, behind the pasteboard frontage and all this set scenery. Then they had gone right through the town, and out the other side, and they rolled out into the weedy, wasted countryside again.

The car laboured up a long slope, drove between two hemming rocky embankments and began a long, gradual straight descent. Marie took hold of George's hand. A squeeze. He tried to settle his thoughts on Leah; on what he would say to her – on what he and she would do back in New York to catch up on the stolen eleven months. But his inner eye kept reverting to the image of that man, stripped to the waist to display his bulky upper body, whilst that woman worked her way over it with a wet sponge. The lit room at the end of the dark, straight corridor. The surgical glimpse past shuttered windows and plaster wall and doors with metal over-frames.

'We're here,' said Dot.

The car pulled up in a tiny village square. This must be Öcalan: a scattering of low-level houses, and rising above them a single fort-like edifice fronted by an imposing double-door. In the middle of the square a fountain poured a quavery thread of shining water into its stone font. There was a single palm tree, leaves foxed and frayed at the edges. Several dozen long-haired men lounged in the sunlight; more strikingly, half a dozen short-haired men sat or stood underneath the palm tree.

'Permit me to go out first,' said Indrikov. Nobody contradicted him. He popped the passenger door, slipped his firearm into his right hand, and climbed into the brightness. George watched him walk over to the palm tree, and stand for a while talking to the men. The group there consisted, George could see, of one big-bellied, doleful-looking fellow with his wrists bound together in front of him, and two burly men at each of his shoulders. A few strides away stood another man, a sailor's cap on his head and the manner of easy command. Two women loitered by the sailor-capped fellow.

Indrikov came back to the car. 'It is OK,' he informed them. 'Please, you shall come out.' As Marie and then George extricated themselves from the vehicle, he added, 'I tell them it is not necessary, but they wish to do it.'

'To do what?'

'It is point of honour for them, they say. I say Mr-Mrs Denoone have no desire for it, but they insist.'

'Lewinski,' said Marie.

'Desire for what?' asked Dot.

'That man,' indicating the man with his wrists tied, 'used to be, here, head-boss. He is to blame for not giving up your daughter. They wish you to witness justice.'

Before George could reply to this, Marie hooted 'Leah!' and started running over the dusty ground. And there, behind the two women, was Leah: wearing a dark grey, long-sleeved dress, her hair black and long, a look on her face of astonishment, or desperate hope, or overwhelming recognition, or disbelief that it was finally all over. A face filled with profound and genuine emotion. Marie reached her, and threw her arms around her crying 'Leah! Leah!'. The two women stepped aside. George picked his step. There she was. There she *was*! Tears pricked his eyeballs, like hayfever. 'I can't believe,' he gasped, to Dot, who trotted alongside him. 'I *can't believe* it's all over.'

He was weeping, actually weeping. He got to his wife and daughter, put his arms around them both, weeping with a strange mixture of pain and joy. It was the sensation of a great pressure suddenly released, a sort of existential abscess to which he had become accustomed, but which gave him the actual, palpable pleasure of relief as it was suddenly pierced and drained. He said 'I can't believe it's over!' and then he said, 'It's been so long, my darling girl.' Leah was crying too, and grasping at her mother's waist.

'Oh, but you're thin!' Marie cried.

Dot touched George on the shoulder. 'Meet the new boss,' she said, as if quoting something. 'We agreed a sum, but he now wants more.'

George blinked in the bright sunlight of his new landscape of joy. 'What?' To think of fussing over sums of money – to, in effect, haggle – was all massively irrelevant to him now. 'More? What?'

'Not much more,' Dot said, drawing him a little further away from his wife and daughter. 'But it is your money, after all.'

'I don't care about that,' said George, his chest thrumming. 'I have my daughter back. I don't care about any of that. She has come back to me.'

The sun was bright as a ball-light. Shadows black as mud clogged the doorways. The whole square felt like a perform-ance space, lit and ready for something, for something, ready for something. The human beings occupying it were fidgety with readiness. George was too, though he didn't know for what. *Money* was a concept from a wholly other world. Readi-ness for what, though?

'I understand,' Dot was saying 'I have a credit chip readied to transfer, though, and only for the agreed amount.'

George said, in a disengaged voice. 'I can't believe you're quibbling over this. Does money matter?'

'Of course,' said Dot, not catching the profundity of George's question. But you can hardly blame her for that. 'Indrikov can transfer the extra money. We'll sort finances back at Tbilisi.' Ever the practical mind.

'Yes—'

He was moving like a man in a trance, walking back towards his wife and daughter.

'The extra *money* is to cover the *justice*,' Dot called after him. But none of her words made sense. None of the world she represented had any bearing. He put his arm around his wife's shoulder, as she in turn shielded Leah with her body, and, together all three, they moved back towards the iCar. Only when they reached the vehicle did George look back, like Lot's wife. The Russian was shaking the sailor-hatted man's hands. Here he was, the new village boss, and he was shaking the Russian's hand. He was smiling, and half-nodding, half-shaking his head. Dot was walking away, strolling briskly towards them across the square. Job done. The sunlight, falling with its preternatural brightness from directly above, gave the scene an unreal vividness.

The prisoner closed his eyes. His wrists were tied so tightly that the fingers (George could see) were turning blue. As he closed his eyes, the new boss came over to him and tapped him on the chest. One of the henchmen, standing behind the victim's left shoulder, drew out a gun. It all happened in a single fluid, hyperreal, continuous take; and *as* it happened, George – however jangled his mind might have been by the extraordinary events of the day – as it happened George understood that it was being staged specifically for his benefit.

The henchman pressed his gun against his captive's head. With a cacophonous report the gun blew a megaphone of blood and matter out of the man's right temple.

George shrieked at the brutality of this sound, at the hurt it inflicted upon his eardrums. Drew his head down into his shoulders. Marie and Leah flinched in unison. But the three of them did not stop, the three of them kept walking, picked up their pace. The open door of the iCar Armoured drew them; the portal into the haven of their transport; their means of escaping that place and getting home to New York, mother, father and daughter. The horrible loudness of the pistol shot had buckled the air, dented it like sheet metal. The sound had tossed a dozen screeching birds into the air. The sound bounced from the roofs of the surrounding buildings. Its din echoed, belatedly, off the slopes of the hill under which the village was located.

In the space immediately beside the victim's head a limb of cloudy scarlet opened up. It spread into an oval. It drifted downward through the hot air.

The felled man slumped, his hands held together in front of him tight as prayer. He fell sideways, spine straight, and he hit the ground with an audible thump. The ground gave up a ghost of dust. The second henchman was stepping nimbly backwards, out of his way.

'Inside,' said Marie, pushing Leah into the vehicle.

George could not bring his head back round. The tableau struck him with great force: the people standing around the prone man; the tree's drooping palm leaves; the bone-yellow ground; the grubby plaster of the walls behind. But he put his head down and inserted himself into the car, and behind him came Dot, and close behind her Indrikov. 'It is done,' said the Russian, in a basso profundo voice, like a preacher. Treading upon the toes of this statement came Dot's low-toned, 'Fuck *that*.'

George saw that the driver had previously pulled down his window, and was resting his chain-pistol on the ledge of it, aimed at the tree. Now he hoiked his weapon back onto his lap, revved the car and they drove straight out of the village. Air poured in through the driver's open window, gushed hot against George's face. 'We've got her back,' said Marie, in a clear voice, speaking perhaps to the whole cosmos. 'We've got her back.'

17

The drive back to the flitter, the flight back to Tbilisi, the wait for the New York ramjet – all this took place in some new variety of time, a mode of experience George had, up to that precise moment, never encountered. It felt hallowed, a solidified, brighter version of the dull flow of moment to moment. More than that, 'moment' was an incompatible concept: this new time could not be chopped or shaved into slivers. It was a glowing unity, a sense of the most profound belonging, as if George – as if even George – were an essential aspect of a work of art, exactly placed according to the logic of aesthetic perfection. The idea that the world was divisible into individual atoms became, under this new dispensation, a kind of monstrous error, akin to believing that the thunder was gods rolling boulders around the palace of heaven, or that the sun only rose because humans excavated hearts from the living chests of other humans. There were, George understood, no such things as *atoms*. There was one atom, the fertile dot, and it flowed to the end of time and back again to the beginning in a gleamingly simple, supple, infinitely replicated motion. Out of this motion only, and not from anything grossly material, the stuff of the universe was fabricated, and this meant that there was literally *no* difference between George and his daughter, it meant that they were literally and actually the same real presence. Her trembling, skinny frame was the same as his corpulent body. The tears that were squeezing between her shut eyelids as she clasped her mother were the same salt that made his neurons fire and nerves thrum. And the spray of that mist of red from the broken skull of the man slain in the village was no dissolution. On the contrary, each of those myriad dots of red was a spark of the essential flame of the universe. The idea of death was impossible, because death was a discontinuity, and discontinuity was not part of the grammar of the cosmos. George had – before – felt himself to be cut off from his daughter, but this had been a misunderstanding, an error, for she and he had never been separated. He pressed his arms around her now, and around his wife, and it reaffirmed what had always been. It would have distorted his state of mind to call it *happy*. It was something more than that. It was a kind of holiness. In the flitter, Marie kept saying: 'Oh how thin you are. How thin, my darling.'

'Her stomach is small, now,' said Indrikov.

'You will need to have a care when reintroducing her to food,' said Dot.

But those sorts of practicalities were so bizarre and alien to the unifying sanctity of George's perceptions that all he could do was shake his head. He shook his head hard, as if to shed the words from his sensorium. Everything that had happened that day existed in a sort of sanctifying superposition. It was all inviolate and imperishable: the granular landscape; the trench being laboriously opened up in the compacted dust by those labouring females. The woman passing her moist sponge over the naked torso of the man, briefly glimpsed down a secret passageway into the heart of an otherwise closed-off building. The red life of the old boss spilling promiscuously into the hot air, in the village square. George's arms around Marie, and her arms around Leah, and the three of them fitting naturally and seamlessly together,

'There are medical experts,' Dot was saying, 'who know how best to handle this sort of situation.'

And the flitter banked over the yellow-brown hills, made

molten on one side by the sunlight. The sprawl of outer Tbilisi was not urban mess, but the hieroglyph of some profound unity. Bulbous clouds were made of pure white light, not water vapour. The ground below was a topography of light. Super-fast, he thought. Miracle engineering, and a thread running through every single distinct thing, like a strand of hair.

18

They parted from Indrikov at Tbilisi; but Dot came back with them to New York. She arranged, whilst airborne, for an immigration official to meet them at Ronald Reagan; and after that she accompanied them back to their building. By the time they were driving through the cubist canyons of the city, Leah had stopped sobbing. She was looking with wonder at her surroundings; an expression compounded of bewilderment at the rapidity of her rescue and the incipient awakening of recognitions. 'You wait until you see Ezra,' Marie told her. 'You wait until you see how he has *grown*. Wait till you see your brother!'

Home, home, home.

For George, though, the coming back to New York was tinged with a strange, not unpleasant, sense of disenchantment. The pure state of heightened Being he had experienced in the air started to fade. The reality of day-to-day existence began to reassert itself. This was mournful, but also, he saw, needful. A human could no more live at that peak of metaphysical insight than they could live under the regime of a continually sustained orgasm. And the afterglow of the illumination was not unpleasant. There was nothing harsh or assonant to it. It was a gentle slide down towards the bottom of the mountain. 'It's not going to be the same now,' he said to his wife, as they got out of the car. Marie, carrying Leah's emaciated frame easily, did not reply.

Behind him, and across the road, some kids in the latest teen shockwear, genitals exposed but legs and upper body, including their heads, clad in tight cloth, ran down the sidewalk, perhaps fleeing the police, or perhaps just for the lark of it. One threw a handball at the side of a Granville Wagon as they passed it, and the sphere rebounded with a sharp crack. George ducked despite himself, and nearly stumbled, as he stepped over his own threshold. The image of a man, his life blowing away in a tomato-red cloud from the side of his head, appeared vividly before him. He saw the man flinch away from this blow, and saw him rotate his whole body about the pivot of the side of his right foot, turning through ninety degrees until intersecting the floor. And then the door to his building flashed brightly, a momentary angle of reflected sunlight as it opened, and the image was banished from George's sensorium.

In the lobby he put his hand on Marie's shoulder. 'Everything will be different now.'

And things did change. One way of putting it would be to say: the renewal of the terms of their family life manifested itself as a studied effort to return everything to mundanity. The key was repetition. The thing to do was to rehabituate Leah to her NY life. Obviously she could not go straight back to school. That very afternoon, as she napped, in her own bed for the first time in eleven months, Marie and George discussed the matter, and agreed that it might be weeks, or even months, before she could pick up where she had left off before the Ararat holiday. Dot had left them, to represent the case to the authorities in person, and explain Leah's reappearance. She had also sent a spreadsheet of the sorts of professionals she considered, in her opinion, competent to help Leah readjust. One was a physical doctor with a specialism in resuming regular eating after a long New Hair fast. Another was a mental doctor – an assertivist, of course (for Dot knew her employer's quirks) – to help Leah mentally. Then there would have to be a teacher to address, one-to-one, the hole in her schooling, and of course a dedicated carer — for there were several reasons why it would be unwise to go back to employing only one person to look after both children. Finally, Dot recommended the employment of three lawyers, one for US law, one for international and one with a portfolio in kidnap victims, in order to cover the bases in locking down the lawsuit; as well as a netchecker, to police any and all references to the affair on the feeds. To all this Marie, looking beautiful for the first time in many months, agreed, excepting only the specific physical doctor suggested. 'There's no reason to bring in a stranger,' she said. 'Dr Baldwin is perfectly competent, and Leah knows him.'

'Agreed.'

Everything seemed possible. The agency sent three possible carers within a quarter hour, and Marie had chosen one before Leah woke up – a short young man called Wilson. Even the alliterative coincidence of their carers' two names seemed to George freighted with a larger truth. That evening, Wharton washed a laughing, thrashing Ezra at one end of the bath, and Wilson carefully soaped Leah's new hair, almost strand by strand it seemed, at the other. Leah sat in the water wide-eyed, staring as if in incomprehension at the people in the bathroom: at the teenager attending her; at her parents standing behind, watching this first ritual performance of the restored family almost greedily. To end her day, Leah was tucked into bed with one of her favourite books. She fixed her eyes on the screen with a familiar avidity that gladdened George's heart.

The following day Dr Baldwin called, and gave Leah a comprehensive physical examination. George watched: Leah was so shellshocked that she could not properly respond to gently uttered medical instruction to raise her arms, to breathe in or to lie down on the settee. An enormous tenderness blossomed in George's heart at the sight. Leah stared into space as if only emptiness interested her any more. Light instead of food, the abstracted aerial existence that had been forced upon her. She was so thin! Eventually, it occurred to George, a little belatedly, that his presence might be some kind of impediment to the interaction of patient and medic. He left Baldwin to it.

When the consultation was finished, Marie came through with a hair-sculptor; or (since that term hardly does her justice) with *Seylon* herself, the medal-winning hair-sculptor. As she sat her subject in a chair, preparatory to removing the vulgar long longhair tresses, Leah showed emotion for the first time since her arrival back in New York. She widened her eyes and emitted a series of yelping little sobs; and Marie had to hold her, and reassure her over and over, just to permit Seylon to crop away the hair.

As this was going on, Dr Baldwin touched George's arm. 'Through here?'

The two men withdrew into an adjacent room.

'She's physically fine. Weak, which is of course what we'd expect. But fine.'

'Thank goodness,' said George. He could hear the hum of the haircutting through the wall, and he could hear little gulping sounds as well, that could have been Leah sobbing. Or perhaps were something else.

The doctor's bland voice continued. 'Reintroducing her to food should be unproblematic.'

'Good,' said George. 'Good.'

'There's been some work on it – research, I mean. Re-introducing photophages to – to the business of eating hard food, I mean. Another thing. Her hymen is intact.'

'It – what?'

'You will, I do not doubt, be relieved to hear it.'

George looked at the medic. 'Of course.'

'Now, she *may* be suffering from the effects of psychological trauma,' murmured Baldwin. 'Now—' he added. 'To be clear. What I mean is: she is not responsive in the ways you would expect an eleven-year-old to be. Responsive to verbal instruction, say.'

'She's been through a lot,' said George.

'Of course she has. That's what I'm talking about. Children are often more resilient in the face of, eh, massive trauma, than, eh. Adults. You'll have arranged for a psychological specialist, of course. But I'll note that she has learnt to speak some of the local language.'

'She was over there for eleven months,' George said. 'It's to be expected.'

'Naturally. Now, Mr Denoone, eh, I've no desire to anticipate what your psychological specialist will say. But this sort of trauma—' Baldwin didn't so much break off his speech at this point as slide it from spoken words into a big beamy smile. He held this grin for some seconds, and then added the umlauts to the U by flashing his eyes wide open. George was a little startled, until, nudged by the persistence of the doctor's smile, he returned it.

'Let me put it this way,' said Baldwin. 'I have been your family's doctor for some years.'

'Yes.'

'I'm grateful, Mr Denoone. Grateful for your trust, and, eh, employment. Of course I am compelled by the terms of the contract I signed to secure my medical school place to – I don't mean to bore you, George.' (Oh, but there was something *jarring* in this new intimacy of 'George'.) 'Law's law, and of course I'm compelled to take a percentage of patients who pay me little or nothing, sometimes through no fault of theirs – sometimes for mortal causes. What I'm saying, what I'm trying in my *very clumsy* way to say is that, is that I'm grateful to you—' And he broke off again, this time in order to laugh a squealy little laugh. George's puzzlement suddenly resolved, in the way an optic-illusory picture can magically cohere as sense, into the comprehension that Baldwin was nervous. It hadn't occurred to him to think it, because he had never known this smooth and professionally accomplished man even had the *capacity* for nerves. But here he was.

Trying to reassure him, more to remove the awkwardness of the man's embarrassment and so relieve his own discomfort, George said: 'It's all right, Ball,' (searching his memory for a first name and not finding it) 'Baldwin, Dr Baldwin.'

'Never talk money to the rich,' laughed Baldwin, as if reciting some celebrated proverb. 'It's a grubby business, I know. And no human, rich or otherwise, wants to think that the respect of others is mediated *only* by money.'

'I don't see,' said George. 'You sound like you're talking your way round to something—'

Baldwin waited several saggy seconds before picking up the hint. 'Talking my way, you mean, *out* of my medical purview? Well, George, if I *may* call you George, I suppose I am – I am, I mean, delighted at your good fortune. Delighted you've got your daughter back! Not as somebody financially beholden to you, but as one human to another. At this fortunate turn up. I mean, the return of. The return.'

'Well thank you,' George put in, positively pained now by the man's embarrassment and wanting the interview to stop.

'You have brought me in today, you have paid me to perform a medical examination on the girl,' said Baldwin. 'You want to hear my medical opinion. You want, in fact, to hear me tell you that *your daughter* is in sound health, good health, as good as can be expected.'

'I do,' confirmed George. He could not fathom why Baldwin had spun the conversation in this peculiar manner.

'That's what – anyway. And I'm very happy to be able to confirm.' He pinched his chin between thumb and forefinger, as if selecting legally precise phraseology. 'Physically speaking, and considering the circumstances, she is healthy and well.'

There was a pause. The hum of the haircutting was no longer audible from the next room. Presumably it was finished. The light coming through the main window threw a Z-shaped area of brightness across an edge of table and the adjacent patch of carpet.

'Good,' said George.

That word seemed to free Baldwin from his odd behaviour. 'Excellent,' he said, in a brisk return of his usual manner. 'I've passed dietary requirements, a comprehensive calendar, to the girl's carer, copying you in of course. Soups to start, but within a week she'll be eating like any other eleven-year-old. I've taken genomic samples. There's always the possibility of unusual viruses, but we have machines to combat pretty much anything nowadays. Even exotic bugs.'

Now that his manner had returned to normal, George felt some obscure gush of relief inside him, as if the impending catastrophic asteroid strike had been luckily averted. But none of it made sense, not his feelings, nor the doctor's manner. It was good to put the oddity behind him.

The two men went back through to find Leah, with decently short-cropped hair now, sucking on a flavoured stick and staring into space. The great Seylon was gathering her things and preparing to go.

Baldwin, stopping in the doorway and turning back to them, suggested as a parting shot that they employ somebody to check Leah's level of in-system Whites. 'They're designed to be self-sustaining,' he said, 'but it's possible they've been . . .' and he considered the right word for a long moment: 'depleted,' he concluded, 'by her experiences.' So George called a consultant from GēnUp. She was, when she came, a smile-faced young woman, her features possessing that slightly *too* symmetrical over-perfection that cheaper treatments can give you. She had some trouble getting Leah to sit still whilst she took a sample; but then, as she crouched over her equipment, the smile withered away and her face became something it had not been designed to be – chill, unfriendly, a mask. 'I must apologize in the most humble terms,' she said, stiffly, to George. 'My equipment is malfunctioning. A GēnUp technician will be here within the quarter hour with a replacement—'

George was not in the least incommoded by this news. But then he felt a familiar creeping anxiety that, judging by her grovelling reaction, he *ought* to be incommoded. Ought, perhaps, to have raged and spouted. But he tried to live his life by one of the core assertivist tenets – being assertive was not the same thing as being aggressive, angry or bullying. So he wagged his head in a deliberately vague way, and left her to it.

The technician came with the replacement equipment in five minutes, not fifteen; and the consultant repeated the test. But now her face looked not blank with professional embarrassment but, rather, puzzled. Odd-looking creases twanged into existence, like impressions from guitar strings, from below her ear to the corners of her eyes. 'I don't understand. She seems to have nothing in her blood *at all*.'

'Check your records?' George offered, vaguely.

'But the records aren't . . . there's no problem in the records. I understand, Mr Denoone, that she has experienced an unfortunate, ah, event. But to lose *all* her coverage! It's unprecedented.' Her eyes looked in all four corners of the room as she (George assumed) calculated the relative professional risks of a lawsuit, a countersuit, the balance of contractual responsibilities. 'This is a very serious situation,' she said, pulling herself to her full height. 'She has been medically examined?'

'Fully,' said George. 'By her regular physician. There's nothing – *wrong* with her,' he added, 'according to our professional medical advice.' He meant, in his awkwardly expressed way, to reassure the woman that, whatever lapses there might have been in her company's coverage, Leah was not actually ill. But the technician looked much more sourly at this news than George might have expected her to.

'I assure you,' she said, 'this state is unprecedented in the professional administration of GēnUp antipathogens. Now, now. Provided it be understood that doing so in no way constitutes a legal admission of any kind, GēnUp will provide a full complement of basic antipathogen coverage.'

'Premier coverage,' said George; not aggressively, but simply because that was what Leah had had in her system before her kidnapping.

'Basic coverage Mr Denoone,' said the consultant, 'in the first instance. Future upgrades to be negotiated as and when – but we cannot load her system with the premier package straight off the pitch. No gWhites in her system *at all*.'

'But,' George insisted with a stubbornness born of indolence and unimagination, rather than negotiatory canniness. 'She had the full premier coverage eleven months ago.'

'These things cannot be dumped into the body all at once, Mr Denoone.'

'I'm telling you she carried that load for *years*. Years and years – until, that is, eleven months ago.'

'In that case,' the consultant said, warily, 'she *ought* to be able to assimilate the premier load. But Mr Denoone: my caution proceeds from the knowledge that to load the full complement into a person with no somatic history of Whites would be medically very dangerous.'

Irritated that things weren't being sorted out with the frictionless efficiency to which he was used, George raised his podgy right hand and flapped it. 'Look, I'm happy with your professional judgement. The regular load if you think that more advisable.'

The expression of relief on the consultant's taut little face seemed to George disproportionate. She proposed a complicated step-up package of regular loading, stepping up over a year to premier coverage. When she left, George felt unaccountably exhausted.

19

Although the psychological health expert came very highly recommended, she made little progress with Leah. At first, Leah refused even to acknowledge her questions. When pressed, she spoke double-dutch in a low, breathy voice, and when that failed to have any effect she clammed up again. She preferred sitting in the square of light cast by her bedroom's west-facing window, even though her hair was now cut. The assertivist doctor, Wu, spent an hour with her, but all Leah did was fidget in her chair, following the sliding rectangle of brightness with her eyes.

It was a few days before the full severity of matters became clear. Therapist Wu submitted a report in which (behind all the usual legal disclaimer boilerplate and after a wearisomely reiterated insistence that insufficient diagnostic data had been accumulated) he offered the opinion that Leah's trauma was much more deeply rooted than had first been apparent. His judgement was that it might take a long time for her previous personality to reassert itself. Marie was not discouraged, at first: 'She lived the life of the village for eleven months,' she said. 'At her age, eleven months is eternity.'

'As a proportion of her life, it's,' George agreed, making a half-hearted attempt at mental calculation before concluding, weakly, 'it's a lot.'

Not everything went badly. True, for the whole of the day following her haircut, Leah was in a doleful withdrawn and despondent mood. But as she was fed little squashy bulbs of sugary water, or more substantial pods of soup, her mood brightened. Three days after returning to NY she was eating with avidity everything she was given; and if she sometimes afterwards lay on the floor and stroked her little globed stomach moaningly, she nevertheless looked forward to meals with unmistakable excitement. And she quickly regained a comfortable intimacy with her parents; her initial wariness went away, and she accepted the cuddles of mother and even of father; smiled in return to their smiles.

But there were downsides too, reminders of the deep-set nature of her trauma. For instance she had apparently regressed to a pre-potty-trained state. To be precise: although Wilson had little difficulty in persuading her to urinate in her bathroom's toilet, one night, about a week after her return, she shat in her own bed. This distressed her as much as it upset her parents, although presumably for different reasons. Wilson cleaned everything up, and patiently explained to her that she needed to use the same special bathroom seat for solid waste as liquid; and Leah watched her carefully as she spoke, and seemed to understand. But two days later she filled her pocket-strides with faeces, and three days after that she stripped naked and shat on the carpet in the middle of her room.

In the second week, when Leah's English showed no signs of reappearing, Marie's resilience began to sag. 'She *does* speak though,' George pointed out.

'Occasional phrases,' said Marie. 'And always in Arab.'

'Farsi,' said George.

'As if *you* know!'

Piqued, George used some language software to try and turn his English to Farsi for Leah's benefit, and to process his daughter's Farsi into English. But the program made no headway with Leah's infrequent utterances. Accordingly Marie brought in a human translator: Ana, a small, m-shouldered woman with dark, lustreless eyes. The three of them sat with

Leah in her room, as the girl watched book after book on her screen. Ana probed her gently with questions, but although Leah occasionally looked sharply at her interlocutor she did not respond. Finally, as one book finished, and as her forefinger hesitated between a choice of sequels on the screenlist, Leah said something. Ana replied briefly, and Leah repeated her statement, before returning her attention to her book.

'Your daughter is not speaking Farsi,' said Ana, adding with muted asperity, 'although this is what your husband informed me she spoke.'

'What language, then?'

'It is neither Farsi, nor Turkish. I believe it to be Kurdish.'

'Oh! So can you please tell her—'

Ana put up her hand. 'I do not speak Kurdish. It is not permitted.'

'Not permitted?' repeated a surprised Marie.

'I apologize. I cannot help you.'

After this lady left, Marie embraced her daughter, whilst George played to them both, or read out, elements of articles about Kurdish, and the Kurds, from various Wikis and encyclopedias. Playing a common phrases program, so that a sepulchral voice chimed out of the Fwn with *hello* and *how is your health?* in Kurdish, made Leah laugh and pick up the device like a monkey, as if to try and get a glimpse of the tiny man inside, as a toddler might.

Matters were worse than they expected. The assertivist had suggested the possibility that Leah's English was merely suppressed, by the trauma of her abduction, beneath a superficial layer of acquired native phrases. But after a Kurdish translator was located (with some difficulty) and brought in, it became apparent that more than suppression was at work. Leah appeared to have forgotten all her English. The trauma of her kidnapping and separation from her parents had thoroughly disordered her conscious mind.

Therapist Wu returned for a new session and spent some time with Leah and the translator. 'Things are clearer now,' he announced, taking tea with George and Marie after the consult. The scalding sherry-coloured water, in its semicircular glass cups, gleamed in the daylight, its surface iridescence fizzing as sugar was added. 'She is suffering from a hysterical personality fragmentation. It is not unheard of – at ten, as I believe she was when she was abducted, the human psyche has not coalesced with sufficient integrity. Human children pass through a phase in which the natural assertiveness of the originary infant is contaminated and diluted – it is present at two, but often by four has become pathologically corroded. The best thing for a child growing is to—'

Marie, despite never having had so much as a half-hour session of assertiveness therapy in her life, broke in here with her own, impressive simulacrum of assertiveness: 'No lectures, please, Mr Wu.'

Wu smoothly shifted discursive gear. 'The best thing,' he said, 'and my advice to you, would be to tutor her in English as if in a foreign language. She is young enough to learn quickly – to relearn, that is. Also, I recommend the company of peers. I understand that you feel a natural desire to protect your daughter, of course you do. But I recommend she be allowed to interact with children her own age as a means of re-socializing her.'

They did this, and Wu's judgement was swiftly vindicated. The old Leah started coming back with gratifying rapidity, not only concrete aspects such as language, but authentic glimpses of her hidden personality, the real Leah.

Life thawed and returned to them all.

George found his daily routine settling into a pleasantly

inflexible timetable. It happened incrementally, and only acquired the look of inevitability in retrospect. It began with coffee, ablutions, and a quarter-hour with Leah and Wilson. Ezra, rattling around on his chubby legs like a miniaturized military Duopod, seemed perfectly able to do without him; but there was tenderness in Leah's clasping little embrace, and fifteen minutes was exactly enough time for George to get his hit of childish affection. Then an hour in the company of Rodion, the owner of the other half of their building – a mild-mannered, elderly man. They took coffee together, and played Reversi, and talked. Most of their conversations concerned the news, a passion they shared. They picked up stories and followed them the way ordinary people followed the instalments of their favourite books, finding a particular pleasure in tracing rises and falls of news profiles. So, for instance, both were interested in the goings on in Triunion, even though, after the previous year's high-casualty strategic blast, reports from that unhappy country had been superseded by news from other parts of the world – Tierra del Fuego, predominantly, but also southern Australia. Nevertheless George would ferret out information, or Rodion would, and the two of them would discuss it diffidently.

Then a stroll, or ride, about town; and a look in the shops; or, some days, he might go swimming. He particularly liked swimming, because it involved a good deal of what actors call *business*: undressing, redressing in his gear, immersion, the shower, drying himself in the big walk-through arch, redressing himself, arranging his hair and person. He always left feeling he had *achieved* something. Then he would return and spend half an hour on his collection: an assemblage of podvigs, ferreted out of obscure sites and feeds. Then lunch, *solus*, in Sun Hall, with whatever nibbles were most fashionable that week. And of course a glass of white wine. Afterwards a sleep, and then an hour of physical exercise in the home gym, or else, if the weather was agreeable, on the roof. Then the day's second shower, and afterwards a book; then a little time playing V, followed by some more time with the children, and a second snack before whatever public event, gallery, balletic performance, musical shug or party was arranged for the evening. He would encounter Marie, usually, only for this last item. Almost always he had little idea how she spent her day. Neither party would quiz the other.

By the summer, Leah's English had come wholly back to her – as if the inner trauma-block had finally been dissolved – and she was fluent again, her talk as fluent as could be desired, and as contaminated by catchphrases from books and Kids Feed, as any kid's. George began to experience a new sort of durable joy, a kind of warmth inside his body. It manifested itself largely in terms of its contrast with what had gone before, but that didn't diminish it. On the contrary. And whilst it was mostly an ambient sensation, there were times when it intruded with joyous sharpness upon his mind. And he would ask himself: could it be that he had spent so many decades of affluent living having everything *except* this experience of somatic happiness? Had he really just been *making do*? Taking his life, and his daughter, for granted? Had he not even known that there was a better mode of being? Joy, he saw now, was precisely not a pure emotion. It was stronger, an alloy of recognizable childish happiness on the one hand, and the pungent and mournful knowledges of adulthood on the other. Consciousness of the time wasted, previously; of the present imperfection, and of future risks. The lack of harmonious emotional balance in his life – a deteriorating situation with Marie, for instance – did not cancel out the happiness he felt at the restoration of Leah. On the contrary, it somehow deepened it, made it more mellow and complex. More, anxiousness at what the future might bring (which, of course, he very often experienced) did not cancel out his present contentment, because that very contentment was bound up with his child, and a child is the living embodiment of what the future holds. He felt that something awaited him in his future, and that the something was important.

He stole odd moments from his daily routine to be with his daughter: slipping quietly into the room to observe her being schooled, for instance; or simply to sit with her later in the afternoon, to embrace her and ask her how her day was going. Before the kidnapping her evening visits to him, just before her bedtime, had been perfunctory. Now he went to her willingly, joyfully even, and drew out the time. More like a playmate than a father, they might sit and gossip cheerily with one another about their day, the people they had met and so on – for tens of minutes. It was a wholly new experience in his life. It would not overstate matters to say: it mesmerized him. He stood on the roof one hot August afternoon, performing his Lithi Ka. When he shut his eyes to the bright world, the sunlight was still visible, filtered pinkly through his eyelids. And this seemed to him profound, somehow, as if the light was so greatly a feature of the universe's goodness that it could not be blocked out.

20

Leah took almost a year to recover her original self. That is to say, it took her that long to recover it all, including all her memories of everything pre-Ararat. But the majority of the restitution happened much more rapidly than that. She fell back into most of her usual ways within the month – endless books, screen games, lolling about and so on. Her English came back to her within six weeks. She spoke, perhaps, in a way that subtly differed from the way she had spoken before, the metaphorical tattoo of her experiences still visible upon the body of her speech. It was not a matter of vocabulary, or accent, or content; and, indeed, after a little while George grew so used to it that the memory of how she had spoken previously became in effect the memory of a memory. But there was a period of a month or so when, every time George spoke to his daughter, he detected a niggling *something* in her voice. She sounded like her – of course, since she was her. But there was nonetheless some sort of crack, or gap, between the like and the was. It was something to do with the way she leant on her sibilances just a fraction more heavily than sounded quite right. Or something to do with her diphthongs. But, see, that was exactly it: because as soon as George tried to pin it down, his diagnosis was revealed as absurd: her pronunciation was exactly what it had always been. Still, the sense of superfine wrongness persisted.

But, anyway, and after all, it didn't matter. He had her back, all of her, and that was the centre of the target. Perhaps there *were* minuscule alterations in her mode of speaking English; or in her body language, or her brief bursts of thrilled excitement at trivial things, or the very un-Leah way she continually fiddled her long, knuckled fingers in amongst her short hair. But if George dedicated any thought as to why these miniature things bothered him at all (and, really, mostly, he told himself, they did *not* bother him) then the conclusion he came to was: they were indices of how deep the trauma of her abduction went. They were markers, subtle but unmistakable, of the horrors she had suffered for eleven long months. And as Wu put it, the fact that she was able to resume *so much* of her previous manner, proportionately much more, was a marker of something more hopeful, something more enduring. The fact that she had been taken away *and then restored* gave a boost to that force in his soul, that great thread, or cable of many threads, linking him to his daughter: that thing bracketed under the word *love*. Such a capacious word! Such a where-opposites-meet kind of location! He had been maimed and not known it; he was cured by the action of chance, without his will, without deserving it.

The other thing, of course, was that Leah was growing up. This additional complication inflected the restoration of her previous personality in unpredictable ways. If we look to children to 'be themselves', we must also acknowledge that the essence of childhood is a process of continually growing out of one self into a new self. Leah soon enough went back to being schooled, and for a month or two she did not properly interact with her half-dozen classmates – the bounds of 'proper' interaction being defined by pedagogic targets and philosophies established by established paedopsychological discourse. But, after a while, she befriended two of the six fellow pupils, and one of those two became her friend in that special way in which eleven-year-olds – going on twelve – are so skilled. And George found this development really touching: deeply, authentically moved in a way that startled him. When he turned the emotion over in order to examine and understand it, he saw its nature. It was *relief*. And with this key, *relief*, gifted to him from nowhere, he bleeped the locked casket of his soul and popped the lid open. He could look inside, and know himself. As he did so he wondered, 'But how have I never looked inside before? How could I be so uncurious?' What he discovered was that all the pleasures he thought he had valued, and which he had expended such energy chasing, were not only unimportant, they were in fact positive irritants to his well-being. What he wanted, more than anything, was the pressure inside the existential abscess to be released. He had not comprehended how anxious he was about little Leah until that anxiety was assuaged. When he put his head in at the schoolchamber and saw her cheerily chatting with little Marthe, he experienced so profound a shift in his heart from pain to relief that it was almost religious.

'Leah seems to have settled well into her new class,' he observed to Marie.

'At last,' his wife replied, her eyes on the screen in front of her. 'Infuriating that it took so *long*, really.'

'Well,' said George. 'Sure.' But *infuriated* was the opposite of what he felt. What he felt was more like a Pauline bright light, the snowbike bursting rapidly straight into the dark spaces of his soul and driving the long spear of its headlight through the night. But it was hardly news that he and Marie were different creatures. What Marie wanted was a return to the status quo, when Leah and her small-scale dramas became the background noise of a life in which she, Marie, was centre-stage. George had been more thoroughly changed by his experience. Now he saw that it was his own life that was the background. This was what he had learned, by having his girl stolen away and returned to him. Leah had proved, quite apart from anything else, a mode of freeing him from himself. She was not one more thing to be fitted, somehow, into a busy schedule. The conversational way of putting this might be 'it had taken her loss for George to understand how attached he was to Leah'; but, actually, that wasn't quite it. What was revealed was something even more core than that. The attachment he felt to Leah was so completely different to the 'attachment' he felt to his collection, or his routine, or his little luxuries that it deserved to have a different name. It was an attachment that freed. It thinned the self, rather than coagulating it. It was a *way out*.

Month followed month, and the sense of something new stretched its roots inside George: he was a waking man yawning, lengthening arms and legs to their full, joint-popping extent. At no point did he ever, quite, recapture the transcendental state of mind he had known on the flitter coming away from the village of Öcalan, when he had first retrieved his beautiful girl. But there were days when he almost recovered that insight of soul, when the soot clogging his spirit got shaken away again. There was for example the first time since recovering her that Leah looked up at him and called him Daddy (looking back, George couldn't remember if pre-kidnap Leah had *ever* called him Daddy). Taking Marthe and Leah to the park together, and observing the two girls' *absolute* delight at the black swans. Marthe, Leah's best friend. 'I thought swans were white,' Marthe said, several times, with a little dent of puzzlement in her perfect white brow. 'How red his *beak* is!' Leah squealed. The huge black wings lifted, slowly, from the beast's back, like a giant beetle opening his shell-casings, and the girls watched hypnotized – until it starting shaking the two great black sheets in the air and they ran away laughing and squealing. Oh, George's heart might have burst with happiness.

Occasionally he would get echoes of his previous eminence; that tragic fame, from the period of deprivation, when he had drifted about the Ararat hotel with a turquoise soul and sorrowfully composed features, and people had whispered together at his passing. He told himself that what he felt now was a completely other thing: that had been a lack, and now he was experiencing a kind of fullness. But there were moments when he acknowledged that the two emotional states had more in common than he liked to think.

Sometimes he had bad dreams.

Sometimes he didn't dream at all, and days would pass without him being bothered by flashes of unwanted memory, or vision. The man's hands were together in prayer. His eyes were closed in meditation. The shape of his holy thoughts leapt from his forehead in a limb of red, like a Greek god born from his brow. The name of this god was Thanatos. Mortality collided into him. And he began to fall, under the influence of gravity, turning about the pivot of his feet.

And *down* we go.

Slower, and

Slower and slower and

It was an exponential sequence. It took him a minute to fall ten centimetres, and then another minute to fall five. A minute to fall two. A minute to fall one.

He's never going to hit the ground at this rate.

He had an insight one lunchtime, over his second glass of wine. Here's what it was: George had been *hurtling* along through his life, propelled by the thrilling acceleration of wealth and privilege, maybe a little anxious at the prospect of his life crashing into something, but not really, because it was all just so exciting. But now he had learned something: it wasn't that at all. He had never been in motion. Life had been moving, not him. He'd been the fly hovering over the freeway, watching each of the separate tonnage-lumps of plasmetal howling past him, every screaming block of death multiplied many times in the honeycomb of his compound eyes. He'd been waiting for life to crash into him. He had dangled, a knot of pure passive anxiety. It was not even as if the cars meant to eat him, howsoever mouth-like their grilles, however intent their eyelights. There was no stomach in these creatures. They were just going through the motions of hunting and devouring.

Shut your eyes. And – *bang*!

The girls, Marthe and Leah, liked wandering in the park. Though, look how peaceful! The black swan *was* a beautiful creature. George sat on the bench and frankly gawped at it. Its beak was so *very* red it looked as if it had been coated with scarlet lipstick. It sat motionless on the taut water, neck curved like a 2, perfectly balanced on its reflection like a Rorschach picture of a black butterfly with gigantic antennae. It made up the number 38. To the right, on a clear expanse of green, the girls were playing tag. George saw Rodion, his neighbour in the building, talking to them. As the little beings rushed past, Rodion would incline his head and call something to them – replying to their questions, or asking questions of his own, George couldn't tell.

George looked about him, at the familiar paraphernalia of the park. It was all new to him. A coiffured tree was a tongue stuck out at the sky.

It surprised him that Rodion had made friends with Leah, not because he considered Rodion incapable of striking up friendships (he was after all a perfectly amiable, if slightly detached, old man) but because George was in that state of pure bogglement at the wonderfulness of his new attachment to his daughter. It seemed to him that his connection with her must be a unique thing.

George wandered over and said hello, and Rodion hunched his shoulders a little, as he tended to do when talking to another adult. Then he smiled wryly. Because their usual mode of interaction was to talk about the news, he said: 'The situation in Mexico is worse than it was before.'

'I saw that,' agreed George. 'Fires and rioting all through the central zone.'

The two men stood side by side, watching the girls chase one another around through the sculptures.

'It is a wonderful thing to have a child,' Rodion noted, shyly.

'OK,' said George. 'Sure.' Then, prompted by he-knew-not-what: 'You have any?'

'No,' said Rodion.

'OK,' said George.

'My wife sadly died. She perished of medical complications.'

'Good grief.' This was a shock! It was as if he had said *my wife was eaten by a sabre-toothed tiger. Medical* complications? How old *was* he? 'I'm sorry to hear that.' Had he married in the nineteenth *century*?

'It was very many years ago,' said Rodion. 'I never cared to remarry.'

After this extraordinary intimacy, the conversation wilted away again. George really didn't know what to say to him.

The sparseness of life.

That afternoon, back home, George watched a long, ill-tempered recorded message from his assertiveness therapist. The gist of the message was: Why have you stopped attending sessions? 'You are of course aware of the profound danger of a half-completed training in assertivity. You are, of course, aware how easily the cruder strategies of assertivity can manifest as violence in the soul. You may feel yourself ready to face the world, but I assure you, George, you are not. I insist you come back. There will be resistance to this inside you, I know. As you listen to this message you will be experiencing fear. Whether you realize it or not, you are afraid, and that is why you are avoiding me. This fear is like a disease in your blood, and you may think of yourself as somebody who has not yet been loaded with the gWhites to keep yourself healthy. I won't lie to you, George, when you come back – because you have absented yourself – it will go hard for a week or two. I will have to go hard with you. I am angry, and you deserve to take the brunt of it. But as a professional I anticipate we can drive this fear out of you, and continue. You need not reply to this message. Simply be sure and turn up, at my therapy suite, tomorrow on time.' That was the message.

The following evening George invited Rodion to join him, and Leah, on the roof to watch the moonlights. Ezra was in bed. Marie was doing whatever she did with her time these days. George really had no idea. A rust-coloured sun had just gone over the western skyline, and the sky's diffraction grating began its slow, enormous tune-down to dark. Rodion came up carrying a little silk bag of flavour-sweets, and passed the pastilles, one at a time, to Leah. The three of them settled into three chairs.

'I'm missing *The Magic Shell*,' Leah said.

'Watch it tomorrow instead,' advised George.

'But Marthe is watching it tonight. All my friends are watching it right now.' Leah took another pastille. 'They'll talk about it in school tomorrow, and I won't have seen it.'

'Perhaps you might watch it later, in bed?' suggested Rodion, tentatively, looking at George to see if this was a permissible compromise. 'The moonlights are definitely worth seeing, though.'

'You can tell your friends tomorrow,' said George, 'that you saw the moonlights with your own eyes. They won't be able to boast anything like that. Won't that be good?'

Leah pondered this, her little chin creasing and smoothing as she worked the pastille. The night was fragrant with New York summer. Away over to the south, a sunkite drifting out towards the sea, a double-diamond shape of blackness against the darkening sky. The masonry of the buildings around them grew more purple, the windows grew more golden. The sounds were of people passing in all directions below them, along all the roads and alleyways, driving and flitting, the city purring. Behind all this noise was the restful and delicate boom and shush of the Hough Wall.

'What are moonlights?' Leah asked.

'We're working up there,' said George. 'Blasting – it *is* blasting, is it, Rode?'

'A form of blasting,' agreed the old man.

'You say, we're working up there?'

'That's it,' said George.

'*We* are not there,' Leah said, looking from George to Rodion.

'I mean the US. I mean *we* in that sense.'

Leah put her lips into the shape of saying 'ah!' Then she asked: 'Up at the moon?'

'Sure.'

'How did we get there?'

'How did we get there? We flew up there, of course.'

'In a flitter?'

It was one of 'those' conversations. Leah was either playing some girlish game, pretending to be ignorant of absolutely basic things about the world, or else this was some late manifestation of the kidnapping trauma, some hole in her memory traceable to that event. Either way, George had long ago decided the best way to handle it was to answer her questions simply and to register no surprise.

'A flitter couldn't fly so high! No, they flew up in a space-ship.'

'Leah,' asked Rodion in his creaky old voice, 'do you know what the moon is?'

Leah contemplated this question for a long time, her jaws moving in a figure of eight, until she had finished the pastille. Then she said: 'Is it a mountain?'

'It is a whole other world, child,' Rodion said.

'A mountain world?'

'A big round ball in space,' he explained in his patient voice, 'just like the earth is a big round ball in space.'

The increasing darkness made it hard to read her expression; but she looked at Rodion for a long time, as if weighing the likelihood that this was an incomprehensible adult joke. But she said: 'OK.' She uttered these two letters with a perfect George-like inflection, and that gave him a twinge of pleasure.

'Anyhow,' he said. 'The US is building big things – up there. On the moon, I mean. And from time to time they blast the ground. Levelling,' he went on, realizing how little he knew about the process or infrastructure, 'mountains, or, I don't know. Filling craters. I don't know precisely.'

'There are specialist feeds,' George said. 'They post the timings. Some people like to watch.'

'If it's on the feeds,' Leah said, 'then why can't we watch it on the feeds? Then I could watch *The Magic Shell* after.'

George's Fwn bleeped. 'It's time!' he said, and reclined his chair. Leah and Rodion followed suit, and the three of them stared at the moon.

'We're on the roof looking at the moon,' Leah announced. 'I think the moon is a roof.'

'How do you mean, my love?' George asked.

'Are the people up there looking at *us*?' Leah wanted to know.

'Use your scope, Leah,' Rodion advised.

'I *am* using my scope.' Leah replied, although she had in fact been fiddling with it in her lap. But she fitted it back over her eyes, and lay there. George put his on too. Magnified, the moon's frost-grey surface revealed all manner of peculiar pore-like detail: interlocking circles like the Olympics Logo, or starburst spreads of lines, frills of ink-black shadow with ragged edges like torn paper. White and cream, pale grey and dark, silver-black. Wrinkles and creases, patches of smoothness. 'Where are they? I can't see them.'

'The big crater near the bottom, to the right.'

'What's *crader*?'

'Those circles on the face of the moon. Those are craters.'

'You should say circles then. Why say crader?'

'Crater,' said Rodion gravely, 'is the proper term.'

'I don't like the proper term,' Leah said, haughtily. 'Marthe and I, we're going to make our own language. When we do there will be no proper in it. Marthe speaks some German, you know. I said she and I will-would make our own language. It will-would be a new language, just for the two of us.'

'What a splendid idea!' said Rodion. 'If you have your own private language, you and Marthe can tell one another secrets and nobody else will know what they are.'

'Yes,' agreed Leah, with splendid force and simplicity.

'There,' said George. They all fell silent. A button-mushroom of sharp brightness appeared on the crater wall, intense, an extraordinary focusing of the moon's own silver light. And then, again, a second blister of bright whiteness. And in quick succession, a string of bright dots ignited soundlessly round the arc of the crater's limit. The first explosion was a glass of light. A string of bubbles. And as the cascade of expansion swelled each in turn, the first began to dim, and little streaks of detail emerged in its orbit, puffs of outward-thrust dust and dirt.

George slipped his scope off, and looked at the lopsided brightness of the moon. Over the course of half a minute the flare on the bottom portion faded and the old regular gleam returned. 'Can we go down now?' Leah asked, in a bored voice. This, George understood, piercingly: this moment, when Leah is abstracted and bored, and I am sitting here replete with the beauty of what I have been watching, this is the perfect moment. Its perfection, a function of its asymmetry, and fashioned of the exquisite, elegiac rightness of the bond between them. 'Yes,' he said. 'Let's go down.'

A sunkite sailed blackly, silently, overhead, on its way to its night-tether, ceilinging them as they walked to the door.

Downstairs, George went through his messages. There was another, full of ire and contumely, from his assertivist therapist, raging at George's continual absence, and heaping all sorts of abuse upon him. He watched the whole of it, up to the moment when the therapist said: 'I shall, of course, bill you for these calls; they and their abuse in particular constitute a valuable therapeutic strategy', when he closed it down.

21

How much longer? A year and a little more, and through-out this fragile perfect asymmetry, Leah's childishness and George's adulthood. Her semi-detachment from him as she found greater and greater focus in her own life and friends; his increasing settlement of all that mattered in the world on her life. They did very little, by the usual metrics of 'did'. Leah improved at English Language and Creative Composition, and indeed showed flashes of genuine talent. George and she took a holiday in Antarctica – Marie was supposed to come as well, but some other pressing engagement kept her back at the last minute. Afterwards Marie, on (George assumed) the principle of equality, took Leah and Ezra both away to Argentina, leaving her husband behind. A week of dinosaur riding and adventure play for the kids. When they returned, George was almost embarrassed to ask Leah: 'How was it?' 'Oh,' she replied, folding her long legs beneath her and settling to a game screen (*just* like old times!) in a chair, 'it was OK.' 'Just OK?' 'Whatever,' she said.

There was a message from Ergaste: he was in NY and wanted to talk. George invited him to the house.

'Can I say hello to Uncle Ergaste?' Leah asked, putting her head round the corner.

'He's not here yet.'

'But I saw him!'

'That was just a message.'

'No,' Leah explained, patiently. 'It wasn't a "message". I *saw* him.'

'It was on the Lance.'

'Oh! What's the Lance?'

'Leah,' chucklingly, 'don't be silly. You know what the Lance is.'

'Oh,' she said airily. 'I've heard people talk of it. But you know, by jiminy, I've never been wholly sure.'

'You remember when Granda was alive, and he would call us on the Lance from Scotland?' She squeezed her eyes between cheekbones and eyebrows, as if staring into a ferociously bright light, so George went on: 'You used to like putting your arm through his chest.' When this elicited nothing, he added, 'Come along, Leah. The Lance makes a picture of the person you're speaking to, in three dimensions.'

'So Uncle Ergaste isn't here?'

'Not actually, not yet.'

'OK.' Leah said. 'Can I have some food?'

'Go ask Walter.'

'Walter's gone.'

George pondered this. 'He shouldn't have. He should still be here. Did you look in the kitchen?'

'I *looked* in the kitchen,' Leah replied, haughtily. '*Didn't* I,'

'Well, Walter is *supposed* to be there. Maybe he'd popped out for a moment. Why not go look again?'

'I *will* look again,' said Leah, as if making a concession. 'But, Daddy, if he's not there, can I just help myself?'

'What – to food? Sure. I guess so. But I'm sure he'll be there.'

She said 'thanks Dad' languidly, and disappeared round the corner. A moment later she was back. 'Dad,' she said, elongating the vowel.

Something prickled in George's pelt. Some atavistic sense of grave danger on the very edge of his well-being. He didn't know what cued him into this sudden apprehension. The little hairs on his arms lifted away from the skin. Naturally, the danger was not of a physical sort. He moved his face slowly towards her. 'Yes, my love?' he said, unable to keep the cautiousness from his tone.

'I was just *think*ing.'

There was a silence. A flitter went past the window with a gushing noise. It was a bright, cloudy day. To fill the gap, George said: 'Thinking is good.'

'Wondering, rather: when can we go see Mother and Father?'

The subcutaneous tingle in George's skin. He felt that caffeiney, or cSnuff-y, sensation of sharpened attentiveness. Something very large was balanced precariously on some teeter-totter, threatening to tumble down. He had known such contentment, the thought of losing it was ghastly. But there was nothing to do but tread very carefully, and hope he did not fall. Through a gummy mouth, George spoke carefully: 'What do you mean, my love?'

'Oh nothing,' said Leah, and George's heartbeat accelerated a little, as if at a dodged bullet. But then she said: 'I just thought, we can fly to Antarctica and Argentina, and Ararat begins with a A.'

'Ararat does begin with an A.'

'I just wondered if we could go there, maybe. I'd like to see Mummy.'

'You can see your mother right now,' said George.

'Other mother, oh it *doesn't* matter,' said Leah, launching into a slouchy gibbon-walk across the carpet in the direction of the window. 'Only, it's only that we never seem to go *there*.'

George swallowed. 'It's not a place with happy associations. After all. Now, is it, my love?'

'I don't mind so much about seeing my other dad, he was a boss and he wasn't very nice to Mummy.' Spoken with disdain.

'But it might be nice to see my other mummy,' said Leah, peering through the window, and showing her teeth to the world. 'It doesn't matter though. I'll go see if Walter's in the kitchen, and maybe he can make me something containing peanut-paste-and-pear.'

She lolled out of the room. George sat in his chair trembling like a man in a fever. But this was an overreaction. Kids say all sorts of idiotic things, after all. There was no point in getting *het*. In getting het *up*. He could see the sky through the window, so he looked at that. He directed his attention towards the bar of mottled blue and white that lay between the roof of the De Hoch Building and the top of his own window. It had a weirdly shimmery quality to it, as if it would not stay in place. But surely we can depend on the sky. White clouds moved, the sun breaking through intermittently and opening a bright claw of dazzle in the window glass. The screen was on, of course, in the corner of the room, sound off; and George turned his face that way for a change, letting his eyes rest on the silent images. It was a news feed, and the visuals were of a large mass of people compressed between two rows of stone buildings, surging and flowing up the passage in a tidal rush, encountering the fat metal posts of military police quadpods and being beaten back in spume-bursts of smoky sprayfire. All in perfect screen silence. The crowd recoiled and shuddered back down its street, and gathered itself, and surged back up again. George found it soothing, in fact: this great systolic-diastolic pulse of people. Forward they poured, in a mass, and back they washed, underneath a sky coloured from the brightest blue pigment. The margins of the images were crusted with infographics, little huddles of people waiting to be pulled out to provide commentary. George took a breath, and waved his hand in the beam to turn the sound on. Then he pulled out the News Genie from the bottom left. To the soothing wave-motion was superadded a white-noise roar and crash, and the Genie's murmuring voice, saying (though George wasn't really following it) 'agromanagerial rebellion' and 'Mexico' and 'violence' and 'hydraulic society' and 'superstructure' and 'containment'.

He placed a hand on his chest. His driving heartbeat slowed. How foolish he was!

Marie came through, looking for something that wasn't him. 'Ergaste is coming to call,' George told her, marvelling at the smooth control he possessed over his vocal organs.

'If you must watch that beastly stuff,' she replied, 'have the decency to turn the sound off.'

He complied with a handwave. 'Marie,' he said. 'Leah just said something strange.'

She stopped, stood straighter, turned her gaze towards him. Her gaze was calm but focused. He could read it. It said: Do not disturb the balance. It said: Do not upset the solidity of what I have, painfully, reclaimed with my daughter. So he said: 'Nothing.'

'What?'

'Nothing.' She looked severely at him, so he added: 'Forget I spoke.'

'If I could,' said Marie, looking about her distractedly. 'If only I could.' And she went out of the room.

22

If George was not precisely discombobulated when Ergaste came in, he was not, as it were, quite combobulated either. He received him in the Blue Room. The big Englishman burlied in and began without preliminaries: 'I'm a Catholic, a Christian-Catholic.'

'Oh,' said George.

'You probably didn't know that.'

'I don't think I did,' George conceded. 'Or – wait. Maybe you did mention it, once before?'

'We *can* divorce, you know, but's frowned on. *And*,' Ergaste added, with almost furious vehemence, '*and* we eat our God. You know?'

'The bread and wine stuff?' said George. 'Of course I had heard about all that.'

Ergaste lowered at him, and then smiled a leonine smile that showed off all the central teeth including his four sharpest. 'We devour our God *weekly*,' he said, again. 'We devour God *every week*,' he clarified, in case George had thought he had said 'weakly'. 'That's the kind of carnivorous religion mine is.'

'OK,' said George.

'Thing about eating,' Ergaste went on, in hectoring mode. 'It has *changed*. Yeah? We don't need to do it for sustenance, now, what? Any of us could get the hair.'

'Yes.'

'So if not sustenance, then what? I'll tell you. Power is what. God is the most powerful thing in the cosmos, top of the pyramid, and *we* eat *Him*, yeah? It's not the other way around, that's the really *important* part of it. Yeah. We're the predator, and he's the prey. That's what it means, now. That's what food is. Strength and force and the wolf's delight is what. Do you understand? *Do* you, though?'

'I'm going to come clean, Ergaste,' George said, scratching an itch in his scalp. 'I'm not sure I do, actually. I can't honestly say I have the slightest notion what you're talking about.'

'Look,' said Ergaste. 'I know how it works.'

'Then tell me. Tell me how it works. Then we'll both know.'

'Fucking is a game, now. I know you and Ysabelle got playful, on the mountain.'

This was not the direction George expected the conversation to go, and it wrongfooted him. 'What?'

'That's the way it's played, I know. That's the *game*. But I insist you regard Em in a different category.'

'Who's Emin?'

Ergaste's sculptural nostrils dilated equinely. 'I insist', he repeated, raising his voice, 'that you regard *Emma*. In. A. Different. Category.'

George flushed red. 'Emma! Of course—'

'I do not come here to say,' Ergaste rolled on, as if addressing a large crowd, 'that you ought to be *grateful*. I do not claim all the credit for returning your stolen daughter. I did not *do this* to be thanked. But to *repay* what I did by – fucking my wife!' Ergaste planted his two enormous feet solidly and, with a conjuror's flourish, brought a handgun out of his pocket. It looked, as these things do, like an augmented Fwn.

George thought to himself: *good gracious*. 'Look, look,' he said. 'Now now.' Those two, for the moment, were all the words he had.

The sunlight came in bright, briefly, through the window; and the room gleamed. Then the clouds muted the beams again, and the lighting shifted back down.

'This is a gun,' said Ergaste, pointing it at George's chest.

'Golly,' George agreed.

'I'm showing it to you. I'm not shooting you with it.'

George pondered the difference between these two things. 'Ergaste,' he said. 'I did not have sexual relations with that woman. With – Emma.'

At this Ergaste turned the gun over in his hand, looked at it, and replaced it in his pocket. Doing this, somehow, seemed even more menacing than bringing it out in the first place. 'The one thing you could do to make it worse,' he said, quietly, 'would be, to lie about it.'

'I'm not lying,' said George.

'You have *seen* the gun,' said Ergaste. 'That's really why I came over. That's why I came.' He brooded for a bit, and peered at the carpet. Then, his voice brightening, and as if it had just occurred to him, he added: 'I bought it in a little shop two blocks from here – just now! Amazing little emporium.' Then the creases cracked his brow again, and he glowered at the floor. 'The idea was: first show you the gun. Second, hope there's no need to *use* it.'

'There's no need,' George assured him. His heart, fashionably late to the party, had begun pumping and hurdling inside his chest. He had the crinkly inner sense of adrenalin fizzing along his veins.

'I can tell *you*, Ergaste,' said George, realizing the truth of the words as he uttered them. 'Marie and I are separating. We'll divorce. We'll be divorced by autumn.' It was an offering, the best George could do. A bowl of jungle fruit laid before the trumpet-mouthed idol. Ergaste watched him distantly. 'It's broken us, the whole thing. You talk about fucking as a pastime – I haven't done that for years. Well, a year. Never with Em, you know, honestly.'

'Then *why* would she *say*—' Ergaste boomed. But he

interrupted himself with 'for the sake of fuck!' at prodigious volume.

'Honestly, in all truth. Not with Marie or anybody,' George went on. 'Not with anybody for longer than a year. Everything about my life is different now. Everything has changed.' He was imploring now. Ergaste opened his mouth. Then he shut it again.

There was a loud bang, like a bass-resonant cymbal crash, in another room.

George twitched. The crackling of his hair-like nerves. Ergaste remained completely impassive. It sounded like something heavy falling down. It sounded like it came from downstairs.

'Show myself *out*,' boomed Ergaste, and spun about like a motorized gun turret.

He was gone.

George's brain's computational capacity must have been a limited thing; for he found he could not process Ergaste's appearance, and the gun, and the realization that he was going to separate from Marie, and the loud crash from another room, all at once. His brain attempted to consolidate all these sense data, but instead of putting them together into a single unified narrative, they blurred and slid. Instead, across his inner eye there flashed the image of a man with his hands pressed together in prayer, a serpent of spraying red leaping from the side of his forehead.

The crash. What?

Had it come from outside the building? Was it just the sound of his own heart beating?

'OK,' said George, to nobody.

Leah came through, looking apprehensive. George expected her to ask what the big crashing noise had been, but instead she just looked at her father with a strange longing in her eyes.

It occurred to George that she knew something, or sensed something, with a child's prescience. Or, he thought, perhaps she had actually been eavesdropping. There was no point in pretence, at any rate. The sooner she knew, the longer she would have to adjust.

'Leah,' he said. 'Your mother and I will be – separating. Do you know what that means?'

'It means being cut up,' she said.

'Yes. Sort of, yes. It means we will live in different houses. But you will still see the both of us.' George's heart was rattling like an old two-stroke. If it went on like this, it was going to shake itself free from the mounting of his ribcage and bounce down into his pelvis. He ran a hand over his face, and breathed deeply, and tried again. 'You will spend some time with me, and some time with your mother. Yes?'

Leah's eyes slipped to the right, and she said. 'I see.'

'It'll be OK,' he assured her.

The gaze bounced back to him. 'You'll get back together after a bit?'

'I don't know about that.'

'So how will it be OK?'

'It will be OK.'

'OK, like, how?'

'It'll be OK because we both still love you.'

'Ez?'

'Him too.' In the moment he had forgotten about Ezra. 'Of course. We still love you both.'

'Will Ez stay with me?'

'Yes. You two won't be separated. I'm going to sit down, now, my love.'

'OK,' she said, as he slumped into a chair. And then, with a rolling drawl, 'O-o-oh *kay*.' She let her arms droop, and performed a sort of sloping, dangling stagger to the right; one step, two steps, three steps. For a moment her limbs were ropes. Then she perked up her stance. 'Later, Dad,' she concluded, brightly, and ducked back through the door.

23

His conversation with Marie was not good. The conversation was powered by bile, a subsidiary of Recrimination Inc. They sat down together for the first time in – oh, months. And George stuttered something about how they couldn't keep avoiding things. They were eating. They were discussing things over lunch. The food was Togliatti and Peach Cider. Marie did not cry. Of course she didn't; that wouldn't have been very like *her*. But her hostility was extraordinarily pronounced. She said right out: it was all his fault. She could not, she said, blame him directly for Leah's kidnapping; but she could certainly point to his manifold failings when it came to supporting her during and after that profound trauma. It was her duty to point that out. As she itemized these, there was a weird sensation in George's stomach. It felt as if it were digesting itself. The words poured down, and he ducked his head as she spoke because that was only fair; but all the time he was trying to locate the nature of this gut-tug. Some sort of cousin to hunger-for-food, like that but not that. A palpable void. It felt like his body decaying from the inside out. It wasn't that. It felt, bathetically enough, more like gas, like something expanding out from his core. Although at the same time it was adrenalized, incipiently exciting, as if something very large were about to happen. It was, he understood with a click, the same sensation he had had upon the slopes of Mount Ararat when he had stepped out in old-fashioned skis. Poised at the top, and about to go hurtling downwards. It felt like that state of mind rare amongst the rich: that the cushion between the self and disaster had been removed. It was the intoxication of recklessness. His life would never be the same. This was the thing itself.

Superfast, superfast, superfast

But it was not like stepping off a precipice. Of course it wasn't. Most of his life carried on in its well-oiled grooves. They hired people to sort out the details, as they did with everything and anything. They continued co-habitation for a short time, barely crossing paths, which was pretty much as it had been before. The fizzing in his gut passed away. George found himself thinking: and how am I *supposed* to feel? He asked himself: what is the standard thing, in a situation like this?

He played Reversi with Rodion, and lost the first game, and the second also; because he could not keep his attention on the pieces. His gaze slid too easily from the board to the old man's face: the woollen strips of eyebrow, the brittle-looking skin, the vermicelli of lines in at the corner of his elderly eyes. His ears were very big, curls and flaps of pink flesh like Danish pastries. His hair was close-trimmed and covered his whole head. This man had been married, and lost his wife. Though the circumstances were different (and of course George was not sure what the circumstances of Rodion's bereavement were, precisely) yet surely there was a kind of bond between them. George turned his line the entire diagonal length of the board, and, on a whim, he said: 'And it's bad news for me, Rodion.' And when the old fellow politely enquired what the matter was, he told him the whole story. The story entire. And Rodion was perfectly old-school about it, and listened with softened eyes, nodding occasionally but at no point interrupting him. And when George had finished, he said: 'I'm very sorry to hear that.'

'I'll tell you,' said George, feeling himself lightened. 'It's not too bad. I guess people's marriages break down all the time? And for most people it is simply loss, and just loss, and nothing else. But, see, not me. But if you ask me, I have to say – I'm . . . content with the exchange.'

'Exchange?'

'I lost my daughter, you know,' George explained. 'She was kidnapped.'

'Of course,' Rodion said. 'I heard about that.'

'But losing her was needful,' George said. 'I couldn't get her back if I didn't lose her first. And getting her back is a joy I never knew before in my life.' He picked up a piece and flipped it over. At Rodion's cough he comprehended that it was not yet his move, and he replaced it on its original square with an apology.

'I've never been religious,' George said.

'No more have I,' said Rodion. 'Though my wife used to pray to Jesus.'

'But it is precisely the religious equation. Isn't it, though? You cannot love something unless you lose it first. Can you? No, you can't. Rodion, my friend, I shall tell you something I have told nobody else.'

At this the old man's Grouchoesque eyebrows slid up his forehead. But he slotted his two hands together, fingers interlocking, and readied himself to hear.

'Getting Leah,' said George. 'I mean, getting her *back*. What I mean to tell you is – something about that. You see, we went to this tiny dirt-poor village somewhere in – Armenia, Turkey, Iran, I don't know. That's where she had been taken, after the kidnapping. We couldn't even flitter to this place because it was too dangerous to be in the sky. Longhairs might shoot at us with guns simply for being aloft. And when we got there we paid money to the boss who ran the village, and they executed the man responsible – apparently responsible – right in front of our eyes! I'd never seen a man killed before. In real life, I mean. Have you?'

'Once,' said Rodion, sombrely.

They both looked at the Reversi pieces. Were they sharing something important? Was that what this was? The more money you have, the harder it is to do so. I don't need to tell you that. You know that already.

'Wow,' said George.

'I don't mean to, ah, upstage your—' Rodion said.

'No, not at all, not at all, no,' George said, speaking across him.

There was a moment of silence.

'It was my best friend, you know,' Rodion continued. 'He was standing as close as you are now, and – well, some soldiers actually, it was some soldiers, and they shot him in the body.'

'Man,' said George. 'That's a terrible thing!'

'Oh, yes.'

'Why did the soldiers shoot him? Was it an execution?'

'As to that, I don't know. He was being arrested, you see, and he pulled out a handgun, which was not a clever thing to do. I've heard people argue that the soldiers had orders to shoot him anyway. I didn't use to think so. But now I wonder.'

George picked up one of the Reversi pieces, held it lightly between the thumb and finger of his left hand, and flicked it with his right forefinger, so that it spun gyroscopically.

'Please continue with *your* story,' said Rodion.

The thing is, George wasn't sure he wanted to. This conversation seemed to have magically unlocked itself, turned into a dangerously intimate thing. But he couldn't think how to shut it down. So he said: 'When I came back from that village, I felt – I don't know how to put it into words. I felt extraordinary. I was floating above the world. It was the purest joy I have ever known.'

Rodion considered this statement for several long seconds, and then he nodded, very slowly. 'I understand,' he said. 'To see somebody killed, before your very eyes—'

'Oh no,' said George. 'Oh, you misunderstand. Oh, no. I didn't mean that.'

'Oh.'

'That's not what produced the great gush of Joy in me. Not that! It was being reunited with my daughter that did it.'

'Of course,' said Rodion. And George couldn't be sure if his tone of voice was actively sceptical or merely reserved.

Of course. Rodion had assumed his euphoria was a result of seeing a man killed, when in fact it had been a function of being reunited with his daughter. Over the following few days this misunderstanding of what he was saying started to niggle. And after a night's sleep, and a morning talking to half a dozen lawyers on the Lance, about divorce matters, the niggle returned. Every time he entertained the thought it enlarged in his mind, like a hole in a sheet out of which he *just can't keep* a poking, exploratory finger, knowing full well that to continue probing is to widen the rip further and further. George's itch was that Rodion might, however inadvertently, have said something true. He found himself thinking back to the flight in the flitter; to the journey by ramjet, with Leah worn out by sobbing and asleep in her seat. What *had* he felt? Uncompli-cated Joy. Or so he had thought. But, now that he came to resolve the matter in his thoughts, he found that he doubted if such a thing as uncomplicated Joy existed. *Uncomplicated* Joy, as much the impossible unicorn of the emotions as uncompli-cated Grief. What *had* the thrill been? The transcendence of it. He had reclaimed his daughter, and for the first time in a year – more, the first time in his life – he had felt alive. And we all

163

know that it is not restoration but death that throws life into the sharpest relief. Was it that he had felt alive because that other, nameless man had died? Perhaps reclaiming his daughter had been only a coincidental matter. Getting Leah back would surely make him happy; but the extraordinary plenum of joy he had known drew from something more profound. More profound, in the final analysis, than the petty resources of his own soul, and that soul's extremely ordinary capacity for *relief*.

He thought again about the summary execution he had witnessed. *For your benefit*, Dot had said. Justice, or something. The fellow's unguessable life all behind him, the bullet preparing to dive from its chamber and thread him through, to knock out his lights. What Leah had said, about going back to Ararat: *my father was a boss*. Oh. Would *you*, knowing that in a few moments all sight would be removed from you for ever, *close your eyes*? Wouldn't you keep them open as long as possible, suck in as much of the world as you could until the very last instant?

And then, what could it feel like? A blow to the head, like a punch; but with a fist inhumanely hard and forceful. Would you feel the bone of your forehead cave in? Would you feel it burst out, on the far side? Perhaps you would feel one but not the other. A brain is a fantastically complicated pattern of cells, after all, and that settles, as one lives on, into increasingly elaborate snowflake patterns along which the body sprinkles electrical charge. A jelly in which fine structure nets, like those thready, flossy fractures you see inside an ice-cube. Pastried about with a globe of bone. The thing itself, unaccommodated man; the horizon of everything that is. And here, *tic*, the trigger clicks. And there, *clac*, the bullet releases an explosive puff-puff of its complicated gases. Rush, and the pellet moves superfast down the pipe, the dot of light at the end swooping up into a blinding surround and the flush of air, and superfast through the cardboard of human bone, and the unilluminated mousse of cerebral matter, and, *pop*, out again into brightness. Superfast.

The crack. The gush of red from the side of the skull. And *down* he goes.

It is as it was. Or put it this way: that red particulate mist *was* the man. It was his mind, brain, soul – strung out of his head like a great red quiff. And time stopped at that precise moment: the man would never hit the ground. His body would, but *he* never would. *He* would hang there for ever, his soul literalized as a bulging scarlet excrescence pendant from his scalp. Perhaps he had been a bad man; or perhaps he had been good, by the mores of his place and time. Either circumstance was as likely as the other, or so it seemed to George. The indeterminacy of life had distilled into that moment. It stayed with George. He could not rid his mind of the image of it.

24

He moved out of the park house and into one of those apartments built into the Chelsea Seawall – smaller, obviously, but with fine views over the Hudson lagoon. Rodion was sorry to see him go, he said. As they played one last game of Reversi, George promised that he would call by and visit often; but over the weeks that followed he only ever met Rodion in the park, never at his house. He was not purposefully avoiding the old house, and of course he had still to deal with Marie (or Marie's representatives) where the children, and financial matters, were concerned. But he was aware that his life had changed in more than mere topographical externals. He was a new man.

The complex he now inhabited was divided into two sets, West and Twelfth, and although George's place was in the southern section he decided – after attending a few West meetings – that he felt more at home with the Twelfth crowd. Their building meetings were more diverse, their exchanges more spiky. Notionally, the idea in meeting was to sort out any problems with the complex, but of course there were no problems. Instead, people met to talk about anything, to preen themselves, to clown about with the grim-faced servants, tripping them as they served coffee, wrapping them in cloth, singing right in their faces – to turn the meeting, in effect, into a café des artistes. The West group was all conventional wealth; but – most excitingly, for George – there were several individuals in the Twelfth group who wore their hair ostentatiously long. It took George a few weeks to summon the courage to ask one such, a thin elderly man called Johan Hartley

Walliam, whether his was ordinary hair or the new kind. It seemed terribly rude. But Walliam was unembarrassed: sure he'd taken the hair bug. It was a statement. It was marvellous to see how much it discombobulated his east-side friends. It didn't mean that he couldn't eat, of course – he still ate, of course. But it was, he said, a splendid show. To walk the city streets with his hair fanned splendidly behind and his matelot trousers and his pepperpot hat and silver beard visor.

George sat in his lounge looking through the glass at the myriad little puckerings on the surface of the lagoon, and seeing how the sunlight took these simple shapes and parlayed them into a thousand different tones and shades of white and grey and blue and silver. The watersprinters folded little creases into the water's surface. A yacht unwound its kite-cable and sped smoothly on. At sunset there was a five-minute window when the water acquired skin-tints, and the million little dints attached to each wavelet looked momentarily like the pores of a giant. And the sun moved closer to the mainland, and the water became darkened and lacquered and mysterious. It was the East lagoon, of course, that had all the wildlife – those ramped-up swan-hawks and the different kinds of fishes. But the Hudson lagoon was where all the sporting events took place, and George had a splendid vantage on that.

On alternate weeks Ezra and Leah came to stay, each with their respective carers. The first few times things were a little stilted, but soon enough George established the thing children value above all others, a routine. Not seeing them for a week meant that each re-encounter was kicked off with George's quasi-grandparental astonishment at how quickly the two of them were growing.

They would do all the things they would do. And Ezra was up for almost anything; fearless, and adventurous, and keen to climb and swim and so on. George delighted in his vivacity.

But with Leah it was something different. With Leah it was more than the conventional, upholstered pleasures of parenthood, and the little thrills, and the comfortable surprises. With Leah he felt some more powerful tug in his soul. It was because, not despite, the fact that his love for her, its almost *edible* sweetness, was mixed with the memories of fear and bereavement. It was, as he knew on some deep level, the difference between the pleasure of taking a lungful of fragrant air in the sunshine, and taking that same breath in that same sunshine after surviving a round of Russian Roulette. The latter took pleasure and made it profound. He wouldn't have put it in such terms, but he understood the truth of it instinctively: his experience with Leah had showed him that the heart is an abyss.

He began growing his hair.

Marie would never have tolerated it, of course; but he never saw her any more. At first he only let his hair grow unfashionably long; he looked disreputable, but it was just ordinary hair. But he woke up one morning, and was aware of a desire to get hold of the Bug, the Neocles Bug, and swallow it. It wasn't hard to get hold of. On the contrary. It was perfectly legal, however infra dig. It would only be a matter of time. He didn't autoanalyse this impulse, not being in the habit of such psychological indulgence. But, instinctively, he knew it was something to do with his daughter. He did not think to himself: it will make me an outcast, somebody seen as an eccentric at best and treacherously insane at worst. But there was some tidal force pulling his soul all in one direction, where the inner waters bunched together in his hollow-earth cranium. It is one of the most persistent and widely believed errors of human life that violence simplifies situations. In fact, of course, the reverse is almost always the case: violence complexifies, sometimes monstrously. But it's only natural that we cling to the former belief, the lie of the Gordian knot, because of course we crave simplicity and we find the prospect of violence exciting and libidinous. It takes courage to see things truly.

George was perhaps the least courageous man in the world. But there are times when even the least courageous surprise themselves.

25

It was Walliam who introduced George to Raphael. But although friends assumed the hair-growing thing followed on from his attending Raphael's performance art, in fact, George knew that his radicalization – if we want to call it that – preceded Raphael by months. Not that Raphael wasn't important too. Which is to say: George's experience was one of resistance to what Raphael was saying, followed by slow acceptance, and culminating in a kind of adrenalized intoxication. It's just that the changes in George's life predated these experiences. What Raphael revealed to him was confirmation, not revelation.

What it was: an extension of his interest in news. That's how he put it to himself when he started attending: he was logging-on to the news in a more than merely contemporary sense. And many of the satisfactions he experienced were just the same as offered to him by the news channels. But there was something more, and that extra quality was something the news never gave him. Belief.

Believing Raphael wasn't a question of content; it was a matter of *form*. It wasn't about whether he agreed with what he said, or not. It was about whether he was ready to become one of *those sorts of people* . . . the earnest people; the laughably genuine people; the religious people; the political people; the *believers*. If Raphael had looked more professorial, he might have been able to tell himself that he had been overawed by the man's aura of knowledge. But he was a lanky, painfully skinny guy, who wore his long hair ostentatiously fanned out at the back in a belt-loom. It was a statement. It was food, also, of course; although from time to time George saw him supplement his diet with little pastries, protein gum, and even little snorts of c:snuff.

On the other hand, what he spoke was *sense*. George couldn't deny it. Raph would sync everyone's Fwns and then run them through a lecture – great sprawling lectures, fifteen or twenty minutes long – about history. 'There's only one subject for history,' he told them. 'Power has told you otherwise, but that's a lie.' (*Power* was his catch-all for the people and institutions and structures in charge of the world: the privileged, the banks, the militarily well-equipped.) 'Power tells you that history is a million little individual stories of people doing this and that, princes and kings, queens and princesses, generals and captains of industry. But looked at properly *they* all go into the dark.'

Dark?

'There's only one subject in human history,' Raphael said. 'Poverty. It's the state most humans have been in for most of the time humans have lived on this planet. Viewed objectively, poverty is massively the defining aspect of human life. Wealth is a recent, occasional and – viewed overall – a vanishingly rare aberration from the human baseline. Is it a coincidence that almost all historians have studied wealth, that almost no historians have studied poverty? This is what they say: it's not that it's not a feature of human history, it's just not a *significant* feature.' And here there would be a blizzard of links to instances of two hundred years of historical focus. 'They say a wealthy king is a more important topic for historians than ten thousand starving serfs. Is he? *He* certainly thought so! But that's not it – the king does not build pyramids with his own two hands, does not wage war by himself, does not personally go into the world and gather wheat and gold and jewels.'

And George pictured to himself a heap of yellow wheat-ears and yellower doubloons and bright red rubies.

'Historians have hitherto worked from the premise that poverty is not as *significant* as wealth. But they don't mean that. What they mean is that poverty does not make for *diverting narratives* the way wealth does. They mean people would rather watch a book with a sexy actress representing Anne Boleyn in a splendid dress, than watch a book about ill-clad peasants grubbing in the dirt. They mean poverty is dreary. And so it is! They mean that poverty is boring. And so it is! So, only understand this: historians look to history for entertainment, not for the truth. They go to be diverted and titillated, not to see how things really are. History,' he said, fiddling with his Fwn so that the slogan was properly isolated and could be sent, 'is like a study of a mighty forest of fir trees that only ever talks about some primroses growing on the extreme edge. History that talks about rich people is a lie. Taken as a whole, mankind *has never been rich.*'

The thing was that George felt people were looking at him as if he, alone of all these people, *he* knew what that mystic signifier 'poverty' actually meant. But his daughter's time in the village now felt like a very remote portion of his past. It had been real, of course. But it didn't *feel* real. Raphael went on and on about poverty as the truth at the heart of the human condition. Conventional history was like a medical study of the human body that only interested itself in the jewelled earrings and hair-gen the person happened to be sporting. It was like study of the great oceans of the earth that talked only about oyster pearls and, more, that pretended that oyster pearls were the only thing *worth* talking about! That the whole focus of the ocean and all its force and depth, its ability to rise up and swallow whole civilizations, its still unmapped abyssal planes, *all* its multifarious life from krill to killer whales – that all of this must be understood merely as the backdrop to some few pearls. Absurd!

'So what do we need instead? We need a history purged of queens and princes, that's for one thing. We need a history that takes a total view, and understands that the being-in-the-world of human beings has always been overwhelmingly non-wealthy.' Raphael proffered a link to *being-in-the-world*, but George didn't follow it. He knew what *being* was, and what *world* was. Why would he need to follow a link that explained those two things?

'Let's start right here, right now,' said Raphael, and the music underneath his voice changed, and it *was* exciting. It really was. George had had no previous interest in history, but still the thought that he was one of a select group of people completely reinventing the discipline, here in Manhattan, was thrilling.

'The first thing we have to do,' Raphael advised, 'is to distinguish between different degrees of poverty. I'm not interested in the upper strata of the phenomenon, of the people with small monies who have been squeezed by society or circumstances – war, for instance. Not right now. We'll keep that history for another day. I'm interested in the old bottom tier. The thing wealthy people don't understand is that, for most of human history, poverty has been something that could always get worse. Human beings would appear to be completely down and out; but they could always sink lower. This was because for most of human history poverty was a subsistence phenomenon. *Poor* meant having the bare minimum. That is to say, it meant having something. And something can always be pared away. Not now! Now a new manifestation of poverty has come into the world – the most significant development in human history since the invention of farming. Now we have *absolute* poverty. And—' adjusting the Fwn again, so that the music is right for the recording of another slogan, 'absolute poverty is absolute freedom! It can't be pared away, or threatened, or warred down.'

George wasn't sure about this, but, like, you know. Whatever.

The following week was revolution; something the rest of the cadre excitedly chattered about on Fwn for days in advance. Secretly, again, George thought this, really, was missing the point – for he had taken to heart Raphael's point (or what he assumed was Raphael's point) that history had so often been hijacked by the dramatically engaging instead of by the True. And of course there was no doubt that revolutions made for more exciting books. He watched the ones they had been advised to watch: two about the American Revolution (there had been an *American* revolution! Who knew?), one about the French Revolution, which involved a lot of inventive decapitation, and three about the Russian Revolution, which seemed to be all about the swarming of crowds. It was hard to follow the narrative in this last one, particularly – a shipful of revolutionaries had docked and then all the crew had rushed about a city and up and down some stairs and . . . what? Something imprecise but very deeply felt. Something intellectually tangled but emotionally very powerful.

'Here's another thing conventional historians have missed,' Raphael said. 'They know that revolutions occur from time to time . . . which is to say, that for long stretches human societies go along without them happening, and then suddenly they happen. But nobody has really worked out what the underlying logic is. Is it an inevitable part of historical process? Does it happen to coincide with famine, or war? Can it be spread from country to country like a disease? Does it happen when tyrannical societies *begin* to reform?' Yeah, yeah, get on with it. 'I'll tell you the truth other historians have missed. What's needful for a permanent revolution? Not an industrial proletariat, and not even a peasant mass. What's needful is a large enough lumpenproletariat.' George was going to check the links on those indigestible words, but he saw that Raphael was morphing the musical accompaniment, which probably meant he was about to utter a slogan, and that would surely boil it all down for him. So he waited, and sure enough: 'A large population of idle people is the perfect kindling for *permanent* revolution,' he said. 'Power keeps adjusting as the People keep trying to rise up against it, and Power has learnt a number of tricks for stifling revolution – strategic concessions, more effective police and army technologies, ideological propaganda. But the best trick Power managed was: keep people too busy to rise up. Keep them tired and distracted. And that kept a hundred and fifty years free of uprising. But the new hair has changed the game. The new hair means that there are *millions* of people who have nothing whatsoever to do with their time. Millions of idle poor, too well-situated to die, but not occupied with any of the tasks or chores of staying alive. The perfect revolutionary class!'

26

He had lunch with Rodion. 'When I sit down to break bread with you, old boy,' he started, but stopped, uncertain how to go on. 'What I mean is: what I always feel,' he said, 'is that you have a secret.'

'I'm sure we all have *secrets*,' Rodion replied, mildly.

They were sipping coffee. George's coffee had a skin of nectar floating on its surface. To drink the coffee, his lips touched the molecule-thin skein, and his tongue was aware of just enough of its flavour to take the brittle edge off the coffee's sourness. It was a beautiful cup of coffee.

'I've come to the conclusion,' said George, 'that the secret in *my* life was – me.' He couldn't help looking at the old man with a triumphal expression on his face, a self-satisfaction, as if he had uttered something terribly profound and original. Of course, he had not. Of course he had only touched on the most mundane baseline, universal feature of human existence. Rodion, though, was too polite to do anything other than smile and nod gently, and lift his own coffee cup (plain black, of course) to his withered lips. His lips were withered because there comes a point where even the most elaborate genetic treatments reach the limit of their efficacy. Otherwise, we would all live for ever.

Rodion waited a decent interval, such that changing the conversational subject wouldn't look too rudely abrupt. In fact he needn't have worried; George wasn't expecting to be probed on his so-called revelation. Had he been politely asked to say more about this secret self he had supposedly uncovered, he would have been reduced to cliché, or to flailing about. Birds flew left to right, over their heads, and right to left, and appeared from behind them. George considered the clouds. They were fishscale silver against the dark blue sky. They were painted-looking. George could almost see the brushstrokes.

'This Florida news is a bad business,' Rodion said.

'What's that?'

'I sometimes wonder why it's so terribly unfashionable to follow the news,' Rodion said. 'I mean, I *am* unreconstructedly old-fashioned, I suppose. Once upon a time, and I don't think we want to go into the details here and now – but once upon a time, you know, I *was* news. So I've kept a kind of weather-eye on it ever since. I just haven't been able to discuss it at polite dinner parties!' And he chuckled to himself.

If he hadn't been so eager to talk about himself, George might have followed up on this *I used to be the news* hint. Instead he said: 'As for my news-watching, well. It's one of my things. I mean, I'm not a slave to the head-in-the-ostrich of fashion.'

'And what *do* you think about the events in Florida?'

'Events in Florida,' said George, nodding. Then: 'Events – when?'

Rodion drew a thumbnail across his bald scalp. 'Over the last few weeks.'

'There was something,' said George, looking into the maw of his white stone coffee mug. 'There were riots, I think. There are always riots, though.'

'Well,' said Rodion, uncertainly. 'I suppose that's true. Not in New York, though!'

'There *was* trouble, back when they cleared Queens.'

'Oh, yes! That's right. I suppose I meant: not in Manhattan.'

'Christ, no,' said George, with feeling. 'Thank heavens, not here.'

'I think,' Rodion said, tentatively, 'that the Florida business was more than just "riots"', you know.' And when George peered at him, with that doll-like intensity, his large black-pupilled eyes like a shark's, Rodion added: 'I think it was more concerted. An attempt at revolution.'

'Really?' Now here was a subject George felt he knew something about!

'Longhairs seized pretty much all the Keys. Lots of people got killed. They called themselves Spartacists – not that,' George was blinking, 'not that it matters what they called themselves. There are hundreds of thousands of them at sea now, in tens of thousands of little boats. Going by that name.'

'At sea!' George, now that he thought of it, had noticed a lot of news imagery of ragged-looking flotillas. But since he was in the habit of watching the news with the sound turned down, and the tickerfeed disabled, he'd not been quite sure what those images meant.

'They can live at sea for as long as they like,' said Rodion. 'A desalinator in the boat for water, and endless sunshine. It's the ideal place for them, really. Anyway, the anxiety was that they were coordinated. They did all this D-Daylike stuff, seized the Keys. Then they started to encroach on the mainland. The deaths numbered in the thousands. In the several thousands.'

'Good grief,' said George

'It's been contained, now, of course,' said Rodion, unsure why he felt the urge to reassure this man. Except, of course, that this man – his hair down to his shoulders, like a teenage rebel – sparked some sort of paternal instinct in him. 'Luckily the authorities have gotten pretty good at containment after Triunion.'

'I'll always remember Triunion,' said George, piously. 'I remember, the riots were going on in Triunion when Leah was kidnapped. The two things are kind of linked, in my memory.'

'Better to watch the news,' Rodion said, 'than get caught up in the news.'

'I like to *watch*,' said George, with unconscious quotation.

'And *those* clouds,' Rodion said, after a while. 'The ones sliding overhead from the east. Now, they look a little too *café noir* for my liking. Shall we go inside before the storm breaks?'

'Yes,' said George, getting to his feet. 'Let's.'

TWO

LEAH

The thing about the fridge was the way it was just *there*, all day and all night, and always full, and always accessible to anybody who just walked up to its door. For Leah it was a continual source of amazement. It wasn't so much the size of it, although it *was* big. Rather, it had something to do with the way the heavy door was perfectly hinged to swing open at the lightest touch and reveal the cavernous wonders beyond it. Shelf after shelf of food and drink. A great, stacked structure of different foods, reaching high over her head. When she opened the door the genie in the box said, *Hi can I help you?*, and after she'd breathed in the lovely cold wafts for a while he said in a deeper voice: *Wow, you're leaving the door open for an age and an age!* So she heaved it shut and the deep-set thunk of its closure was very thrilling to her. It sounded like some lost portion of the cosmos reclaimed and clicked into place. It was much bigger than the fridge in the village, but that was hardly a surprising fact, when you came to think of it. When she had been kidnapped, as she had learned, the Big Man in the village had a fridge, in his house; and there was that one time she'd gone into the house with Shabine to do what Aga H. had told them to do – retrieve a knot of plastic leads and cords from the room behind the kitchen, for whatever incomprehensible purpose Aga H. had needed them. The two of them had passed the humming monolith. 'You know what's in there?' Shabine had said to her, and she had replied: 'Go on, open it – take a strawberry.' This had been a joke between them, because the day before Shabine had told her that strawberries were a kind of crunchy straw, of the same family as the splinterish blades that grew all over the narrow field behind Isman's. But Leah had said, no, she'd seen a picture show with strawberries and they were red as lips. And, lacking any strawberries, real or imaginary, against which to test their disagreement they had moved on to other things.

Now, today, in New York, Wally came in the kitchen, and *wsht-wsht*ed her away. Wax, mother called him. Leah could tell from the way she said this that it was one of her jokes, although she didn't understand it at all. So she went away, and went up to the roof instead. It was a hot afternoon, the sort of weather that still sometimes made her feel a little homesick, although, mostly, she'd gotten on top of all that nonsense a long time ago. And homesick was a stupid word, anyway. The feeling that people called homesick wasn't in the least bit a nausea, nothing sicky-of-gutty about it. It was more a tingling, or kindling feeling in her heart. And it had nothing to do with 'home', for wasn't she home right now, standing on the roof of her home and looking about her at her city? It was for something else that made her soul fizz with yearning; an idea of something, a simple loss, like the chopping off of her hair. Where was that hair now? What did people do with hair when it was cut off? Did it go in the organic waste chute, or in the plastic chute, or in the compressibles? Which category did hair belong to? She lolled about the roof of the building, and checked out the cityscape, making sure everything was in their proper places. Overhead a sunkite lay sprawled on the air, two linked triangular sheets spread over an invisible mattress. Leah didn't understand why they had to be so big. They had done sunkites at school a few weeks earlier, so she understood the principles involved; but she still didn't understand why they had to be so *big*. They were doing Antarctica tomorrow.

Her father and mother were going to divorce, just like Tercier's parents, and Kelly's. But there was a difference, because this was her fault. She broke the fridge, and it made her parents break-up – though not because they were cross with her, because oddly enough they didn't seem to be cross with her. But there was, obviously, a connection. She had told her father that Wally was out of the kitchen, although she didn't say that he was in Trotters again. He went there to kiss-and-cuddle, she knew, but she liked not telling any-body – except Marthe, of course. She had no secrets from Marthe.

How it happened, was.

It was still an astonishing thing to her, even after all these years. To think that food filled every shelf of this huge box, and that the door was not locked. She'd said that Wally wasn't in the kitchen, and Daddy had said to go back down there and look again. So she had. She'd considered this a permission. Alone in the long room, she had stood before the fridge. Stainless-steel-coloured dolphins played endlessly across its wide door; shaped by the waters they swam in, as pebbles are shaped by the millennial stream. A purple-blue sea. She flicked the door with her thumb and the images changed to another of Wally's presets – she assumed Wally had preset these, for who else would have done so? Breakers on a beach, curling like peeled rinds and crumbling in a blizzard of white spray. What was it with Wally and the ocean? Did he have, like, a thing for it? Another thumb-flick and another preset: the constellations of myriad globular jellyfish, pulsing like hearts, like wafer-walled, transparent hearts, against a green-blue background. Talk about boring. So, postponing the moment of actually opening the fridge (because she *was* going to open the fridge, and because it *was* pleasant to prolong the anticipation), she pulled a menu out of the pictures and scrolled through to something a bit less *gique*. She found a scene from a new book, *Angels and Pain*, and let that roll for a while across the door: Mica, who was the coolest angel, soared through rainbow clouds chasing Aer, who had killed Mica's mother. They shot heatrays from their wings.

She got out her Fwn. She had begged Daddy not to get her a Fwn. Fwns were so *over*. But he had got it for her anyway, with that vague expression on his face that was so completely him. There was a small burden of shame involved in speaking to Marthe on a Fwn, knowing that Marthe was speaking to *her* on a Helio. 'So, Marthe, you know strawberries?'

'You're damaged,' Marthe replied. 'Of course I know straw-berries.'

'Red, yeeah?'

'Your *brain* is the strawberry.'

'Odd they're called *straw*, though? Straw not being red.'

'Your *brain* is red,' Marthe said.

'Later.'

'Can't wait-a.'

She tucked the Fwn away, and pulled the mighty door open. How smoothly it swung, how perfectly poised on its heavy hinges! *Well hi–hello there* piped the genie. *Long time no see*.

He wasn't tall, not especially, Wally wasn't. So how-ow-ow did he get to the *top* shelves? There must be a command to pull down a ladder, or something, but Leah couldn't make that happen. She asked the fridge for a staircase but it did its *I'm only a dumb machine* thing, in a squeaky voice. And who knew how long Wally would be at Trotters? So she used some initiative. She clambered up using the shelves as ladder-steps. It went OK for the first few, although she put her left foot in something squishy. But her hand on a high shelf she tried to lever herself up, and the fabric of the thing refused to take her weight. The shelf lurched. It didn't break, it *slid* towards her, and before she could think what to do she was falling. Everything came down in an avalanche of things – the whole shelf came free and flew, wing-like, over her head.

She landed on her b.t.m. and banged the back of her head too on the hard floor – it was pretty sore. But more alarming than the impact was the sound she produced. The liberated shelf struck the floor just behind her and rang with a great gong noise, and then bounced, and then hit again with enough force to boom throughout the whole house. And all around her, and on to her also, food and pots and plastic moulds and scoops and fruit and everything rained down. And the fridge itself didn't help matters: 'Ow ow ow!' it called, 'you're ripping my guts out!' it shrilled. What good did that do?

Leah got herself up and brushed as much of the food off her front as she could. Then, scowling at the sharpness of her aches she tried to pick the shelf off the floor. But it was too heavy for a kid to lift one-handed. She only succeeded in raising it high enough to mean that dropping it again made a *violent* racket.

So she retreated to the corner of the kitchen and surveyed the mess – the really pretty impressive mess – that she had made. There was no way of avoiding responsibility for it, she could see. Even if she could somehow get the shelf back in the fridge, and stuff all the spilled food back inside, many of the viands were all scuffed or squashed. And who knows what system Wally had. Perhaps the thing to do would be to persuade Wally to take the blame? 'Wax', Mummy called him. Why, though?

She got out her Fwn. 'Marthe?'

'Hello, girl with a red-red strawberry for a brain.'

'I think I broke my parents' fridge.'

'Nohow!'

'True. How can I get Wally to take the blame for it?'

'Who's Wally?'

'He's the kitchen guy. He's the food dude.'

'Tell him he's gotta take the blame, or you'll shave his head and kick him out.' This was Marthe's joke at Leah's expense, and went way back to a conversation they had had, like, *months* ago, about the other country. Marthe wouldn't let it go, she wouldn't. *She* thought it was funny. It wasn't funny. But the more Leah pointed out that it wasn't funny, the more Marthe went on and on.

'You're, one, a help, or two, no help at all.'

'One.'

'*Two*, Ma-ma-Marthe. Later.'

'Can't wait-a.' said Marthe.

'It's our fate-a.'

'It'll be great-a.'

There was nothing for it; so she made her way upstairs to confess everything to her father. She had to ask the house where he was, because he wasn't where he'd been the last time they spoke. Blue room, the house said. And when she went into the blue room she could tell that something big was *up*. Instead of his usual sweetly dopey face, which Leah rebuked him for as molasses, though she thought, secretly, it was *pretty* sweet, actually, instead of that Daddy had the eyebrow-scrunched expression he got when he was feeling sorry for himself. Leah's stomach writhed with *he knows* and *uh-oh*s.

She let her arms dangle. The house told him, maybe; or Wally saw and rushed straight up to tittle and tattle. So she came into the room expecting – not knowing *what* to expect, actually. But instead of anger, her daddy started bla-a-athering something about separation. Then he asked her if she knew what the word meant – as if she didn't *do* words, hundreds of them every week, meaning *and* spelling. The word was 'separation'.

'It means being cut up,' she told him.

'Yes,' he said, gravely. 'It means that your mother and I will live in different houses.' Cottoning on a little late – which, as Marthe said, was Leah's extra *special* talent, the thing with which Providence or Genes or God had gifted her – she realized that Daddy and Mummy were divorcing. Exactly like Kelley's parents! Except that Kelley's parents had taken her on a special holiday, just to break the news to her, and Kelley said it was strange because although it was a superspecial resort, in one of the Antarctic bubbles, with tunnels and slides going on for kilometres, and although they'd deliberately taken her there – nevertheless her parents grew cross when she *had fun*. They had told her the news in that place to stop her being too sad, but when she *wasn't* sad they got huffy. 'You will spend some time with me, and some time with your mother,' Leah's daddy was saying, now; but that was pure chaff. He had to say that of course.

Then it struck her. He would never say so right out, of course; to spare her feelings, so she wouldn't blame herself. But it was the fridge. Of course. She turned her eyes like Vision-Man, as if she could see right through the walls and the floor to where the contents of the fridge were scattered over the floor. 'I see.'

'It'll be OK,' he said, in a when-you've-cleared-it-all-up sort of voice.

'So you'll get back together afterwards?'

He shook his head, with that bitter little trembly way he sometimes had. Leah knew it wasn't the fridge, of course. She wasn't an idiot. She wasn't one of those Hance-Men souped up on neurogenes that walked around with the weird expression on their faces like they were normal people when everybody knew they weren't normal people at all. But still, the fridge had something to do with it. It was an allegory. It was an icon. It was an emblem. That was the way of it. Something had yawned open and smashed in her parents' relationship. What could it be, if not her? What did it go down to, if not her greed for food?

'I'm going to sit down, now, my love,' Dad said.

She had to tell Marthe; but she couldn't do that directly in front of Dad. So she said goodbye and ran – really *ran*, full pelt – through the hall and up the curly-stair to her room. She didn't know why, but she felt *crammed full of energy*, all of a sudden. She was ready to burst! She couldn't sit still. 'Marthe?'

'Whaddaya whaddaya?'

'You'll never guess what my parents are getting a divorce and that's for real!' She was breathing so fast she sounded like a flitter about to take off.

'You are lying to me with your mouth!' squealed Marthe.

'Not.'

'No way!'

'No no-way.'

'*No* no-no-way.'

'It's true, my dad just told me, they're going to live in separate houses, and I'll tell you something nobody else knows.'

'What?'

'They're doing it because I broke the fridge!'

'You *told* me you broke the fridge!' Marthe yelled.

'I *did* tell you I broke the fridge!'

'You were on the Helio, like, seconds ago!' This was a little dig, because although Marthe had a Helio, since day-before-yesterday, Leah only had a Fwn, and Marthe knew it. But she was so excited she let it go.

'I know!'

'A nailed-up *fish* on the *cross*,' cried Marthe. 'I can't *believe* that's why they're getting divorced! That's the deekiest reason to get divorced!'

'Well,' said Leah, the shine of excitement coming off her mood a little. 'I guess it's not just the fridge. I mean, maybe the fridge is like, you know that phrase, about breaking the back? Last strawberry.'

'Last *straw*, crazy-o,' hooted Marthe. '*Strawberry*! I'd say you have grass for brains!'

'Straw's what I said!' said Leah, growing cross; because, after all, Marthe wasn't being very supportive for her in this, her time of trouble. 'I said straw.'

'Shall we just run that past the All Seeing Eye?' said Marthe. That was the catchphrase from the new Q&A prize show, *Quoz*.

'Anyway, I've *got* to go,' said Leah, darkly. 'The whole world is coming to an end here.'

For a while she lounged and flailed languidly about on her GelBag and watched a book. Her excitement was all disappearing. It was all vanishing through whatever spacetimeportal governed Mood, and only leaving her the beginnings of despondency. The poverty equivalent of feelings. Hateful, that. A hatful of hateful. She watched another book, but despite super 4D explosions and a lead with eyes the size of shields her attention kept wandering. 'This is it,' she told herself. 'It's happened, it's over.' But these words didn't really connect either. If it were over, how come she was still breath-ing, blinking, thinking?

She thought about who else she could tell. Marthe was no good. Marthe had only made friends with her from pity. She had said so. Really she had. You were kidnapped, Marthe told her. You were stolen by poor people, and they infected you with the poor people bug. Leah squealed at this, and said not fair, but it was nothing but the truth. Her hair was different to normal people's hair. She could rub her hand over Marthe's trimmed hair and feel how soft it was, like moonlight, or magic, so soft. Her own was stiff as bristles. 'You had proper soft hair once,' Leah informed her. 'Then the poor people grabbed you and fed you the Bug, and now you've got leaves for hair.' This wasn't right; leaves would have been gross-o the most-o. But the thrust of it was spot-on. She wasn't normal. Marthe really only made friends with her because she had the weird religion, which she had because her parents had the weird religion, and other kids made fun of her for it. But having a weird religion wasn't the same thing as having the Bug. Once, Leah had asked her dad – but tentatively, because it had been drilled into her, in her time in the village, that losing her special hair was tanta-mount to death – whether they couldn't take the Bug out. She knew (she wasn't a Pretard) that 'Bug' meant millions of fantastically small machines all up and down her strawberry-coloured blood, and all inside her pale lymph, and clinging to the threads of her nerves. But she couldn't quite shake the sense that it was one squat Bug, living somewhere in the rose-tinged darkness of her insides, with goggles for eyes and cutlery mouthparts and two laptop covers snicked shut over its curved back. Exuding evil. Put a hand in there and pull it out. I'm afraid not, honey, Dad said. Can't be got out. But it doesn't do you harm, it just means your hair has this—

'tever, Dad, she had interrupted him, and dashed off somewhere else. The Bug was stuck inside her like the fruit in the
rhyme:

> *There was a young woman who swallowed a fruit*
> **She** *didn't want to, a* **snake** *made her do'it.*
> *The fruit changed her spirit from goody to bad:*
> *And sun that set happy rose up again sad.*

What was *snake*? Her Fwn told her: a legless reptilian creature
common in desertified scrub and parchlands. She looked at the
pictures. They looked horrid.

No, she couldn't chat with Marthe about this right now.
Who else? There was always Rodion. It was a little apocalyptic,
having a friend as old as Rodion, but he was good to talk to.
She remembered her first proper conversation with him, in the
park. He had introduced himself to her, gravely, as if communicating something very important. 'Good afternoon, my
name is Rodion,' with an accent you only heard in books.
'You're the other person who lives in our building,' she had
said. And Marthe had said: 'You're older than some dead
people.' He had laughed at this. Rodion had offered to buy
them ice cream. 'Strawberry,' Leah had demanded.

So they had strolled to one of the vendors, and sat themselves at a round table. The vendor came out with a giant
bullfighter's cape and flourished it ostentatiously in the air to
let it settle over the tabletop. For a moment it lay plumped on
its cushion of air, and then the air came through the weave and
gravity sucked it tight about the underlying shape. Rodion
ordered three bowls, and they were all strawberry. All strawberry all the time.

'I will tell you something interesting about strawberries,'
Rodion announced. The girls hunkered down, eating the

creamy chill paste with their tongues only, it seemed: for nothing seemed to go into their stomachs. 'People think that the fruit eaten in the garden of Eden, eaten by Adam and Eve, was an apple. But not so!'

And Marthe was already bored. Nothing is so boring as the stuff you don't comprehend. 'What's Eden?'

'Oh don't you know *anything*?' Leah asked, who at least knew this.

'I know Adam's the dude in the Deep Sea Battle books,' Marthe replied, defiantly.

'Did you never hear the story of the Garden of Eden?' the old man, Rodion, asked, in a mild voice.

'Never did never will,' replied Marthe, leaping up. 'Later, oldster.' And she was off.

'*I've* heard of the Garden of Eden – and the apple,' Leah assured Rodion.

'But that's exactly it,' said Rodion, looking about him with a vaguely baffled air. 'It was no apple. It was a strawberry. It says so, in the Bible.'

'Strawberry in the Bible, got it,' said Leah, hopping to her feet. 'Got to find my *friend* now.' And she ran after Leah, singing with delight.

'In the heeb,' Rodion hooted mournfully at their retreating figures. 'Rue!'

Whatever street *that* was. But Rodion was all right, and what's more he was always there: the same bland, blithe friendliness, the same distractedly cheerful manner. He offered Leah another strawberry ice cream the next time she was in the park – just her, this time, and her new carer, Josephina. 'Are you one of those pie-doughs we're warned about?' she asked him.

'Gracious *no*.' He looked actually shocked.

'A pie-dough would say no, though.'

'But so would an honest man.'

Of course, that was true. 'They say in school that pie-doughs are everywhere, and want to get their grubby hands on little children. Little girls especially.'

'Not I. And anyway, your carer is right there.'

'Oh *her*? She's a sullen beast. She doesn't like being a carer at all. I don't know why she doesn't go off and do something else with her lifestyle and being-in-the-world.'

'Perhaps there's nothing else for her to do? Perhaps she has no choice?'

'Well *I* don't know, do I?' Leah retorted.

'You could ask her?'

Leah considered this. 'If she were proper poor, I could talk to her. Or if she were rich, obviously I could. But she's a kind of inbetween, and I don't talk to *those*.'

'What do you mean, proper poor?'

'I mean like the people in my village.'

'Interesting that you call it *your* village!' Rodion smiled at her.

'It's not like I'm pretending I own it,' Leah said. 'Anyway, it hardly matters. Daddy came and pulled me out of *there*. Where's my ice cream, though?'

They went to get the ice cream.

Leah could hardly go tell Oldion Rodion that her parents were splitting up. That would be sadder than the saddest.

And in the event, the break-up was smoother *than* smooth. Dad moved into a stony flat in the Seawall apartment building overlooking the Hudson, and Ma moved to a house on First Street, and – well, Leah had no idea what happened to the old house. Maybe they sold it, or maybe it just sat in darkness, the windows turned to black, the carpet bots making curlicues in the dust, and at the heart of it all the fridge, the enormous fridge – still (though this made no sense) packed with every kind of food, and murmuring to itself all day and all night with its voice like a housefly's buzz. The god of the house's peculiar, New World *plenitude* of silence. The Fri. The Idge.

At any rate, Leah never went back to that house.

Her time, now, was divided between Ma and Dad. Schooling went on – though Marthe's parents moved to one of the New Zealand islands (the one with the big siege wall all about it, like one of those collars with which they neck sick dogs – can't remember the name of the island right now). They still stayed in touch, of course. Most everybody had Lance, now; it wasn't just for special occasions. And Leah made other friends, like Freda and Lucy, and she kept on seeing old Rodion. She and Rodion had an ice-cream date every fortnight, in the park, and never missed it. Dividing her life between Ma and Dad became the larger rhythm of her life, and soon felt as natural as day-night or the swap of seasons.

She liked the interchange the best, when the flitter collected her from First, or from the Seawall, and hoiked her up into the sky. She liked to look down and see the city modelled, transformed into a bristling art-installation on the topic of Plenty. The rectangular green gap in the middle, and all around it, like a cluttered formation of crystals and basalts, an artificial giant's causeway, pink and cream and grey. It was the Fridge, made stone. It was the Fridge laid on its side with the door removed, and all the bursting, thrusting fullness solidified into something permanent. Her insides would spangle, and the little hairs on her neck wriggle like the seeds in the book about the big peach. The waters would shimmer, and the antique bridges gleam, the suspension wires taut like bowstrings. And then the flitter would swoop and she would be deposited, with Adrianna, her new carer, Adrianna of the open mouth, who would puff and gasp as she manhandled Leah's case out of the trunk.

Switch off the screen and what have you got? The huge white door. No images moving upon it any more. Only the great block of blank door, like a monolith of milk ice cream. My god it's full of – food? Is it? Stars, is it?

Stars. Food.

Towards the end of the year she became aware of a generalized *pressure*, in a psychodynamic sense of the word. It had to do with the imminent embarrassment that she might have to spend *another* year learning, like a mong, like a kaka, like the *poor* have to, because they can't afford the braingeneering. But it was all all right. She had a sit-down talk with Mama – she always had more sensible conversations with Mama – about her age of majority. It was one of those 'as you know' chats. 'As you know, Leah, it's a privilege of wealth to be able to attain legal adulthood at fourteen.' Leah didn't know anything of the sort, but knew better than to say so. 'This is not an automatic thing, of course,' Mama was saying. 'It is that a child of means is able to mature more quickly. And your time in – the thing that happened to you – took a chunk out of your schooling.'

Leah contemplated this phrase: the thing that happened to you. 'Papusza says that there's a new tweak . . .'

'Now, my darling,' said Marie. 'We don't need to rush after any strange new treatments. Your tutor says you're very quick – that you're making very quick progress.'

'Sure,' said Leah.

Papusza was her new best friend.

Mama was doing more and more of her gardening work. She loved gardens, Leah knew, although Leah couldn't imagine why. The city was a work of art, as far as Leah could see.

Gardens were just smartified wildernesses, and she'd seen enough wilderness and weeds and scrub in her life to last her for ever. But she tried saying this to Mama once, and got snapped and snarled down. Queens was more than a wilderness.

They went for a holiday to New Seattle. Everybody agreed – all of Leah's friends, anyhow – that holidays in the tropics were totally *over*. It was uncool, all the swarming poor with their long black hair, clustering on the beaches like a beard of bees. The resorts were cleared of them by security, of course, except for those few vetted for work as, you know, waiters and that. But you saw them as you flew over. Papusza made an 'eew' sound that was higher-pitched than you would *believe*. It was almost up where only dogs could hear it, oh my *god*. Leah had never before in her whole entire life laughed as much as she did with Papusza. And Mama and Papusza's two dads got on, so they all went to New Seattle together for a holiday. If George could have come it would have been even better. Not that it was bad, of course.

'Come over here Lee,' Papusza cried, from the right side of the flitter.

They were all in Wasj's private flitter, double trunk, with its own shower and fridge and everything. Leah rushed to the right side and looked down. The flight path was north over the ocean, and all the little dints and wavelets in the water were carved in light. It was easy to make out the old coastline – the land north of SF, this would have been once, where the sea had encroached deepest. *Under* the water, roads and houses and dead tree stems like the piles for vanished piers, all clearly visible. The new coastline was, variously, gentle upslopes and sharp ravines where waves ground themselves into a froth, but in either case the landscape was dotted, or crowded, or *teeming* with longhairs. God they were everywhere! Mrs Ficowski said you weren't to call them long-hairs, because that betrayed a vulgarity of condescension, or something. But that's what they *were*! They just milled about, or lay there, or sat in groups, or fought with one another, or kissed and cuddled and pornoed together, and Papusza made her 'eeew' noise again, and Leah shrieked with laughter, until one of Pap's dads told them to shush with the banshee stuff. They flew past stretches of new coast that were properly fenced off, where real people had their houses and gardens and so on; but the longhairs had no respect for fences. As they went by Leah counted three estates where the fences had been breached, and where longhairs were scattered about the property, eating the flowers, or just laying about. What could you do? There were so many of them.

The fatter of Pap's two dads came over to the window to see what they were making so much noise about. 'They come up from So-Cal and *Mec*-hico,' he said. 'Lord knows why. It's not as if there's more sun up here. Less, rather.'

'They should make the fence between America and the South stronger,' said Papusza, imperiously.

'They come in waves,' said Pap's dad. 'It's to do with religious sects. I've also heard it's drugs, there's proponents of both explanations. But anyway, a great mob of them gathers, time-to-time, and they just bust through. Provided they have water the desert's no barrier to them. On the contrary. All the sun in that desert? Desert's a restaurant to *that* lot.'

'We should,' said Leah, excitedly, rubbing her own close-cropped scalp unconsciously, 'block the sun for a few months! Put up a space filter – I saw a book about, about it, science fiction it was. You put it in space directly between the Earth and the sun, and stop all sunlight for a few months, and clear them all out.'

'You come up with the *most* idiotic ideas,' snapped Mama from the other side of the flitter.

But Pap's dad chuckled at Leah's idea, actually *laughed*! So it can't have been a bad one. And as he laughed the fat on his neck trembled like a rapid pulse. 'It's sure a radical solution,' he said.

'They're weeds,' called Pap's other dad across the aisle of the flitter. 'Poisonous weeds. And that's all there is to say about them.'

'You quiet your Nazi noise, Tishani,' said the first dad, and laughed again.

'I know it seems like the problem is a long way off when you're in New York, kids,' said Tishani, addressing the two girls. 'But it's getting worse. It's worse because the authorities won't seize the nettle. These longhairs come over with guns you know. They're like cockroaches, real hard to kill, and mean as hell.'

Ez, who had been immersed in his game, perked up at the mention of guns. 'Hey,' he said. 'Do they send in the militia?' God he loved *guns*, that boy.

'They did that two years ago,' said Tishani. 'There was a mob assault on the LA fence.'

'Did they send in the Striders?' Ez asked, growing more excited.

'The kit, the caboodle, the lot,' said Tishani. 'Men, robots, the whole lot. It was a mass–a–*cre*.'

'Cool!'

'I never heard of it,' said Mama, crossly, from the back of the flitter.

'It was all over the news,' said Tishani. 'But who watches the news?'

Leah wasn't stupid. She knew nobody cool watched the news, because it was all vulgar nonsense. And she knew that if she'd said: 'My dad watches the news' it would have made Mama angry. So she held her peace, and looked out the window again. The crowds of poor became sparser the further north they went. Of course they did. The further north you went, the less sunlight there was – everybody knew that.

Secretly, Leah wished she could watch the news too. Just to find out what was going on. She could watch on her Fwn, of course; or on the house screen when nobody else was about, but then Mama would see it on her records, and she'd get into trouble.

'If you blotted the sun out,' Papusza said to her, 'you'd kill all the crops. Fruit trees and so on.'

'I guess.'

'Maybe your science-fiction book hadn't thought it all through?'

'I guess not.'

Pap sounded very complacent and wise and clever-old-crone-y as she added: 'It's all interconnected, you see. You can't just snip out one section. It's all part of a complicated interconnectedness.'

Oh, they had a *great* week in New Seattle. They were in a house and all around were fields of grass; red and yellow and pink and green. Pap and Leah used to lie down between the long stems, their arms around one another, and listen to the noises made by the breeze. Like the whole world was trying to whisper something to them. They played games, and ran about, and saw real live livestock and real live wildlife, and pretended to fight one another. She never laughed so much in all her life before.

Mama took samples of these new grasses with a handheld device. It had something to do with her Queens' garden. Sometimes Leah tried asking her about all the gardening she was doing now, since the break-up with Dad, but if she tried to ask Mama generally snapped at her. About her nose. Which is to say, nosiness. She seemed to get pretty angry, these days. That was the truth of it.

She was pretty sad when the week had to end, and that's the truth.

Back in NY she introduced Papusza to Rodion. 'My good God he's *old*,' Pap shrieked, right there, right in front of him. It was, like, the *rudest* thing.

But Rodion only chuckled. 'Ice cream, ladies?'

'Ice cream is for tiny kids,' said Pap, grandly. 'I want a coffee. Are you more than a hundred?'

'I am,' said Rodion, getting slowly to his feet and curling his book into a scroll.

'Are you more than *two* hundred?'

'I am not. Would you like a coffee, too, Leah?'

And this was a dilemma. Coffee always made Leah think of the village; the Big Man had always had a cup of coffee in his hand, so far as Leah remembered. When she made a mental picture of him, in her head, there he was, holding the little cup of pungent-smelling black liquid. It looked like hot tar, and the tiny cup might just as well have been carved from stone. The Big Man would be sat there, in one of the rooms of his enormous house (though it was hardly enormous by *actual* standards; it was only enormous by the village standards, and that wasn't saying very much), and he'd open his mouth in that big croco manner he had, and he'd be holding his coffee cup in his right hand, or else perhaps he'd be balancing it on his spherical belly. Little wisps of steam would be coming up out of it, like threads. Aga H. preferred Shabine, but mostly he liked having both of them there. 'You know why I like you girls?' he said, once. 'You don't pester me for food.' Leah's job had been to hold the Big Man's big belly out of the way, so Shabine could work properly, and it used to make her *arms* ache. It really was a large mass of flesh. It didn't seem part of a human being, somehow; it felt like a water-filled piece of furniture – like a mattress. 'Grown women are lovely,' the Big Man had sighed, fitting his words into Shabine's rhythm. 'But they always have an *agenda*. Food, food, always food. Hoarders. They want to. Have babies. So it's food, Aga, please, food. Oh they'll do what I *want*. They'll do things you *can't*. Oh, uh, uh. How I get sick of the nagging!' At this point Shabine disengaged her mouth and put her head round the side of his belly: 'Oh I'd love to try some *food*, Aga, can I?' 'Hey!' he boomed. 'I didn't tell you to stop, did I?' 'I've never tried any *food*,' Shabine had insisted. 'I've love to try some sugar! Could I?' But the Aga had smacked her on the top of her head with the flat of his hand. 'Get back to your work, kid! What do you want food for? You can't have babies for years yet.' There were tears in her eyes now, because the smack had not been gentle, but Shabine persisted. 'Oh, please, Aga! Just a little taste – just a taste of your coffee, there?' Leah had caught on, though fearful of getting a smack too: 'Ooh, yes, Aga, can we just have a taste?' He had growled, like a thunderhead, and said: 'I'm the only food you're to put in *your* mouth.' Shabine, always bolder than Leah, snapped: 'Swallowed that once and it made me want to *sick up*,' she said, wriggling from between his huge hairy legs and darting away. 'It tasted like death! Bitter like death. I want something *sweet*!'

'Come back here!' he bellowed. 'You shitless creature.'

At this, carried away by Shabine's small rebellion, Leah had dropped his pendulous belly and rushed over to her friend.

'Shitless, the *pair* of you,' the Aga had snapped, sitting

forward in his lounger. But he switched immediately to wheedling. 'And if I give you a sip of my coffee, will you come back here and finish what you *started*?'

'Oo,' squealed Shabine. 'Coffee! Coffee!'

'You come here now,' the Big Man had said, settling back, 'or I'll shave your fucking heads right now, and throw you on the mercy of your aunts.' But even this hadn't deflated Shabine's excitement. She and Leah had squirmed back over the fellow's body, and taken turns at the lip of his little cup. Shabine first, Leah second. The liquid was lukewarm, gooey, and it made a weird contrary jarring confusion on her tongue. There was something sweet about it, she thought, much sweeter than the time Nada had brought some stems of wild beet back from the wasteland and Leah had licked at the broken end. But the predominant flavour had been horribly *bitter* – even more bitter than the Big Man's gunk, which was horrible-tasting enough, and which even he never expected them to swallow (sometimes Shabine did, mind you, though it never had good consequences). It was so tart a flavour that it set Leah's face into a rictus, and she gagged. Shabine endured the coffee a little better, but even she made a face like a rat, pushing out her lips and wrinkling her nostrils. The Big Man had found this very amusing. After that, he had pressed sips of coffee upon the girls on several occasions, and Leah came to associate the ghastly combination of sweetness and toxicity with those sessions.

'I'd rather have an ice cream,' she had told Rodion.

Pap mocked her, and they had one of their instant fallings-out. The black swan thrashed the waters languidly with its wings; not wanting to fly, apparently, but not wanting simply to sit still either. Rodion always looked pained when Leah bickered with one of her friends. 'Perhaps a compromise?'

he suggested. 'They do a very lovely coffee ice cream, I believe.'

'I would prefer strawberry, Rodio, *if* you don't mind,' said Leah, scowling and crossing her arms. She was cross about Pap and the coffee, though Pap of course didn't understand why she was. Pap wasn't the one who had been kidnapped, after all. But by the time Rodion came back to them the two girls had made up.

Then it was Ezra's seventh birthday, and he had a party, and Mama insisted that Leah join in. She pointed out that she was way older than any of Ez's stupid friends, but Mama got cross with her and wouldn't hear a word of excuse *about it*. Snappity snap snap. So there she was, sat scowling amongst all these *little little* boys. She watched a portion of some book or other on the lap of her smartdress, one of her own, and tried to pay them no mind, but her carer kept hissing that she was being rude. Like she cared! Not even Ez cared. A vampire pursued a woman over the folds of her dress hem – but a *good* vampire, who didn't want to eat food, but instead made up blood-substitute from water and iron and stuff. Then the little boys all got in a ring and she had to join them. Even though she was way older, some of these boys were almost the same height as her! It was pretty humiliating. Back in the village she'd been one of the tallest – her mother had taken a pride in it, and kept feeding her milk as long as she could snatch scraps of food to keep the supply going. She had had the memory of milk, long before she had ever tasted a Central Park ice cream. She'd been *much* taller than Shabine, say. The Big Man had done *all* the uncomfortable things to Shabine, because – well, why wouldn't he? But he'd been more restrained with Leah, telling her that, being so tall, there was a future financial margin in keeping her unmolested. And it had been her height that had singled her out (nobody had *told* her this; she'd worked it out for herself) and it had been her height that had meant that her mama and dad had driven up to the village in a car the size of a house. And the ride in the flitter, and the plane. But then she'd got to NY and discovered that she was the shortest girl in her age-year!

It was humiliating.

The memory of milk. The taste of stars.

Ez was like an alien monster, anyway; like the creature in *Hyperspace Horror*. He looked like a Homo sapiens, but he had no interest in normal human things. He didn't like books, for instance. He only liked sports, and even then his attention only held for the start of the show. Then he'd get too excited and run off to imitate the players – to hurtle his ball against the walls, for instance; or to smack the cleaning bots with his Harding Stick.

Mama wasn't angry with her *all* the time, of course. Sometimes she'd be really affectionate, and fold Leah in a great hug and cry tears into her hair. But *most* of the time she was snappish. 'You Mama has a problem,' was Pap's opinion.

'I know!'

'I know you know!'

'I know you know you know!'

'Wrongo!' Pap. 'You should say *I know you know I know!*'

'I said exactly what I intended to,' said Leah, regally.

'You know Kelley's parents dee-eye-vee-ohed? And, and, Kelley's dad had a catastrophic personality breakdown afterwards! Maybe that's what's happening to your Mama!'

'Maybe,' said Leah, though cautiously; because it seemed to her that Mama kept to a pretty even keel, most of the time. But what did she know?

And then it was announced that there was going to be a new

Angels and Pain book, and with the same actors! There'd been talk of number seven being the last one, but now there was going to be an eighth! Everybody Leah knew was more excited than it was humanly possible to *bear*.

THREE

OF QUEENS' GARDENS

1

The three years after she separated from her husband were the happiest of Marie's life. This wasn't cause and effect. This was not exactly cause and effect. It wasn't that she had been miserable with her husband and *therefore* happy to separate from him. Rather, it *just so happened* that becoming single again coincided with new substance entering her existence. She had no wish to be unfair, or to blame George for everything. These things might have happened whilst she was still married to him. It was just that they hadn't. Or, to be particular, the one thing that *had* happened – she got her daughter back – had turned out to be the catalyst for ending the marriage. And as she said to her friends, she had not realized how much she loved her daughter until Leah had been taken away. But everything else had come afterwards by serendipity. Her glancing association with the Queens Rewilding Project had blossomed (good word!) into something truly fulfilling. Her friendship with Arto had grown into something special, the authentic emotional and sexual connection she had always craved and never known. She had come to an understanding of her trauma, and that in turn had unlocked its *creative* potential. You didn't realize that trauma could be creative? Plus, she had a new circle of friends. That awkward transition from the friends one has as a couple (those awful people they'd met on Ararat, for instance) to your *own* friends was miraculously shorted. She took up the standing invitation to join the Project Steering Committee – the cabal, they called themselves. And there she was, chatting by Lance with Imlah, or Lehmann, or 'the Minotaur', or meeting in person with Moniza Stainer, who represented the Five States administration, or handsome Arto – who claimed to be a *spy*, the big kidder – or with Fainlight. Fainlight was the sole member of the cabal who had to work for a living. Nobody called her a jobsucker to her face, of course; that would have been vulgar. But it's what she was. Her business was to liaise between the cabal itself and the lower strata of labour collectives and frontages, to ward off the 'news' horrors that would otherwise contaminate the work of the Project. All the messy how-to things. Obviously, Marie didn't socialize with her. But the rest of the cabal provided a very useful new set. People to drink with, to chat, to play.

With some people you just click, you know?

Marie moved into an eastside lagoonfront apartment; smaller than the house, of course, but with a redemptive view past the southern promontory of Roosevelt to the new possibilities across the water. Limes and the towering vacuum-bamboo fringing the old Brooklyn dockworks. From time to time a dinodozer lumbered on its fat mechanical legs pursuant of some task or other. By the time they were finished the whole of Brooklyn would be forested, and that forest – haunted by sunbeams, rich in shadow and gossamer and butterflies – would be part of the larger project of the Queens Garden.

She didn't *entirely* drop the Gunesekera Organization set – that was still an important charity. The people who organized it were lovely people. Gunesekera worked to bring education to the disadvantaged, which meant (practically speaking) to the deserving longhairs. Actually, donations had somewhat dried up lately. There'd been the riots down in Florida, and public sympathy had migrated elsewhere. Marie didn't know the details, because (unlike her ex-husband) she was not prepared to debase herself with news. Obviously, she wondered at the stupidity of longhairs, biting the hand that was trying to help them. They could hardly think it helped charitable enterprises like the Gunesekera when they went wild and smashed everything up.

But the truth, for Marie, was that she simply had less time for the Gunesekera people than she had once had. The garden had taken over. Because, although providing educational opportunities to the disadvantaged was important work, it wasn't directly creative, the way the Rewilding project was directly creative.

Queens was *art*.

She knew Arto didn't agree with this. *He* thought the project was pure politics – a twenty-second-century Clearances – to move a population of potentially dangerous low-earning types further *away* from the city itself. Not that there were exactly *herds* of the actual poorstruck over there. Mostly the area had been home to those hardscrabbling lower-middle-class types who serviced the threescore menial jobs that couldn't be automated. A resentful, sly crowd, envious of the ease of the truly wealthy. Plus, of course, the various longhairs such people retained in various service capacities – and everybody had some of those. 'It'll be a buffer zone, quite apart,' Arto said, briskly. *Quite apart!* He meant quite apart from its *aesthetic* value as nature – he knew that was where Marie's soul was. She flew over the water and landed at Station 3 to meet him for cocktails. Two workwomen, long black queues dangling and QRWP on their jacket-backs, were loading a planter with StoneRoot shrubs. I suppose you could say that Marie and Arto were supervising them, although they hardly needed supervising.

A warm day in late spring, and the sky was a clean grey-blue. Marie was wearing a Sheena Pugh overshirt, and smartcloth trousers. Her handbag threw up a skein to shade them, and they sat on Project chairs sipping their drinks. Arto was – well, the thing about Arto was more than just good looks. What do good looks count for, these days, anyway? George had been good-looking. Had been, that is, before he'd let himself go to seed, holed up in his breakwater apartment growing his locks like a longhair. It wasn't Arto's looks, precisely: although there was clearly nothing *wrong* with his tidy nose, his pistachio-green eyes, his firm flesh. His body was plump without being flabby, his clothes were always perfectly chosen. But it was more than that. It was that Arto had a self-assurance, a confidence that was not arrogance. He had the air of a man with a secret. Something about the way his eyes smiled.

Above all, Marie and Arto *shared* something. Others on the Rewilding Project – the cabal, that is – used it as a platform for social eminence. But Arto and Marie were both drawn to it because they wanted to remake the world. In a phrase, that was the core of Marie's rebirth: her new understanding that life could not be passively endured, but must be actively engaged. The year when Leah had been taken away from her had been a continual agony of helpless waiting. When her daughter was returned Marie knew that she could never be passive again. She must *do*, must create, must produce. Gardening was the finest and purest articulation of this creative urge, a literal remaking of worldly chaos into beauty. And the Queens project was the biggest gardening scheme in the world!

Arto meant something different by 'remaking the world', of

course. Something grander, he would say. 'It's been half a century and we still haven't come to terms with the hair,' he said.

They sat, in company chairs, sipping their drinks, and breathing the warm air. All around them the old stone was being broken up, and earth that had been stifled for centuries was being rotovated to the air again. That smell of loam. Still so much to do! Station 3 was mid-island, located at the − of course wholly *un*forested − Woodland. To the south the derelict airport was mostly under water, only the upper sections of its towers above the waterline, constituting a series of art-installation islands, cuboid, multicoloured, and with, of course, longhairs lolling on the roofs. There was some discussion in the project coordination meeting as to whether all the submerged buildings ought to be demolished. Some said they should. Others liked that all manner of aquatic life had found a new home in amongst the underwater portion of the structure. Marie did not have strong feelings, one way or another.

'What's that?'

'I said we still haven't come to terms with it − Neocles' hair.'

A brightly coloured bird, a parrot, a macaw, a rainbow gull, whatever it was, hurtled from east to west and disappeared into the foliage hundreds of metres inland. Marie surveyed the world. The land was a confusion of half-demolished old buildings and juvenile vegetation.

'Oh, *you're* a bit obsessed with the hair,' she joked, her attention only half on what he was saying.

'I'm serious about it, if that's what you mean. It's a Frankenstein whatname, isn't it? Though? Monster, is that the word I mean? Am I the only one who sees that? What are we to do? Either we address it, or we're going to end up squeezed out, living at the poles, six-month-long nights and everything dreich and cold.'

'I think you *like* spinning yourself melodramatic storylines,' she said. Of course, she didn't believe there was any *way* the longhairs could force the world's powerful and wealthy elites away from wherever they chose to live. Chase them to the poles? The very idea! 'Apocalypse and impending disaster,' she drawled. 'I believe it adds spice to your life.'

He made a chopping gesture, as if to silence her; but he was grinning. 'Oh *you'd* wither under the artificial lights!' he said. 'You're the sort of fine bloom that needs actual sunlight.'

'Artificial lights?'

'Like they have in the polar – oh, but you're mocking me! Look, though! We both agree the world needs to be remade. *You* think it needs to be re-Edened. To be remade for purely aesthetic reasons. I'm more practical, that's all it is.' He shuffled his chair closer. 'Ring the city with wilderness – and some farmland too, of course, since we need food. Fence the wilderness about; police the whole zone. Then *let* the longhairs swarm over the Midwest for all I care! We'll have *our* sanctuary.'

'Fences don't make the problem go away,' she replied, although mostly she was thinking how *ugly* the big rooted-fences were: slabs of orange a hundred metres high, spiderbots crawling up and down by the hundred thousand like maggots on a corpse.

'Yes there are more radical solutions,' said Arto, matter-of-factly. Marie breathed in, and breathed out. Oh, when he pretended to that kind of ruthlessness, this genocidal unflinching purposefulness, she felt a flutter of erotic excitement underneath her breastbone. People were having this particular conversation a hundred different ways all over the developed world. But for the sake of form she said: 'We can't simply exterminate them all, now can we?' She threw in a little laugh. 'What about the bodies? Think of the smell!'

'After what happened to your daughter,' he said, distantly, 'I wouldn't have thought you had any sympathy for *them*.'

From anybody else this would have been a too provoking thing. But, somehow, from Arto, it didn't upset her. 'You worry too *much* about the longhairs,' she told him.

'The danger isn't the longhairs,' said Peter. 'I know people get anxious about them, of course. The great mass, the great unwashed. But they're not the true danger.'

'Oh no?'

'No. It's the middle-earners. It's those who struggle through their lives earning just enough to buy food, the ones envious of the well-off, desperate not to fall into the sump of the truly poor. They're the ones we should watch.'

'You don't really understand the fundamentals,' Marie told him.

'Oho!'

'The danger *is* the poor. You see, we have a way of controlling the lumpenbourgeoisie. We have something they want. In point of fact, we *are* what they want, what they want to become. They won't destroy us, because they aspire to be us, and to destroy us would be to exterminate their own dreams. The poor are another matter. There's nothing we can offer them as inducement, and nothing we can withhold as punishment.'

Arto leaned closer to her. 'I'm going to come out and say this,' he said.

Marie waited.

'Would you like to have sexual intercourse?'

'Yes,' she said, laughing. And as he moved closer, surprised delight on his face, she added: 'But not with *you*.'

Just a moment his face fell into the most hilarious mask of dismay. But then he was laughing, and she was laughing, and the two finished their drinks and strolled, arm-in-arm, around the area.

2

Over a year, the project cleared a swathe of built-up land from the Nassau fence right down to the Jamaica Bay dyke. The trick was *variety*. Some of the buildings were straightforwardly pummelled by dinodozers, or cracked and dustified by detonations. Others were deliberately overgrown with NeoIvy, or flowering nettle. Some of the roadways were planted with Rock Roots, and the job of breaking up the stone was left to the plants.

This was at the heart of her life now. Purpose, creativity, joy, wonder. The steering committee debated whether to call the finished area 'Queens', or to break with the stagnancy of the past altogether and go with 'Paumanok'. Occasionally other names were proposed. It was an on-rolling, never-ending discussion. They'd break it off, and then resume at odd moments, when more pressing project business didn't intervene. Otherwise her routine was sweetly regular: hot lamb petals and pea-sized potatoes in the winter; cold lamb jelid and chilled pea-sized potatoes in the summer. A Liquid Leisure for breakfast. Early afternoon check-in with the cabal, by Lance or in person. Siesta and the preparations for the evening's entertainments.

She wasn't like George. He had been almost completely untouched by the absence of Leah. For the whole of that time when Marie had been most cast-down and desolate, he had trundled along in his passive, cheery little groove as if nothing had happened. *She* had been the one to feel Leah's loss, not him. The irony was that, after Leah's return, it had been

215

George who had gone off the rails! Lurking in his apartment with his hair all long. She had been renewed. Misery was so habitual to him that he couldn't cope with happiness.

Not every night was restful, of course. Let's be realistic. Most of the time she slept just *fine*, thank you very much, but every now and then she'd have a night when sleep just refused to come. She didn't mind the crying so much. The crying had a psychologically emetic function. Or so she supposed. It couldn't be a pointless exercise; evolution must have designed it with a purpose. Catharsis, or emotional autoimmunity, or *something*. She was prepared to believe that the crying was good for her. But sometimes the crying would leave her physically exhausted – weeping for hours is hard *work*, after all – and still she couldn't sleep. She spoke to her medic, of course, and she in turn suggested a number of fine tunings of her load. She'd been carrying extra GēnUp 'Psyche' ever since the initial trauma, the kidnapping. To help her cope. Just to tide her over. She'd thinned the load when Leah was returned to her, of course; but oddly enough this opened the door to long sessions of despair, to weeping and bitter feelings, to stabbing her forearm with a divot-knife and leaving a dozen or more little puckered scars. When her medic – her *then* medic – had suggested going back on the prior Psyche dose, she had grown furious with him, really, *really* angry. It had been a puzzling thing, actually, just how intense her animadversion had been. She's screamed at him, abuse, obscenity . . . well, not screamed exactly. Screaming was hardly *her*, was it, now? But the rage had possessed her. Tried to poke him with a fruit knife, though he'd interposed furniture between himself and her. Oh, but she'd given that squirming, middle-class job-sucker a piece of her mind. Listen: she had got her daughter *back*! She – had got her daughter – back. And he had the nerve to sit there, and tell her she needed GēnUp's shitty anti-melancholics? He was telling her that getting her daughter back had made Marie *sad*? Oh, the coffee had been projected at the wall, cup and all. No mistake there. And of course he wriggled and danced about the room as if electricity was passing through the frame of it, and tried to stutter out apologies or whatever. She was superb. She felt superb, felt the vril of it, surging through her. 'You have no conception,' she yelled at him, 'of the bliss I have felt at being *reunited with my beautiful daughter!*'

That was the end of her association with GēnUp, and no regrets. Ghastly corporation. Most of its customers worked for a living. She felt stupid that she'd ever retained them at all.

She was happier? Of course she was happier.

She retained a different company – CellMech – with a much better-mannered personal agent, and tried a different regimen, which helped a little. Not anti-melancholics (because, as Marie explained with brittle emphasis, she had *nothing to feel melancholy about*), but an older model of mood stabilizer. She had a greater proportion of good nights. Her joy at being able to spend time with Leah– literally that, at just being able to spend time with her – was so intense that often it manifested as a kind of jagged snappishness. But Leah never cried, or complained, or rebuked her mother for ill temper, so presumably she understood the intensity and complexity of the emotions involved.

And then, as the year turned around, she finally broke it off with George. Dear, foolish, hopeless George – sweet-natured, but hopeless. Incapable of deep feeling, that was the truth. A shallow individual. And divorce was like a new injection of youth. She really felt now, what was it the characters in that book said, when the earth stood all before them – or whatever the line was. Her life was getting better in every way. It was the very perversity of life that this development brought with it whole days – sometimes whole *stretches* of several days together – when she couldn't get out of her bed. She felt so drained of life-force. Whatever this experience was, it wasn't unhappiness. She was honest with herself, over a solitary bottle of grape vodka. There was no point in anything except honesty, after all. If divorcing George made her miserable, then the logical thing would be to bring George back into her life. But when she contemplated such a move, her spirit sagged within her. And when she looked at her prospects without him, she felt only a sort of spacious gladness. It wasn't that the divorce had made her unhappy.

It was her new medic who provided her with the answer to this horrible, counterintuitive tangle. Wiczek was her name, a compact, pleasingly fleshy woman with the scent of ginger about her. She explained something to Marie that had simply not occurred to her before. Coming to Marie's new apartment, listening to the narrative of the previous three years, she nodded very slowly at Marie's insistence on her happiness and her repudiation of the need for anti-melancholics; and eventually she spoke:

'People don't understand it, and – if you'll permit me – you haven't understood it yourself yet. But happiness is a trauma. Especially a great and sudden happiness. It is as disorienting to the psyche as great sorrow.'

With a gusty feeling of sudden comprehension, the dark side of Marie's moon became suddenly bright. Finally, she understood. 'Of course!'

'Yes,' said Wiczek, and nodded again, thoughtfully. Oh, the force of her explanation zigged and then zagged through Marie's consciousness. 'Of *course!*' she said. 'That's why being reunited with my daughter has brought me so many – tears.'

'If we say *tears of happiness*, then we don't get it quite right,' Wiczek said. 'For the tears do not feel happy as we cry them.

But it is happiness that is behind then, nonetheless. The happiness that works like an earthquake in our lives, toppling our old architecture.'

This described Marie's situation so perfectly her mouth fell open. It was as if this person had opened the blast doors and peered into the heart of Marie's life. 'Exactly,' she said, in a soft voice. 'Exactly.'

Wiczek prescribed a new regimen. 'If you look up the serial codes, which you can do in a breath on your Fwn – your Helios, rather' (this correction offered with a self-deprecating smile that was perfectly winning) '—if you look it up, you'll find it's described in the same terms of the most common anti-melancholics. But don't let the superficial similarities fool you! This prescription is individually tailored to address the excesses of *happiness* in your recent life.'

'I trust you completely,' said Marie.

And the regimen did help! Of course it did. The number of sleepless nights was reduced, and she was better able to *enjoy* her newfound joy. In one of the follow-up sessions, Wiczek mentioned assertivism as an avenue worth exploring. Marie's reaction surprised even her with its vehemence: 'My ex-husband was an assertivist – a lot of toxic nonsense! The least assertive person I have ever met, and assertivism just bedded in his inertia.'

'I quite agree,' said Wiczek, smoothly. 'I was not about to suggest actual assertivism, but rather to quote some of the wisest words ever uttered on the subject of living with the aftermath of trauma. You know Voltaire?'

'The electricity inventor?'

'Writer, philosopher. Voltaire said: We must cultivate our gardens. Do not fret and internalize, but rather busy yourself with pleasurable, creative activity.'

Once again, her words connected immediately, profoundly,

with Marie's soul. How could Wiczek possibly have known about her love for gardens? Conceivably she meant the phrase metaphorically – or this old Voltaire fellow did. But gardens were amongst the places where Marie felt happiest. And she'd been involved in the Queens Rewilding Project from early on. Losing the seaside portions of Brooklyn and Queens to the rising waters, and the possibility of further incursion by the sea, had driven the better off out of the area anyway. There'd been some talk of extending the Hough Wall all round the coast, build up the dykes properly, but that was never going to be cost-effective. So the area was already in the process of dereliction, and there wasn't as much difficulty in moving the last real people out – those workers who still clung to their respectability, and ate food however expensive it was. Naturally there was some trouble, and the QRWP Coordinating Committee – the cabal – had to hire a couple of quadpods and a platoon of riot police to clear them away. Quite apart from anything else, there were lots and lots of longhairs, although in the end they all got moved on easily enough.

None of the real-estate management stuff really interested Marie. She joined the cabal, and put her money forward, with a view to the actual rewilding itself; the planning and gardening itself. And it so happened, thank Providence, or thank Happiness, that the clearances were pretty much completed, and spiderfencing erected to keep out itinerants, before she began her treatment under Wiczek. That was one reason why her words struck so powerfully. This Voltaire had it right; the garden would heal the land over on Queens and Brooklyn, and heal her traumatized spirit too!

Whatever else was true, she had the garden. Something to work for. Something to work in.

'Thank you,' she said. Who was she thanking?

'Thank you.'

'Thank you!'

The cabal met several times and scanned through hundreds of VR possibilities for how the completed project was going to look. It was going to be a thing of real beauty. Marie liked the meetings; she liked the feeling of godlike omnipotence. But she liked being actually in the zone better – to see it happening around her, to watch the groundworkers toiling away. See it taking shape. *Shape*, she thought to herself, sitting beneath one of the project sunshades and drinking a Gap cocktail, was the secret of the universe.

To be *doing* something! She was happier than she'd ever been.

She brought Ezra fairly often into the project zone. To him it was a giant playground, and no sooner would the flitter door open than he'd run off, whooping and hallooing like a gibbon. She brought Leah sometimes too, but the girl was going through a difficult phase. Marie sometimes thought, honest to Providence, that Leah preferred books to real life. She'd find some stump to sit on and unroll yet another brightly coloured book. Marie just couldn't get her interested in the great design. 'It's the grand project of our age, sweetie,' she would explain, and Leah would look up with her 'whatever' expression. Often it was simpler not to bring her into the zone. It would only result in Marie losing her temper with the child.

And then there was Arto, who shared her belief in the importance of the rewilding, and whose sly, knowing glances acted as catalyst to her new life.

It was about her happiness. She had never been so happy! But it was more than that, it was about the careful management of her happiness, the keeping of her happiness within manageable bounds. So much of her joy was tied up with the garden. Making the new world new again. Was it fair to ask her – she who had been through such a lot, who had suffered so much trauma – to ask her to *contaminate* her good feeling? And Leah's sulky dumb-insolence *was* a mode of con- tamination. Ezra couldn't care less about the aesthetic possibilities, of course; but at least he took a primordial joy in the environment. Leah always had this fish-out-of-water look in the wilderness, as if she couldn't wait to get back to the city. She had no larger vision. Took after her father, of course. That had been the fundamental incompatibility between the two of them, Marie now saw: his inwardness, as opposed to her receptiveness to the world outside. She did not pretend never to have loved him. Obviously she *had* loved him, once: and not just for his good looks and louchely attentive sensuality. But he was a radically *passive* individual, content to let things happen to him. Where she, of course, was radically *active*. She was a doer, a go-getter, a maker. Once upon a time, perhaps, she had found his inertial being-in-the-world oddly charming. She had believed it complemented her own more assertive nature. She could hardly have coexisted with another such as herself. But it was too much, in the long run. It was too provoking. She couldn't be with him any more. It turned out he really wasn't very interested in *her*.

Now, the thing about Arto was that he was *actually* inter- ested in her life. 'So you've got *two* children?' he asked.

'That's right.'

'Tell me about them?'

'Ezra – my boy – is shaping up to be a sportsman. He loves any kind of running, or kicking, or climbing, or jumping. Brom – that's his carer – took him underwater last week, and he loved it. I've never seen him so excited! And he gets excited, you know? These waterlungs . . . we never had them when I was a child.'

'Oho,' said Arto. 'They're all the rage, though, aren't they?'

'Aren't they though? I think they look daft – stomping

around the bottom of the pool in weighted shoes with those things flapping after you like loose sheets! But Ez loves them. He says he wants to do the lagoon race – I mean, the footrace across the Hudson basin, not the Murdoch event. Water-lungers running in slow motion the whole way! I've told him next year, maybe.'

'How old is he, though?'

'He's nearly eight.'

'And your daughter?'

'My lovely Leah,' said Marie. But the tingling in her heart was a chill. It was a sort of contraction. It was a puzzle, but that must be because *she* was a puzzle. 'She's not so physically active, I'm afraid. But she loves her books!'

'I heard the terrible story—'

'Oh,' said Marie, briskly (for there was no point in being evasive). 'Yes, it was a horrible thing. We were on holiday at the Ararat resort, and she was snatched. They just grabbed her. And the police were worse than useless.'

'Corrupt?' Arto prompted.

'Take *that* for granted. I had to hire a private agent to locate her. She was gone for ages! The poor thing, I shudder to think . . . but she's back now.' The way happiness, in its proper home in the heart, burns like anger. That's the truer joy.

'Your husband?'

'We're separated now. I'll tell you the truth, Arto.' She leant in a little closer, feeling the pleasing anticipatory tingle. 'I don't think he has ever quite recovered from losing Leah for those months.'

'Months!'

'Oh yes, it took *months* to recover her. It caved him in, I'm afraid. He's tender-hearted but weak, you see.'

'I can see you're *not* weak, though,' smiled Arto.

She took this in her stride. 'Caved him in,' she said. 'He hasn't been the same. He lives pretty much as a hermit, now. Do you know he's taken the Bug?'

'The Bug?'

'The hair thing, I mean'

'Gracious. Really?'

'It's some obscure form of self-punishment, I think. Grown his do out like a longhair. It's a bit tragic, really.'

'He still sees the children?'

Having painted George as a mild lunatic, this question rather incommoded Leah. She had to say, 'oh, yes,' of course; but she didn't want it to sound like she was abandoning her beloveds to the care of an insane man. 'He's harmless. He's good with the kids, actually.'

'Won't Leah be fourteen next year?'

How did he know that? Perhaps she'd told him on some other occasion. 'Yes.'

'She could decide to live with him full time?'

The thought of this had never crossed Marie's mind. 'Oh she wouldn't do that.'

'She's friends with a man called Rodion?'

This was when the warning bing-bing sounded, as it were, inside Marie's head. 'What?'

'Rodion VanderMolen – I believe he used to live in the other half of your parkfront building? Before you moved, I mean.'

She scowled at him. 'What are you getting at? How could you possibly know?'

He returned a perfectly shaped smile. 'Can I let you into a secret, Marie? I'm a spy.'

'You certainly *sound* like one.'

'I'm not joking.'

She eyed him. The pause was just long enough for a crinkly

smile to come into being on his face, and the moment dissolved into bonhomie. 'Nobody's tried this hard to get me into bed since I was fifteen!' she said. 'I mean – seriously! Don't you think that maybe you're working *too* hard to impress me?'

He took hold of her right hand, and kissed the knuckles with an exaggerated smooching sound.

3

That autumn there was trouble along the south stretch of the project, up and down the seafront and in Jamaica Bay. The monthly project security budget doubled. Longhairs were everywhere. The root problem: many of them had taken to living on rafts. As Arto explained, with grim satisfaction, it was perfect for them. With a simple desalination unit for their water they could live a completely open-ended, floating exist- ence. This was a relatively recent development, at least off the US coast, though Arto said that the Indian Ocean had been lousy with longhairs for decades. But it *was* a problem, a real and present one. They'd walled the Nassau boundary with spiderfence – at vast expense. They could hardly fence the entire coastline as well. The coastal dykes could perhaps be raised, but that wouldn't be that much cheaper, and probably wouldn't keep them out either. What to do? 'Exterminate all the brutes,' was Arto's grin-flashing solution. Obviously some- thing a little more practical was required. Some of the long- hairs had actual boats – Marie had to wonder how they got hold of them, not legally she supposed – but most of them had cobbled together makeshift rafts from anything that could float, loosely roped together, planked or covered with plasmetal sheeting, junkyard junks, rubbish heaps.

To look at a map of the whole of Long Island was to think: oh, but the Rewilding Project is a modest undertaking! But, here, on the ground, she was continually struck by how *huge* the job was. So much human clutter had been squeezed into such a small space! Uncovering some of the hills that urbanization had overwritten. Where giant subterranean knuckles pushed up the latex. Supine profiles, hawk nose and snub. The detritus of centuries of human habitation.

Important milestones were reached. Forest Hill was fully reforested! The entire cabal flittered in, personally, to enjoy a feast. The theme was greatness; the food (cherries the size of a beachballs; toast you could shelter under; sugar grains big as dice) appropriately gigantic.

The problem with the seaborne longhairs kept pressing. They hired a dozen wardens to patrol the southern coastline, to keep the longhairs from landing, but the work required endless vigilance. Workers, machinic or human, kept stumbling across vagrants living in the shells of as-yet-undestroyed buildings; or clinging to the tops of trees like monkeys. The sea-approach was the tricky one.

Arto addressed the cabal with a proposition for a string of oceanic platforms and automatic guns. Program them to shoot anything that moved. Place them far enough out to sea that if they did malfunction they couldn't shoot anybody on land. After some exemplary executions the ragtag longhair flotillas would get the message and stay away. But 'malfunction' was the wrong word to use in this context; it spooked the meeting. 'What do you mean, malfunction?' Arto tried his grin: 'Well, nothing's perfect.' But the cabal didn't like it.

Leah and Ezra came back from the week with their father telling strange stories. George was now a fully tressed longhair. He had taken them to a radical Christian meeting, which (so far as she could tell from Leah's sulky and unforthcoming summary) had proposed a solution to the problem of the longhairs via missionary work and Christian conversion. 'So your father hasn't become a Christian, has he?' she asked.

'Oh no,' said Leah. 'At least, I don't think so. But he was talking about some hermit guy.'

'What hermit?'

'I don't know his *name*,' said Leah, with prodigious disdain.

Ezra, bless his heart, was at least *pleased* to be back in Marie's apartment. None of that mopy selfish sulking for him – he *ran* from room to room at top speed, his new carer, Moore, scurrying anxiously after him, fearful that something would get broken.

'I don't know,' said Leah, turning her flank to her mother and writhing as if all her joints had come undone under her skin.

'Leah!' Marie snapped. 'Please act like a civilized human being, not a jelly*fish*.'

Panting, Ezra smacked to a halt against the wall, turned to his sister and mother and said: 'I say we ship all the longhairs to the moon! Plenty of sunlight up there, *and* water at the poles!'

'Not very practical,' said Leah.

'We need some sort of radical solution,' said Marie, putting her arm around her boy and squeezing him affectionately. 'I couldn't agree more.'

4

But, oh, the active engagement with the world! A midday with Arto, out on what had previously been the Brooklyn-Queens border. A roto had been through the whole district here, pushing over rubble and crushing it, and now a mulch machine was being guided through parallel sweeps of its snouty head, dragging a long waterpipe behind it. Two workers – longhairs, with their hair out behind them (women, of course) – were walking alongside, making sure the waterpipe didn't snag, and that the mulch mouthparts didn't choke on any unexpectedly large pieces of rubble. The raw mulch didn't smell very nice.

That was the autumn the poetry charts were dominated by Zuleika:

> *And write out the words,*
> *and link them in art,*
> *that people might read them*
> *and break up their heart.*

It was Marie's life! It was her life in a poem! The joy of heartbreak.

The sky was motley: pale blue and pure to the west; a paintpot roil of purples and storm-blacks and dark grey to the east. 'A rainstorm,' Marie said, as if she were any sort of expert on weather. On *weather*!

'There's a storehouse a little way over there,' said Arto, taking her hand. Taking her hand! Her heart was buzzing like a fly trapped behind a glass pane. Along they trotted together, like kids. Three hundred metres across yet-to-be-developed waste; then between low bushes, and over green grass, and past various splendid trees, and the stumps and chassis of old architecture, ivy and nettles, legumery. Sunlight spent itself prodigally amongst the leaves. The world so various, and beautiful and new. The corduroy of a fingerprint. A lacy girder, with diamond spaces punched out. This Jackson Pollock sprawl of tangled wiring. The unique pattern of swirls and line of a human face.

Eastwards the sky was increasingly occupied by the coming stormcloud. It was solid shadow, tangled with the etching lines of distant rain.

Clean odours of incoming storm.

Marie stood, the wind fumbling and mussing her shirt about her body. The cloud moved visibly; the gods fitting the lid to the box of the world. The air was cooling, and the wind increasing in strength. On the roof of the building was a five-states banner, the asterisks-and-stripes. The wind was trying persistently to shake crumbs from this flag, the rope slapping the flagpole with a rattlesnake sound.

Overhead, the fjordy coastline of the cloud shifted its aerial tectonics, and swallowed the sun. For a moment its high-above beaches glowed lit gold, and even its inland mountain-ranges, granite-purple and black, lightened and gleamed. And the cloud moved westward and the last gleam of the sun was smothered. It was much cooler now, dark as dusk at noon.

'So thrilling!' Marie called to Arto over the wind.

Look!

A fishbone of lightning, discarded by the cloud. It made Marie's breath stick in her throat. Scaldingly white, coldly white, and then vanished. It was a bone picked clean, bleached clean, washed clean by the oceanic sky, glimpsed clean, and gone.

One, two, three seconds later: the cosmic empty-belly rumble.

'Shall we go inside?' suggested Arto.

A dozen or so longhair workers were inside the project shed, gathered over by the window and playing cards. The light was on, but the intermittent flickers of lightning lit the window more brightly than did the glowball inside. Arto marched over: 'Clear off.'

All twelve stood up. Though none of them came up higher than Arto's chest, they had the advantage of numbers, and for a moment Marie felt a fleeting fear. What if they all ganged up? But they didn't. Of course they didn't: they looked at Arto's muscular, plump torso; his long legs; his cropped hair, and they filed out into the trembling chill of the newly falling rain.

In thirty seconds they had the whole place to themselves. The storm threw a million glass beads at the window. When Marie and Arto embraced, the rain on the roof sounded like applause – like *thunderous* applause – like *raptures* of applause. Marie kissed him; pressed her mouth against his. He responded to her passion. There was ozone in the air. He pulled her trousers off; and then dropped his own pants and stepped his left foot out and kicked them away with his right, like a sportsman. They fucked, naked only from the waist down, a partial nudity that made Marie feel, oddly yet excitingly, like a child again. She braced herself against a wall of packing boxes and he took her from behind. Then he sat on one of the chairs and she spread herself upon his lap. At one point he took hold of her ankles and lifted her feet up, so that she tipped backwards and her head touched the carpet. His long, fat arms opened wide, and Marie was conscious of her shocking, delicious openness – her delicious, shocking helplessness, upside down at forty-five degrees, dependent upon this large man to prevent herself collapsing. It wasn't a very comfortable position, of course; which meant that she couldn't come. But after a while they shifted again, and she laid her spine on the carpet and he got on top of her and she brought the palms of her feet together, yogalike, above the small of his back. And finally she felt everything shift and slide away into that place where nothing mattered any more and everything was blessed with heavenly pleasure. And – she was there, she was *there*, she was there.

Afterwards, she clutched him, both of them lying on the carpet and sharing their warmth. She dozed a postcoital doze – minutes, no more, but long enough to dream. It was a strange dream. She was watching the moon coming down to earth, but the closer it came the smaller it seemed, until it approached her face as a white bubble of light, small enough to tuck itself into the bed of her fingernail.

Her finger gleamed.

She woke up with a little hiccoughing twitch of her whole body. Arto was fully dressed again, and standing at the window looking out. 'I fell asleep!' she said, sitting up and looking for her trousers. 'How long was I asleep?'

'Not five minutes,' he replied, not turning around.

And here were her trousers. 'Oh,' she said. 'I had a weird little dream.'

He grunted.

'The moon!' she said. But she didn't elaborate.

The rain was still coming down as white noise on the roof and sides of the little storehouse. Marie pulled her trousers on, dialled the colours up and changed the design of show. 'What are you looking at?' But, joining him at the window she could see what he was looking at. The dozen longhairs they had shooed out of the building had taken shelter – or approximate shelter – under a twenty-metre planar tree a little distance from the hut. They were bunched together, some of them hugging one another, others standing awkwardly with their arms pressed at their sides. All twelve were looking in the direction of the storehouse. Staring, really.

'They're looking at us,' Marie noted, redundantly.

'You know what they're thinking?' said Arto, in a strange voice.

'What're they thinking?'

'They're thinking how much they'd like to eat us.'

She snickered at this, as at a joke, and draped her arm round the back of his neck and over his plump shoulder. But he wasn't joking, and the more Marie looked at the twelve women, all of them looking back at her, the more sinister they appeared. 'Not literally eat, though,' she tried.

'That depends what you mean by literally,' said Arto. 'Food is a pastime for us. But it's an obsession for them. They want what we have got, which is to say they want to *be* us, which is to say, they want to *internalize* us. They're so numerous, the poor, you know? They are so many and we so few. Soon enough that fact is going to embolden them. And then what? There isn't enough food in the world for everybody to eat. There hasn't been for a hundred years. So let's say they're successful, and sweep us away; they eat our supplies of food and it lasts them a day. Then what? Us.'

She didn't know what to say to this. 'What a horrid notion,' she said, quietly.

And he turned to her, and embraced her properly, and spoke in a warmer tone: 'I don't mean to be gloomy!' he said. 'I'm sorry. That was such a lovely thing we just did. Being put in touch with such joy prompts a kind of equal-and-opposite reaction in my head, perhaps. But the world is still a lovely place.'

She looked through the window, deliberately ignoring the

knot of surly longhair women under the tree, and instead looking across the spacious prospect; broken old buildings yielding to the green of nature. It *was* beautiful. Spawning strands of water eeled through the beautifully inconstant skies.

'Lovely!' she agreed.

There was no point in trying to avoid it. She was in love. She wrote him upon sheets of paper, like a character from Shakespeare. Love letters. My heart is with the butterflies, she wrote, for they can only be and move in the world by folding themselves in half, over and over, like a letter that is finished to be tucked into its envelope. Butterflies live in the crease; they are the living crease; and so am I.

He didn't write back. But he did send a Helios message, and they arranged to meet again. It made Marie thirteen years of age all over again.

He came to stay over at her place, and they made love in the bed and in the shower and back in the bed. Afterwards she watched him sleep. He was a restless, fidgety sleeper. How could anyone, she wondered, regard sleep as *repose*? Watching him reminded her of the *urgency* of sleep; of how *effortful* and *strenuous* it can be. It's a puzzle how anybody could confuse, even for mere poetic effect, sleep and death. Not siblings, those. Not related at all.

Later they talked about her previous life, and she felt a cartilaginous protrusion, somehow, on the inside of her throat. It was hard to talk about it, and she didn't want to talk about it. But he asked, with his big ingenuous face. She didn't want to talk about it, but she did. 'Your husband,' said Arto. 'He was hardly faithful, though. The rumours – you know.'

'I know. And I knew.'

'And didn't it bother you?'

She thought about it. 'It might have bothered me,' she said, in a queer voice, 'if I had desired him more.'

Arto's eyebrow came up like a sideways question-mark. 'You didn't.'

'At first I did: when we were young. He's quite handsome. And he used to be more handsome, when he had the sheen of youth on him. But he's – a kid, really. And I fell into habits of – mothering him. I suppose I did. And that kills desire, you see. It ended up with him having these flings, and me indulgently, I don't know, noting them, giving him permission.' She didn't add, because she didn't think she needed to, or perhaps rather that she hoped she didn't: *that's not how our relationship will work*. Arto was man, not boy. Apart from his silly spy play-acting. But that, Marie told herself, that would go away.

5

The spy stuff didn't go away. One day Arto was at her apartment, and Marie took a Helio message from Rodion, the old man who'd owned the other half of their previous mansion-block. She still met up with him, from time to time, in the park.

'Who was that?'

Arto's tone was sharper than usual. She might easily have rebuked him for the rudeness of this; but instead she only said, 'An *old* friend, just arranging a time to hook up.' *Old friend* was to distinguish him from the newer friends she had made since her divorce. Although of course, it was a stretch describing Rodion as a *friend*.

'Friend?' said Arto, suspiciously. Was that jealousy? Dimples appeared in Marie's cheeks.

'It's not like *that*!' she said, cajolingly. 'He's more a friend of Ez and, and – Leah. He meets them in the Park, buys them ice creams.'

'Rodion?'

The dimples dissolved back into the flesh. 'That's right.'

A peculiar expression took control of his eyes. 'Can I come?' he asked. 'I'd like to meet him.'

She wasn't sure why she felt uneasy at this. And of course there was no reason to deny him. She said: 'Sure.'

They all went to the park. There was Rodion, with his old-fashioned tunic, and his big bald head, at once fragile-looking and brutal, and his absurd black eyebrows like two simcards stuck over his eyes. 'Rodion,' Marie said, 'may I introduce my friend, Arto?'

'Let's not be bourgeois,' said Arto, bouncily, shaking Rodion's hand with vigour. 'Marie and I are lovers.'

Rodion's eyebrows slid a long way up his big wrinkly forehead at this forwardness, but he mumbled 'Good to meet you.' Although he didn't meet Arto's eye. Then he bowed down to bring his face closer to the level of Leah and Ezra: 'Would you like ice cream?'

Ezra gave voice to his opinion: 'Ice-cream is yucky.'

'Oho! So you don't want any?'

'Strawberry,' Ezra said, looking pointedly past Rodion at the sky.

Rodion went to the booth and returned with two globes of coral-pink iced goo. Leah, at least, thanked him. The three adults sat on a bench and watched as the children, self-consciously, ate their treat.

'Has Marie mentioned me, to you, I wonder?' asked Arto, beamingly.

'I can't say she has,' Rodion replied in an embarrassed voice.

'No matter. She's a special human being, Marie.' He patted her knee. It was all very embarrassing. Indeed, it was so embarrassing that Marie almost literally couldn't believe it. It had that weirdly jointed clumsiness of dreaming. Perhaps Arto was playing some peculiar game.

'So, Rodion,' he said. 'You don't mind if I call you Rodion?'

'Not at all,' Rodion said.

'How old are you? More than a hundred, I'd wager. You have the look of a three-figure fellow.'

'Arto!' Marie cried.

He turned an ingenuously wide-eyed expression on her. 'What! It's an achievement! It's an index of vigour. Now I've always said,' he added, expatiating for the general benefit, 'that one thing we can bring to the cosmos is the vigour to live long and well.'

' "We"?' queried Rodion, mildly.

'The wealthy. Oh, the longhairs sometimes *hang on*, I know, for ages and ages, like – moss or something. But I don't call that really *living*. And in my experience jobsuckers wear themselves out, like components in a machine, with their ceaseless activity. They don't usually live long. *We* are the pinnacle of existence, though, aren't we? We're what existence is *for*. We're the overmen and the overwomen.'

'I was a jobsucker myself,' said Rodion, unassertively, 'for many decades.'

But Arto bounced straight off this implied rebuke. He was beyond shame. 'Our eminence carries with it certain responsibilities, you know! Certain duties and responsibilities. Do you travel much, Rodion?'

'Are you drunk?' Marie asked.

Arto laughed at this. 'It's an innocent question, my love. There's a lot of world to see! I bet, Rodion, that you've seen a good deal of it in your time?'

'I did travel, a long time ago,' said Rodion stiffly.

'But you don't travel nowadays? Wise of you, Rodion. Manhattan, Manhattan! Wouldn't you agree, Rodion, that Manhattan has all that a person needs right here?'

Rodion sat straight up on the bench at this, and looked more closely at Arto. Then he said a strange thing: 'You're one of *those*, are you?'

Arto didn't stop grinning, but he did stop talking. In that moment Marie was simply grateful that her lover (shudder!) had ceased embarrassing her. Only afterwards did it strike her as strange that Rodion's mildly spoken words would have such an effect on Arto's impregnable ego. But the weather was nice, and the sound of the ocean rubbing itself, catlike, upon the

Hough Wall was a pleasant distant susurration, and the air tasted clean, and for a while Marie just sat and permitted herself to enjoy the moment. She let her eye drift over the great bank of blooms opposite. Properly beautiful flowers, a well tended horticultural display. All the reds and purples and pinks. The great variety of greens. The empty skullcaps of the hyacinths. The cabbage in-folded pinks of roses. The purity of lilies. The long grass-coloured tubing through which the bind-weed blew its effortless white trumpet.

'We've finished our ice creams,' said Leah. 'Can we *go*?'

Later, back at the apartment, after a strenuous but oddly unsatisfying session of lovemaking, Marie asked him: 'What did Rodion mean when he called you *one of those*?' Arto was face down on the bed, and his reply sank inaudibly into the mattress. But Marie wasn't in a mood to let it go. 'What did he *mean*? One of *what*?'

'Spy,' said Arto, turning his head.

'This nonsense again?'

'A spy,' said Arto.

'You said Manhattan has all that a person needs, and he replied that you were a spy. That hardly makes sense, now, does it?'

'Oh he recognized me well enough. Which is to say; he recognized my type. He's had plenty of run-ins with people like me.'

'Spies?' Marie sneers.

'People telling him not to leave the city, I mean.' With a heave and a *hup*! Arto was off the bed and padding towards the shower, his bulgy buttocks wobbling. Listen! Those tender little smacking sounds, as his thighs chafed step by step: the somatic percussion of affluence.

Marie lay on her back. 'Why can't he leave the city?' she called; but the whoosh of the shower had started up and she couldn't be heard. So she sat up and thought about the idiocy of Arto's game-playing, and how infuriating it was, and how infuriating *he* was. When he came back, dribbling water from his naked body all over the floor, she was waspish: 'It doesn't impress me, you know.'

His tone was mock-innocent. 'What doesn't?'

And she saw that a fight was coming. More, she welcomed the possibility. 'Your nonsense about being a spy,' she said, belligerent. 'You do it to impress me. Well, I'm not impressed. You can drop it.'

He stood at the foot of the bed, dripping water. 'You have no idea.'

'Don't I?'

'You're an innocent. You don't have the faintest *notion*.'

'You're so condescending,' she returned. 'You know nothing *about* me! You don't know what I've gone through.'

'The world is one lit candle away from going up in flames!' He was yelling, he was really shouting. 'You have no idea now precariously we're positioned! You don't know what we do to keep you safe.'

'To keep me safe!' she cried.

'You are like a *child*. All you people, you're like *children*. You've no idea what the grown-ups do so you can sleep safe and sound at night.'

This was too much. She leapt straight up, standing on the bed. 'Don't talk to me about the dangers of the world! You're not the one who spent a year of your life in misery, in purdah, because your child was stolen from you. You tell me that I don't understand? Tell me *what*?' She felt the fury pour through her, like a poet from the ancient world visited by the Muse. She was channelling it. It was too powerful a force for the filigree structure of words to carry. 'The cruelty of the world – the cruelty – hammering right into the heart of my life—' She wanted to convey to him how deadly, how harrowing it had been, the violation of the family. She wanted to say how, when she looked at her daughter now, she saw a stranger. As if she could see the Bug living inside her. As if she could only see George in her face, and not herself in it, at all, any more. But all of this was too fiddly to express, there, then. Instead she howled. Wolf.

She jumped from the bed onto the floor. She was looking for something to throw at him, to batter him with. She wanted very acutely to hurt him, to mark him. But there was nothing to hand, and he was shouting something at her, his face weirdly, almost ecstatically, coiled and distorted. She could not even hear his words.

Then she was at him, slapping and punching, and he went down under the abruptness of her attack. A face possessed by surprise looks very like a face possessed by anger. And then, belatedly, he was countering her blows, trying to grab her wrists. She got in two or three satisfying thwacks to his big face, and wrung a twist of delight from her sluggish soul to see his astonishment, to see the skin blush with the blows. But then he had her – he was bigger than her – and he rolled. He was gasping out a series of 'ah! ah! ah!' noises. He pinned her under his bulk; and when she darted her head forward to try and . . . whatever, bite him, headbutt him, she didn't know. He lifted himself up on his hands, on her wrists, to get out of range. She was aware of his belly sagging upon her own, moving as he shifted position. With a shriek she struggled, and struggled, and they were kissing, aggressively kissing, and before she knew it his cock was inside her again. She twisted her legs out and round to grip him, and he was squirming heavily in her arms, pushing his splodgy manhood into her over and over. They rolled over onto their sides, and then she was on top, and the roll continued. Out of the corner of her eye

Marie saw a figure in the doorway – Leah – and then another figure, swooping her up with an adult arm and pulling her away, her carer. Then Arto was on top again and gruntingly thrusting, and she lost track of her surroundings, and herself, and she was pushing her own pelvis up to grind against his, and

bye-bye

bye-bye

bye-bye

Afterwards, since it wasn't comfortable lying on the floor, they got onto the bed and lay, side by side, staring at the ceiling. For a long time neither said anything. Then Arto said: 'I haven't come twice in half an hour, like that, for years!' And he laughed. Marie reached over and patted his stomach. 'It's been a while for me too,' she said.

'You're a very special person,' he said.

She felt that some significant change had occurred, that afternoon, in that room. That there was now no going back. She wasn't sure if this was a good thing or not. She thought of his face, uglified with anger. She remembered the profound satisfaction she had experienced as, unrestrained, she had punched at him. Leah's face, blankly observing, flashed into her mind, but she put it aside. 'Arto—' she began to say.

He was chuckling, still. 'You're special to me, Marie,' he said. And when he said that, she understood that he wasn't chuckling at all. He was sobbing.

'Arto, what's the matter?'

'Oh Marie!' he said. 'Oh! Oh Marie!'

This was unexpected, and it wasn't very pleasant. Really it was very far from being pleasant. 'My dear man,' she said, awkwardly, unsure what to do. Then, dutifully, she slid one arm (with some difficulty) underneath him, and laid the other over his broad chest. 'It's all right.'

'I've done such things,' he gasped. 'I've done such things!'

'What things?' she asked him, not because she wanted to know, but because she couldn't think of anything else to say, and felt she had to say something.

'I was in Florida, on a Standship,' he said. 'The sea was so thick with bodies you could have walked to the beach. You could have literally walked to the beach!'

'There there,' she said. 'Shush, shush.' This wasn't right. She didn't want to be the mamma. She didn't want a full-grown man in her arms who was nothing but a supersize baby. But what could she do? He was hysterical. She wanted him to stop.

'We killed so many of them. I did, I killed so many.' His sobs had settled, and now he spoke in a sort of breathy mono-tone. 'I expected to be shocked at killing them, and at first I was shocked, but after a while it stopped being shocking and became just boring. Became a chore, you know?'

'I know,' she said, although of course she knew nothing at all about it. But what else could she say. 'Shush, shush.' Why wouldn't he shush?

'But that's a different sort of shock, though?' He seemed to be getting his sobs under control. That was a relief. 'A what do you call, a meta-shock? It doesn't dawn on you at first, but then when you look back, you know? I got tired of the killing, but it had to go on.'

'Shush all this talk of killing,' she said, in as kindly a tone as she could. She could hear her own voice. She could hear that it wasn't a very kindly tone at all. 'Don't upset yourself. It's all nonsense, this talk. You didn't kill anybody.'

'Only longhairs,' he said.

'Shush,' she said, stroking his chest.

He coughed, and ran a fat hand over his face. 'You're right,' he said. 'It's crazy. But honestly, Marie—' His voice sounded more normal now. 'Honestly, it was like a slick.'

This made no sense. 'Slick?'

'You know. Like an oil slick. Just a mess of arms and legs flopping over one another, hair swaying in the water like seaweed. Paved with faces. The ones that live at sea wear floats, you know. In case they fall in, I suppose. So they don't go under.' He shifted his position. The crying had stopped now, and the tone of voice was more controlled. He was explaining, not confessing. 'Some of them have proper buoyancy waistcoats, or whatever; some just have plastic or sealed bags tied around them. They're in the water a lot, you see. But it means, the bodies don't sink.' *Sink* was uttered with a worrying catch to his voice, so Marie spoke up briskly, to stop him dissolving again.

'Let's have a drink, yes?'

'Oh yes.' He stretched out his arms and legs, like a cat, stretching. 'I'm sorry, sweet-bread, I'm sorry for losing it.'

'Don't be silly,' she said, firmly. She meant it.

So they had cocktails on the balcony, and watched the waterracers coming darting round the shoulder of Roosevelt and making the surface of the lagoon shiver. Arto talked a little more about his work with the government. Marie didn't especially want to hear all this, but at least he wasn't actually sobbing any more. So she listened, as politely as she could, and sipped her drink, and let herself unclench inside. She couldn't evade the knowledge that this new intimacy made a difference to their relationship.

'I haven't spoken to anybody else about it,' he said. 'Only you. I haven't spoken to another solitary human soul. Not since the army psychiatric debrief, I mean.'

With a little tingle of insight, she understood the ground of their new connection. It was trauma, and it was the way life's flow gets twisted into tourbillons and eddies by the interruptions of trauma. She and he had it in common. Tentative, she explored the ground.

'What anti-melancholics did the army give you? Not GēnUp, I hope. There are much better treatments on the market than GēnUp, believe me.'

'There's a government-only branding, Forward.'

'What?'

'You ever heard of that?'

'I never have,' she said.

'It works pretty well.'

'Forward,' said Marie.

'Sure. Forward. The trick it has: it makes it so that you don't mind, any more; but – and this is the clever wrinkle – you do *mind* that you don't mind. If you see what I mean. It doesn't produce that zombie thing. That, uh, affectless blankness some of the other treatments give you.'

'Perhaps,' Marie suggested, 'it doesn't hold up so well in the case of sudden, strong emotion?'

'Oh, well,' said Arto, looking across the water at a dinodozer churning up some old building on the far shore. 'I suppose none of them are too good at that.'

'I suppose not.'

'It doesn't bother you?'

'What?'

He swirled the last of his cocktail in the glass. 'I'm not used to talking like this, you know.'

'Does it *bother* me. You're asking if it bothers me. Do you mean,' Marie asked, 'does it bother me that you've killed people in your time?'

'Not that,' said Arto.

'No?'

'Well, no! I know you well enough Marie. I know you. You have the soul of a warrior. You have the soul of a warrior. It was war, after all. It *is* war. You know that much, though. I'm not asking: does it bother you I *killed* people.'

'So?'

'I'm asking: does it bother you I had a breakdown?' Ugh, what a word!

'Breakdown?' she snapped.

He nodded, mournfully. 'Nervous breakdown, after Florida.'

That was a cold-water shock to the soul, to Marie, and no mistake! So, so. She lost a portion of his next sentence, and when she tuned in again Arto was saying: 'They posted me to the Queens garden project to help me recover, true, true. There are levels of stress that – well, anti-melancholics only go so far, don't they? Sometimes the spirit is simply drowned by the weight of . . .'

'Now, *don't be silly*,' she told him, fiercely.

Below them, the water was changing colour as the sun descended though the sky. There was a jellyfish tremor in the bulk of it, and the light slickly blushing. She sat next to him, conscious of the fact of this intimacy between them, a new importance. Falling in love, she thought, was a magnifying of importance. People in love were more important than people who were not in love. And the trauma they shared, she told herself, was more complex and ensnaring than she had at first thought. Because her trauma was not that she had lost her daughter but that *she had got her back*. Hers was not the misery of loss but precisely the happiness of reunion. And his trauma was not the violence. And she wasn't a *monster*, she wasn't interested in knowing all the horrible details, like some sort of voyeur, like a peeping-Tom, like a news-junkie. His violence was something else: not that the violence had shocked him, but precisely that the violence had not shocked him. Their affinity was more than elective.

He was what she deserved.

'I love the way dusk comes out of the east,' Arto said. 'I love the way dusk comes out of the same place dawn comes. Do you know what I mean?'

'I know what you mean.'

6

She knew exactly what he meant. This, rather than being with somebody when everything had to be spelled *out*, this was the genuine currency of love. Wasn't it? Arto's home was somewhere else in the Five States, Connecticut or somewhere, but he had a base in the city, in the Lower East Side, so as to be at hand for the rewilding project. A bare boxy space, uncluttered with the usual appurtenances of day-to-day. On occasion Marie would stay the night, and some sort of instinct would wake her before dawn. She might lie there, in his bed, listening to her lover breathing scrappily through his nose, as the white room filled up with light. She contemplated the way love comes into a soul, as light comes into a room. She felt a motionless horror, a sense of great misery pressing down upon her. The prospect of this new emotional greatness inside her was alarming rather than liberating. Shouldn't it have been freeing? It wasn't. Not that there was any mystery about what was going on. She went back to her therapist, Wiczek, who had done such a good job before, tweaking her prescription. 'You said how great and sudden happiness is as disorienting to the psyche as great sorrow.'

Wiczek nodded, smiling a knowing smile.

'I think it has happened again. The first happiness was getting my daughter back, of course, and, yes, the drugs I was on did stabilize my happiness. But now I'm experiencing a new happiness.'

'Really?'

'I have fallen in love. I'm in love. I think it has destabilized my medication, because I feel full of a kind of . . . dread.'

Wiczek nodded again, more slowly. 'Is that not part of being in love?'

But Marie wasn't going to put up with any nonsense. 'I'm not talking about butterflies-in-stomach. I'm talking about a kind of misery – depression, I mean. I want you to rewrite my prescription to take account of this new thing in my life.'

Wiczek wouldn't meet her eye. This really was the last thing she had expected. 'I am really not sure, Ms Lewinski, that it is best to smother your feelings with medication.'

Marie felt like she had been slapped. The words came to her almost exactly as if she had been struck in the face! 'Smother my feelings!' she gasped.

'You are in a new relationship,' the woman said. 'You need to attend to what your feelings are telling you. How can you judge whether this is indeed love, if you squeeze out your natural reactions?'

Marie got to her feet. She stood a little unsteadily, wobbly-wibbly, wibbly-wobbly. It was like a blow to the solar plexus. 'I trusted you,' she said. And then: 'If I understand you correctly, you are saying that I do not love this man. Without knowing anything about him, without even knowing his name, you have the nerve to tell me that this is not the man for me!'

Wiczek was also on her feet, with a gratifyingly horrified expression on her thin little face.

'How dare you! You don't know anything about it!'

'Not at all, Ms Lewinski, I assure you, I was not . . .'

Her grovelling came too late, obviously; but it at least gave a kind of strength to Marie's own anger. 'Be quiet! Shut up! I trusted you, I came to you for help! If a person came to you with a broken leg, begging you for a painkiller, would you smugly instruct them to pay attention to the message of their nerves?'

There were tears in the stupid woman's eyes now. 'Please! Please!'

'We're through,' said Marie. 'I am happier than I have *ever* been, do you hear me? How *dare* you tell me I am not! You don't know anything about me, you skinny little jobsucker. What can you possibly understand about a person like me?' Her anger elevated her. 'I'm only surprised I ever thought you had any expertise,' she said.

The woman just stood there looking poor and drawn, her face ruddy, wet with tears. Marie left her like that, and went home. There was so much resentment in the world. There were so many people who could not bear the happiness of others. Pettiness and hate.

At home, Ezra and Leah were watching a book. Marie kissed them both on the tops of their heads, feeling the ferocity of pure love thrumming inside her. *Her* kids! Out on the balcony she drank a beaker of grass wine down in one great gulp, and poured herself another. A sunkite was sliding overhead like a huge autumnal leaf. Its shadow seemed wholly disconnected from it; a double diamond of grey sliding over Roosevelt and over the lagoon. The edge of its shade was doing that disconcerting quantum-leap thing: now adhering closely to the street, now jumping suddenly on the roof of the adjacent building.

Leah came out. 'Ma,' she said. 'Carol wants to know if she should cook now?'

It took a moment to remember who Carol was. 'And she can't ask me herself?'

Leah shrugged, slouching half in at the door and half on the balcony. There was something particularly provoking about her posture. Ill-disciplined, loose-limbed. As if she weren't taking things seriously enough. 'Ma,' she said again. 'The charity you work for?'

'*What*, Leah?' she said, tipping the beaker to get the last drops of drink into her mouth. She sounded a little more peevish and annoyed than she intended. 'What is it you want?'

But her tone had cowed the girl. Look at the restlessness of her long limbs! She slouched most of the way back into the apartment so that only her left leg remained on the balcony. The fact that Leah could so easily be browbeaten by her mother's anger, paradoxically, only made Marie angrier. She made an effort to control herself.

'You mean the Queens garden? You mean the rewilding project?'

Leah's expression was incomprehensible to Marie.

'That's not a charity, my love,' Marie said. 'Come here.'

Leah obeyed, in her slackly fidgety way. She sat herself down next to her mother, and permitted herself to be embraced. 'What do you want to know about it?' Marie asked.

'Not the garden,' said Leah, in a low voice.

'Not the garden?'

'The Gunes-what-you-say.'

'Oh!' Marie said. 'You mean the Gunesekera Organization?'

'Yes.'

'What about it?'

It took a moment for Leah to come out with it. 'Could I do something for it?'

This was a very strange development. 'Do something for it? What do you mean, do something? What do you think *you* could do for it?'

Leah shrugged again.

'You do understand what it is, don't you? It provides educational opportunities for the children of the very poor,' Marie explained. 'The absolutely poor, you know.'

'You're still involved in it, right?'

'Well, yes.' Marie. 'Although most of my time is taken up with the garden, now, to be honest. But I'm still on the committee. Oh, my love, do you *really* think there's much a twelve-year old could do for the Gunesekera people?'

'Thirteen,' said Leah, staring at her own feet. 'Ma – are you going to marry Mr Arto?'

'Yes,' said Marie, surprising herself with how easily the word came out. 'You see, he and I have fallen in love. We are going to get married, my dear. That's what people do when they're in love.' Trying without complete success to put a wry and funny inflection on her words. She waited for Leah to follow up with a question about her father, but instead she said: 'I'll go tell Carol to cook, then,' and wriggled free. Away she sloped, drawing her long limbs fluidly after her.

Marie watched the lagoon, and the sky, and the buildings. If she were any happier, she'd die. If she were any happier she'd expire. If she were any happier, if it were even possible to be happier, then she would break down in a blizzard of cold tears. Stand in the place where you live, is good advice.

7

Arto asked: 'Are you planning on seeing your friend Rodion any time soon?'

'What *is* it with you and Rodion?'

'Oh you know,' he said, smiling. 'Spy stuff.'

'That attempt to put a twinkle into your speech,' she said, coldly, 'is, I have to say, a *complete* misfire.' She took hold of his hand. 'You know, a more suspicious woman might get the impression that the only reason you spend time with me is to get close to that old man.'

'Sweetheart!' he laughed. 'How could you think it? The spy in me is interested in Rodion, but the *man* in me is interested in you.'

'And why,' she said, only partially placated, 'would a spy be interested in that dried-up old man? He must be a hundred and fifty.'

'He has historical importance.'

'History!' sniffed Marie. '*No* such thing. An abstraction – by very definition it is past and over and dead and inexistent.' Was that even a word?

'Sometimes history pops up in the present,' said Arto, 'like a zombie.'

'So Rodion's a zombie?'

'Might become one. But we'll keep an eye on him, and make sure that doesn't happen.'

One night, she had a nightmare. It took place in the Queens garden, and it was completed and it was a place of rare, Edenic beauty. She was there, and Arto, and George too – though, why him? – and Arsinée, who had been one of Leah's carers years and *years* before (why think of *her?*), and a dozen or so other people. It was as if everybody had gathered for an opening ceremony, and she was expected to make a speech. But she couldn't think what to say. So she looked around the crowd. Ezra was there; but she couldn't see Leah. She looked about at a complex tapestry of greens and green-blues, olives and emeralds, with bright red and bright blue flowering blooms, the loveliness of neoEden. Then she looked into the sky, and she saw a great fleet of flying machines, filling the sky from horizon to horizon. And as she gazed upward she saw one break away from the formation and swoop down through the air. It didn't look like a plane or a flitter; and it didn't look like a military aircraft, although that was clearly its intent. It looked, rather, like a comet. An oval chassis with a bright light at the nose, and streaming away behind it a huge wind-sock tail of brightness. It came closer, and Marie could hear the rapid click-clack noise of its approach. At the very last moment, and with abrupt terrifying horror, Marie understood that it was coming down to destroy the whole of the Queens garden. She saw it was coming down, although nobody else seemed to. Everybody else was stupidly placid, and uncon-cerned. She tried to open her mouth to warn people, but her mouth muscles did not work. And then the whole area, every-thing, everywhere, was a great tangle of fire – explosions all around, lifted by her imagination directly from books: rosebud knots of flame unfolding and swelling; and spiky bursts of smoke and fire, red and white and black and a hideous tempest roar. The plants were all burning with the intense heat of—

Awake.

She was lying in her bed, and Arto was snoring beside her.

When she thought back to that dream, it seemed to her that it happened on the night before the garden was overrun. But this was her memory telescoping things. In fact, there was more than a week between this vivid dream, and the events in the garden. Still, there was some symbolic point to the compression of time; for together they marked the point at which everything in the world toppled over.

Leah. It was a conclusion that felt inevitable once she had reached it. It felt, in fact, as if she had made the decision a long time before, but had through some clumsy oversight not realized until this moment. To look into her eyes was to see George, and not see herself at all. Ezra was different. Ezra was not a stranger to her. She wondered if this was how men felt, looking into the faces of their offspring and registering the impossibility of knowing, for certain, their paternity. She felt like the first woman in history to have that sensation. There was nothing for it, Leah would have to go and live with her father. Leah would have to go to George, with Marie's blessing – with her love. But she couldn't stay in this place with this person.

Her new life was beginning.

She had a row with Arto. He was drunk, again, and kept saying in his most braying voice that marriage was vulgar, that love was vulgar, that love was for the fucking longhairs, that it was all *empty* air and *free* light and nothing real. 'I can't believe you want to *wound* me like this!' Marie was yelling at him. 'I've opened my heart to you! I can't believe you want to lacerate me like this!'

'You haven't seen where it all ends up!' he cried. He was crying! Oh Lord, look at that! Tears squirming on his face. All the wah-wah-wah. And now there was nothing but scorn for him in her rage.

'Are you a *man*?' she boomed at him. 'Are you a little baby, crying for your Mamma or are you a man? God, you make me *despise* you. You've turned all my love for you into contempt.'

He was on the floor, sobbing, and his tears and slobber made a darker patch on the rug. 'You haven't seen where it all ends up!' he kept repeating. 'And I have! I've seen where it all ends up! Love? Love? You haven't seen where it all ends up!'

'There *is* a connection between us,' she told him. Or perhaps she was telling herself.

'If you could see where it all ends up,' he was saying – or something like this, it was hard, it was hard to understand what his words were, they were slurred, 'you wouldn't talk about love and marriage if you could see.'

The wine pours from the bottle, the fluid moving out of the cylinder and through the glass pipe neck. The wine is a twisty rope. To the glass. It is toxins that give it that red hue. The wine is the red snake that leaps down from the bottle writhing in the sunlight to curl in the glass.

Later, she took charge: moved him to the bed (which wasn't easy, because he was a big fellow), and soothed him with her mouth. He came very quickly, with a little, squeaky series of gasps. She spat her mouthful of quicksilver onto the mattress. Her head felt full of light. There was a spacious, mystic, cosmic quality to her drunkenness.

One Clear sorted her out the following morning, but Arto needed two, and even then it was a struggle getting him to take it. 'Leave me to my misery,' he groaned.

'Come along,' Marie told him, putting on her brisk voice. 'Don't be foolish: you're very obviously suffering a very bad hangover.'

'Leave me! It's all that I deserve!' His sobbing sounding like the ticking of an antique clock: slow, deliberate,

He took the two Clears eventually, and they sat in silence on the balcony drinking coffee. When the Lance chimed, Marie had an intimation that it could not be good. Fainlight appeared, shimmery, on the balcony; and her heart sank down.

Fainlight had never presumed to Lance her before. And although she was straightaway apologetic, her briskness of manner suggested insolence behind the polite form. 'I am sorry to intrude into your apartment, but I have alarming news.'

'The garden?'

'I'm afraid so. There's been some kind of mass action.'

'Mass action?'

'*Thousands* of longhairs. Thousands! The Nassau fence has been breached in half a dozen places, and many more have landed from the water.'

'Shit,' said Arto, pulling out his Helios.

'I'm letting all the members of the Steering Committee know,' Fainlight said, with just the faintest touch of smugness. 'It's probably best not to flitter into Queens, not until the situation has been addressed.'

'Shit,' growled Arto. 'Shit.'

'What about our security people! What were we paying them for?'

'I'm afraid,' said Fainlight, 'that they were just overwhelmed. I'm afraid the numbers were just too great.'

She shimmered away into nothing, into the blank morning air, and Marie's gaze moved over to Arto. 'It's happening,' he said to her. 'It's happening, and they're cutting me out.'

She was going to ask: *Who is cutting you out?* But the question would have been redundant. It was obvious enough. She looked at him and tried to identify what it was that had made him seem so *strong*, when first she knew him. It was only too obvious now that strength had nothing to do with him. All she could see now was a special assignment soldier dropped by his army after a nervous breakdown that had nothing to do with counter-terrorist action. That had been in fact only the manifestation of the fractures running right through his soul.

He looked so bereft. 'They've frozen me out.'

'Never mind, baby,' she said.

Later that day, as the first sounds of gunfire rattled through the rectangular canyons of Manhattan, Marie was hustling Ezra and Leah and Arto too up onto the roof to take a flitter to – anywhere but here, obviously. Well, it was as she was doing that that she found herself thinking: *But how have I ended up with* three *children to take care of*? Nobody was taking her calls, but that was presumably because there was nobody *to* take calls, because everybody was scattering, getting out of the city. 'You've a place in Connecticut, yes?'

'We need to get out,' Arto was saying. 'We need to go!'

What she bit back was a yell: *What do you think I'm doing?* Because, obviously, yelling at Arto was going to be no better than yelling at Ez. He'd only crumple, and that would make it harder to shift him. Her plan was to fly over the garden, and hope that the hordes of longhairs that had crashed the place weren't armed with anything that could shoot down a flitter, and then to zip northeast, and hope the flitter had the range to get to Connecticut. She needed the code for his place, and she wasn't sure she had the patience, in the panic and frenzy of the moment, to coax it out of him. Why couldn't he just tell her?

'We'll go over the island and follow the coast,' she said.

'We need to get out!'

'Sure. What's the code for your Connecticut place?'

'They're going to eat us alive!' he gibbered.

So she gave up on that. 'You'd better be able to guide me in, when we get up to your place,' she told him. But Arto was only gabbling, wide-eyed, get-out-get-out-need-to-get-out; and there was no deriving sense or use from him.

As they emerged on the roof something very substantial exploded, over to the west of the city. There was a horribly cacophonous rending noise, fringed about with the sounds of things splintering and shattering. All of them turned their heads at the same time. A tar-black smoke cloud was bulging upwards, over intervening roofs.

'Our flitter is gone,' said Leah.

And it was true. Somebody had stolen their flitter. Marie's outrage at the betrayal of trust – for it *could only have been* somebody in her employ, somebody who knew the lockcodes – almost overwhelmed her panic. How were they to get out of the city *now?*

She had children with her!

'What are we going to do?' Arto asked, in a blank voice.

Ezra, somehow impervious to the general mood, ran over to play on the glassy surface of the flitter's recharge pad, running to pick up speed and dropping at the last moment to his knees to slide, slide. He picked himself up, and took another run at the vacant pad. Arto had his Helios out again, and was trying, in vain, to connect with somebody. Anybody. Marie looked around her. The snip-snap of gunfire in the streets below was weirdly lugubrious. The sun was directly above them. Up, down. The sun was directly overhead.

FOUR

ODYSSEA

Preacher said: 'Hair's made all men preachers, now. Made all men preachers or else lazy dogs in the sun. Hair took our work, which had sustained us for millennial generations. It took our power over women and our power over the things of the Earth. These things were ours, and the Hair took them away.'

Issa was ready to yawn at all this chatter. But Rageh loved it. He was amazed. He wanted it unpacked; which is to say, he wanted it elaborated, so as to make it more real in his imagination. 'We used to have *power over women*?' he asked.

'Surely we did. We said go, and a woman go.'

'And if she did not?'

'We strike her with our hand,' said the Preacher, gravely. 'And she do it.'

Issa couldn't really believe it. She saw Rageh's eyes popping out, like boils, at this amazing fact, and there was no mistaking the fantasy of power it represented to him. But the men *they* knew were skinny as a new moon; scraping together their energy from the sun, combing out their hair strand by strand to maximize the surface available to the light. Enfeebled and stringy men. How could (say) Ari, or Moh, or Atil strike with their hands at – Mam Ann, to take one example only? Mam Ann pinned the ends of her hair to the hem of her shirt, like the splendid array of a bird. Mam Ann who snatched actual food from here and there and everywhere, and had grown superb upon it. Who had the Waali's trust and did the Waali's work? She knew where the best bugs were to be found, and she had the strength of stomach to chew great mouthfuls of plain soil, not the little crumbs here and there that Ati sucked on. If Ati ever tried striking at Mam Anna with his hand, she'd land a blow in the middle of his forehead would knock him lips-down in the dust.

But the Preacher insisted: 'In those days, when we had the food the rich eat, men grew up stronger than women.'

'Why?' Rageh asked. 'Men didn't hold the growing young inside they midriffs, did they?'

'No,' said the Preacher, with his slow, considered manner. 'No, it was women who did that.'

'Then why did the men grow stronger than the women? What *use* was they strength?'

This, Issa thought, got to the nub of the matter. This was the really crucial question. And for a moment the Preacher looked uncertain as to how he was going to reply. But then his expression settled into its gaunt placidity.

'They strength was the *glory of God*,' he said. 'Ra, the father. Saturn, the father, God the father, Christ the father, Muhammed the father. And anyway, they needed strength.'

'Needed howso?'

'To delve.'

'What's delve?' Issa asked.

'Delve is Adam's business,' the Preacher replied, not looking at her. 'Spinning cells in the womb was women's business, but *delve* was man's.' The Preacher nodded once, twice, thrice, fource; one for each of the quarters of the world. 'Was the way of it.'

As to what delving meant, Issa was no clearer.

'And power over the things of the Earth?' Rageh pressed.

'Gifts and raw materials. Called raw, as food is, for it was to be cooked: metal ore cooked to metal, plastic ore cooked to plastic. All a man did was lift the hem of his shirt, at front, to make a pouch; and the things of the Earth stood ready to fall into it. Gold and equipment electrical, and raw ores filled with gems. But the Hair come, and all is taken away. The rich live as they always have, and the poor gone poorer.'

The thing with the Preacher, Issa knew, was that he did not speak plain. It was not that he lied outright, but that he used language in a certain way. More like poetry than history. But being poetry did not mean it wasn't truth, after a manner.

Preacher used to say: man shan't live by Sun alone.

Issa considered what it took to become strong, like Mama Ana. For one thing, she had the knack of lust; which is to say, the knack of pretending it, which was the best way. So Mama Ana got scraps of food from the Waali by having his dicks into her mouth, or otherwise doing the sexual thing with him; or sometimes with his gunmen too. Her diet was meagre, by richman standards, but at least her body was habituated to food. On the rare occasions any of the village men – or any of the village Skinny Girls – get hold of food, or alcohol-drink, they would gobble it and then struggle to keep it down. Nine-times-from-ten it come up again, retching with a *reeah* and a *tch*! But Mam Anna, and the others like her; that was a different matter. They'd get tidbits almost every day, and they could supplement what they were getting with bugs from the weeds, or garden salad if it grew. So they become stronger, and

263

so the men and the Skinny Girls hit the bottom and get weaker and soon enough die out.

The village stood in the highlands, with views westward pretty much all the way to the sea – or more, or less. Most days the haze was such that the view was a descending arpeggio of rock and dust all the way to the end of things. But some days it was possible to see a thread-thin line of azure, laid precisely to effect a seal between the body of sandy ground and the cap of monomaniacally blue sky, and that was the sea. Nor was this simply a picture-book vista. The Waali in the village made money by moving people about, as most Waalis did; but Abda, the big Waali, did more than move people. He shipped water, moving a green Zeppelin-balloon, bigger than any of the houses – almost as big, Issa thought, as the whole village – down the roads to the coast. There, according to Rageh, it drank, like a cow, from the seashore, and then it ambled more slowly back up, its belly sloshing with millions of litres. Issa was probably the only person in the village, aside from Abda, who knew how to use the word million with some precision, rather than vaguely as a signifier at the end of a one-two-many sequence. Taking the blimp down was easy; and hauling it back up was hard, for it became swaggery in the air when it was filled with its cargo, desalinators fizzing, load heaving back and forth. And if it were to scrape against a sharp enough rock, or roll itself ornery-fashion upon the sharp peak-points of dry mountain firs, or if malign idle men found some way of spearing or shooting the membrane . . . well, then, all the water would spill out and be lost, and the blimp expensively damaged into the bargain. So it was a precarious trek, bringing the water back up. Since it was the source of Abda's wealth, that made him grateful to the mothers who accomplished it, just as it would make him murderously angry if the blimp were damaged or the water lost. His gratitude was the one valuable thing in the village, and his wrath the more fearful.

It was only ever mothers who escorted the blimp. Only ever mothers, and occasionally (perhaps one trip in four) Abda himself, and a couple of fat-bellied gunmen. In her dreams, Issa saw a poetic rightness in that fact: the great pregnant air belly of the blimp, as if the sky itself were gravid. But in her waking hours she saw, rather, the practical benefits. Mothers left their children behind in the village, and that made them less likely to simply abscond. Issa had never been down to the coast, but the rumours were that Preachers and Jihadists and Spartacists of all sorts roamed, offering extraordinary inducements to peasants to join their revolutionary causes. They rarely came up into the hills, and, young as she was, Issa found it hard to imagine what those inducements might *be*. But Abda worried enough about it, certainly.

And, though she *was* young, Issa understood why Abda got so worked up. She saw things from his point of view. The water was gold and jewels. People could be bought from all the wide lands to the west and east, and passed down to the factories and orchards of the south, where things were grown and made for the wealthy of the world. But they had to be moved over the desert, and in the desert the dust was grey with dryness, and there was nothing whatsoever apart from the wind-gathered piles of plastic, or the sheared-off stumps of concrete posts, sprouting wires at the top like hairs from a wart. Concrete walls bitten down by time, and buildings over which dunes of masonry dust moved slowly, filling the spaces with sand. Some of the old houses still stood, up near the rocky prominence, roads and small squares intact; but lower down, where the scrub and dust had moved over, everything was ruin, and waste. There was not so much as a single date tree, or the stubble of grass. There was some poison in the air, too;

although there was plenty of good strong sunlight, and all that was needful was enough water to see the phalanx of trudging people down through to where the weeds started growing again. Rageh thought there were probably a dozen places, like this village, where Waalis like Abda made money supplying that water to people-movers. That was as it might be. This one village was enough of a horizon for Issa.

At the centre of the village Abda's house was a compound with its back to Beard Height; and Beard Height was a knobbly prominence of bare rock, pink and grey and sand-coloured, that glowered over the whole village. Issa had no idea why it was called Beard Height; it looked nothing at all like a beard, as far as she could see. The gunmen and sub-bosses had smaller houses, running along the downslope, of various sizes and with various examples of luxury attached to them. But Abda's was the largest and highest. If ever a flitter passed overhead, buoying itself along through the yielding air on the cushion of its own rattle-buzz, then it was on its way to Abda's place, nowhere else. If strangers came to town, it was Abda they had to talk to.

Abda ate any food he fancied, and liked to throw good food away, just to show he could afford to. He kept dogs, too. He'd fed his dogs the sunlight bug, and although they were a short-haired breed, the fact that fur covered their whole bodies gave them enough energy to live. And he kept chickens, in a run at the back where nobody was allowed to go; and the chickens were fed on real food and scraps, to make sure they laid eggs.

Of course there was a village shrine to Neocles, who made the Hair. Neocles the saviour. This was tolerated rather than encouraged by the Boss, and frequented by only a few regulars. But most of the people in the village would go to it in times of trouble: a concrete altar, and roofed over with plastic, with an icon of the Man Himself – a motion icon, playing over and over again, the moment of his martyrdom, with his arms flying out to his sides and his chest turning to fluid red. Arms at sides, chest of solid flesh – arms outflung, chest bubbling blood: one, two; one, two. When Issa first came to the village she often used to go to the shrine just to watch the icon. Soon enough, of course, she got bored by it. It was the same thing over, over, over. Where's the fun in that?

Issa had been purchased from a woman in the highlands. Ali Salih had bought her, and then moved her westward. They'd travelled a long way by train: eight trucks carrying food, each with an AI-gun on the roof; and a dozen trucks full of people. Issa had been hypnotized by the way the motion of the train slid the whole landscape around and beneath her.

Anyway, Ali Salih had sold her to Abda. That was the way of it: Abda bought her from Ali Salih, who had bought her from the woman, who had originally bought her – from her mother, presumably. But settled living worked its amnesia into the texture of existence. Soon enough the routine of life in the village overwrote Issa's memory, to the point where she could barely remember what lay at the back of the chain of past recollection. There was a kind of shimmery dream-life, something white and immense, a distant place where she had been more than just a girl – a city, a shining place. For a long time, until she knew better, Issa assumed *everybody* had something like that at the back of their memories. It was hardly even worth talking about it. Wasn't that just life, though? The day-to-day is laborious and draining, or it is pangs in the stomach, or it is a blow to the head, or it is insects swarming at the mouth and eyes, or worse. But memory possesses a golden quality that the miseries of the present cannot contaminate. Why else would this be, except that behind everything else the mind remembers the glory of how existence used to be, before birth?

Everybody has dreams like that.

On the other hand, there were days when her past life came back to her in astonishing detail and fine excess: all the particularities, all the names and places. But she was canny enough to know that that would only make her pine, and pining was no use to her. So she put her thoughts elsewhere.

As to why Abda had bought her – well, it was obvious she was special. It was not that she was beautiful, or accomplished; but she was *tall* . . . taller than anyone else her age. One day Rageh asked her how she came to be so tall; and she realized that she had no answer. It was just one of those things. Except she wasn't stupid; and she knew that kids who ate nothing but sunlight didn't grow tall. That meant that, before, somebody (her mother, maybe) had fed her plenteous real food. Hard to see why she'd do that, if only to sell her on. Perhaps, Rageh said, she did it *in order* to sell her on; but that didn't make sense to Issa. Whatever else she was, she was a logical girl; and she knew the investment in hard food would have had to be maintained for *years*. There was no way you'd get the money for that sort of an investment back by selling on. So perhaps there was some other story there. Perhaps her mother had never intended selling her, but had made her so striking and handsome by making her so tall that it was inevitable Issa would be stolen away. Stolen away felt right to Issa, chimed with her nebulous behind-memories, although she couldn't put her finger on specifics. Although the woman in the plane-lands hadn't been her mother. Although she used to say she *was*, sometimes. But that woman – she had told her various kids many different things about her name, so nobody knew what she was really called – had gotten sick. The sickness was a horrible thing, and it smelt horrible, and it made all her skin come up with boils like the bubbles in dirty bubblewrap. She'd sold Issa to Ali Salih in a hurry, and for less than she could have got. And Ali Salih had almost wrecked his acquisition by settling down with Issa that very night, drunk on grass wine, and not understanding why he was having such difficulty sticking his thing in. He did realize, eventually, for all his drunkenness, and he did desist. Probably he couldn't believe his luck. At any rate, when he sold her on he'd *certainly* got a lot more for Issa than he'd paid.

So it was she'd ended up in the village. Abda had waited three nights before putting it in, between her legs. Perhaps he'd been in two minds as to whether to keep her himself, or sell her on. But once he'd had her, and she'd lolled around the compound for a week, he more or less lost interest. That's the way of it, with male desire. She was tall, it was true, and striking-looking; but she was quite skinny, unprepossessingly so. Abda's favourite girl had sweetly plump shoulders. She went to wash her hair at the watertrough, and when she bent over the skin of her belly smiled a deep fleshy smile. Issa couldn't match that.

It was possible Abda had so much money that he simply lost count of what he had. That was possible. Water was a lucrative business. At any rate, Issa didn't stay in his house for very long. She tried to keep out of everybody's way, but Abda's other wives chased her out. Galla had an electrical cord that she used, with wicked effectiveness, as a whip. But it didn't matter. Issa was taken in by Mam Anna, and ended up sleeping under the big plastic sheet, pinned on one side to a garden wall and on to the other to a series of metal posts, where Anna and her friends lay. It was Mam Anna who showed her how to carry a piece of plastic – the kind of plastic didn't matter, it was the shape that was important, bitten and trimmed to a particular shape – up inside her to prevent conception. It was strange that she pressed this upon Issa, since one thing everybody agreed about Mam Anna is that she'd had more children than any other woman in the village. She herself said she'd had enough to know better, now.

Petal, a pale-skinned girl with a gaunt, oriental face, thought it all nonsense and a waste of time. 'If you get a child,' she said, 'it's going to fall out anyway, except that you eat hard food.'

'So?'

'So – don't need Mam Anna's plastic.'

But Mam Anna took Issa in a flappy-skinned embrace and told her that it wasn't as clean or easy as Petal made it sound. Better not to go there. 'You understand this, my tall girl,' she said. 'You need to do it properly. Pick your time, and make sure you've got the food. Kids are what make us up strong. We keep a hold on when we have them.'

First days in the village, the thing that surprised Issa most of all was how much freedom she was given. Back before, Ali Salih had kept her cuffed with a plastic band to hold her back from running away; but neither Abda nor any of the gunmen seemed to pay her any mind. She thought, this hour, or that hour, of escape, sometime; but didn't know where she was, or where she might go. There was the sea, of course; and to sit on Beard Height and gaze – it was best in the morning, when the sun was behind you – was to imagine what freedom might feel like. But nobody else in the village fretted about freedom; and in her bones Issa understood that it was a toxic meme, some-thing alien to the way life is lived, something she had picked up somewhere but would have been better without. What would she do if she went to the sea? She knew nobody down there, and she had no aim or plan. More, she comprehended, without being able to put it into words, that the freedom thing worked better as a thought in the head than a reality underfoot. It was better to see the sea as that azure thread, stitched so tightly against the horizon it almost wasn't there. It would have poisoned the purity of this line to have got any closer.

Life in the village settled into a tolerable rhythm. The worst things happened early on, when her place in the network of things was not as yet fixed. She slept under Mam Anna's sheet with a dozen other girls, and that was safe; but walking around in the daytime she had to run the gamut of crowds of idle males, lounging in the sun and staring at her, calling after her, making sexual suggestions, or sometimes masturbating openly as she went. Though she was a kid she understood all this well enough, and it was no fun. Sometimes, as she ran some petty errand for Mam Anna, or as she went up dog-alley to the water trough, men and boys crowded about her, jostling her, urging her to perform one or other sex act upon them, singly or together. She wriggled free, mostly, though it made her blush. It was the blush, probably, or the combination of the blush and her great height, that meant she became the focus for so much male attention. The other girls experienced it too, of course; but not to the same degree as Issa.

Well, she was not stupid. Why have sex with these no-good hairy men, who had literally and absolutely *nothing* they could give her? The village had a dozen powerful men, below Abda, who had stores of hard food and alcohol and trinkets to dole out.

Mam Anna, though, took what seemed to Issa a surprisingly lenient view of the men. 'After every-all, what do they have?' she asked, as they all lay together one evening in open air, and the evening sky grew thicker and thicker with darkness, and the stars toyed with the idea coming into clear view, and the cicadas hissed all around them like steam escaping, and mosquitoes shrieked and stopped. Mam Anna liked to smoke a snuff-pipe, and her girls huddled around her to catch a whiff of the patchouli and lavender scent of it. 'What do they have?' Man Anna said. 'We've the bellies to grow kids, and they have not. They sit around all day soaking sun, and drinking at the trough, and going through the field looking for bugs. And apart from that they have nothing, but talk, and all they talk about is us. You could feel sorry for them.'

'Or,' said Petal, 'maybe not.'

The worst happened within her first month. A young man called Adel Bary and another called Oma, ambushed Issa one afternoon, in a shallow, dusty valley south of the village – it was called Road Valley, although Issa couldn't see evidence of any road. She was individually taller than either of these men, and had it been one-on-one she would probably have fought any of the men off. But together they were able to overpower her by dint of leaping on her and bowling her over. When she was down, they rolled her over. They pulled her arms over her head, and Oma sat on them, hooting in her ear and keeping her still by punching the back of her head. He had a pebble concealed in his fist, which made blows very painful. Adel Bary, meanwhile, yanked her trousers off, and slid his right arm under her belly to pull her hips upward. It took him a number of clumsy stabs with his member, jabbing her leg, or the dirt, or her ass, before he got inside her; and then almost at once he did a ridiculous male epileptic seizure performance, a bird-rapid thrusting and lots of gasping. It was over. Then the two men ran off. Issa didn't know why Oma hadn't taken his advantage also. Maybe they'd been interrupted, or maybe they'd been afraid of being interrupted, or maybe their high spirits had just bubbled over into flight. It seemed to Issa that she lay there dirt-dazed for a very long time. It took a deal of energy and coordination to retrieve her trousers and draw them up over her trembling legs. She would not have thought it possible that the sun could have seemed brighter than it did before the attack; but somehow it did. Its glare was acid. A palpable pressure of dry heat. But here was Mam Anna, squatting beside her with a plastic beaker of water.

Adel Bary was only the second man she had been with.

But it was the aftermath of this experience that was most instructive. So, Mam Anna sent four girls, and a blade, and they grabbed Adel Bary behind the nettlefield. All the rest they girls come to watch. Mosa and Atene held him down, and Petal grabbed hair and hacked shreds off with her knife. How Adel Bary wailed! He was, Mam Anna said, like any toddler. But his wails lost force soon enough, he was sobbing more than anything, and his whole body shook with feverish little sobs. Petal had the biggest knife, and she cut at his hair, and cut, and left him with nothing but a few tufts, and a scratched and bloody scalp.

After that Adel Bary went to beg hard food from Abda, to tide him over till his hair grew again. And Abda called Mam Anna to come tell him what occurred, so Mam Anna went up, with a hipsway in her step that the girls could read for confidence. She was there half an hour, and at the end of it Abda himself had been persuaded that justice had to be done. The girls gossiped about what lewd thing or things she had done for Abda; or whether the power of her rhetoric had been enough. Then Abda had two of his gunmen grab the boys, to contribute his display of public justice to proceedings. He liked to do this, every now and then, just to remind people who was in charge. First Oma, although he was let off lightly. Lev, one of Abda's right-hand men, cut the soles of his feet with a knife. But Adel Bary was punished properly: bound with cord so that his elbows touched behind his back, the last of his hair was shaved clean. He wept piteously whilst this went on, and afterwards he was cut loose to wander the village. How freakish he looked, bald and teary-faced! But his former friends knew better than to associate with him. He tried begging for hard food with everyone. He must have understood this was long odds, longer than hope. But he tried it nevertheless. What else could he do? One strange thing was that he came to Issa first of all, weeping, not apologizing for what he had done to her, but trying to sell her an incoherent plan that she could seduce one of the gunmen in return for just enough hard food to keep him alive till his hair grew back. Issa felt no particular anger as far as Adel Bary was concerned, and neither was she aware of any internal callousness, or any of the satisfactions of revenge. But she felt a complete disconnection between him and her. The idea that she would work to keep him alive was not outrageous so much as it was baffling. At any rate, he gave up bothering her, after a while. By the end of the week he was so weak that he could hardly walk without staggering. He left the village anyway. 'He should have walked away as soon as he was shaved,' was Mam Anna's opinion. But Issa knew why he hadn't; because his mind was perfectly empty of *where he was going to go*. A bald man, absolutely poor, trekking the friendless road.

'Don't pity him, no,' said Mam Anna. 'Pity is a scarce resource. You hoard it, girl, keep it for your later.'

And not all the men were as bad as Adel Bary. Rageh, for instance, who didn't lounge about with the other men, and didn't join the huddle. The other men mostly talked, or else played cardgames with greasy plastic cards.— Creased and seamed items, these, despite the UNCREASABLE! boast-logo printed on the back of each. Rageh wasn't part of that crowd. He preferred going off by himself, liked to spend time observing the world. Round to the north of the village, behind Abda's compound, a hefty metal tether had been set in the rock of Beard Height. This was where the blimps were tied. They leaked a little, because everything in the world leaked a little and nothing was absolutely tight; but that meant that the fields here were woman-high with weed. Wild rhubarb, bolted, extruded-looking, white as picked-bones curling in amongst masses of dark green nettles. Rageh told Issa that, no question, this was where the best bugs were to be found. Since it was impossible to penetrate the thicket, Issa had to take this on trust. There were certainly many flies – too many for Issa's comfort, really. The thicket, and the sewage tunnel that didn't go anywhere half-set into the downslope of the hill, were the worst place for flies. Switzer had somehow obtained tomato seeds – *tomato the most beautiful food God ever put on the planet, red as strawberries but more luscious, the original fruit of sin of the Garden of Eden* she claimed, which led Issa to believe that she'd never actually *tasted* tomatoes. She had tried sowing them in at the open half-pipe of this sewer. But they had not prospered. Switzer had pulled the weeds clear to give the tomato seeds a chance, but the weeds had grown back too quickly and choked them. Or else the seeds had been duds. That was very possible too. Tomatoes remained an abstract and imaginary food.

She kissed Rageh. Oh he wanted to do sexual things, naturally enough; but she was clear that she didn't, yet, and he was ruled by her. Nevertheless it was an interesting thing to kiss him: kissing mouth to mouth, for long long stretches of time, kissing until her lips went numb. They liked to go behind the shrine, down amongst the grass there, and lie together, innocent as Adam and Eve. If Adam and Eve had ever been innocent.

One day some Spartacist wanderers stopped at the village in their ongoing travels. They soon gathered a crowd down by the roofless fac; mostly men, but some women too who wandered down to see what the fuss was about. Three Spartacists, each taking turns to speak, although one was a much more effective orator than her two fellows. 'What strength is given to us!' she cried aloud. 'More than the rich – our strength is greater than theirs! We can go where we choose! Hunger cannot consume us, as it does the wealthy. We are stronger, and gifted, and pure! So why do we live as slaves?' Issa's heart beat faster at this, and little sparks of hope gleamed anew in her mind; but people around her muttered as if the answer were obvious, and Astra, whose two-year-old clung about her neck, walked off in disgust. But the Spartacist woman grew more and more passionate as she went on. 'We are many, they are few,' she said. 'We are strong and they are weak. We can endure, where their life is pitifully contingent! Why do we not simply rid ourselves of them? Join with us, live with us and for us and for the greater cause! Become something bigger than yourself! Rise like lions after slumber! Comrades, the revolution *is* coming.'

Bolted nettles, growing behind her, swayed in the breeze, an intense green colour in the bright sunlight. Their shadows trembled and pulsed at her feet.

Then Abda's men came down, waving their firearms and hooting at the Spartacists to fuck off. The three of them went away, blithely enough, singing some song in a foreign language about colours and flags – a kindergarten song, perhaps. That afternoon, when the sun was hottest, and Issa's blood tingled with all the sugars in it, she retreated under Mam Anna's canvas roof. Several of the women there were talking about the coming revolution; how likely it was, or how unlikely. The visit had stirred the soup, and no mistake. 'What do you think, Anna?' Issa asked. 'When is the revolution coming?' Mam Anna took the pipe from her mouth and said: 'I remember Triunion.' But none of the others knew what this meant, and pestered her to explain. 'I mean,' she said, eventually, looking weary, 'that they tried their revolution not many years ago, in Triunion, which is a place over the Western Sea. These Spartacists, they hoped to kick all the rich and bald out of that place, and they spoke big and grandly about going on from there to seize all the tropics. From Cancer to Capricorn was they slogan. But did – not.'

'What happened?' 'What happened?'

'The poor had the bodies, and the voices, and the right-eousness. But the rich had the guns. And guns count for more than righteousness, or voice, or body.' She shut up, then, and when prevailed upon to say more, all she added was: 'It broke this Spartacus movement, is what it did. Now they's just a few wanderers and hermits, like those who spoke today, who don't understand that it is over.'

The next day Issa went off with Rageh, right round to the far side of the Beard hill, in amongst the bushes of scrub, the two of them kissed. Rageh broke off repeatedly to beg her to touch his manhood, or plead whiningly to let him do it to her, and each time he did so made her laugh more than the time before.

After the punishment of Adel Bary, Abda took an interest in Issa again. One day Lev poked his big head in under Mam Anna's canvas ceiling, massy bone sphere and boo-boo eyes, chin and upper lip velvet and shiny half-fuzz cranium. 'Abda requests the pleasure,' he said, in his low voice. Issa might almost have thought the ceiling thrummed with his voice, but it was only the hot wind. So she stepped out into the blinding heat of midday. The two of them made their way, walking slowly because it was so parchingly hot, up to the compound. Lev was a man who spoke little, as a rule, and since none of the women in the village knew what he did for sex he was assumed to be gay; although if he had sex with any of the men in the village, *they* didn't talk about it. Perhaps he simply did without, although that seemed unlikely.

But having summoned her Abda had no use for her right away. It was too hot for him and her to be slamming their privates together. So she lolled about in the cool big empty rooms of his house, and did nothing for a long while but watch. She watched people come and go; and some of them stopped to pass words with her, or some of them put their faces in another direction rather than look at her. Abda's two dogs came over, skinny as furred skeletons, to sniff at her. Their noses were shaped like flitter snouts. Their breath smelt of dust and darkness. Then they were bored with her and away they trotted, one behind the other like a slinky-bodied eight-leg beast.

After that Abda's kids came hurtling through into the room, moving as a pack, racing fast despite the heat. They came to crowd about her. The youngest was two year old; the oldest – Nik – old enough to be a man in any other situation, but not in Abda's house, obviously enough, because Abda was the man in this house. As for Nik: well, Issa could see by looking at him that his main pastime was trying to get a nasty fury properly on the boil inside himself. He leered at her, and then ran off and the kids ran off in a straggly line after him, pied-piper-ish. But ten minutes later he was back, standing over where she was sat, her back at the wall. He just stood there and glared.

'How old are you, anyhow?' Issa asked.

'My papa has brung you here as a present for *me*,' he replied. He pulled down his pants and brought out his thing, starkstiff with lust. He held it *at* her in his right hand. 'This going to hurt you hard,' he promised.

'Yeah?'

'You won't forget this in no hurry,' he said.

She might have been scared, for he was the Waali's son, after all. But she didn't feel it in her to be scared. So she said: 'That little thing, I'll hardly notice going in.'

The other kids laughed, and for a heartbeat Nik laughed too. But then he remembered he was supposed to be mean-at-heart and a killer, so he bit his laugh off and put his young manhood away and spoke all the bad words he could at her. And by speaking them, he worked himself up into something like a rage. So he taunted her with what Adel Bary had done; and she retorted by asking where was Adel Bary now? This got Nik into a bigger tantrum rage, and he started trying to slap and scratch her. She had to jump to her feet and hold him off. He was Abda's son – not his oldest son, for others, older, were elsewhere about the world – but his son nevertheless, and he had the habit of eating hard food. But she was still taller and stronger than him; and he wasn't used to being fought back against, so she soon enough got the better of him. She caught his hand and swung him about on the pivot of it. He went hard into the wall, and left a bugsplat of blood on the plaster. Then he sat on the floor for a little, little dribbles, tomato-red, seeping from his nose, and he cried a little.

Soon enough, he got up and ran away. The other kids did not follow him this time, but lolled about the room with Issa, or wandered off on their own. He came back, of course, this time with Lev, and bearing the accusing finger. But Lev laughed, and called Issa a fine little devilla. So Nik went off in a rage. Issa cared nothing for that. After a while her blood started tingling with hunger in the dimness of the room, so she went up to the roof – by the main stairway, like a houseguest, and no slave – and lay in the sun. There were some splotchy white clouds against the blue, like blots of chewing gum flattened upon a pavement. A year before, and Issa might have wondered why she thought of chewing gum, something she hadn't seen since she didn't *know* when. It was a hard food people bought and ate even though it gave no nutrition *at all*, the ultimate in conspicuous consumption.

When the sun drifted listlessly behind the western places and the stars came out like a bright pox, Issa went back inside the house. She could smell food being cooked, and it made her mouth gush. So she joined the scrum of all the folk in the house, the guardsmen and wives, the kids and hangers-on, all trying for a crumb, or a lick. A light bulb snapped out, its filament fusing. It was one of two, and when it went the illumination all fled to the other side of the room, which gave it, somehow, the feel of a space that was tilted. Abda spotted her in the crowd, and came shuffling over in his huge red velvet slippers, and his psilk gown. He put his big hairy hand about her neck, from the front. 'You fight with my son?' he boomed.

Issa, torn between begging for forgiveness as piteously as she could, and replying with boldface heart, chose the latter. 'Your son? I took him for your daughter.'

There was the merest – *hup* – pause, when nothing happened, and the space allowed in the uprushing fear that he was going to be very angry at this, and was going to squeeze her throat until she choked to death. But then Abda started laughing a proper Jabbahutt laugh. He removed his meaty hand from her neck to pat her on the back. 'Maybe I didn't *altogether* waste the money I spent on you,' he grumbled. 'I heard he showed you his stabber, then?'

She had to work to bring out the smile and the flickering eyelid coyness, because her throat was raw from where he'd gripped it. But she kept her wits. 'Just the tip of it, unless – no!' She grinned. 'Never tell me that's the *whole thing*?'

Again, Abda did the Waali thing, making her wait for an instant before revealing whether he was going to manifest displeasure or pleasure. But then he was laughing again, and bringing her past all the others and through the kitchen door. 'Have a taste,' he instructed her, and he dipped the handle-end of the big wooden spoon in the soup, and slipped it into her mouth like a dick. It was scalding heat of it, and she 'oo-oo-oo'ed, which made Abda laugh louder.

Later, after he'd eaten, Abda took her back to his big bed and hammered her against the mattress for ten long minutes. She didn't need to simulate her gasping, for he was so heavy and bore down on her chest so mercilessly that he forced the air out like a bagpiper. Afterwards he rolled off with a pleased look on his face. She took this for a good thing. He lay, face upward, eyes closed, and muttered something for a minute or longer, but not in any language Issa could understand. Then he was asleep.

She stayed four days and four nights in the house. For most of that time she was in one of Abda's bedrooms, which wasn't ideal. The door was locked, nobody thought to bring her any hard food, and she had to lean out of the window to warm her hair in the sun. Each night Abda came to her again. He didn't want anything too elaborate, sexually speaking: her on top, facing away from him, bouncing up and down so that her bony ass bounced against the swell of his big belly. Or else he got her to lie down, which was a little tricky, because his weight was pretty much smothering. But he finished up soon enough, and then roused himself, slapping his stomach with his big hands. He got al-Schawarma, his cook, to bring up many metal plates of sizzling food, and an extraordinary mess of odours steamed the room. He ate, and drank from a litre plastic bottle of white wine, and filled himself; and he permitted Issa to have little licks of his spoon, but no more. Most of the hard food was like acid upon her tongue, and she had to gulp water. 'How can you eat this?' she gasped. She was proper amazed. 'It is like eating fire.'

'Oh, *you're* the fire-eater,' he laughed. It took a while to understand what he meant. The sun, the sun.

He fell asleep eventually, his sphere-stomach creaking and burbling like a bathysphere squeezed by abyssal pressures in the deep ocean. Issa dozed at the side of his bed. She had a dream in which the sun spoke to her. It said: I am a fish, the greatest leviathan. It was orange as a goldfish, with a peripheral fringe of flame-shaped fins all about its face. Its voice was like the

Preacher's voice, only echoier. And the sky was as blue as any ocean. 'You are fire, and how can you be a fish?' Issa asked the dream. 'Fire cannot swim through water.' She looked again, and the fish had the face of Mam Anna, and its passage through the cold waters sheathed it in a great mantle of steam the colour of white gold. I am fire, said the sun. And you eat me.

Briefly, Issa was the Waali's new favourite. The bedroom door was no longer locked during the day, and she had the run of the house and roof.

One morning he chivvied her about her inability to eat any of his previous night's curry. 'When you get big with my child,' he said, 'you'll have to get the taste for hard food. Besides, you are too skinny.'

'Skinny as a sunbeam,' she said.

'You must plump up!' he declared, gravely.

And for a week or so she settled into a new rhythm. Rather than hang around the house, where there was nothing to do, she ventured outside. Abda didn't seem to care. Preacher and Mam Anna were walking up and down in the intermittent sunshine, talking. When she saw Issa, Anna embraced her. 'How is things?'

'I am the new Waali-wife.'

Issa told her everything, and didn't even mind the Preacher loitering, eavesdropping. Mam Anna was pleased for her. 'I am worried about Nik, though,' Issa confessed. 'He has a hatred for me, and he is the Waali's son, after all.'

Mam Anna waved this worry as if were flies. 'He's a fool. Abda has three older sons, and they are in the world, and they are making their ways. Abda do nothing but despise his son Nik.'

'Children are the only wealth in this world!' intoned the Preacher.

Mam Anna slapped him twice to drive him away at this; and settled Issa in the crook of her armpit, as they both lay in the sun. 'Don't be fearful of Abda. He may look like a big feller, but he's the weakest of the Waalies in this part of the world. I been up and down to the sea, with the Blimp, more times than I can recall. You see other Waalis run their villages rather different.'

'How so?'

'Oh,' said Mam Anna. 'Look at how Abda leaves all the men just lying about in the sun, or playing cards! Other Waalies take their men into a militia, train them up. To defend the village, or maybe attack another village, or to hire them out as soldiers. But Abda is too lazy to be bothered organizing a militia. He's too lazy even to order *Lev* to organize a militia.'

Issa thought about that. 'So the village isn't defended?'

'You're quick, you've a wit,' said Mam Anna, indulgently; 'and later you can go over my feet with a wet cloth.'

'So why don't some nearby Waali come take it, if they've a militia and we've not?'

'Because Abda's brother is a minister in the national government,' said Mam Anna. 'And all the other Waalis know it. If they try, the government would make a media show of bringing in actual army. So we rub along, and we do rub along.'

Issa understood: Abda was weak. Of course it was true. But she deduced a different moral from this. Mam Anna thought not only that a weak Waali was one she could manipulate (and so she could), but that this made life more comfortable than it might otherwise be. Issa had a wordless comprehension that a weak Waali was a less stable Waali, more vulnerable to outside pressure, and more capricious in his own power.

Still, who was she to challenge the authority of Mam Anna?

For a couple of weeks things went well. She picked up

283

various sorts of tidbits, and her stomach got used to the stretching sensation of having stuff inside it. She got so used to having food in her that on the days when she didn't get to eat she felt the shards of actual hunger inside her. When Abda came in her mouth she could swallow it down without indigestion. One evening, post-coital, he said to her: 'You are too skinny. But you're young, and that makes up for it. Make up some way.' She was emboldened by this to ask him: 'How old are you, Abda?' 'Sixty,' he said. 'Sixty years of age.' He said it with pride.

The sun turning over in the sky, day-slow, bending the shadows one way and then another.

The dogs were drinking out of the water trough: a noise like two men clapping.

The exhaustless sun.

But then everything went wrong. It happened in a moment.

At night, in Abda's bed: she was on her knees and elbows and Abda was taking her from behind. The irony of it was: she was actually thinking, in that pride-goeth-before way we humans are good at: 'Better this than him on top, squashing me.' Although she was only thinking it in an idle sort of way. Abda was pulling himself a long way out and pushing himself a long way in, making the sort of noise that Issa knew meant he was about to come.

Then he screamed. He reeled back, pulling entirely out of her, squealing like a braking train.

She was very scared straight away, wriggling round on the bed to sit, holding her knees to her chest. 'What have you done, woman?' he bellowed. He was clutching his manhood, bent over. 'What have you – have you *bitten* me?'

She couldn't stop herself crying. 'What? What?'

'What have you *done*?'

'What's the matter?'

'By the food of God I'll burn you on an *open fire*, you bitch!' he howled.

'What?' she wept. 'What?'

He hobbled over to sit on the edge of the bed, still clutching himself, and swore at her some more. She could see that his cock was bleeding. 'Lev!' he bellowed. 'Lev!'

Lev came in, went out, saw what had happened immediately, and went back out for wipes and a bandage. By this point Abda had calmed down, but this made Issa more scared than ever. She clutched herself. She was shivering hard with pure fear. 'Fuck, the *fuck*,' Abda gasped, 'what the fuck', and so on, and so forth, as Lev – impassive – tended his cut glans. Right on the end, bisected by the cut to give him a cross design there.

The whole house was roused by his noise, of course. Al-Schawara brought in a bottle of brandy, and Abda guzzled it like fruit juice. Issa could feel the wall shake behind her naked back as people thumped up and down stairs.

When Lev had finished, Abda came over and grasped Issa by both shoulders. 'You cut my flesh, woman,' he said. 'On a most delicate place. I cannot forget it.'

This shocked her out of tears. She went very still, expecting a neck-breaking blow, or a gun to her head. But instead he let go of her and turned his back. He left the room, with Lev behind him. Issa sat on the bed, and started shivering again. It was not cold; in fact it was a very hot night. She clutched her knees to her body. She stared at the wall, at the duckbeak shadow cast by the lampshade upon the plaster, and thought: a shaved head is the least I can expect, here. She tried to anchor her terror in practical considerations. If she were shaved, would she throw herself on Mam Anna's mercy? Or would she leave the village and try her luck whoring for food down by the sea? But her mind's grip on practical matters kept slipping. What had happened? How had she hurt him? She could not work out what had happened. She could not see how she had caused this sudden maelstrom of outrage and anger.

Galla, one of Abda's house women, came through eventually and wrapped her in an old poncho with the Olympic logo on it. She led her out of the bedroom and took her downstairs to a basement. The bottom layer of the house, underground, where no sunlight ever penetrated: a barren set of rooms. 'He's a fury,' she said, quietly. 'What did you do to him?'

'I don't know,' Issa wept. 'I honestly don't know. I genuinely don't know.'

'Did you bite him? He had a girl once called Elen, she had a epileptic condition. One day: sucking his cock, had a fit, bit him. There was no blood, but I'll tell you what he did. He laid her on the bed until her fit passed, and then he beat her hard on the skull, beat her so hard he got bits of skin with hair on between his knuckles. I saw it! She went simple after that beating.'

This story might have fuelled Issa's hysteria; but instead, fire fighting fire, it quelled it. She felt calmer. 'Will he beat me? How will he punish me?'

'I don't know what you *did*, lover-child.'

'I don't know either.'

'How did it happen? Wait—' She put her handsome head on one side, listening to the above stairs. The sound of commotion, muffled, from above. 'Wait – there's yelling. I'll be back in a peck.' She went out. The door banged shut, and a moment later it clucked to itself. Issa didn't bother checking; she knew it was locked. So she wrapped the poncho around her, and lay on the narrow bed. The aircompressor motor was down in the room with her, making its continual slow drum-machine chug, and eventually she fell asleep to its shushing.

She woke as the doorlock was unsnibbed. Galla was back,

with another one of Abda's women: Dani. Both looked very sombre. 'Tell me exactly, as exactly as you know, what happened,' Gallas said.

'He was having me from behind,' said Issa, matter-of-factly, her voice still blurry with sleep, her mind not entirely logged-on. 'Then, sudden, he wailed aloud, and kept wailing.'

'You've got something up there?'

'Up there?' said Issa, thinking this a reference to the topography of the house.

'Up,' said Dani, patiently. 'There.'

'Mam Anna put in a length of hard plastic,' said Issa.

'Lie down, my dear,' said Galla. 'No, on your back. Yes, I'm going to have a feel up there.' She wore no glove, and used no lubricant, so it was indeed an uncomfortable examination. But the physical discomfort took Issa's mind off its anxious dread. It woke her up too, and as she lay there she regretted telling them about Mam Anna. She shouldn't have mentioned her name. She could have said she put it up herself on her own. Of course, there was nothing they could do about it now.

Galla had her whole hand up Issa, and was pulling the face of somebody pondering a philosophical conundrum. Then the expression changed, and she got hold of the device and drew it out in one single movement. 'He pranged his cock on that,' said Dani. She sniggered. Then she stopped.

'Maybe it came a little loose from the inner skin,' said Galla, judiciously. 'Or maybe it was just the angle, and the depth of his penetration. But he surely caught himself hard on it, on his most tender place.'

Issa had pulled herself up sat on the narrow bed, trying to braid her left leg around her right. More than the discomfort, and the lingering ache, she felt a new and horrible sense of diminishment. It was to do with being so horribly opened up.

'His rage has altered,' Galla said, wrapping the plastic device in a piece of plastic cloth. 'It's gone cold. That isn't good for any of us.'

'Dangerous times can be opportune for ambitious people,' said Issa.

Dani looked astonished that Issa had uttered this sentence. But Galla said nothing to this. She looked hard at Issa, and then went out. 'I think,' said Dani, following, 'that she was expecting *sorry*.'

The door shut with a slap and the lock clucked again. But only a few minutes passed before it was opened again, and Gallas came back in. Then she and Dani brought Issa out of the room. The bare soles of her feet slapped on the ascending stairway. She came before Abda, in the main hall, where he was sitting upon a big metal chair. All the house workers had assembled, the children as well. Lev was there of course; with his gun in his hand. The two dogs lay with their chins on their paws. There was murmuring in the room, but it stopped when Issa was brought in.

The windows were sheened pale with dawn. One fly, alone out of the whole kingdom of his kind, was terribly excited by the window pane. The creature danced upon it. It swerved away only to rush back to do his lucky-strike prospector jig once more.

'This is a wake-up,' Abda said, as soon as Issa was standing in front of him. 'A wake-up for me, and all.'

Issa didn't know where to stand. Lev was standing just to Abda's right, and holding a long-barrelled gun. Kemel, one of Abda's other musclemen, stood behind the chair, his clothes tight as a scabbard on a sword.

'Mam Anna had no business fitting you with one of those,' Abda said. 'I bought you, didn't I?' He leant forward at this question, and Issa understood that he expected an answer.

'I guess you did,' she said.

'Nobody *else* bought you, no? It was just me.' He wanted an answer to this, too; but at this point Mam Anna was brought in. She came into the room with her slow swagger, moving weight from hip to hip. Hers the walk of a person aware of their own strength and heft. But Lev put a gun on her and some of her confidence fell away, and when Abda started talking she began to shiver with her own fear.

'You put a plastic stick up this girl's twat?'

'Abda!' she said.

'I know you did. It sliced my meat across. My cockend look like a fucking screwdriver now, you cunts.' There was some sniggering at this, from his men, though it dried up when he looked round in fury.

Issa, even standing behind her, could see Mam Anna summoning her courage. She was tall and strong, and she had courage to match. Her shivers left her. She straightened her spine. 'On account of your cock being too *big*, though, Waali,' she told him. 'You think *I'm* the one not knowing it? Think it again. You wave it about, you're going to knock stars off heaven.' Abda did not smile. 'Some those stars got sharp edges, too,' she added, looking round the crowd.

Everybody was silent and still.

Abda said: 'This girl *ask* for the plastic stick?'

'Her? This child doesn't know.'

'What doesn't she know?'

'She does not know anything about anything.'

'You sure, now, Mam Anna?' said Abda leaning forward. 'If it was *your* idea, I must punish *you*. But if it was her idea, then maybe it goes different?'

At this Kemel stepped out holding plastic cuffs. Mam Anna started to shiver again. 'You *really* that angry about a little nick on your little cock, Abda?' she said.

'You know that's not it,' Abda said. And Kemel cuffed her

wrists behind her back, and, pressing on her shoulders, made her kneel down. 'You did it to steal children from me,' said Abda. 'That's the crime. That's for-why you need punishing. For stealing from me.'

Mam Anna, when she spoke, had a different tone in her voice now. It was wheedling, 'But, now, you *got* lots of children already, Abda.'

'Oho?' he bellowed. And everybody flinched. Every single person in the room. 'You *say* so?' Nobody moved. The pause button had been applied to the image. 'I've been too soft on everybody, it seems. I've been too *soft*. You think I wouldn't find this out? Look at my kids—' And he flung his arm out to the right. The youngsters cowered at the vehemence of the gesture. 'Fucking sprats, the lot. This girl, this Issa, she's a big strong girl, she'll give me some big strong kids. You don't have the right to steal those *from* me.'

'Pama turned out OK,' said Mam Anna. 'He's a good son to you.'

'He's had ten years away from the village to make it, and I hear nothing about him but drinking and fucking and gambling my money,' yelled Abda. His face had changed colour. 'Pama? You bear me *one* son, Anna, and think I'm going go on my knees to you in gratitude? What ever else you do me but daughters? And I've been too too soft on you, and too soft on the whole town. I've let you get away with too much.'

'Don't shave my head,' said Mam Anna, her voice all woe now, and the tears dripping (Issa could see) from her cheeks and chin. 'I'm asking on my knees, don't shave my head, Abda. Don't make me beg scraps.'

'You think I *shouldn't* punish you?' Abda said, his voice dropping in volume. 'You think I shouldn't get a grip on this town again?'

'Punish me, maybe – but not the bald head.'

Abda sat back, and sucked a long breath in, and then let it out. 'I won't take your hair off,' he said. 'You can keep your hair.'

He nodded at Kemel, and the big man took a grip of the hair on the top of Mam Anna's head, and then with his other hand took a fistful of the long hair, behind her back. Then, though a big man, he trotted, danced about her. He drew the hair all the way round her neck, and she was pulled to the side and overbalanced. Unable to steady herself with her hands she fell, but she did not smack the floor, because Kemel had twisted the rope of her own hair around her neck. She made a noise like *ocsh*, and *ocsh*. Her face blushed with the shame of not being able to breathe. Kemel's hold slipped, and then Mam Anna's shoulder hit the floor. He tried to twist the hair into a rope as she struggled, and kept losing his hold of it. 'Do it,' said Abda, in a loud voice. 'Why you waiting?'

'Hard to grip it, boss,' grunted Kemel.

Lev stepped forward, the barrel of his gun resting into the crook of his left elbow.

'What do you think you're doing?' Abda snapped.

'I'll finish it,' said Lev.

'Wait,' croaked Anna, hauling herself over onto her back. 'Wait, Abda.'

'I'm *not* happy about this, Anna, killing you and all,' said Abda, without looking at her. 'But what choice do I have? You've been undermining me. It's my authority that's in question.'

'No,' Anna gasped. Her eyeballs had grown a little bigger, so as to block off the tear ducts, or else she would surely have wept. 'Never undermined you.'

'Of course you have. I'm not an idiot.'

Kemel was trying to hook a rope of twisted hair under her chin, and she was resisting him by pressing her chin into her chest. With a goat-nimble little leap, Abda was out of his chair; he went down upon one knee beside the prone woman. He batted Kemel away. 'In *a* sense,' he said, confidentially – although the whole packed room could hear. 'In a sense it is unfair. Because I knew, and didn't care! Maybe I encouraged it, even, because you kept the women in line, and that kept the men in line. I was happy the village was running nicely. All I wanted was a peaceful life, and the chance to grow my family. That's not too much, is it? But now look at where we are! You wanted power, that's all.'

'No,' gasped Anna, pleadingly, raspingly.

'Sure you did! Oh, I don't blame you for it. You accumu-lated yourself a little bit of power here, and a little bit of power there – that's natural. That's natural to humanity. But a body can only have one head. And this place can only have one Waali. And that's the lesson, my friend. Come: if you eat power, you shit death. That's all.'

Issa's voice came back to her. She couldn't have said where it had gone, all this time. 'Don't do this,' she said.

Abda ignored her. Or perhaps she hadn't spoken at all. The theatre of it. She might have expected her pulse to be hurrying, her heart lolloping faster, but in fact a weird calm had frozen her innards. None of it was real. Everything was a lie. She had tumbled out of the paradise of tall towers and sunshine, the Eden of which all children are aware, just behind their backs, in the blindspot no amount of spinning around will disclose. The intimations place. The light of setting suns. Perhaps she had only thought to speak and hadn't got the words out. So she drew in a breath. 'Don't do this,' she said, stepping forward, putting volume into the words. How to make a world: speak it, with enough conviction. 'Don't.'

Kemel stepped in front of her and put his hand out, with a casual gesture. His palm jarred onto the bone of her forehead like a bolt-gun. She reeled back. There was a mortar blast and pain in her head. There was a flapping sheet of light inside her eyes. She stumbled against something behind her, and the collision tipped her over, and without any great sense of her orientation in the largest scheme of things. She leant her shoulder up against the wall, except that it wasn't the wall, for she was lying on her side on the floor.

There were hands upon her. They lifted her and carried her through to the terrace of the house. Migraine lights flickered inside her eyes. The air tasted cool and sweet. The early morning sky was syrupy with light, yellow and jam-red with milky spills and patches. She lay on the ground until her head stopped throbbing, and then she sat up. Presently she got up, and went down to the water trough to wash her face and drink a little. The sun was like a hole in the sky from another dimension altogether.

Later that day there was a deal of shouting on the out-road; Abda down with Lev and Kemel, shaking up the men, scattering their playcards, beating whoever they could land a blow on. Some of the women went down to spectate, but Issa just lay in the sun. She ate the sun. Her belly had got used to food, and that meant that it burned a little flame of hunger, a soreness in the core of her. But she relished her hunger. It was truly hers.

In the afternoon there was another commotion. Kemel had Rageh by the wrist, and was trying to haul him up the hill. 'It's not true,' the lad was wailing. Despite being by a good deal the smaller of the two, Rageh's desperate writhing was making it hard for Kemel to move him. 'I never touched her.' 'You're coming along with me,' Kemel grunted. 'She never *let* me!' Rageh cried. 'You're to come,' Kemel said, heaving him on, 'with *me.*'

Eventually Rageh was brought up to the house and disappeared inside. Issa watched in a sort of torpor. Silence settled again. Two birds, very high up, moved in an oval path round and round the crown of the hill. The cicadas were the sound of the scrub scratching an endless itch. Issa dozed. A loud snapping sound woke her up.

She knew what it was. She didn't want to think what it was.

She took a long drink at the water trough. The enemy was lassitude. She knew that. But it *was* hard to rouse herself. The stick-snap that had woken her. She knew what that had been. And there was Lev, strolling about the village with a grave look upon his face, holding his gun in his right hand, resting the long barrel in the crook of his left elbow. He carried it that way. That was his look. Except immediately after he discharged it, when the barrel was too hot to rest there.

Preacher came and talked with her; but there was something different about him to the way he had been before. The play-acting was gone. He asked how she was doing, and her reply was to look through him as if he were a man-shaped portal into somewhere else. 'It's tough,' said Preacher. 'He's been King Log. Now our risk: he'll get a taste for being King Stork.' He was Abda, of course; but she didn't know about Logs and Storks and what all that meant. 'Neocles teaches that there's a gift that undoes the logic of giving,' the Preacher went on. 'It's a mystic gift, a magic gift, and once given nobody is in debt to anybody else ever again.' Perhaps this was offered by way of consolation, but Issa didn't see how that was supposed to work.

It took a palpable effort in her to get the words out, but she asked: 'What did they want with Rageh?'

'A kissing thing,' said Preacher, looking at the sky.

'It was all we ever did,' said Issa, with a great weight of tears behind the words, somehow managing to hold them off.

'That's what he kept telling them. But Abda – he has a point to make, now. So to prove his point, they made him kiss Lev's gun.'

The stem grows straight until it is snapped.

This made Issa withdraw for awhile. She still lacked the energy to move physically away, but she blocked out the Preacher's words and lay still, supine, letting the sun feed her and put sugar in her blood.

The Preacher talked at her, for a bit. 'I come down from Denmark,' he said. 'Nobody ever ask where I come from, or why I speak funny, but there you go. I never tell body else, until you, but there you go. It don't matter. I come through Europe, and down to Black Sea – many adventures. But you don't want to hear the adventures.'

She didn't say anything.

'The thing about God,' said the Preacher, 'is that He only interested in those who eat and drink. That's in the Bible. After all. You *got* to eat and drink to please God. That's the Bible. Drink his wine and eat his bread. But this is what happen: mankind got too numerous, and then there was a choice. The choice was: humanity could die in famine and go to God, or it could use its clever to save itself, and never eat no more, and leave God behind. It chose the latter. That's why we're here. That's why things *are* the way they *are*. Now Neocles, maybe he set up a new god. A foodless, breadless, unwined god. But maybe he never found his time to do that.'

Later Preacher said: 'You beware revenge, Issa, you know?'

That word woke her up, at least a little.

'I know you're going to want to revenge, and to hurt Abda, and his people. That's natural. But you must not. Whatever they crimes, you must not. You know why you must not?'

She looked at him.

'You must not,' he said, 'because you don't know how. I don't say it be wrong – it's not wrong. But you need to know how to do it, and you don't know how to do it. You maybe try to stab him, say, and miss, or scratch him. Then he'd snuff you out. How would that help anything?'

She digested this. It was probably true.

'Keep in your thoughts,' said Preacher, standing and readying himself to go off. '*Everything* are supposed to be different to the way they are, now. That's the one thing to keep in your mind at all time.'

He went. She never saw *him* again.

That very evening Galla came to find her. 'He wants you,' she said. 'He wants both of us together.' She took her by the hand, like a sister, and together they climbed to the big house. 'It's just to make point, you know,' she said. Issa could think of no reason at all why Galla would want to reassure her, but here she was, trying to diminish Issa's dread. It was almost humane. 'Like a dog pissing its territorial marker,' Galla said. 'Just to – you know.'

'How is his willy?'

'Oh it's fine. It got a scrape on the end, nothing at all. He wouldn't be going to stick you with it if it really hurt.'

Afterwards, when she looked back on her time, Issa might have wished she had decoupled her hand from Galla's then and there and made a dash for freedom. To have made her stand against passivity, straight off, instead of being chucked into it. Not that the experience with Abda was especially bad; which is to say, it was no worse than any of the previous occasions: she lay, in effect, in Galla's lap; the other woman wrapped her legs about Issa's legs, and the two reclined on cushions, whilst Abda brought his bull-weight to bear on them both. His cock went up her hard, for as Galla had said he was looking to make a point. He came quickly, too, and then he stood back from her, and his member did its little shuddery drawbridge lowering thing. Then he went out, and Galla hugged her a little, and finally she went away too.

Issa was alone.

She lay on the bed, and thought about things. Or she didn't think about things. It was exactly the same. Finally she had a sort of vision, the kind that comes to a person halfway between sleeping and awakening. Those stiff, stacked rising polygons, they were buildings. Blocks and square-edged columns, or table legs without a tabletop. Or casino chips balanced high in piles that did not totter. And here was the wide green rectangle in the middle. New York, she thought.

She got up and made her way through the darkness of the house. One room was full of people drinking, and the light fell out of the open doorway on the floor like a tombstone knocked over. She skirted that. Here was the kitchen, and the door wasn't locked. Issa went in, and found al-Schawarma drunk as a stone, lying with his flung arm for a pillow on the ceramic flagstones of the floor. His other arm stuck straight out, along the floor, like a salute. An empty bottle lay on the tiles beside him, mocking his posture with its long neck. What was clear to Issa was that this was a special night. Things would not be good after this night. She went through to the back entrance, and it was shut tight, but the key was in its keyhole. It looked as if the lock was smoking a pipe. She turned the key, and opened the door, and there was the night, all its stars, and she thought: each one is a window into a New York apartment. The evening air wobbled with warmth and moisture and the wheezy sound of night insects. To the right, the rocky cranium of Beard hill blocked out a portion of the sky. Down to the left, over the roofs of the chicken house, was one plastered wall, like the ghost of a wall in the light of a quarter-moon. She went down there, and looked, and soon enough she discovered a dufflebag, or pile of old clothes bundled together, or perhaps a heap of earth, that had been left by the wall. Except for a single spread-finger hand that visibly protruded, like a star, it could have been a large bag, or a bundle of clothes. She trit-trotted down to the wall. This one was Mam Anna. Ten metres further along, near where the garden door was, lay another tangle of shadows. That would be Rageh.

The trick with any big decision is to *finesse* it. Don't force it. Turn your face away and the decision has made itself.

She went back into the kitchen, and locked the inner door. Because she had no animus against al-Schawarma, she dragged him by his heels out through to the back, to leave him under the sky. It wasn't easy, because he was large and she small. But she managed it. Then she went back inside again, wedged a chair under the handle of the door between the kitchen and the hallway, such that anybody coming from the rest of the house into the kitchen would find their way blocked. Then she opened the kitchen windows. She gathered combustible materials and piled them on the stove. She poured cooking oil over them, and laid rags out in several directions. She went to the fridge. It sat there, enormous, sat on a stone shelf. It was like a god, from the old pagan days, humming to itself its holy hum, all day and all night, and all of it pure. Singing of other worlds than these. A utopian drone. She summoned her resolve and pulled on the handle. The great door swung wide, and its seal between warm and cold broke. The timbre of the hum shifted, went down a semitone. Cold air spilled down upon her. This is what the air of heaven will be like. After the baking heat of life heaven will be as cool as a chilled silk cloth drawn over the body. It stands to reason that heaven is a fridge of vast size, to keep souls preserved at their best for eternity. And its waste heat is piped down a silver chute the diameter of the sun, studded with amethysts and sapphires, all the way down to hell. Those souls who are cruel, and murder and despoil must bake for ever in the overspill heat of hell; but those who are good walk in landscape of cool food for ever and for ever: eggs cooked hard with the shells chipped away, the most perfect whiteness. Jars of many colours. Crisp green salad leaves, more perfect than banknotes. Issa would have prayed, if she could remember a prayer. She thought of all the times she had talked with the Preacher; but he never said prayers, and had never taught her any ritual speech.

She didn't have too much time. So she pulled out what she was looking for: a litre bottle of water, cold as gemstones to the touch, and with little pure watery carbuncles all around its neck and torso. Then she took two tins of Virgin Beer and a carton of milk. There was a drawer in the corner crammed with old plastic bags, white and orange, the logos scuffed and rubbed to illegibility. She took one of these and put the drinks in it. The handles stretched when she tried to hold it, so she put the bag in another bag, and – for good luck – put that inside a third bag.

She wondered whether she ought to close the fridge door, or whether it was better to leave it open. She closed it.

Then she turned the electric cooker ring on, heating the piled combustibles. She took the backdoor key with her, locking up when she was outside. She smelt smoke as she went by the open windows to the wall, but saw no flames. After she'd scrambled up and over the wall, and hopped down the other side, she began to wonder if she hadn't done it properly. But down the dark road, and looking behind her, she saw a blur of shining orange. Soon enough the shouts and cries of men were carried down the sounding board of the hillside to her. She was out of the village altogether, walking down the road and miles from the house, but she stopped and looked back. By now the fire was clearly visible against the dark sky, red and yellow, orange and tan, like stained glass in motion.

She walked for a long time, and it felt like an excursion. She walked until the glow of the burning fire was no longer visible behind her. The sun came up. The journey stopped feeling like an excursion and began to feel like a chore. The day was bright, and there was enough sunlight to mean she could walk pretty much continually. But she got worn out anyway, and had to take more rest-stops than she liked, especially through the afternoon. Not as healthy as she might be. The worst of it was the weariness that afflicted her arms. As her arm grew tired from carrying the bag of drinks, she shifted the burden to the other arm; and as that grew tired and she shifted it back. But soon enough both limbs were on fire with fatigue.

That night she slept at the base of a broken concrete wall, overspread by an intermittent ceiling of leaves. It was an abandoned roadside shrine to Neocles, but the icon was gone, and the shrine as a whole had been allowed to fall into disrepair.

She dreamed of New York. All the buildings were towering, massy fridges: blocky and sacred. In the dream she wandered through deserted streets, and the buildings all around her murmured to themselves.

The next day dawned clear and grew very hot very quickly: early autumn weather. She started as soon as her hair had warmed up, swinging the plastic sack at her side. The bright blue sky, the wide, hill-rich land. Only cicadas disturbed the silence. She heard a vehicle barrelling down the road from behind her: the noise alerted her a good time before it came into view. Prompted by the sound, Issa wondered if Abda had sent people out looking for her. As soon as she thought how foolish it had been of her not to have thought of it before, she got off the road, and went up into the hills to her right. But the climb was tiring, and she wrung her ankle on an unsteady stone as she climbed, so she couldn't go on, and was forced to take cover behind a thornbush. The car came through, by and by, and followed the curve of the road downhill with a loud *rear-ear-ear* noise. Then it was gone. Eventually the quiet settled again, and only the cicadas remained. She listened to the staccato trill for a long time.

After that she stayed away from the road. But the going was tough on the uneven ground. Her ankle flared with pain whenever she put too much weight on it. She got up the hill, and started off in the general direction of the sea, stopping to take sips from the water bottle when she grew thirsty. Slow, slow and painful. Come nightfall she had to lie down in the open, and it was very cold. Why hadn't she stolen more clothes from the house? Through the night she dozed, woke, dozed, woke again. In the morning her limbs were stiff and painful. She wanted to get going at once, but she was too sluggish and underpowered to move. Rather than wait for the sun to power her, she decided to drink some of the milk, and use the food energy to go. But when she unscrewed the bottle, it smelt foul. She drank a mouthful, and then forced another mouthful down, but it wasn't pleasant. As the sun disengaged itself gingerly from the eastern mountain jags, she decided to try the beer instead. Her assumption was that beer was another kind of food drink, like milk. She cracked the lid, as she had seen Abda himself do on many occasions; but instead of giving her access to a drink the whole tin exploded in foam. She screamed and instinctually flung the grenade away. Straight-away she rebuked herself, and crawled after the thing. It had fallen between stones and was pumping foam like cum in gushing spurts. She plucked it from the ground, held it up-right, and watched the strange cream of its content subside. Her first sip filled her mouth only with foam; but with the second she got some fluid, bitter and bite-y from the bubbles. She swallowed it, and got a second and a third down. Then, she sat and waited for energy to come to her, idling the time by trying to work out how to replace the ringpull to preserve the rest of the liquid.

Energy didn't come. Instead her stomach roiled, and boiled, and soon enough she had vomited out everything she had drunk. The sour milk and beer came scorching back up her throat, but afterwards she felt immediately better with an empty gut.

She lay in the open, spreading her hair, and feeling very sorry for herself. The nausea went away eventually, and the sun perked her blood a little, and soon she was able to go on her way, limping only a little. She left the milk and the opened beercan behind her; but she took the as yet unopened tin, and washed her mouth with the water.

She spent all morning climbing a prominence, resting, climbing, and was rewarded at the top with a fine view down to a broad lake. The rim of the waterland was crusted with signs of human habitation. Across the water, in the V of the horizoning hills, she could see through to a glimpse of the sea.

She was woken up by two men; and she jumped from sleep in a panic, thinking they were from Abda. But they were just wanderers, their long black hair dusty, plastic bags for socks poking up out of fat plastic shoes. One had close-set blue eyes in a wrinkled dark brown face. The other's face was longer, smoother and darker. 'Didn't mean to startle you,' said blue-eyes.

'You didn't,' said Issa, sitting up and clutching her bag to her. 'I knew you were there.'

'I'm Coco,' said the first of these men, squatting down with his back to the morning sun and separating the strands of his hair with his right hand. 'This is – he don't speak at all, or he hasn't to me, so I'm not sure of his name. But I call him Pal.'

'Pleased to meet you.'

'You got an accent there, I'd say,' said Coco.

'Everybody has one, I would imagine,' said Issa.

'True, true. What's in the bag?'

'My stuff,' said Issa.

'We're not going to rob you,' said Coco. 'That's not what *we* do.'

'I'm glad.'

Coco patted her elbow, and pointed. 'See?' She looked in the direction of his gesture. A hundred metres distant, standing completely still, was a long-haired cow. 'It broke from a farmer's compound over lakeway,' said Coco. 'It's a hairy beast, don't eat nothing. It's only the wealthiest farmers can afford to give their animals food – that's for the luxury market. Makes the meat more tender and delicious, they say. This beast was for the middle classes. You know what middle classes are?'

'Yes,' said Issa, although if she'd been pressed for a definition she would have had a hard time.

'Merchants and fly-commuters, down in Trabzon. People too proud to realize they're poor like us.' Pal made a grunting noise at this, presumably in agreement. '*Everybody's* as poor as us,' said Coco. 'Save only the super-wealthy, and they're so different they're hardly human any more. Everybody's poor as us, only some don't realize it. People in Trabzon, merchants and fly-commuters – half of them *have hair*, you know? They could live on the sun like we do. But they take food for the status. Only for the status of it! I could believe, easily, they don't even like the taste. Light-reared cattle is supposed to be pretty tough and flavourless, see. But they slaves to their status, see.'

'Slaves,' said Issa. She was feeling her sore ankle with her left hand.

Coco gave her a canny look. 'You've got it, sister.'

'Why are you after the cow?'

'It's stupid,' said Coco, looking at the beast. 'It don't need food save sun, but it need water, and it don't know it. There's no water here, so soon enough it will die.'

'And then what? Will you eat it?'

Coco's laugh was instantaneous. Pal laughed too, belatedly, with chunky little gasps of amusements. 'Not that! Not I!'

'Why, then?'

'To sell it, of course. For money, of course!'

'Oh,' she said.

'And where are you going? You're not a wanderer, I'd say, by the look of you. Village girl, eh?'

Issa looked at him.

Coco stood up. 'It's crazy to be up in the hills like this, a crazy location for a village girl. You should stay on the road.'

'*You're* not on the road,' she pointed out.

'We're following the cow!'

'I am about my own business,' she said. 'Why are *you* doing the work, though?'

'Why us? Who else?'

'Women, of course.'

'Oh! We're not like most men. We're hard workers! We have a *cause*.'

'I see.' Issa got to her feet. Her ankle still hurt. Standing, she was the same height as either of the men.

'Oh you're tall!' said Coco. 'You want to help us? You could definitely help with the cow!'

'OK,' she said. 'But my ankle is hurting. I can't run.'

'Oho!' said Coco. 'If we can't rely on our ankles, then on what can we rely? Is it both your ankles? Ankles, plural?'

'Just the one.'

'You'll be fine. Come along.'

The three of them approached the cow. The beast eyed them placidly. From a distance Issa had thought she had a sense of it, but coming closer it loomed much larger than her depth perception had led her to expect. It was, she thought, simply *too big* for an animal. Why did it need to be so big? 'Will it bite me?' she asked.

'You've never seen a cow before, that's obvious,' said Coco. 'It won't bite you. It don't eat. Look at its hair.' Pal coughed at this, as though Coco were omitting the truth. But there was something fascinating, to Issa, in the creature: the unhollow heft of it, the unsettling combination of nobility and imbecility in his eyes. The giant folded purses of its outsticking ears. The double curl of its nostrils, branching in two plump arches from its snout like the top of a Greek column.

Pal danced forward and slapped the beast's rump, and Coco began hallooing and hallooing, wordlessly. Sluggishly the cow lurched forward and trotted cumbrously away. They followed. If it looked like the cow was going to stop, or when it stumbled on the uneven upward slope, Coco would dance, shrieking and flapping his arms to get the cow to move on. Issa, hauling her bag with her, found it hard to keep up. There was a problem with her energy levels, but she did her best to push through.

After a while they stopped, and Issa shared her water bottle with the two men. 'Where are you down from, then?' Coco asked her. 'Livera, is it?'

'Is that the village? I don't know the name of the village.'

'Up the road. They had some trouble, night before last. So I heard.'

'How did you hear that?'

Coco looked terribly knowing, and winked his eye. 'That stone?' He pointed. It looked like a regular stone: grey granite shaped like a two-metre wide bald head, with a ruff of green weeds growing behind and around it. 'That stone is a door to a magic kingdom. Pull it aside and walk down the stairs to a land of— No, I'm only joking.' Pal was laughing big, silent guffaws, like a man choking on a fishbone. 'I have a Fwn,' said Coco, proudly, with heavy emphasis on the pronoun. He brought out a scuffed, battered old-model device.

'How do you have one of those?' Issa asked. 'Are you a Waali?'

'Me a Boss? The idea! My sweet flower, I have this Fwn to put an *end* to Waalis.' He put it away again. 'So, you, you don't know anything about a fire?'

'I used to have a Fwn,' said Issa.

'Oho, *you* were a Waali, is it?'

'When I was younger, I lived in a town where everybody had them.'

Pal started up his conniption-fit silent laugh at this fantastika, and Issa blushed and grew quiet. 'Well,' she said, getting up again. 'Where are we taking this cow, then?'

'Not far now,' said Coco. 'That ledge, and over.'

'Over?'

'Sure. Live cow won't do us any good. Live cow can be tag-traced. Dead cow, all chopped up – well that can be traced, too, but who's going to the bother of tag-tracing a stringy old burger? Come on.' He stretched his arms, and groaned. 'If *we* lived on hard food, we'd have the energy for continuous physical exercise,' he said. 'Like the workers of the golden age. They were strong as He-Man, and could work without respite all day and all night like Prometheus! Heliophages like us are puny by comparison.'

Issa didn't know the word, but didn't ask what it meant. 'Come on, then,' she said.

So they ran at the cow again, disturbing its placid standing-around once again. They slapped it, and shrieked at it, and got it moving. Pal threw flints at it. He had a knack for finding sharp-edged stones that, evidently, really stung the big beast. The idiot-savant look of its bovine eye took on a long-suffering look of accusation. After the third or fourth strike, Cow kicked both his back legs up like a double-punch, and lurched towards a line of low bushes. Issa didn't realize that this line marked the edge of a precipice until the beast dropped suddenly, its wide chest giving the rim an audible knock. The cow mooed, struggled, its back legs danced up again. Issa was struck, as if for the first time, by the shape of those legs: the chunk of muscle at the top, the walking-stick-tip of the hoofs, the crick in the line of the leg like a knight's move in chess. Then the whole creature toppled forward and slid from view. Holloing with joy, Coco rushed forward; Pal too. Issa came more gingerly, still clutching her bag. Peering over the lip made a tingle go all through her torso, and filled her stomach with prickles of dread. It was a long way down, not sheer but hideously steep, and the cow's passage had left a visible trail. At the bottom Issa could see two individuals pushing a handcart up towards the beast's carcass.

'Straight down? Round there, I think,' said Coco. He set off immediately, twenty metres along the cliff edge and down into a gully – still so steep that he slid down on his backside amongst a fuzz of dislodged grit. Pal went after, and Issa, despite misgivings, didn't feel she could stay behind. Getting down was alarming, but soon enough she was there.

Coco introduced her to the two pulling the handcart: women both, one called Issa (like her), the other a bindi-marked old woman, her skin tan brown and wrinkly as bark, called Sudhir. She seemed to be in charge. 'Your name?'

'Issa,' said Issa.

'*Her* name is Issa,' said Sudhir. 'Try again.'

'It's a coincidence that her name is Issa. Because my name is Issa also. It's not an uncommon name.'

'Not good enough,' said Sudhir. Issa did not understand her suspicious hostility. 'Pick another name.'

'Leah,' said Issa. It was out before she had time to think of it. And once she had said it, she felt a rush of shame to her chest and face, a feeling that she had, with horrible finality, somehow blasphemed.

Sudhir glared at her.

'She's OK,' said Coco, stepping forward. 'She shared her water with us.'

'Did she share her private parts with you too?'

'No!' said Coco, wrongfooted. 'It's not like that. I just think she's a good kid. We could use her.'

'And you just *happened* to bump into her, up on the high ground?'

'You have trust issues, Sudhir,' said Coco, chuckling. 'She's fine. She can come with us.'

'I don't know if I want to go with you,' said Issa.

'That's a little better,' snapped Sudhir. 'But still lame. Go back to your espionage master and tell him to train you up better.'

'I'm no spy!' said Issa, surprised how shocked she was by the accusation.

'You're no spy, but you share water with my people unbidden and you're not sure of your own name. Go on, fuck off.' The other Issa had strung a rope harness around the cow carcass, and now the three others joined her in order to haul the beat onto the handcart. Issa had no energy in her body at all. She watched, silently.

'I'm sorry,' said Coco, once this task had been performed. 'Sudhir's the cadre leader. Maybe in another life! For you *are* very pretty.'

'Where shall I go?' Issa asked. It felt like some supporting strut, vital to the integrity of her inner world, had cracked and sagged. She didn't know what, or why. It surely was not that these strangers, having been friendly, were now shunning her.

It could hardly be anything so trivial. But what else *could* it be? She felt ready to cry. She no longer felt like a brave traveller, heading out alone along an inviting path. She felt like an abandoned kid.

The four were pulling shoulder harnesses on, preparatory to heaving the cow away. 'Wait,' Issa said. 'Don't leave me.'

'Fuck off, kid,' grunted her namesake.

'Where will I go?'

'Find a spring in the mountains and live off water and sunlight,' was Sudhir's advice.

'Longlake is just down there,' said Coco, pointing. When Sudhir, in harness next to him, slapped the back of his head he said: 'What! What? We can't stop her from going to Longlake, surely.'

'Go straight on to Trabzon, why don't you,' said Sudhir, not looking at her. 'Blag yourself onto somebody's raft, and try sealife. Just don't pester *me* again, or I'll fucking rip your hair out, fistful by fistful.' She yelled a mark, and all four of them pulled together. Issa was trembling, she didn't know why. She sat down on the gravelly dirt and watched the handcart haul down the track and round the bend.

The sun went down over the screeslope and the flank of the hills. Something – the sunset or some other panic – threw into the sky the loose stones of many birds. They made the friction-noises with their beaks. After flocking, and circling, they eventually settled again.

It got cool in the valley, and then cold. Issa was torpid. This was solitude. Only one bird remained, and this was not a real bird, this was a metaphorical bird. Its name was misery and it nested down for the night, inside her breast.

Issa buried herself as best she could into a bank of bushes. The leaves were scratchy, but after some wriggling she got comfortable enough. Then, sipping a little from her water bottle, and just lying there, she fell asleep. She woke with the cold, fell asleep again. Woke, dozed, woke. At some point in the midst of all this she had a conversation with herself. 'Where will I go?' she had asked the others. Sudhir had said: To Trabzon, to sea, to oblivion for all I care. She asked herself the same question. Where will I go?

New York.

What is New York?

I don't know.

How do I get there?

I don't know.

Where am I now?

I don't know.

She drifted into a state between waking and sleeping where the mantra throbbed in her mind I *have* nothing I *am* nowhere, I *have* nothing I *am* nowhere. She was woken by a mountain hare, sniffing at her face. When she opened her eyes, and gasped, the creature leapt backwards with a scuffle of grit and was gone.

She extricated herself from the hedge. It was very early in the morning, the sky pale but the sun not yet visible over the tops of the hills. She was shivering with cold, and no matter how hard she rubbed her arms and legs she couldn't seem to get any warmth into them. She needed to get up and move around, but a massive inertia, deep inside her bones, prevented her. She could not move. She lacked all energy. 'Perhaps if I open the tin of beer in the bag I am carrying,' she thought, 'and drank it. Perhaps it would work like hard food, and give me the energy to get up and go.' But she knew that on three days of empty stomach the beer would go down and come straight back up again. With a monumental effort she got halfway to her feet, moved into a more open spot and sat on the ground.

The sun would come over the lip of the valley soon enough.

She looked up. The moon, almost full, was visible with preternatural clarity against the early day sky. It looked imprinted upon the blue like a seal of official authentication for the sky.

She watched.

The line of sunlight moved down the mountainside, slow, slow, superslow. Issa's shivers had subsided. She watched the coming of the light with a mix of feelings. At first she was aware of impatience: *come along, hurry up*. Then she fell into a mood of rebuking herself: if only I had stayed on top of the hill, the sun would even now be soaking into my blood. Why did I come down into this valley? What fool's errand did I think I was on? But, when she looked at the moon, those feelings went away. She began to feel a weird, potent sensation of *peace* slide into her soul. Before these last few days she had never been alone, not ever, in her life. There had always been somebody with her. It seemed a crowded sort of past. And it seemed to her now that there is nothing fearful in solitude. The moon is a goddess, and this is her song: I *have* nothing I *am* nowhere.

Presently the sun touched Issa's head. She closed her eyes.

When she had enough energy she continued walking. She followed the road down out of the valley, and soon enough, with numerous rests, she came to human habitation. The road led down towards a lake, small visible sections of which were bright in the distance. But before Issa came to any buildings, she came upon people. The further down the road she went, the more people there were. Longhairs packed the roadside, or gathered in crowds on the east-facing hillsides – hundreds of them. The sight of so many people was oppressive. Some of them called after her, with questions, or lewd suggestions, but most simply lay there placidly. She passed a few structures: concrete sheds, and some walled spaces, all filled with longhair humanity: all the roofs teeming, all the doorways, longhairs in chairs or prone on the ground, their hair fanned out. Then, suddenly, she was in the town itself. Flat paved roads, buildings on all sides, and some bald-headed people in fine clothes moving jostlingly through the crowd. Turning a corner, Issa came upon a view of the lake – a great perfectly horizontal sheet of water, smooth as plastic, fitting with a pleasing neatness exactly into its slot amongst the hills. Away to the left an island was visible, with two sharptop towers upon it like rockets ready to launch, and a white temple.

The streets of the town ran down to the water, but the way was blocked by a barricade, with armed guards looking blankly about, or using their rifles as props, seating themselves on the stock and the barrel jammed into the ground. Issa rested on a step – it was in shadow, and so unoccupied – to observe the set-up. There was a gate. Various well-dressed, short-haired or no-haired people came and went, some displaying passes, some simply waving confidently at the guards. At this, the gate was opened and the people passed. Longhairs lounged, and gazed, but none of that kind went through.

Somebody came and sat next to her. 'Hello,' said this stranger. 'What's in your bag?'

'Nothing,' said Issa. 'An empty water bottle. I was hoping to fill it in the lake. It *is* freshwater, the lake?'

'Good luck with that!' scoffed the stranger. 'My name is Roxan.'

'Mine is Issa.'

'Pleased to meet you,' said Roxan. 'New here?'

'Yes.'

'Well, you might get past the barricade: you're pretty. But you'd have to shave your head.'

Issa looked at the woman. She was a few years older than herself, with wide-spaced, clever-looking eyes. But her face was quite badly scarred: two long downward lines on the left side, and scuff marks, buckles and weals in the skin on the right. The skin, drawn tightly over the cheekbones, revealed where the bone underneath had been chipped and pocked. It was in Issa's mind to ask: *What happened to you?* But that seemed too personal a question for somebody she had only just met. So instead she said: 'I wouldn't last very long with a bald head.'

'That's right.'

They sat together for a while, watching people come and go. At one point, a policeman came up the hill towards them. He was carrying a long staff, which he used to clear away a dozen or so longhairs lolling on the sunlit side of the street. He spun the stick about his head like a Jedi, clearly very impressed with himself; but the action was nothing more sophisticated than battery – the noise of wood connecting with the stone walls, or with the more yielding heads of the people. Some shunted or shuffled away; some yelled or cried out. After they had all fled, the policeman sauntered back down the hill to the barricade.

'They don't want us going down to the lake?'

Roxan ducked her head. 'Listen, Issa, if you really want to go down to the lake, you can go round the shore. It's all fenced, to discourage us, of course. But crowds will push the fence over when they get thirsty enough, and you can usually get down to the waterside. They'll come by soon enough to chase you away, and then you'll need to be lively enough to dodge the bullets. But you've more chance there than here.'

'Why don't they want us down by the water?'

'Cluttering the space up for the nice people – people with

money, and their nice lakeside apartments.' Roxan ran a fore-finger up and down one of the vertical scars in her face. 'They don't want us anywhere near here. Don't want us within a hundred miles of here. They'd like us to fuck off up into the highlands. But there's no water up there. So we come down here. Every now and again, when the mayor can get hold of a Walker she'll try and clear the town of all the longhairs. *Then* there's lots of shrieking, and some bloodletting. But she can't get hold of a Walker very often. She has to borrow it from Trabzon.'

'What's a Walker?'

Roxan looked hard at the girl. 'You're straight off the boat, aren't you, my truelove? D'you *really* not know what a Walker is, or are you jesting with me?'

'I don't see why I'm not allowed to go down to the lakeside!' said Issa, growing annoyed. 'By what right do they prevent me?'

'Right.' said Roxan. 'Are you for real?'

'I'm only saying.'

'*Fair* is Spartacist talk.' This was said guardedly, with Roxan peering closely into Issa's face. Issa stared back, ingenuously. 'I'm thirsty,' she said.

'We're all thirsty,' said Roxan. 'But what can you do?'

Issa didn't like the sound of that. After a while she said: 'I have a tin of beer in my bag.'

Roxan opened her eyes wide. 'Where did you get that?'

'Out of a fridge.' Issa read Roxan's expression as disbelief, and so brought out the tin to prove her possession of it.

'You're either very canny or very foolish,' said Roxan. 'To show me that.'

'Maybe if I give it to the guards on the gate, there, they'd let me pass?'

'Maybe they'd just take it, and beat you back with a stick.'

'But I would give it to them as a deal,' Issa explained. 'The deal would be: I'd give them the tin of beer and in return they'd let me through.'

'Deal,' repeated Roxan, colourlessly. 'You *actually* a holy fool? Or is this some complicated pretence on your part?'

'I don't understand.'

'Why should they honour any deal? Particularly with a longhair? Put it this way: if they took the beer from you and then refused to let you through, what could you do?'

Issa thought about this. 'I'm being naïve.'

'You're an odd mix of clever and dumb,' agreed Roxan. 'And what about me? You don't know me. Why wouldn't I simply take your tin, when you showed it to me?'

Issa thought about this, too. 'I see what you mean. That was naïve of me too. But you *didn't* simply steal it from me.'

'No,' said Roxan.

'Why not?' Issa asked, simply.

Roxan put her hands into her hair, and pulled the strands out tight, like zither strings. Then she let it go. 'You see these scars, here?' Issa nodded. 'I'll tell you about these scars. They mean I have no love for the rich.'

'I think I see,' said Issa, gravely, although it wasn't really true.

'Well,' said Roxan, 'you have honoured me with your trust. And if it's the trust of a holy fool, well that's an even greater honour. It would demean me to betray you. So here's what I suggest: I know a man called the Nudnik. His name is Sergei, but we call him the Nudnik. He'll buy the beer from us, I think. And if he gives us a little money, and we can buy a little water – why not? It's your beer, so it'll be your money and your water. But perhaps, if you're truly a holy fool, you'll share with me.'

Roxan led Issa up through a series of antique, narrow streets,

315

bent with odd little twists and curves, like rickets. The sunlit side of each street was crammed with longhairs, so they moved through the cool of the shady side. Many of the buildings they passed were fortified, their doors blocked in with metal plates, barcodes of metal rods covering the windows. Most of the other houses were in varying states of dereliction. People thronged the roofs. They passed round a corner and up a staircase of wood so old and crumbly it reminded Issa of biscuit. Through an open door. Inside it was a dark, lengthy room, brushstrokes of sunlight on the floor at the far end where a shuttered window let in a little light. There was hardly any furniture and the place reeked of birdshit. But it was inhabited: for a man with a very strange hairstyle – a great sticky-up crest of hair, like a circle of metal embedded vertically right through his skull – was lying in the corner. Who would wear their hair like that? Neither enough surface area to make for good sun-eating, nor the ostentatiously shaved cranium of the high-status, hard-food man.

'Here's a girl called Issa,' said Roxan. 'Has something to show you.'

'You're Sergei, then?' Issa asked.

'I'm in love with her already,' said the crest-haired man. His accent was heavy, as if he were chewing the words in his mouth as he spoke them. 'She doesn't think of me as a Nudnik. Uses my actual name!' He was lying on a messy tangle of sheets, and spoke to them without getting up.

'She's got a tin of beer,' said Roxan. 'Will you buy it?'

'And how did she obtain such a thing? Theft, is it?'

'There's only one way to get things in the world,' said Issa. 'It's just a question of whether the thieving is large-scale or small.' She was not happy with how squeaky and ordinary her voice sounded: how unlike a Preacher. But it was what it was. 'When a longhair steals it's theft. When a rich person steals it's—' And she wanted something to round the sentiment off grandly, but couldn't think of the best word.

'I see,' said Sergei, getting to his feet. 'You've picked up some Spartacist patter. Is that why you want me to buy your tin of beer? So you can turn a few cents over to the grand revolutionary reserves? Changing the world costs money, I suppose.'

'We're thirsty,' said Roxan.

'If you're thirsty, why not drink the beer?'

'You obviously don't know much about *beer*,' said Issa, unsure, actually, as to the status of the person she was speaking with.

At this Sergei began to laugh. 'Little Spartacus,' he told her, 'I spent my twenties *swimming* in beer! I was pickled in the stuff, like an onion. Of course, not everybody likes onion. I don't touch that stuff any more.'

'We only want a few cents,' said Roxan. 'Or we'd swap it for, let's say, twice the quantity of water.'

The Nudnik continued, supine: 'Well if you're thirsty, why not say so? You're welcome to drink with me. There are some bugs in my garden you can eat, too. Stay. We'll make a little bower of bliss for ourselves.'

Roxan was silent for a few seconds, and then laughed brashly. 'Oh you're not interested in *my* scratched-up old face, Nudnik.'

'I love you both. But I love you *more*, Roxy,' said Sergei. 'Look at your new friend, the Little Spartacus: she's so pretty, and so tall, she might be a rich kid from Stanbul who's grown her hair out for a lark. But you're the real deal, Roxy. You're the irresistible lure of disenfranchisement.'

'You want to stay here, Issa?' Roxan asked. 'You got somewhere else you'd rather be?'

'New York,' said Issa.

The two of them were silent for a while.

'The city?' Roxan asked.

'Hey,' put in Sergei. 'You want to go to *New York*?'

'Yes,' said Issa.

'How you going to get there, Little Spartacus?'

Issa hadn't worked that out yet. 'Fly?' she hazarded.

Roxan and Sergei both laughed, as perfectly synchronized as if they had rehearsed it. 'You spread your hair in a big wind, and away you go!' said Sergei.

'There are jets and geldarm, gelderms,' Issa pointed out. 'Jets.'

'You gather a chip topped with money, shave your head and buy some rich-woman clothes, maybe they'll sell you a ticket,' said Roxan.

Issa saw what she meant. 'I'll find a way,' she insisted.

'*Why* do you want to go to New York?' Sergei asked.

She hadn't even asked herself this question before that moment. She thought about it. 'It is,' she said, the thought striking her with potency only as she put it into words, 'my city.'

Sergei laughed again. 'Good for you, little Spartacist! You claim that city for the revolution!'

Issa stayed. Sergei, as she came to understand over the days that followed, was the son of a moderately wealthy Putingrad businessman. 'Enough money to keep us comfortable, though not enough for me to ski through life,' Sergei put it. 'I was supposed to learn a trade. It's cut-throat, though. Cut-throat in the sense of competitive. But cut-throat in the sense of destroying people. Anyway, I rebelled.'

Roxan and Issa slept in an annexe room on a bed of blankets. Sergei made his sexual advance that first night, but was perfectly unruffled in the face of Issa's rejection. It occurred to her that this was his thing, actually; that he had made rejection his great life's project. 'I probably wouldn't have known what to do with you if you'd said yes,' he confided, settling back with his snuff pipe. 'But I had to try, you know?'

Issa shrugged.

She and Roxan slept wrapped about one another. Roxan was affectionate, but Issa didn't mind that. By day, she sat in the sun, and drank as much as she liked, and listened to Sergei go through his repetitious life-story. It was interesting the first time he told it, dull the tenth. 'I started hanging out with the Putingrad Spartacists – some religious folk, some driven by ideology, and some honest-to-goodness Black Sea longhairs. There's a problem in the Spartacist movement, though. Because they despise the rich, and they want to destroy them. But their kind of revolution needs money, and so they're compelled to fraternize with the wealthy – or the moderately wealthy, like me.'

'So you're a Spartacist?'

Sergei's head-shake was lazy and prolonged. 'I left the movement after Triunion.'

'Why?'

'Do you have to ask?'

Issa thought about this. 'Yes,' she said, seriously.

'Because of the bloodshed. So many dead! Because I understood then what I hadn't before, that Spartacism *depends* upon the bloodshed. The rich have all the advantages but one, and that one is, numbers – it's the longhairs who have the numbers. It's like an antique battle, where you throw wave after wave of sacrificial soldiery at the enemy.' A lazy draw on the pipe. 'Tell you what. That's very – not me,' he said.

On occasion, to alleviate the tedium, and if there was enough sunshine to give her the energy, Issa wandered about Longlake. The outskirts were swarming with longhairs. Most were rootless, shuffling round and round or simply lying there.

Some fragments of incipient community were visible here and there. A few enterprising women were selling water out of this house or that, with male, or sometimes female, muscle to protect the resource. The properties were in various states of dereliction.

On the lakeside of the fence was a resort for the reasonably off. It was not especially high-class, as Issa could see, peering through the slicewire. One afternoon she saw a mob of long-hairs attempt to storm the main entrance: a hundred or so people pushing forward in an ill-defined way, accompanying their own motion with a series of whoops and holloahs. Nobody seemed to have initiated the movement; and nobody coordinated it. It happened spontaneously. A much larger body of longhairs, several thousand people, stood or sat, watching. In many ways Issa found this latter group even more interesting. Theirs was pure spectatorship: unengaged with the attempt at breaching the perimeter except, Issa presumed, in the opportunistic sense that if a breach was effected many of would hurry through to get to the water. But otherwise they lolled, observing with the purest, idle indifference.

The knot of people dashed at the guarded gate. Issa could see the faces of the guards on the far side, stark-eyed with panic. There were various hurryings to position; then the snip-snap of weapon fire. The first shots made no apparent impact on the press of people, and the crowd's collision with the gate made a loud crash and sent tremors up and down the fence. For a moment it looked as though the weight of people might simply push the barrier over. But it held. And on the far side the guards were aiming and discharging their firesticks. A police flitter, bright green, leapt over the farside roofs and plumped itself down on springy prongs on the police side of the fence. Its belly cracked open, and police tumbled free. In moments armed men were clotting behind the gate, focusing their weapons fire. And moments later the cohesion of the mob dissolved, and longhairs were scattering. After it was all over, Issa counted a dozen bodies.

The sight of these dead bodies did not disturb her; although she was a little disturbed at how little she was disturbed. They were human beings, after all. And now they were dead.

Roxan was more practical. 'They should have organized it better,' she said. 'There's no glory in stupidity. That's just giving the guards drill practice, that is.'

Sergei gave a disjointed, rambly lecture on what he called the real lost opportunity. 'A dozen martyrs – wasted,' he said. 'If they'd broken through, and filled their bellies on water, so what? But a dozen martyrs, wasted! Martyrs are gold. We don't even know their names.'

For the first week or so, Issa wondered what the milling, itinerant population of longhairs did for water at all. There was a black economy in the stuff, for those who could scrape together a few cents. The women – always women – queuing at the metal-barred-windows in amongst the derelict buildings; picking up bottle or beige-coloured water; or else little packets of hard food to help them through late pregnancy. But the majority of people, and all the men, lacked even a few cents. What did *they* drink? When it rained, people became frantic as fleas, and all manner of containers and plastic sheeting was brought out. But this went sour and dangerous in a day or so, and the long stretches of dry weather must surely parch people to death. Sergei, who received a stipend from his family, had water delivered in torso-sized plastic barrels, along with small boxes of hard food, though he ate very little. Issa drank in the morning and again in the evening; and Roxan drank even more frequently than that. But the others? The conclusion at which Issa arrived was that whilst some found spits and spots of water here and there, others, having come here lured by the prospect of lakewater, were driven away by the impossibility of access. What looked like a constant population was actually a continual turnover of new people. And of course, some must die. The numbers of longhairs was so great, milling or lounging, that natural wastage must produce many dozens, or perhaps hundreds of deaths daily.

'What do they do with the dead bodies?' she asked Sergei. He was stroking gel into his great plume of headhair, teasing it upwards with his fingers' ends.

'Collected by the waste agents,' said Sergei, dreamily. 'The law requires that they be held three days for family to collect them. Then the bodies are sold to farmers, who undertake to bury them in arable.'

'In what?'

'In fields, where hardfood is grown!' said Sergei, opening his eyes prodigiously wide. 'They fertilize. They are fertilizer.'

'I cannot stay here for very long,' said Issa. 'I cannot stay for ever.'

'I know,' said Sergei, wafting dotsnuff about through the air in front of his face. 'You must go to be Queen of New York.'

'I need to know the way.'

'West,' said Sergei, drifting off. 'West of here.' She thought him asleep, but he lurched awake, and blurted: 'Spartacism needs bodies to fertilize its revolution too! Spartacism is arable too!' And he laughed, in an unhinged manner, before drifting back to stupor.

West was vague; but it was better than nothing. Since flying was out of the question (and why had she even thought it possible? She was no bird!) she would have to walk. She could set out in the sunset direction, and ask for further direction as she proceeded.

Sergei was not always devoured by snuff-induced lassitude. Some evenings he roused himself, and went out. 'My pretty

322

girl,' he told Issa. 'I fully intend to show you that Spartacism's not the only game in town.'

'Are we going out?'

'I'm going to *take* you out!'

So she went with him, along a series of bafflingly tangled small roads, to a one-storey building. Judging by its tattered advertising paraphernalia this had, once upon a time, been a shop. This night it was lit with iWicks and filled with several dozen people. Sergei brought Issa in at the back of the audience. 'This is the weekly meeting of the Siblings of Islam,' he told her. She asked him: 'Is this your group?' 'Oh no,' he said, looking past her. 'But I like the way they're planning to build heaven on Earth. I like the way they plan to do so without resorting to the blood-soaked nihilism of the Spartacists.'

Several people came up to greet Sergei, and they seemed pleasant enough when he introduced them to Issa. Soon enough a woman stood on a chair and delivered a speech. Issa *mostly* followed what she was saying, despite her rapid delivery and a lot of unfamiliar vocabulary. She was talking about fasting, and about how fasting had always been a distinctive and central aspect of Islam – not merely during Ramadan, but at any time of the year. Mohammed taught that abstinence was an ever-shining sun of infinite virtue and invaluable soul-strength: it teaches the spirit moderation and willpower, and divine patience and modesty and selflessness. For by fasting, a Muslim feels the pains of deprivation in order to endure them patiently and so demonstrate love for God. No Muslim should fast upon 'Eid-ul-Futr, of course; or upon any Friday. But this did not mean that Muslims ought to *gorge* on hardfood on those days. It was enough to nibble a little clean earth, or take the vitamin supplements that even longhairs required. For the prophet specifically said: the worst thing a man can fill is his stomach. And he meant, it is better to fill the soul. Peace be on him.

Issa found all this interesting, as far as she could follow it, although it seemed short on specifics. When the speech was finished, and questions were solicited, she put up her hand. 'I am a stranger, and I apologize if my question is foolish. But what is your *practical* programme for undoing the injustices of the world?' Everybody was looking at her, and she felt, belatedly, self-conscious. A blush warmed her face from the inside. This prompted her to add: 'Last week I saw a thirst-maddened crowd press at the gate that leads down to the lakeside. The guards shot a dozen people dead.'

There were murmurs. The woman who had spoken said: 'It is a great wickedness, and it displeases God.'

'I do not understand,' Issa insisted, feeling a point of stubbornness inside her soul and pressing out against it, 'how *fasting* addresses the injustice.'

The woman said: 'Fasting is forced upon longhairs. But despite being forced on us, it can be voluntarily chosen. And when the rich and the hardfood-eaters embrace it too, and swallow the Bug, the whole world can join in a sacred union of fasting. When this happens, all wickedness and oppression will cease; the whole of creation will be a great Ramadan. The Bug is a gift of God. The inventor of this drug was a Muslim, you know. The West styles his name "Nick", but in truth he was called Nuh Kareem ibn Muhammed. He was a Cypriot Muslim.'

Issa said, 'Thank you' and said no more. But returning with Sergei to his place, she found herself cross. 'The rich will not willingly give up their food. That will never happen.'

'Isn't it a beautiful utopia, though?'

'I want something more practical.'

'You *are* a little Spartacus!' he laughed. 'Well, I won't give up. I'll convert you, don't worry. Or at least I'll *di*vert you from the violence of Spartacism. There are other games in town. Not all as God-oriented as the Siblings, there.'

The following day Roxan told Issa that she was pregnant. Issa was alarmed at how shocked she was by this news. 'Is it Sergei's?'

'Of course!'

This was enormous news. Issa didn't know what to say. 'What will you do?'

'I will need a great deal of hardfood. Not all at once, but over the period of the pregnancy, and afterwards, whilst I feed the little thing from my old breasts.'

Issa realized that, despite several conversations with the other women, back at the village, she had no idea what practicalities were involved in pregnancy. 'How will the baby grow its hair? Will you have to feed it the Bug?'

'It will get the Bug through my milk. But to make the milk I'll need a great supply of hardfood.'

'Sergei can get you the food.'

Roxan shook her head. 'He slept with me because I sleep with you. It was his way of getting close to you. He's not interested in having any children. He's not interested in anything to do with that.'

'Are you sure? Have you asked him?'

She shook her head again. 'I can't stay here. Not here in his place, not here in Longlake. There's nothing for me here.'

Issa digested this information. 'Where will you go?'

'I must have the hardfood. There's no helping that. Usually women plan to get pregnant, and work for a year or more to save the money they need. But I haven't planned anything for this.' Then, a little shyly, she added: 'I've heard that there are Social Missionaries who give out hardfood to pregnant women in Stanbul. So maybe I'll go there. Will you come?'

'Me?'

'Sure! It's closer to your New York, though I don't know by how much. We can keep each other company on the way, we can look out for one another. And maybe, when you see the baby, you might even want to . . . to stay with me?'

Issa pressed her lips very tightly together. 'Hmm.'

'We could be a family, you and I.'

Issa tried to think of a way to decline without hurting Roxan's feelings. But nothing immediately occurred to her. So she deferred that problem, and gave Roxan a hug. 'A baby!' she said. 'That's enormous news!'

That evening Sergei roused himself for the second day running: a record for him. 'Tonight,' he told her, 'you shall meet a different sort of apostle. A famous person, in this town. She holds court in this town once a month, and her gospel is directed only to longhairs.'

'Unlike the Muslims.'

'Oh, you only heard the Siblings! There are dozens of different Muslim groups and organizations, all with various plans and ideas with respect to the longhair problem.'

They were descending stone steps, the concrete edges rubbed smooth by long usage. The sun was going down amongst clouds the colour of oxygenated blood, and Issa's belly was full of water. 'I would say,' she put in, 'that there is no longhair problem. That what we are talking about is a problem of the rich.'

Sergei glanced over his shoulder at her, grinned, and said: 'I wouldn't want to contest the point with you, my little Spartacus. But Maguelone has a radical solution that cuts through all that.'

'Maguelone?'

'The woman we are going to hear speak. She is one of the most prominent Aquatics. She tours the region. I mean, she goes all along the Black Sea coast, and she even goes inland, sometimes.'

They walked for ten minutes, the crowd thickening around them until they were pushing through the midst of a big mass of longhairs, going through opened double-doors into a large hall well-lit with iWicks. 'She's popular?'

'Some longhairs call her the Redeemer.'

'So?'

Sergei opened his eyes wide as Issa had ever seen them. 'You don't understand?'

'What do you mean?'

'Redeemer is what they called Neocles. The man who invented the Bug, you know. That people are using the same word – well, it's like a *sacred* word, an important . . .' But the crowd heaved, and Sergei was pushed away from Issa. She could no longer hear him over the babble. In fact, the crush was uncomfortable. She was taller than most of those around her, which meant that she could use her elbows to lift herself out of the mêlée a little. But she didn't like it. The possibility of claustrophobic panic nibbled at the edge of her mind.

For a long time the crowd simply filled the hallspace, pulsing like a single, gigantic, breathing organ. Eventually, a very elderly woman emerged on a tiny wooden internal balcony, halfway up the far wall. This, Issa supposed, was Maguelone. She was extraordinarily ancient, perhaps as many as seventy years old, her skin wrinkled like a cabbage leaf, her hair white – white! – and down to her calves. The crowd grew, slowly, quiet. When she spoke, her voice was clear and strong, more singing than speaking: 'Fellows! Comrades! Longhairs!'

There were no interruptions, and no questions after she had finished.

'The future is the sea,' sang Maguelone, 'as the past was. Simple tools – a raft to sit on, a unit to turn salt to drinkwater and, every few weeks, a net or a piece of string to catch a slimy thing or a fishy thing from the water, and suck some minerals and vitamins in your mouths. What else do you need? Only your hair, the hair that defines you! Come to the sea – you will never be thirsty again, for you will be surrounded by water. Come to the sea – you will never be oppressed again, for the sea is freedom. Float away from the envy of the rich and the savageness of the soldiery, to the absolute freedom that is your birthright! Come to the sea – for I have had a vision! The Redeemer gave us our freedom, but he died before the whole of his gospel could be communicated. He set us free from food. He meant to set us free from the land as well! He was a Greek Christian from Kos. He *came* from the isles of Greece, jewels of the Mediterranean, the realm where sea defines land and land always faces the sea. If he had lived he would have said: take my great gift! Leave the hard and stony land to the rich. It will be their punishment! Remake yourselves as seafolk, and live on the sunlit blue roof that stands five miles above its ocean floor and that will never fall down to it. Remake yourselves as seafolk, and follow the great currents of the Atlantic and Pacific and Indian oceans. Remake yourselves as seafolk, and never set foot upon the land again!' At each reiteration of 'remake yourself' the crowd cheered, and she waited until the yelling died down before going on. With this final exhortation the whole hall, Issa included, banged their feet and shouted, in an unbroken oceanwave roar. But it was dark, and longhairs grow sluggish when the sun has set, so the boisterousness did not last long. When it subsided, Maguelone, visibly tired, rounded off with a practical peroration: 'You will need to band together and obtain money – for you will need to get yourself a raft, and a desal device, and you may want a pulse motor to propel you. But the expense is less onerous when it is divided between two dozen people, or four dozen, or a dozen

dozen, if you think big enough! Organize, and return to the sea!' She had to be helped off the rickety little balcony at the end of this, and the crowd, similarly exhausted, but buzzing, began to exit the hall.

It took a while for Issa to decant out, and she stood to one side as the crowd dispersed waiting for Sergei. Whilst doing so she saw, unmistakable in the crush, the bindi-forehead and crumpled face of Sudhir, the Spartacist leader she had met in the uplands. She was pushing through, angry-looking, and did not see Issa. But Sergei, coming up and clutching her in an embrace, did. 'I see you noticed your cadre leader, there?'

'You know her?'

'I told you. I have a history with the local Spartacist crew.'

'Then,' said Issa, disentangling herself from his grip and starting down the road, 'then you must know that I have no connection at all with the Spartacists here.'

'Oh I haven't been to any Spartacist meeting for several years,' he puffed, jogging to keep up with her. 'I'm not plugged in any more.'

'Well: then you must take it on trust from me. I'm no Spartacist. In fact, I was hoping you might take me along to one of their gatherings – like you did for the Siblings and the Aquatic lady.'

'But what did you *think* of her?' he said, eagerly. 'Wasn't she inspiring? To live at sea for ever, like Captain Nemo! Outflank the land-dwellers, let them gather as much wealth as they want! What did you *think*?'

They were making slower progress now, up a series of freakish ascents and turns: Sergei unused to exercise, Issa growing more torpid as the night settled in her blood. 'I would have liked,' she panted, going up the incline, 'more detail. More practical strategy.'

'Oh,' scoffed Sergei. 'Detail! Where's the passion and romance in your heart?'

'What about storms?' Issa pointed out. 'And how are we to raise children on rafts, with nothing but a piece of string to catch a fish every three months?'

'Details! You think longhair wit can't solve that kind of problem? But think of the future!' He sat himself heavily on the top step. 'Longhairs take the sea – the wealthy don't need it any more. It's exhausted, mined out, fished dry, large parts of it are polluted and poisoned. The rich do without it, and continue their life on the land. The longhairs take the ocean. And after seven generations a mighty longhair nation has grown up, a seafaring people, living all the year in mighty seagoing rafts and yachts. I picture them gathering a vast armada, a spread of ships reaching from horizon to horizon, and sailing up the Thames Estuary to sack London, or sailing into Sidney Harbour to burn Sidney!'

Sitting beside him, Issa put her head back. Geometrically pared by the buildings, in the transverse fissure of two rooftops, gently angled towards one another, she could see a thousand stars. Two thousand. Three thousand. The more she looked, the more stars she could see. 'I don't see how life could be maintained for seven generations,' she said.

'Life will find a way.'

'I suppose you think we could live for ever on the waters?'

'Why not?'

They roused themselves, and started back along towards Sergei's place. 'It burns when I piss,' he told her, apropos of nothing. 'I suppose it does with you?'

'No.'

'You have an admirable constitution. I envy it. I think I have an infection down there. And Roxan's got some illness. I don't know what, she won't tell me, but I can tell something's up.'

They were at the wooden steps to Sergei's doorway now. The stars pressed closer here, like the cosmic dizziness filling the unlit inside of the sky's vast skull. Without premeditation, Issa said: 'She is pregnant.'

Sergei went through into his big, dusty space; and Issa followed. He more fell than sat on his divan. Roxan was asleep in the corner. Issa felt it wash through her, that great weariness that immediately precedes sleep. As she started towards her shared bed, Sergei said: 'Mine?'

'Of course.'

'I won't believe it of that whore.'

This hurried Issa's heart a little, the tone of it, the offhand violence of it. But she carried on walking towards her bed. There may have been a part of her that was thinking *say nothing more, just go to sleep now*. This, though, was unlikely to prevail against her larger character. 'She said you would take that attitude,' she told him.

'What attitude?' He sounded sulky.

'She said you would want to have nothing more to do with her if you found out. I should not have told you.'

He was fiddling with his snuff pipe, trying it in one nostril then another. 'It's not like that,' he said, eventually. He sounded almost plaintive. 'I'm very happy for her.'

If she had had more experience of men, Issa might have spotted the danger in this whininess. But she was still very young.

'Good,' she said, telling herself that there was no crisis, after all. She sat on the end of her bed. Roxan was sleeping a deep, vegetative sleep. And Issa was ready to join her. But she wanted to put a few items of blithe smalltalk between her and this long-boned, rangy man before she went to sleep. 'I enjoyed tonight. Thank you for taking me.'

Sergei looked at her with one eye, sniffed, and said: 'Don't mention it.'

'Will you take me to a proper Spartacist meeting tomorrow?'

To this, Sergei only looked at her.

'Joking aside,' she said, feeling uneasy, although she did not quite understand why. 'You do know I'm not actually a Spartacist, don't you? It's just that I'd be interested to see their take on the whole situation.' When this produced nothing, she said: 'It's been an education, meeting you, Sergei. I've learnt a lot.' She did not know that this was the worst thing she could possibly have said.

Sergei took another sniff. Then, he started talking very quickly – so hurriedly, in fact, and in such a low voice that Issa had trouble following him: 'Always loved you, and it's OK that you treat me like a hardfood turd, because that's why I love you. You and I can wait until she gives birth and then raise the child between us. Did she tell you why I'm here?'

'What?'

'Did she tell you why I'm *here*? Did she tell you why I'm here? Did she tell you why I'm *here*?'

'In what sense?' She almost added: *Why are any of us here?*

'Did you think I was letting you stay here rentfree and drink my water and not even asking you to twang my cock like a guitarstring – what, out of pure charity? Do you think I'm a holy man? I did it because I love you, because I love you, although you treat me like a fucking hardfood turd. And *she* will not destroy what I have built here. She said to you: come away. Didn't she? She said to you: let's go to New York where you can be queen and I can raise my child and we'll leave fucking Sergei wallowing in his snuff doze. Did she tell you why I'm *here*?'

Issa had gone very still. Her heart had woken up and was running on the spot. 'She didn't tell me anything.'

'Why do you think I'm *here*, Issa, rotting in this lakeside hovel, and not in a big comfortable house in Putingrad?'

Issa checked the distance to the door. She would have to get past Sergei of course, but he had taken two snorts of snuff, and would be sluggish. She was feeling sluggish herself; but with a little help from her friend adrenalin, she figured she could do it. The worry was Roxan. She couldn't just leave her here, could she?

As if reading her mind, Sergei sat upright. From underneath his pillow, he brought out a small, plough-shaped object. It was a gun. He aimed it in her direction. Everything slowed down inside Issa's head.

'Why?' she asked. She swallowed, then said: 'Why *are* you here, Sergei?'

'I shot a woman with this gun,' he said. His eyes were bleary. 'I shot her in Putingrad. On the outskirts of Putingrad is the world's deepest hole. Did you know that? It's an energy borehole, and goes seven kilometres into the earth. You can go down two kilometres as a tourist. It's a very deep hole. After I shot Katerina, I wanted to go and throw myself into that hole. But my parents talked me round. Or forced me. Or . . . What does it matter? They had to smuggle me away. I was in Trabzon for a year or so, stoned out of my wits – so stoned my wits were a fucking *dot on the horizon*. In those days I lived a conspicuous expat life, and that was not clever. So there was some business there, and and and I had to come up the road.'

Issa concentrated on trying to keep her breathing calm and level. Oddly, although she was genuinely terrified – although she had no doubt that her life might end at any moment – it took an effort of will to stop herself falling asleep.

'She told you to go away with her,' said Sergei. 'Don't deny it. It's what she would do. She is in love with you. She gets to sleep with you. I don't get to. Wouldn't it be sweeter if I killed all three of us now?'

'I wouldn't like that at all,' Issa said, in as matter-of-fact a voice as she could muster.

He narrowed his eyes, then he opened them very wide. Then, abruptly, he slumped back on his divan and fell instantly asleep.

Issa sat watching him for a long time. The sensible thing, now, would be leave and never come back. Of course. Get out of there. Escape with her life. But she did not move. She could not have told you, if you'd been in a position to ask her, why she did not move. The rational thing would have been flight. But Issa did not do the rational thing – because she was drained of energy, or because some existential inertia overcame her, or because she was foolish, or because her karma was to remain there. Instead of going away she surrendered to her exhaustion. She lay down and slept. And the following morning, sitting at the open window letting the sun warm her head, she was perfectly aware of how peculiar her behaviour was. When Sergei woke, he looked at the weapon still in his hand with puzzled eyes, before tucking it away under his pillow. He got up and shook himself all over, like a wet dog.

Roxan woke as blithe as a songbird. She drank water, and Issa drank, and they chatted together, and Sergei joined in. Then, afterwards Sergei and Roxan went out, laughing, and Issa sat on the floor in a parallelogram of sunlight. She asked herself why she was still there. Might this not be the moment to slip away, to take a bottle of water and make her way down to the coast? But she did not go. She did not know why she did not go.

In fact she stayed a further four days. Every night was a period of low-level anxiety, as Issa lay there, conscious of the fact that Sergei had a gun right there, under his pillow. But she did not say anything to Roxan, or to anybody else. And life continued in its regular, lassitudinous groove. What had nested inside Issa was the germ of passivity, and it was growing its bindweed complexities in amongst the branches of her spirit. Her life was a soil in which this seed could take root, as any life is. She thought about this, but part of the cunning of this decay is that it feeds precisely upon our self-absorption. She told herself: 'He could kill me at any time.' She felt the force of the threat. But she didn't do anything. Or to be precise: what she did was to cycle through a series of notionals. Maybe she should get them all to talk about it, compel Sergei to talk through whatever it was he had done in Russia. Maybe she could offer to have sex with him. Maybe she could steal the gun when he was asleep and somehow dispose of it. But she did none of these things.

On the third evening, the three of them chatted with seeming good humour about Roxan's state. 'We'll live together here and raise the child,' Sergei announced. 'The three of us will make a utopia-in-little. Utopia will be we three.' Roxan blushed. 'You're such a Nudnik,' she told him. But there was an unmistakable flavour of threat in the word *three*.

How does it go on? Breath stains the glass. The view is the same in the morning and in the evening. The sun slides a tray of light over the floor. When it rains, the streets fill with dancing longhaired figures, and pots and pans are waved, and plastic boxes and bags are held out at arm's length. The world is slightly heavier after the rainfall than before.

Issa watches a religious parade – a dozen ragged-looking longhairs dancing along the street down below, carrying an icon of Neocles, who made the Hair.

Sergei fucked Roxan right there in front of her, on the floor of his shabby one-room hideout. She watched without interest. Afterwards the two of them slept on Sergei's divan and Issa stared into the corner of the room. It was the afternoon; cool but bright. There was nobody there, of course. There was nobody in the room except Issa, Roxan and Sergei. Except that there *was* somebody there. It took Issa a long time to bring him into focus. It was Rageh. 'What you doing?' Rageh asked her.

'Just sitting in the sunlight,' said Issa, but quietly, because she didn't want to wake the two of them up.

'Where you going?'

'New York,' she said, although it took an effort to get the words up.

'Why there?'

'Because I am its queen,' she said. The words were plastic and unreal on her lips, but she mouthed them anyway.

Rageh stepped forward a little. His face wore an unusual smirk, as if he were laughing at her. But then she saw that the back of his head was all broken open, the edges folded out in petals of bone, like a tin sheet through which a fist has punched. He turned to look at the couple asleep on the divan. Issa could see inside, could see right inside: scooped and void, clean as a washed gourd. When he turned back to look at her, she watched the distortion in his front-face with renewed fascination. There was a tiny pale-pink hole, like a button, on the bridge of his nose. There seemed no connection between this shallow filled-in circular depression and the monstrous distortion at the back of the head.

'How are you getting there?' he asked.

'By air, or water, or land,' she replied.

'Not by lying here,' he noted, looking again at Sergei and Roxan.

'No.'

The uncanny moment prolonged itself.

'I'm sorry,' Issa said, at a loss, 'that I got you killed.'

'Did you get me killed? My memory isn't vivid.'

'You don't remember them emptying your head, with their gun?'

'I suppose. I suppose I do. Distantly. It felt like – I don't know. This is what I remember: a big wind was blowing in both my ears. A big wind, the biggest. It started with a dog bark that stretched into a rolling breaker crashing on a long, straight, black-sandy shore. But it was all very gentle, really. But it was a slow sort of drawing-out.'

'I feel responsible.'

'You remember that Nature Fact Book you watched, the one about the giant bull seals?'

Issa couldn't bring her mind to focus properly on this statement. 'What?'

'Sure you remember it. You watched it, like, a hundred times. There was this big colony of these huge seals, like long massive rubber sacks filled with jelly, with dog faces on one end. Whiskers and everything. And the biggest male had these great tusks, like walking sticks, poking out of its mouth. They were huge, these creatures, metres and metres long, big as a flitter. And the biggest male kept all the women in a harem. And if any of the younger males tried to creep up and *schlup* one behind his back, he'd get really furious, and flail around and sack-race chase the challenger over the beach, and head-hammer those teeth into the rival's fleshy back, like big knives.'

'Schlup doesn't sound like the sort of word you would use, Rageh,' she observed.

'You *do* remember that book. It is the nature of the universe, that book. The only way for the younger male to get any women is to get fat enough to fight the old guy and kill him. The youngster needs to grow his teeth long as a sword, and then sheathe them in his rival's flesh. The women just flop around, whilst the males fight over them.'

337

'How can you know about that book, Rageh?' Issa asked. 'I saw that long before I ever knew you.'

Rageh looked at her, and something shivery went through her heart, so she said: 'This is, like, a hallucination, isn't it? I'm hallucinating you.'

'You don't drink enough,' he chided. 'And you need more minerals. You need to get your energy levels up.'

She was going to reply: *It's not easy*! But she was going to say so in a whiny voice, and she squashed the sentiment before it emerged. Whining wasn't going to help her.

'You know I'm right,' said Rageh, indulgently. 'More water. And a little hardfood! He's got money, why doesn't he buy you a little, from time to time? All this lounging about!'

'It's in the way of me getting up and going.'

'Get up and go,' agreed Rageh.

'I just . . .' said Issa, searching for the elusive truth of it. What, though? 'I just – I don't know. I feel an attachment.'

'But he threatened you with a gun!' said Rageh, looking disapprovingly.

'Not just him. Roxan. Can I just abandon them?'

Rageh laughed. When he opened his mouth wide, it was possible to see the far wall right through, on the other side. This, more than the laughter, made Issa tremble. 'That's the *easy* abandonment! You've had the giving-up of food thrust upon you, that's the hard part. Perfect freedom is almost yours! But you keep getting tangled up in new addictions. Glued down by them. People!'

'It's natural,' she said. 'It's the human thing.'

'And you're content with that,' said Rageh, in a sly voice. He came a little closer. 'Queen of New York? Or just some girl?'

Issa breathed in through her nose. 'What must I do?'

'Drink more. Eat as much as you can get your hands on. Energy levels! See that spider?'

'Spider?'

'There. Start with that. Just that, and then you can go.'

This spider was all elbows, and a self-important manner, lodged in the corner of the ceiling. It tasted shockingly bitter, *howlingly* bitter, and made her tongue stretch and *gah*. She drank a gutful of water after, and then spread himself flat in the window's patch of sun and fanned out his hair. The aftertaste of the spider was foul, but she'd done a good thing by eating it. She looked around and noticed that Rageh had vanished.

She stole two bottles of water and left.

It was easy enough making her way along the Trabzon road, skirting the western bank of the lake. It was late afternoon. Crowds lined the way, shifting reluctantly every few minutes. The setting sun, going behind the eastern peaks, pushed shadow further up the slope, and the crowds shuffled to stay on the light. Issa kept her head down, and ignored the various hoots, or hellos, or offers of sex, or pleas for a drink of water from her bottles. There were many of these, some aggressive. Issa wished she had cached the bottles in a bag or sack, to disguise them a little, rather than having to carry one in each hand. As the sky darkened and deepened overhead, and the first stars jabbed the points of their needles through the cloth, she found a place to rest and sat down. People were all around her, all of them settling for the night; and Issa fell into conversation with a woman called Ayşe who was walking in the opposite direction up the road. This woman stood out because she had a backpack. She was from Rize, she said, and was trying to get enough money together to buy hardfood to see her through a pregnancy.

'Aren't you scared somebody will steal your pack?' Issa asked.

'At this time of day,' she replied, 'people get sluggish, and it's not usually a problem. But I have a *gun*,' she added, bringing out a small iron pistoletta red with rust. 'And I'm careful. I'm travelling the coast, buying and selling in a small way. I pick up a euro here, a euro there.'

Issa held up one of her bottles of water. 'Would you buy this?'

'I'm on the way home,' said Ayşe, cautiously, 'so I'm more interested in selling than buying.'

'I'll give you a good price,' Issa pressed, eager to be rid of the weight of the thing. 'I don't really want it, anyway.'

'You shouldn't tell me that!' said Ayşe, laughing. 'That's no way to bargain!'

'I'm not skilled at bargaining,' said Issa.

'Your accent,' said Ayşe. 'I can't quite place it. Where are you from?'

'Several places,' said Issa.

They sat down together and each drank a little from the bottle in question. Ayşe talked a little more about the challenges involved in raising the money to have a baby. 'I wouldn't try it in spring or summer. With the stronger sunlight, and after months of enforced winter sluggishness, all the men go a little crazy. Leaping about, grabbing at you – rape, even. They wouldn't think twice about stealing anything I was carrying. But look at them now—' She gestured with her right arm. 'Late autumn, they're much quieter. It'd be even safer in the wintertime, but then I'd end up eating half the food I collected, just to keep going.'

'You can't, you know, *do* it on insects and leaves?' Issa asked.

'No,' said Ayşe, gravely. 'I mean: this will be my first child, so I'm not speaking from experience. But speaking to the older women in my village, it takes a *lot* of energy to bring a child to term. And then you've got to feed it, with milk. It comes out of the nipples, on your front!' Ayşe shook her head at the strangeness of this. 'They come out bald. Have you ever seen one?'

'I have a brother,' said Issa, remembering very vaguely the arrival of a blue-rompered little creature, all red in the face.

'Well then you know!'

'And the Boss of your village wouldn't help with food?'

'We don't have a Boss. There's a ruling cadre. It's much more progressive. We were cited by the national government as an example! Imagine that! But there's not much they can do to help us, when it comes to caching food. Still,' she smiled at her new friend. 'It means I'll be able to pick the father.'

'How do you mean,' Issa asked, ingenuously, 'pick the father?'

Ayşe explained: 'I mean, it doesn't have to be the Boss! I can choose whichever boy I like!'

Issa nodded slowly at this. It seemed to her a marvellous, a spacious and illuminated thing. Choice! 'Do you have a boy in mind?' she said.

'Oh, one or two,' laughed Ayşe. 'But I like to keep them dancing attendance. You don't want to give it all away. It's hard enough in this world, being a woman, and a longhair woman at that. You need to make the best of what you have. What about you? Where are you going?'

'New York,' said Issa.

'Where's that? I don't know where that is.'

'It's away in the west,' said Issa, and that was information enough.

After a while, Ayşe agreed to buy the bottle of water they'd shared for twenty cents. It was four-fifths full. 'And I'll get forty cents for it from the right buyer. As much for the bottle itself, as the water. Are you sure you won't feel ripped off?'

'Do you have a bag you could let me have?' Issa asked, thinking of the other bottle she was going to have to carry. 'A plastic sack, or something?'

'A plastic bag and fifteen cents for the bottle and the water,' offered Ayşe.

'Deal.'

When they parted it was dark, and all around people were clutching one another to keep warm through the night. Some few had sheets of cloth or plastic, but most did not. The sky was the colour of the deep water beneath the ocean. The Milky Way gave no energy to the blood. Issa pushed on for another mile or so through the night air before she had to stop from exhaustion and lie down. The thought had occurred to her: What if Sergei comes after me? He might do. And he would ask himself: Which way would she go? Not south into the mountains, or west or east into the wilderness, but north to the Black Sea. So he would come up this road, with his gun, and his unpredictable rage, looking for me. But as she lay down, and pulled her arms inside the body of her shirt, and tucked her legs tight against her tummy underneath the material, she thought to herself: He would never have the gumption. And then she thought: And even if he did, how could he spot me, amongst all these people? The sheer populousness of people was her shield. Her prop and stay. Her sword and spear.

She slept.

In the morning she took a drink, just to moisten her mouth, and walked on; slowly at first, but more energetically as the sun warmed her head. The sky was pale blue; white trilobite-shaped clouds crawled, occasionally intermitting the sunlight and causing Issa to slow. But by midday she came over the crest of a hill and at last saw the Black Sea. It was so beautiful a sight her heart danced upwards like a flame. Water, as far as the horizon!

She stopped for a rest and took a long drink from her bottle in honour of the sight of it. There were no fences forbidding access (the water was brine, of course). She could see the new road, a fat concrete line linking the eastern and western horizon. The old road, clearly visible under the water, ran alongside, as if in spectral homage.

She watched the sea for a long time. There was something hypnotic in it, in the mélange of illumination and shadow. The magic eye. There were no hawks. There were neither hulks nor icebergs. Nothing dropped violently down from the white sky. All that happened was that the Black Sea butted its blue head gently against the shore, and the wind went all in one direction, endlessly, above it, and people sprawled in the sun. Earth and sky. Suds on the surface of the atmosphere were clouds, erratic and baggy or tight as bolted cloth.

The sun set and there was no sun.

The following day, with almost all her water drunk, she walked westward. She talked to a few women, and ignored, or rebutted – or in one case wasted valuable energy fleeing – sexual advances from idle men and boys. The main event of that day was passing over a river. The river flowed in a ragged-sloped valley through land the colour of burnt toast. The road passed over it, a flat slab of concrete.

A great scrum of longhairs packed the riverbank, like ants on honey. Issa tried to get down to the water and fill her bottle. Down towards the sealine there was some order amongst the longhair masses, but as she tried to penetrate the press to get to the water a tall man demanded she pay a toll. Wishing not to spend her fifteen cents if she could avoid it, Issa came away and instead tried to get at the free and flowing water upstream. But here the crowd was bad-tempered and aggressive. She eventually got down the side of some gritty rocks and reached down to hold her bottle in; but it was only half full when a beak-nosed woman tried to snatch the vessel from her, and it was all she could do to scramble away. The whole thing was so energy-intensive that, after scuttling half a kilometre further along the rocks, she had to lie down in the sun, the bottle underneath her body, and spread out her hair. After that she left the road and mounted the southern slope, until she found an empty spot with a reasonable angle on some sunlight. All around her, people were settling, or settled, like puffins on a cliff-face.

She was close to a man, who sat with his knees pulled in at his chest, staring out to sea. Normally she would stay clear of engaging conversationally with a man, but the way this fellow shyly held back from approaching her endeared him to her. After a while she asked him his name. When he didn't reply, she turned to look properly at him, and saw then that he was dead, motionless, his eyes hemmed by a living, clotted mascara of flies.

She found another place to rest.

By the time she properly had her energy back it was late afternoon. She walked a few hours, picking her way along the western highway. Occasional cars passed, their horns set to head-denting levels of loudness to try and clear a path through the milling pedestrians. The sound of their engines accelerating when they broke through to clear freeway was a monster hound growling fit to rend meat with its jaws. And then, diminishing into the distance, leaving behind the sound of waves lapping at its new coastline, hungry in a different and more implacable way.

Issa chatted with another pedestrian, called Alia. She was going to Trabzon because she had heard that there were

Christian missionaries who handed out free water and vitamin pills in return for listening to a sermon. 'And if you can convince them you're pregnant, they take you off to a special hardfood facility and stuff you for a year and a half with ice cream and roast chicken.'

This didn't sound very likely to Issa, but she didn't want to contradict Alia, a tiny, fidgety woman with wrists thin as breadsticks. 'Are you pregnant?' she asked her.

'No,' she replied, 'but that's easy enough to arrange. First I want to check the story about the ice cream and the chicken is true, though, before I get myself into that interesting condition. I haven't saved anything up for a baby. My cousin got pregnant by accident, and it killed her.'

'How?' asked Issa, experiencing that familiar unease at her lack of anything except intellectual curiosity in the face of such a horrible personal circumstance.

'She did her best,' Alia said. 'She lay in the sun all day, and she *drank* a lot, ate as many insects and dirt and grass as she could. But the baby just drained all the meat out of her arms and legs, and she got so that her eyes bulged like her skull was trying to shit them out of their sockets. Then she couldn't keep the baby going, and lost it, and there was a lot of blood. Then she got hot and shivery and died.'

There was a long silence.

'I'm sorry,' said Issa, in a neutral voice.

'I wasn't especially close to her,' said Alia, looking out to sea. 'And people said it was her fault for getting pregnant in the first place. But I don't think that's fair. It shouldn't be a crime, getting pregnant.'

'No,' agreed Issa. 'Not a crime. Not a death sentence.'

'Ah!' said Alia suddenly, pointing out to sea. '*There's* a raft!'

It was a foreshortened dark rectangle, away near the horizon, like a black rug laid over the water. The sun was low in the sky, so Issa sat down with Alia and watched it. It moved gradually to the shore; as it came closer Issa could see how crowded it was.

'I'd love to get on a raft,' said Alia. 'The open sea!'

'It looks rather crammed,' said Issa. 'And I thought you were going to become a Christian and get ice cream?'

'Oh,' said Alia, 'it pays to keep options open, don't you think? And there's no harm in dreaming. We could be dead tomorrow.'

'A morbid thought.'

'I was speaking to a woman from Batumi who said that they'd invented a new disease, especially for longhairs.'

'Disease?'

'Sure: makes your hair fall out and your skin come up in blotches, red and black. Kills you in days.'

'They invented this?'

'Yes.'

'Who are "they"?'

'Oh, you know,' said Alia. 'The wealthy, I guess.'

In the morning the two walked on together and by noon they were at the outskirts of Trabzon. The town sat in a series of linked wide concavities in the coastline, the remains of the old harbourfront clearly visible beneath the chemically blue waters. The town itself was fenced, of course, and longhairs were discouraged; although, resting after her walk, Issa watched one crocodile of longhair women, dressed in black, showing IDs and being permitted through. There were the usual dusty crowds of longhairs loitering on the scrubland outside the fence.

Issa rested, and got talking to a group of Georgians. Their talk was all of the new bioweaponry, targeted specifically to attack longhairs.

'They hate us. Ever since Flowrida.'

'Flowrida was worse for us than them!' one man said. 'Tens of thousands of our kind died at Flowrida'.

'Florida,' Issa corrected. 'And what happened in Florida anyway?' A few glowered at her, as if she had made a joke in bad taste.

'It goes back further than that,' said another Georgian, a young woman with very wide-spaced grey eyes. 'It goes back to Triunion.' Everybody murmured their agreement. It was the opinion of everybody that Triunion was where the problems had started, and the blood-deep hatred of the wealthy for the longhairs was born. Issa, not wishing to invite mockery by admitting she didn't know what Triunion signified, held her peace. 'They treat us like animals – they treat us worse than animals,' said somebody. 'Then they mustn't be surprised if we act like animals – and devour them.'

Somebody asked her where she was headed.

'New York,' she told them.

There were gasps, some laughter. 'Good luck! But what will you do there, little longhair lady?'

'It's mine,' she explained. 'I own that city.'

People nodded, hugged their knees to their collar bones, adjusted their hair to gain the best purchase on the light.

That evening, as most people were settling for the night, Issa overruled her exhaustion and explored. The guard was changed on the gate; the day soldiers carted away in a landcar, the night guard brought in. Issa wandered towards the sealine. The lights itched and shivered on the water. One tall white-lit glass skyscraper, visible round the bay, looked to be built on the foundations of a trembling, watery, inverted version of itself. Flitters passed through the city's sky. An eerie mix of sounds, blended into a clanging, choral, mumbly noise. A hundred thousand people with money, folk who owned things and ate hardfood, going about their lives in the young night.

Issa found a place where the fence had been underdug, and thought about sneaking into the town. But she couldn't think of anything she wanted to do in there.

The next morning Alia went off with three of the Georgians, and Issa made her way around the south of the city, up and down an arthritic topography of hills and descents. She passed many derelict and semi-derelict houses and innumerable longhair bodies, variously prone, supine or upright. Her own throat was dry as sand, as thorny as a kaalbush. Her insides felt bleached. Little sips from her bottle did not alleviate the horrible sensations, so, impulsively, she drained the last of her water. The relief was temporary, of course, as it always is. By the end of the day the inside of her throat was again dry rubble and dust, except that now she had no water at all. She sat on the roof of a Neoclean shrine – two solid planks of concrete set into the rise of the gradient, leaving a space below into which people came and went – and stared at the sea. Strange how beguiling the sea is to look at.

She dreamt that night, or else it wasn't a dream but a genuine ghostly visitation, that Rageh sat beside her, with his ridiculous cranium like a crimped-rim ear trumpet. 'Will you go on a raft?'

'I don't see how I shall get on one,' said Issa. Either in her dream, or in real life, she started weeping. The tears were exhaustion, and weariness, and physical suffering (for her throat's lining felt like a hot puff pastry). But as soon as she started crying, she stopped: for crying made her feel foolish, and weak, and she didn't like feeling either thing. 'I may die of thirst this night, or tomorrow,' she said.

'You *do* need to guard against despair,' agreed Rageh, as if she hadn't so much as mentioned the physical condition of thirst. 'That's the one thing that will sink us.'

Us. 'Will I get on a raft?'

'Of course you will. The real question is what you do when you have come to the king's palace.'

'What king's palace?'

'New York, of course. You'll come floating back in, like the big space-bubble baby in that book. But will you come to destroy, or save?'

'Nonsense,' she muttered, slipping past her physical discomfort into deeper sleep. She had a dream then, or had another dream, depending on whether her encounter with Rageh was or was not a dream. She was Moses going down the mountain with horns upon her forehead. She came down to discover that the water had flooded the whole world, but the horns upon her forehead meant that she could breathe under the water, like a deep-sea diver, they were magical like that, or they were technological like that: grasping her two ingots of stone to help her sink down, readying herself to encounter the grotesque forms that sealife takes upon the abyssal floor.

She was woken by rain. The sky was pre-dawn grey, but filled with shimmers and lines. At first she lay on her back with her mouth wide open, but this barely got enough water into her. She waved her bottle about, and cursed the idiotic design of bottles that made the mouth and neck so tiny compared with the belly of them. But cursing was fruitless. She got up and danced. Then she slipped out of her dress, sodden with water, and wrung it out into her mouth. Water had never tasted so delicious. The water was cold, and the air was cold, and so she shivered. But she danced nevertheless in an access of joy that amounted almost to ecstasy. Spreading her dress meant that it soon soaked with water again, and she was able to squeeze some into the bottle, although most dribbled down the sides. Finally the rain died away, and the silver-grey clouds brightened with full dawn. Issa dressed again, and hugged herself to try and prevent her shivering. Her dancing had worn her out, and there was little sustenance in the cloudy sunlight. But the water had had a reviving effect, and by mid-morning she was able to gather herself and walk down the slope towards the waterside.

On her way she ran into Coco, the wandering man she had met when she first left the village. He was in a large crowd, and he recognized her straight away, although it took her a moment to place his intense blue eyes and wrinkled skin. 'Fate means for us to be together!' he said.

'Oh, hello. Where's your friend?'

He looked momently puzzled. The clouds were scooting through the sky behind his head. 'I've got lots of friends. Oh, you mean the man I was with when we met last time?'

'Yes.'

'He's away at sea. That's where I'm going.'

'A raft, is it?'

Coco stood up taller. 'My raft. My cadre. My wife, too.'

'You have a wife?'

'I'm sure I mentioned that. But don't let that put you off. Lots of men have more than one wife. Do you want to come on my raft?'

'Yes,' said Issa, and her heart galloped a little. But she took a deep breath, and let it out, and tried to get her pulse under control.

'I'm the captain,' said Coco. 'You'd have to do what I said.'

'You mean, I'd have to have sex with you.'

'What else are wives for? But it's more than that. We're not a pleasure cruise, you know. We have a mission – we are Spartacists.'

'What would Sudhir say?'

Coco's eyebrows lowered. 'Maybe you'd better come meet her.'

'I don't think she'll be too keen.'

'Oh, we need bodies! Bodies. Our strength is numbers, and numbers can always be bigger.'

He started down with his jerky little walk. Though she felt tired, Issa went after him. 'What do you mean, bodies?'

'I mean lots of people. I mean enough people to cross the river and retake West Stalingrad. I mean hordes and crowds of people.'

'I don't know where you mean by Western Lingrad,' said Issa. But very soon they had come to a makeshift gateway: a barricade between two roofless buildings, and a great many hard-faced people. Coco talked to one of these for what seemed to Issa a very long time, and eventually they were let through. Down they went into the interior of a large building. People were actually up, pulling away rooftiles to let the sun into this space. A great impression of bustle, and action, although of course the majority of the people there were lounging about, trying to get as much sun on their heads as they could.

Coco led Issa to a corner, told her to wait, and went off. She sat for a while, and then took a sip of the water in her bottle. It tasted strange, iffy, but she drank it anyway. Shortly she dozed. She woke to somebody kicking her foot. It was Sudhir. 'You're persistent,' she said. Issa sat up, and Sudhir sat beside her. 'Tell me why you want to go on one of our rafts,' said Sudhir.

'I want to go to New York,' said Issa.

'Now, why would you think the raft is going to New York?'

'I don't suppose it is. But it'll surely take me closer. Maybe it'll take me all my life to get back there. If it does, it does. If I can't go on the raft, I'll walk.'

Sudhir seemed less hostile than the last time they had met. 'Sit down my dear,' she said, and the *my dear* didn't seem hostile or ironic. They both sat on the floor, with their backs to the wall. 'You understand why I'm anxious?'

'You think I'm a spy.'

'I can't be reckless. I can't take risks. To be a Spartacist is to be dedicated to the struggle. Do you know what that means?'

'It means your life,' said Issa, gravely.

Sudhir looked closely at her. 'It does,' in a quieter voice. 'This is the great war of our age. The wealthy have the hardware, and they are ruthless. But we have the numbers, and justice belongs to us. And those are the two most important things. The rich have realized, although it is only belatedly, that they must eradicate us, or perish themselves. And so they are planning eradication. The latest thing is a targeted disease, one that affects only longhairs. That is only the first of what will be a whole series of assaults. They are planning the greatest genocide the world has ever seen. Should we not fight back?'

Issa thought about this. 'Is it really so dire?' she said.

'You don't think Triunion showed that it was dire? You don't think Florida did?'

'I know where Florida is,' said Issa, unsure what else to say, since she still didn't know what had actually happened at those places – beyond her general understanding that they had been places of massacre. 'What *did* happen there?' she added, feeling it better to ask than to carry on in ignorance.

Sudhir did not answer this. Instead, she said: 'If you are a spy, then you have been extraordinarily poorly prepped for your mission. Or perhaps it's a sort of brilliance. Maybe it's a brilliant strategy.'

'Or maybe I'm not a spy.'

'I know what you mean when you say that,' said Sudhir. 'You mean that I am looking for spies, because I crave the attention of my enemy.' Issa had neither meant that, nor, really, understood what Sudhir meant by it. But she didn't interrupt. The older woman went on. 'It is demeaning to think that my enemies have such contempt for us that they're not even bothering with counter-espionage. But I prefer to see that as their weakness. Will you commit your life to this struggle?'

'Hmm,' said Issa, looking at the floor. 'What struggle, precisely? What commitment am I being asked to make?'

'You see,' said Sudhir, 'a spy would immediately say yes, yes, I commit. And a spy would have some prepared boilerplate about the horrors of Triunion.' She poked at one of her own teeth with a forefinger, wobbled it. 'Except, except. *You* mentioned New York. *Why* would you mention New York?'

'I am the only living Queen of that city,' explained Issa.

'Let me tell you this, Issa,' said Sudhir. 'I'm lowly.'

'Lowly?'

'I'm very far down the hierarchy of the organization. I'm very far from being at the heart of this operation. So if this is some elaborate attempt to infiltrate the mission, then you've picked the wrong person.'

'I don't know anything about that.'

'Do you *want* to go on Coco's raft?'

'You mean, do I want to have sex with Coco? Of course not.'

At this Sudhir laughed, and her face was transformed. All the severity and suspicion vanished. 'Oh well said!' It took her a moment to gather her serious face again. 'So it comes down to a judgement,' she said. 'Conceivably my enemies are stupid enough, or think they are playing a cunning enough double bluff, to send a half-wit right into the Spartacist camp babbling about New York. If so, I should probably kill you.'

'Probably?' echoed Issa.

'But I don't think so. You can come on the main raft.' She stood up. 'Our strength is in numbers, but numbers mean nothing without unity.'

Issa, who didn't like Sudhir standing over her, stood up too. 'I don't know what you mean by that.'

Sudhir, about to turn away, looked back with amused astonishment. 'What?'

'What do you mean, unity?'

'Ha! Wonderful. I'm surrounded by people who use that word all the time, and never question it. But you ask a good question, of course you do. By unity I mean all of us working together. No.' She put her hand to her cheek. 'No, I mean all of us *fighting* together. I mean putting an end to ten thousand different movements, to Islamicist longhairs and Christian longhairs and Marxist longhairs and Capitalist longhairs and neoCasteians and Gandhians and Abdullans and Chavists and Ferdinandists and Wedgers and Moral Forcers.'

'The Seafolk?' offered Issa.

'Oh they have a point. It's only a point though. We do thrive at sea, provided we have only a float and a desal device. But we're vulnerable there, too. '

'I saw Maguelone speak,' said Issa.

'Who?' said Sudhir. 'Never mind that. If we could coordinate all the longhairs in the world to act *as one*, then we would be unstoppable. Do you know what is the most profound piece of political wisdom ever uttered?'

This pricked some distant memory inside Issa, something buried under the glacier weight of her day-to-day existence. 'Do as you would be done by?' she suggested?

Sudhir looked frankly astonished at this. 'You need to learn not to interrupt so much,' she said. 'At your age! Listen and learn. Don't speak so much. The most profound piece of political wisdom ever uttered. It's attributed to Neocles himself. It's this, in English: *Ye are many, they are few.*'

Issa digested this. The sound of a dozen or so people singing was audible outside. It wasn't clear what they were singing. 'What's *ye*?' she asked.

'You understand the English then?'

'Yes. Apart from *ye*.'

'It means: there are many more of us than them. Many more. If we all act together we will beat them, even though they have the machines and the money. Do you see that?'

'Well,' said Issa. 'Not wanting to interrupt, or anything. But it seems to me that people are too awkward to get them to do what you want.'

Sudhir looked at her again. Then she said. 'Where did you learn to understand English, then?'

'New York,' said Issa.

There was just enough of a pause before Sudhir started laughing to indicate that she had decided to take this harping on the name of the city as a running gag. 'Come along,' she said. 'You can come on *my* raft.'

There were two weeks of waiting, down by the waterside, before Sudhir made good her promise. But they were weeks with plenty of water to drink, and many interesting conversations to eavesdrop upon. This was a camp, a group organized towards one large-scale project, and the levels of excitement were unmistakable. Issa began to understand that there were pleasures in submerging one's individual self in the larger group. Everybody around her seemed so purposeful! Several of the men made advances towards her, of course, but none of them pushed themselves physically upon her, and most of them took her rejection in good temper. A couple more lectured her about her outdated, shorthair morality, and advised her that having sex with many people was the truly revolutionary behaviour. 'When we've overthrown the short-hair tyranny,' a man called Kal told her, 'when we've driven them out of the tropics to live in the arctic deserts, then we'll all spend our days sunbathing and fucking.' He was a tiny man with ricketed armbones that curved like ribs, but there was a

355

sparkle in his eyes. Issa smiled and nodded and didn't believe a word of it.

Lots of people talked about Florida, and the strategic lessons to be learned from that *débâcle*. She thought *débâcle* was an English word until somebody explained to her that, actually, it was French. A few people claimed to have access to the higher echelons of the movement: to be privy to the secrets of the campaign. A broad assault on the eastern coastline of the United States, millions of people pouring from the sea to the land – but all this only a feint, a ruse, a piece of distraction. The actual aim was a single man, a token, a figure of enormous symbolic potential. To capture him, and use him to unite all the longhairs of the world. To connect the movement with the aura of Neocles himself. 'Neocles is dead, though,' said Issa. Nobody contradicted her.

She saw Sudhir from time to time, but the older woman was very busy. Their conversations were inevitably truncated: and then the day came when all Sudhir said was: 'Get on the raft now. Porro will take you.'

Finally she went down to the seashore, and got her legs wet walking out to the raft. From the water's level it was a reef of plastic barrels. When she was hauled up by those already on the raft, she stood to see a great undulating floor of plastic boards and wood. There was a shed near the centre, and beside it a heap of plascable and bits and pieces. Around the peri-meters three separate desal devices dipped tubes in the water. She didn't see it straight away, but soon enough she discovered the solar motor: its top portion was a fan of solars; the motor itself of course below the waterline, a metre-diameter white tube. Apart from that, the only things on the raft were people. There were a great many people.

Having finally boarded the raft, Issa sat cross-legged and waited for departure. Nothing happened. People came and went. The sun went down. Issa tucked her limbs about her as best she could and slept uneasily, waking as much from unsettled dreams as from shivers of cold. The next day the raft's population unwound from the torpor of darkness and arranged itself to make the most of a haze-thinned sun.

The day passed with people jumping off the raft to wade back to the shore, and more people – sometimes different people – splashing out to the raft to clamber aboard. Nothing else happened. Issa fell into conversation with some of the other rafters, but all they wanted to talk about was the coming revolution.

'At Florida so much of our blood flowed into the ocean that the seas there are red now,' said one twitchy woman. 'That's why they changed its name to Florida – for all the blood that flowed there.'

'I don't think that's true,' said Issa, although nobody heeded her.

'What we shall have,' says somebody away in the crowd, 'is vengeance. *Venge*-ance!' There was a cheer at this, and a few people shouted, 'Vengeance for Triunion!' and 'Flo-o-orida!' and there was a quantity of ragged dancing. But longhairs tire easily, and it soon died down again.

That night, Issa introduced herself formally to a group of mostly older women, some as old as forty, and was permitted to cuddle in with them. She slept much better, in large part because she stayed warm. These old ones spread their hair luxuriously in the sunlight of a hotter day, and chatted in un-hurried, uncontending voices about many things.

'Do you know where we're going?' Issa asked.

'To sea,' said Mam Luda. 'To live the life God intended us to live. Surrounded by free water and basking in the sunlight!'

'I thought we were on our way to advance the revolution?' said Issa.

'Don't mind Luda,' said Mam Chen. 'She's ready to do her part. But it'll be *years* before we get anywhere near that.'

'And what's the hurry?' said blue-eyed Mam Elessa, who had the apexes of an isosceles triangle in three moles on her brown cheek. 'It will come when it comes. Until then, the thought of all the water in the world is enough for thinking.'

'You know what the revolution needs?' said Mam Sofia. 'Bodies. Yours, mine, lots of them. So here we are!'

The conversation moved on to rumours about the latest anti-longhair viral plagues.

'How do they make these things so that they attack long-hairs but leave the rich alone?' asked Mam Elessa.

'Oh that's easily done,' was Mam Chen's opinion. 'We're the ones with Nick's Bug, after all.'

'I don't see how a virus knows if you're rich or poor,' Mam Elessa persisted.

Mam Sofia said: 'I heard this one kills you in three days. The first day you feel poorly. The second you feel worse. The third you start to feel better – then you fall down dead.'

Sudhir came aboard that afternoon, and there was a good deal of shuffling and agitation amongst the rafters. But even her appearance was not the signal for departure. She went into the cabin with her three deputies and didn't come out.

'She doesn't mind staying out of the sun,' said a pigeon-chested young lad, younger even than Issa. 'She's got a *larder* in there. You know what a *larder* is?'

'Yes,' said Issa, disdainfully.

'It's where you keep hardfood,' the boy explained, super-fluously, keen to impress her with his knowledge. 'She's got a *frodge* in there, full of hardfood.'

'Fridge,' said Issa, 'and I don't believe you.'

She moved away, but the boy came after her capering and hooting 'Fridge-frodge! Fridge-frodge!' The raft was not big enough for Issa to escape him, so instead she hugged her thighs to her chest and pressed her face into her knees whilst he danced about. He got tired eventually, and went away. But there were plenty of people on the raft who gossiped about Sudhir.

'She's having the Nick Bug removed, you know, so she can pass as a rich woman! It's all part of the plan for revolution,' said one frizz-haired woman.

'That's nonsense,' said a young man. 'They can't take the Bug out. Once it's in, it's in.'

Two days later the motor was started, and the raft moved slowly away. There was a mild panic as too many people moved to the shoreside to watch the receding coastline, and the whole structure bucked and twisted, threatening to capsize altogether. But soon enough order was restored. Officers ran to and fro yelling at people to move back. Folk found places and settled. Soon enough a more-or-less spontaneous form of deck-order emerged: where if one person moved to one side, another would make her way to the other.

The land vanished, and then reemerged on the left-hand side, and then vanished again. Issa understood, from raft chatter, that navigation was being undertaken by Sudhir herself, aided by her magical Fwn technology. Issa thought of telling people that she had herself had a Fwn, once; but she decided the fact might not endear her to her new companions. The sun set in front of them, and rose behind them, and Issa set herself the task of adjusting to her new mode of life: the uneasy quake and jelly shifts of the raft's floor; the sound of water hissing and smacking the superstructure. Waves flapping like many flags. There was, most of all, a constant queasy motion in everything. It took Issa a couple of days before she became used to it, but eventually she did. Some others never did, and spent their time hugging themselves and moaning, or lying on their sides curled up like a conch. They would take their turn at one or other desal pump, fill their bellies with water, and then almost at once vomit the fluid back up.

The weather improved: sunnier days, and so more energy for everybody. The mood on the raft lifted: people chatting animatedly, even dancing, couples trying to find discreet places to have sex. Issa spent most of her time watching the great gleaming ground of water, all about them, and the extraordinary sheen of colours folded into its generalized glaucous blue, like the iridescence just visible in pigeon feathers. For one long day, the last clear day of the year, the sky comprehended one concept only: blue.

Then nature got bored with its own monotony, and bleached the sky, and turned the western horizon to crimson. The heartbreaking clarity of western skylines. This is the stuff that lungs wrap themselves round.

The next morning it rained, as if the heavens were jealous of the sea, and wanted to imitate both its wetness and its symphony of shooshing and flushing sounds.

After that one perfect blue day, the weather became increasingly autumnal. The air became colder, and the rafters got into the habit of huddling together.

From time to time they would chance upon other sea-travellers. One day they saw another raft – much smaller, tiny by comparison. This craft was faster than they, and soon pulled alongside. There were, perhaps, forty longhairs aboard, mostly women.

'Do you have anything to trade?' the newcomers called across.

'Join the revolution!' people called back. 'Come with us!'

At this the other raft became disrespectful, and ribald. 'Oho, what are you – Marxists, or Spartacists?'

'Spartacists!' yelled several on the bigger raft.

'Spartacists! Idiots! Fools! Off to waste your lifeblood on the beaches at Florida!' the others hooted. 'Goodbye, good riddance!'

Some rubbish was thrown, in anger, from the larger raft, but the smaller craft was much more manoeuvrable, and easily pulled away. The mewing of their laughter came over the low swell of the water for a surprisingly long time after they had departed.

If the weather was nice, rafters would dive in the water and swim about. The trick with this was to blow up a plastic bag and tie it around your torso, or else to get hold of one of the swimming vests piled by the cabin. Without buoyancy swimming involved a continual threshing of legs and arms that very quickly became exhausting. But with a little help floating, it was a pleasant way to pass the time.

One day they saw a huge structure, a pyramid of metal and plastic half a kilometre long, making its noisy way from west to east. They saw it at dusk and its various lines of dotted lights were both bright along its side, and smeared and shaky reflections in the black water below. Issa strained to listen, wondering if she could hear the sound of rich people laughing and enjoying themselves on the upper decks, but all she could hear was the drone of the craft's giant engines.

A few days later they spotted another longhair raft, a boat at least as big as theirs, or even bigger. They went after it for a while, but it was travelling at an angle to their own route, and moved as fast as they pursued, and eventually they gave up.

The sky sometimes played host to planes, or flitters, and it rolled the noise of their flight around like a stone in a bowl.

It didn't take long for Issa to lose track of how long she had been on the raft.

Day by day it grew colder, the sea more boisterous. Some of

the swells were hill-sized humps that lifted the raft towards the sky and then slidingly dropped it dozens of metres. Having become accustomed to the constant movement, Issa became unaccustomed again, and felt the vomitous bulge of nausea pushing upwards from her empty stomach. Clouds owned the sky. It rained in violent, grit-hard bursts, and when it did the sea fizzed all around them. Some days it was calmer, but there was never quite enough sunlight to lift Issa's energy levels to strong happiness. Most days were entirely dominated by the forceful tremor of the swell, the prodigious ebb, the head-butting intermittent forward motion of the voyage.

One morning, when the sea was all gentle wallow, a fluid landscape of lowlands, a proper boat came out to meet them. It pulled alongside and fastened itself: a sailor jabbed a spike in the plastic body of the raft, and pulled his craft alongside on the attached rope. When they were docked a shorthair disembarked, wearing a little beret, as tight over his bald head as the cup of an acorn. People milled about him. He might have been a unicorn, they were so fascinated; but he went straight into the cabin in the middle of the raft and didn't come out for half an hour.

When he did emerge, it was with Sudhir. They kissed, as the crowds on the raft watched. Then the stranger lifted his arms. 'People!' he cried. 'I am here to let you know: not all shorthairs are indifferent to your sufferings, or hostile to your cause! Some of us, men and women like me, are disgusted by the oppression you have suffered, and will do our best to help you. Justice! Justice!' Nobody cheered, not because the sentiment was unwelcome, but only because it was all unexpected, and early in the morning, and people were sluggish and tired. He looked a little nonplussed, but went back to his boat. Two more shorthairs appeared on the deck, and between them hauled a large plastic crate from their craft onto the raft.

Sudhir organized four women to carry this to the cabin. 'What's in it?' people asked. 'What's the deal with the crate?' 'Guns,' said somebody, and the word ran all about the raft like the aftermath of a broaching wave. 'Guns! Guns!' The visitor got back on his boat and zipped away.

The following day Issa saw, like half-kilometre-wide pterodactyls, sunkites hovering above the horizon; and she knew that they were approaching a city.

That was the morning when, whilst she was waiting her turn at the desal pump for her morning drink, a couple of lads grabbed her and tried to get her trousers down. Some of the women around her moved away, or stood and watched stupidly; but a few of them slapped and pushed the boys to encourage them to desist, and eventually the two guys gave up and went away. The incident left Issa shivering and gulping air; more from the unexpectedness of it than anything.

The horizon thickened; the blunt serrations of mountains rising a millimetre or so towards the sky. 'Stanbul,' was the buzz that went around the raft, and the flock of sunkites certainly suggested a large conurbation. Overnight they must have moved quite a bit closer to the land, because the following morning they were near enough to see the hordes of longhairs filling the hillsides, and mobbing the beaches. Many waved, and some ran splashingly into the sea towards them and began swimming. It seemed a very long way to swim, to Issa, and she watched with distant interest as individuals gave up and returned to the shore. Some few struggled on. It wasn't a very sunny day. It must have been *exhausting*. They must, she realized, have been desperate.

That was not a happy thought.

A military flitter overflew, and then came back. It zipped low over the raft, crossing the side opposite to where Issa was watching. She saw the rafters on that side leap and dance in defiance, throwing things at the plane. It didn't seem like a very clever way of proceeding. Nor could she see what they were throwing, although they must be throwing something, because their projectiles, falling short, were going into the water with big gloopy splashes. She looked again. Something about the picture didn't add up. She was still trying to work out what was happening when she saw a young woman – Bala was her name – spin three-sixty, unwinding a scarf of liquid blood from her neck. The flitter banked and turned and the screams from the far side came into focus in Issa's mind. Then she understood. People were leaping into the water, and trying to push their way clear of the strafe path. It came over again. Great chunks of plastic leapt high in the air as the flitter went overhead, and Mam Chen did a crazy high somersault, kicking her legs and landing on her back in a splash of blood. Issa pushed forward, but the press was against her; in fact she was carried against her will towards the edge of the raft and over into the water. It was cold and salt and engulfing, and Issa wasn't wearing any buoyancy. She struggled not only against the water but against the tangle of wriggling bodies that had come into it with her. Eventually she kicked herself to the surface and grasped the edge of the raft, but it took several minutes of draining effort to pull herself over the lip and on again. By then the flitter was a speck in the south sky.

Nine people had been killed, and two more must have drowned, because when everybody in the water climbed or was hauled back onto the raft they could not be accounted for. The raft had some manhole-sized holes in it, and a portion had been broken away from one corner; but it still floated. The women most skilled at the task did their best to repair the damage, with whatever material was lying around.

They watched and waited, for further attacks. But none came. As the sun went down, Sudhir made a speech. She sounded more weary than outraged. 'Let none of us doubt that we're at war,' she said. 'Let none of us forget our honoured dead! Mam Chen! Helena! Bella! The others!' There were murmurs, but everybody was too tired and drained to respond more energetically. 'We are going to New York,' said Sudhir, and Issa's heart leapt up – despite the horror of the afternoon, and the shock of the sudden bereavement, she felt some great wriggling joy inside her. They *were* going to New York! 'We are going to seize the great emblem of the revolution – Neocles' best friend himself!' Sudhir was saying. 'Rodion! His *right-hand man*! The last living remnant of the great Redeemer! We are going to liberate him from the prison of New York, and he will become the figurehead of the Third Spartacist Rising! We're going to smash New York and free Rodion! With him as our banner, longhairs everywhere will join us! All who revere the Redeemer! With him as our banner, we will sweep the world in a united mass, and avenge the deaths of, uh,' but her energy was fading, and the sun had buried itself behind the world, and the speech petered out. Life on the raft sank to muttering and shuffling and sleep.

Rodion, thought Issa. *New York* and *Rodion*.

The next morning Sudhir spent her time going from group to group, from individual to individual. This is what she said: 'I wasn't supposed to reveal our mission until we were past Gibraltar. But you know now, so we're all in this together. The deaths shocked me, and I couldn't keep it to myself any more. We're going to smash New York and release Rodion! We're part of the most important mission in the history of humankind!'

'I think I know your Rodion,' said Issa, when Sudhir came to her.

'Of course you do – and you're the Queen of New York.'

'But I actually do.'

365

'I thought,' Mam Elessa put in, 'that Rodion *betrayed* the Redeemer?'

'No, no,' said Sudhir, firmly. 'It wasn't like that. That's a *lie* put out by the forces of evil. He was the Redeemer's best friend! He was *himself* betrayed by the wealthy, who manipulated him and tricked him to reach the Redeemer.'

'Yes,' said a young man called Mika, with limbs skinny as rope, his knees and elbows like knots. 'I heard that.'

The land came closer, and the rafters watched the skies anxiously. There was no trouble for three days, by which time land was visible on both sides of the water. Sudhir was very agitated, and kept running from one side of the raft to the other. The Fwn was always in her hand. 'The bottleneck!' she said. 'The bottleneck!'

So: they had entered the bottleneck.

The land was scrub, pale brown and exhausted yellow-green. New houses, many built on elevator platforms – stalk-legs glinting in the sunlight – overlooked the waterway. From time to time it was possible to see the inhabitants of these expensive domiciles watching them from their terraces. Once, a figure aimed a rifle at them and fired – a little ragged ball of white smoke, as if he were puffing on a long thin cigar, and the crack of the shot seconds later – but he didn't hit anything. With the following day's dawn they discovered that another raft had come up behind them. It was just as densely packed, but was smaller; and its size gave it an advantage in terms of speed. During the course of the day it overtook them. 'I wish we had their speed,' cried Sudhir, in an ecstasy of agonized waiting. And it *was* agony; the knowledge that there was nowhere they could go, and nothing they could do but carry on down this narrow channel, vulnerable to any attack that might be launched against them, existed for Issa like a sort of toothache of the mind. She never felt rested; sleep at night was fitful, dozing during the day would inevitably end with her jerking awake in blank fright.

The land to the west and the east closed in upon them like a press. And then they were drifting right down the middle of Stanbul, the sunkites sliding their shadows over the water, the land on either side crowded and busy, flitters in the air. The old Bosphorus road was visible just below the waterline. They floated between the two towers that had once supported the old road bridge; and then, an hour later, with a sense of déjà vu, they drifted past another set of submerged road-bridge towers.

They watched the sky anxiously, of course, but the flitters all seemed to be civilian, or at least uninterested in them. Night fell, and Issa drifted in and out of sleep to the sound of water's incessant slurping and knocking, and the more distant, melodious distortions of Stanbul's noise echoing off the flat. She woke properly when people started yelling. A flitter was coming. As it moved through the air, it opened and closed two massively elongated mandibles of light in front of it. The cones of these searchlights moved over the raft, and something dropped noisily into the water some metres from the raft. It sounded like a diver, leaping from the flitter to divebomb the water. And (count one, two, three) *then* there was a huge angry-god roar, a grinding cacophony, and a huge tree-trunk of water upthrust from the sea, white as bone and gleaming in the moonlight. The raft, entire, was lifted and shaken like a sheet. The shutter flash, like disco lights, snapping people in succession of frozen wrought postures, hands reaching, mouths screaming. Issa fell down. Everybody fell down. As she tumbled, her arms went between two sets of barrels – part of the fabric of the raft. It was this that prevented her from falling into the water. But the night was full of people yelling and splashing into the sea. Then the raft was laid back down flat upon the water, as a rug laid on a floor, and the great tree of water broke up into crumbs and splotches and fell as rain down upon Issa's back. The sound was a million tons of gravel poured onto the ground.

She looked up, and saw these two slender cones of light closing and opening as they passed over the sea. Soaked and shivering, she got to her feet. She watched as the flitter located the other raft. There was a flash, and the yellow-white bubble of an explosion, and the raft began to burn. As it shone, the flitter circled it and dribbled blocky chunks of fire down upon it. She could hear the sounds of detonation and conflagration, almost covering over the screams of people. She could feel the heat of it across the water.

People were splashing in the Bosphorus all around her, calling for help: people from her own raft. So she went to the edge and did her best to help them back aboard the structure. After a while she was too exhausted to carry on, and she fell asleep like that, with her arms over the side.

She woke in the dark with everything quiet, save for one girl weeping. She dozed again and woke with the dawn. The girl – Tapa – was still moaning. Issa went over to her, and discovered a knot of older women already there: it seemed Tapa had broken her arm during the attack. There was nothing to be done, of course, but she could not be induced to stop groaning.

In the daylight it was possible to take stock. The raft had lost much of the cargo stowed upon its surface, including the crate that the shorthair had delivered. Four people had gone, although Sudhir insisted they had not drowned. 'It's a short swim to the shore,' she said. 'They'll pitch up on Stanbul, and they'll be fine.' Issa wasn't so certain. Nobody else was injured, with the exception of Tapa – a remarkable thing. There was no sign of the other raft, which had evidently not been so lucky.

They were not attacked that day. Perhaps Issa had reached a point beyond anxiety, for she found she no longer fretted about the possibility. Flitters passed through the air behind them, but did not approach. The land withdrew on either side. A pleasure boat, a hundred metres long, skimmed past on its splayed hydrofoils; the decks busy with shorthairs filming footage of the raft.

Another night and another day, and the land withdrew completely away on both sides. People on the raft began to talk as if they had passed through the bottleneck. Sudhir was exactly as agitated as before, however. 'It is only because we are a small raft,' she told people. 'That is how we have slipped past their notice.' A *small* raft? Issa tried to imagine what a large raft would look like.

Tapa's arm swelled up, and went black as eggplant. Her fingers sank into the boxing glove of her own flesh. Her whimpering quietened, and then it stopped altogether. Some said they should simply pitch her body over the side and into the water. Others said that they should weigh it down, although it wasn't clear what they would use. 'It's more respectful,' said the weighers-down. But practical considerations intervened. Almost all the junk that would have been heavy enough had been knocked overboard in the Bosphorus. They said a prayer, in the name of the Redeemer, and sang to the sun, where God, Christ and Allah would welcome her. Then they pushed her body in. But it floated, buoyed by its distended and monstrous-looking arm. Worse, it seemed to follow them as they moved into the Mediterranean. People muttered that it was a very bad omen to be followed by a corpse, but though they poked her off with poles, and a few enterprising people swam out pulling her body further away, whatever they did she still bobbed and followed in their wake. They tried altering their course, but, as if tied to the raft by an invisible thread, the

369

corpse followed. Only when they sailed, slowly (it took hours) right round in a great O, circling the dead girl, and heading off again did they eventually shake her off.

So it was they passed southwest, into the Greek seas. One day a tiny raft, no bigger than a double bed, approached them. There were seven longhairs aboard. When they were close enough to talk to by shouting Sudhir brought out a gun – a rifle, no more than a few decades old – and held them at bay.

'Did you know she had a gun in that cabin?' Mam Elessa whispered to Issa.

'No,' Issa replied.

'What do you want?' Sudhir called over the water.

'Our desal is kaput,' said one of the newcomers, in a raspy, accented voice. 'Can we come on you?'

And they did look like a ragged band, their mouths crusted with sores.

'Where are you from?'

'From Stanbul, or just down the coast at Stanbul. My cousin, she helped another woman steal the motor. It's a good motor! You can have motor, make your raft double fast – if only we can come on board and drink! Our desal is kaput.'

Sudhir thought for a time. 'All right,' she said. 'One at a time.'

Two women tied the little raft tightly alongside. The seven new folk staggered, or were helped, over to one of the desal pumps, where they drank like babies at the teat. Six fell asleep straight away, and the one who had spoken before – Sabah, she was called – stayed awake to tell their tale. She spoke in a very weary voice. 'Things very bad for longhair in Stanbul now, much hate.'

'More than usual?'

'More than that. They clearing us out from areas. They do

fire, burning fire, and gun. On the northern shore they spread special sickness. Very bad!'

Sudhir, though, seemed pleased. She inspected the new raft's motor, and declared it sound. 'It won't double our speed,' she said. 'But we will go faster.'

Rather than remove the motor from its housing, Sudhir and two women lashed the new boat tight to the side of the raft.

'Faster' was still very slow, however. They drifted day after day across smoke-grey waters. Issa watched the black-bearded stormclouds clashing on the horizon, shading the space between them and the sea with rain. The clouds became bigger, the hissing sound of the storm upon the water, and then the clouds were above them, and the lightning was around them, and thunder dinned, and water flew in every direction. The sea was shrugging itself, pushing humps and jags up that palpated the whole raft, and the only thing to do was to grab some of the strapping that held the elements of the craft together and hold on. But the storm didn't last for ever. Issa found herself thinking that this was the truth at the heart of things: that nothing *does* last for ever. That the only skill a person actually needs, in fact, is endurance. She stood, the deck of the raft misty in the sunlight, her own clothes steaming, looking back in the direction they had come. The storm was still tormenting that one patch of Mediterranean with its mindless hostility.

Life on the raft settled into its particular social geography. Everybody knew everybody, of course, but not everybody spent time with everybody. The men tended to keep separate from the women. A crowd of younger men and lads spent their days as idly as any male land-lubber, gawping at the sea, eating as much sun as was possible. One of them, Niki, owned a pack of cards, so filthy and ragged that it was possible to tell the identity of pretty much all the individual cards from their backs. But it was all the group had, by way of pastime. The rumour was that Niki charged his friends to use the cards – two wanks or one blow-job – but since nobody ever saw the boys sexually interacting with one another, and since privacy was an evident impossibility on the raft, maybe this wasn't true. Sex did happen, of course. But it was a low-key, rather restrictive affair.

The women, socially speaking, fell into three groups. There were those who were closest to Sudhir, or at least considered themselves close to her. There was a group of older women who spent the days chatting and reminiscing, and who attracted a group (about as many again) of younger girls. Issa was one of these latter. The mood of this group was indulgent, accommodating, pleasantly gossipy. And then there was the largest group, consisting of many variously disaffected women of various ages. This last lot were motivated, it seemed to Issa, by resentment, and they spent their time rehearsing the evils of the world and the most effective way of remedying them. Since what they talked about, inevitably, was Spartacist doctrine and strategy, Sudhir approved, and spent a good deal of time with them. But Issa's own private judgement was that they were a flaky bunch, interested more in opportunities to vent their individual frustration than in the coherent political vision Sudhir preached.

They saw another raft, but made no attempt to go towards it, and were not themselves approached. One day the dawn rose over a shield of land laid flat upon the water, with brand-new rich-people dwellings built at the brand-new waterline. A single sunkite floated over the peak of the island's centre, its tether catching the light like a geometrically purified everlasting line of lightning. This, Issa knew, was a Greek island. She had done the Greek islands at school, eons and ages before, and was frustrated that she did not know the name of this one. Sudhir steered the raft away from the landmass, and continued southwest.

In the night everybody was woken by the sound of a flitter passing overhead; but it did not attack. Issa lay awake for a while, staring at the stars. It was the oddest thing. She looked, and they seemed very far away, infinitely distant, lost in the immense space of the world of *Angels and Pain* and all those spaceship books. But then she would blink, and she would be possessed by the certainty that the stars were close enough to touch . . . that if she just reached up her hand she could get her nails underneath one of them, a yard above her face, and prise it loose. This would leave – what? A hole? And through the hole – what?

She did not raise her arm. She went back to sleep.

The next day, the Stanbulis began to get sick. It happened to all of them at once, which was the worrying thing. The rafters set them all in one corner, and crowded closer together to leave as much space between them as possible. Some said now was the time to put them back in their boat and cut them loose – taking their motor, said others. But no decision was taken, and by the end of the day nobody would have agreed to go close enough to them to carry them across to their own craft. They looked hideous: big raspberry-coloured sores visible on all exposed skin, the scabs around their mouths big and white as knucklebones. They lay too ill even to moan. The whisper went around the raft: 'They'll die! Push them straight in the water!' But nobody had the hardness of heart to do it. Or perhaps nobody had the stomach to go closer to the revolting symptoms of disease.

The following morning, they were still alive, but looked worse than ever. 'Somebody should give them water,' was Mam Elessa's opinion; but when one of the boys retorted 'You do it, then' she turned her back on him. Issa went as close to them as she dared. The sores had grown bigger in the night, and now looked like sliced tomatoes laid upon their skin. Three were lying on their backs, and she watched their chests looking for movement. It was hard to tell.

By sunset the general opinion was that they were all dead. 'We can't just leave them there to rot,' said Sudhir. 'We have to dispose of them.' Three lads offered to throw them overboard, if they got blow-jobs from the girls of their choice as a reward; but older women beat them on their heads and faces with the flats of their hands and chased them away. In the end Sudhir and two of her associates wrapped scarves about their mouths and kicked the bodies overboard with their feet.

That night, Issa lay unable to sleep, thinking that the bodies were following the raft as Tapa had done. She dozed, woke, dozed. Rain fell and woke everybody up. When dawn made the eastern cloud-cover gleam dusty silver, the rafters scanned the waves, but saw no sign of the Stanbulis.

Three days and nights passed. Sudhir altered the direction of the raft, so that now they were travelling directly west, heading for the glory of sunset every evening. Issa sought her out. 'Show me your Rodion,' she said. 'On your Fwn.' Sudhir observed her for a while, and then wearily complied. 'I do know him,' Issa confirmed.

'I'm too exhausted for your make-believe now, Issa,' said Sudhir.

'It could be of use to the mission,' said Issa, although she could not imagine exactly how. 'I could be an asset.'

'Go away.'

The next day they saw smoke from beyond the horizon: a great spectral skyscraper of black tailing off near its roof into streamers and puffs of grey. By the afternoon they discovered the source of this smoke: land. A wildfire was burning upon that place, although whether it had been started deliberately or accidentally it was not possible to tell. There were no signs of civilization. The fire was a bowstring of brightness drawn across the scrubland, and it sent a huge amount of smuts and dust upwards. As they passed, Issa could smell it. The smell stayed with them for a long time.

Two days later a storm pounced on them like a panther, and the cabin was struck by lightning. Nobody was hurt.

Two days after that, the first rafter showed signs of the Stanbuli sickness.

The plague went all round the raft rapidly. The first day everybody except Issa had boils about their lips, and complained of thirst and pains in their eyes and sinuses. The second day some rafters got worse, and some better, and Issa permitted herself to hope that things might be all right after all. But on the third day several rafters had sores on their chest and neck, and by the fourth everybody on the raft was afflicted except Issa. Some women hissed that she was a witch or a demon, or promised her that her suffering was just around the corner. Most did not have the energy for that. Issa did her best, carrying water all about the raft, but the whole group grew sicker and sicker. The sores were disgusting, although she found she got used to them. They looked horrid, and smelt worse, but it was possible to look past them, and see the individual underneath.

The first rafters died on the sixth day. When she was bringing Sudhir water, inside the cabin, the older woman grabbed hold of her wrist. 'I know why you're not sick,' she rasped.

'I do too,' said Issa. 'I used to wonder why so many people got ill – like poor Tapa with her arm. Or when I was back on the mainland. They got sick and I never did. But it only really sank in these last few days. None of you have gWhites. It's such a crazy thing! No gWhites!'

'You have them,' gasped Sudhir.

'Of course!'

'*Of course*,' laughed Sudhir. She looked a terrible sight.

'I thought everyone had them. I thought they were like – teeth, or something.'

Sudhir asked solemnly: 'Do you know Rodion – really?'

'Yes.'

'I wish I'd known about you. Or. I *did* know. I knew something was wrong about you. I thought you were a spy.'

'I'm not a spy.'

'We could have used you!' She retched, coughed, and lay still. Issa watched her intently, thinking that perhaps she was stopping breathing. But after half a minute, her chest started going up and down. 'Sudhir,' said Issa, in a small voice. 'Everybody is going to die. What will I do?'

Sudhir looked at her with crusted eyes, but didn't speak.

'I'll be alone,' said Issa to herself, feeling a wash of sorrow and self-pity come up, like the ocean swell, inside her.

Sudhir closed her eyes.

Issa went back out onto the deck. It was not possible for her to say whether the waves slid and danced under the action of the wind, or whether it was the fluid wash of tears across the global surface of her eyeball. She drank some water from the desal pump. Some of the women had dangled fishlines over the side of the raft – for those moments when sudden cravings for some nibble of hardfood became particularly acute. Nobody was tending them now. Issa laid her finger against one, and felt the thrum of a trapped creature.

She felt intensely sorry for herself, and that, of course, is not a pleasant sensation. But worse than that was the sharp apprehension of her own weakness. All bundled in together, feeling bad and feeling a harder kind of worse that she felt bad in the first place. She could not have put it into words, but she had the intuition that this was a dangerous state of mind, a sort of emotional short-circuit that might burn the tender membrane of her consciousness. And instinctively, she withdrew from it. Feeling sorry for herself was stupid. *She* wasn't sick, after all! She wasn't in such a bad situation as the others. The thing to do, she realized, was to stay active.

The next time she went into the cabin it smelt worse. Sudhir was dead. She lay with her arms and legs starwise. One of her people was propped against the wall with his head so slumped his face was virtually pressed into his stomach.

She went round the whole raft with a beaker of water, offering it to those who were still alive. But those who were still alive were barely alive, and would not be so for much longer. Nobody had the energy to drink. Still, she did not feel she could be idle, or the tears would come back. So she cleared a space in the corner of the raft, moving bodies out of the way. She didn't have the strength, in herself, to pull the larger corpses, so instead she waited until the swell lifted that portion of the structure, and pushed with her legs to roll the bodies away.

By evening she did another tour of the raft, but as far as she could see nobody at all was left alive. That night was not pleasant. It kept returning to her that she was alone on a ship of corpses. It was eerie, and made more so by the way the clouds spun through the heavens intermittently illuminating the heaps of bodies. She told herself: *Imagine they are only sleeping*, and that made it a little better. But the air was very cold, and there was nobody she could cuddle against to warm herself. So she slept only a little, and greeted dawn with stupid tears of idiotic gratitude.

'This won't do,' she said aloud, speaking English for the

first time in – a long time, she couldn't say how long. She went back into the cabin and searched for Sudhir's Fwn. It was in the last place she looked, which was actually underneath the woman's dead body. She brought it out in the sunlight and sat cradling it for a long time. She wondered, vaguely, about using the Fwn to call for help: but as she sat there she found herself thinking: But who should I call? And besides, of course the Fwn was locked.

Clouds kept dimming the sun, but after an hour or so she had gathered a little more energy. She tried to focus her thoughts on practical matters. She went over to look at the raft's main motor. It was a large cylinder set underneath the water that passed water through it to propel them onwards. She understood, more or less, that this was how it worked; and understood too that changing the vector of water passed through altered their direction. The controls panel looked simple enough. But how would she know which way to steer? West, she supposed. But surely she would collide with land at some point.

She started crying again, as the comprehension that she was perfectly alone passed violently through her soul. Utterly alone. Fully alone. Then, suddenly, she was gripped with the irrational fear that all this crying was wasting precious water. So she stopped crying, and put her mouth to the spigot of the desal. When she finished, Rageh was standing next to her, with his bizarre open-trumpet crimped skull.

'Exactly what I need,' she told him. 'More dead people.'

'There's no need to be like that,' he replied, calmly. 'I can't help being dead.'

'And I can't help being alive.' It occurred to her that she was speaking English, now, and that he was understanding her perfectly. But Rageh didn't speak any English. So that meant he was only a creation of her imagination. That was logical, and it didn't upset her. Would it have been better if he'd been a real ghost? Probably not. Probably worse.

'What do you mean, worse?' Rageh asked her.

'I didn't even say that out loud,' objected Issa.

'Of course you did.'

'The worse thing *is*,' she told him, 'being all alone. In the middle of the ocean! On a raft full of corpses!' It sounded ridiculous to her as she said it; which is to say, being true didn't stop it being ridiculous. She laughed into her hand, and felt better.

'You're not alone,' Rageh told her. 'You've got me.'

'It's sweet,' she said, falling out of English again, 'and you're sweet. But you're not real. You're only a part of my mind.'

Rageh's face, twisted out of true though it was, gave her a sly look. The curtain was drawn back inside Issa's mind. She gasped.

'Do you see, now?' he asked.

'I do.'

'Being alone,' Rageh said again. 'Kids do that. This is because kids don't fully exist by themselves; they're not whole beings yet. They feel the isolation of being separated from friends or family much more acutely. But a grown-up can be alone quite happily, because that's what being a grown-up means. A child is half a person, an adult a whole one. Loneliness is a kind of amputation. You can amputate an arm; but you can't amputate an entire person.'

Issa looked about her, at the many dead people. 'I don't need *them*, I suppose.'

'You don't.'

'Family,' said Issa.

There was a long pause, and the water slurped at the sides of the raft. 'Why did you say that?' Rageh said.

'Just – I don't know.'

'It's all behind you,' said Rageh. 'You're free of all that.'

Issa nodded. 'It's a funny kind of free, though,' she added. 'Stuck on a raft in the middle of the ocean.'

'It's a sea,' said Rageh, 'not an ocean.' But when she looked up at him, to rebuke him for his pedantry, he wasn't there any more.

She found a plastic blanket in the cabin, and wrapped it around her that night to keep warm. It crinkled and rustled like popcorn when she moved. The sea was unusually calm, and there were very few clouds. Almost all the stars were out. She had to decide what to do. She was a grown-up now, after all. She was in charge. This thought formed a membrane inside her head that kept the tears back. It was remarkable, really. She tested it, as it were, by bouncing a test-thought off it: 'I'm alone and stranded at sea on a raft of corpses.' But it bounced back. She was alone, and that was fine – what good had it ever done her, really, hanging out with other people? Even on the raft, which hadn't been all bad, there had been those boys who tried to pull her trousers down. And in the village, being with other people had meant being in a place where other people could upset her. So that was OK. Then: stranded at sea: but she had all the water she could drink, and all the sunlight she needed. She was better at sea than she had been outside Trabzon – just as that old preacher women had said. What had her name been? No, gone. Didn't matter. Then: corpses. That *was* a problem, true, but it was a practical problem. She would have to push them into the water. It wouldn't be easy. But it wasn't impossible. She had plenty of time, after all.

Morning brought the sound of gulls, which in Issa's half-awake mind sounded like the quarrelling of angry ghosts. Standing up, she saw a slab of land on the horizon, and boats visible in a bitten-out-chunk of a harbour, and lots of houses like mah-jongg tiles. She ran to the motor and swivelled the circle on the little screen. Slowly the raft responded, turning to miss the island.

She went over to sit on that part of the raft that gave her the best view. This happened to be where the Stanbulis' boat was strapped to the side, and looking at it made her wonder why she hadn't thought of it before. Instead of removing all the corpses from the raft, she could decouple and take this much smaller craft. It would, she supposed, be harder to cross the Atlantic in a boat that size; but − did she need to cross the Atlantic? She'd planned to get to New York by way of going home. But according to Rageh, home was what had made her feel the loneliness and the upset in the first place. Could she not choose her own destination now, and leave all that debilitating pain behind her?

But where would she go?

The sound of an approaching flitter distracted her from these contemplations. Her heart ran and jumped with fear. The craft flew close enough for her to see that it was a civilian flitter, and she almost relaxed; but then one of its door slid open and somebody inside began shooting at the raft. Issa heard the snap, snap, snap of the gun, and saw shreds of flesh bounce up from one of the prone bodies. The machine overflew. Issa lay down. If she stood there, the only upright figure, she would be an obvious target. The flitter's sound diminished, grew again, and passed over with some more snap-snap sounds of gunfire. She lay very still, and hoped not to be hit.

The flitter made one more pass, and then flew off. Presumably the people aboard were disappointed that the raft provided them with no live targets. Issa lay there for a long time, listening to the sounds of the water, and her body was raised and lowered by the undulations of the raft on the water.

When she decided it was safe to sit up, the island was no more than a thick line between sea and sky, away behind her.

Rageh was there. 'Will you go to America?' he asked.

'I suppose you're asking me that because I'm thinking it,' she said. 'But look, this is stupid.' She reached out to touch him, half-expecting her hand to go right through him (wasn't that what happened with ghosts?), but surprisingly he was palpable and solid, if cold, to her touch. She took hold of the torn petals of head at the back and bent them back into shape. It was like moulding plasclay, or manipulating something in a Virt. The pieces all went back, and with a little pushing and pulling of his cheeks his head was restored – almost – to its former state. Like a mended pot.

Rageh gave her such a sweet look that she laughed with delight. 'Thank you,' he said, gravely. 'Really – thank you very much.'

Later that same day she saw a boat, coming towards the raft. It was a wide-bodied barge of a craft, low in the water, but clearly well-built and with powerful engines. Issa wondered if she should try and steer away from it, but it was soon apparent that it was steering directly towards her.

She waited.

It came within twenty metres, or so, and slewed round to present its lengthy broadside. Faces were visible, watching her over the side. They were, she was relieved to note, longhair faces. A woman stood up near the prow and shouted: 'Are you Issa?'

'I am!' she shouted back, startled.

'We'll not come closer. Swim to us.'

Unsure she had heard correctly, she replied: 'What?'

'Swim across to us,' yelled the woman.

Issa looked around at the raft. It was a shabby thing,

ramshackle and ruined, and covered with dead bodies. She didn't even think twice.

The only thing she took with her was the Fwn, which she tucked into her trousers. The water was gaspingly cold, and salt water went in her mouth and down her throat before she really got going, so her threshy crawl was accompanied by a series of coughs and splutters. But she reached the side of the barge soon enough, and took hold of the bottom step of a plastic ladder lowered down to her. Climbing up was onerous, but she managed that too. Finally she was on the deck, and surrounded by longhairs.

The woman who had shouted to her introduced herself. 'My name is Li,' she said. 'I'm in charge here.' Her English was smooth, though slightly accented.

'You're a Spartacist?'

'Of course,' said Li. 'And you are Issa.'

'How do you know?'

'Sudhir was one of mine.'

'Oh,' said Issa. She looked around at the rest of the crew. 'I'm afraid she's dead.'

'I know. I spoke to her just before she succumbed.'

Issa brought Sudhir's Fwn out of her trousers. 'On this, of course. Here,' she said.

'Keep it,' said Li. 'She told me the whole raft was dead or dying, except for one person. And she told me that person's name. It's easy to see why you're well, and it's easy to imagine the backstory. But she told me something much more remarkable even than that story. She told me you knew Rodion.'

Issa looked around herself again. 'I did,' she said. 'He lived next door. He was a friend of my father's. He used to buy me ice cream.'

'In that case,' said Li, smiling at Issa, 'you can *certainly* be of use to us.'

Li took her down into the insides of the barge. 'The crew don't like coming down here in the daytime,' she said. 'They don't even sleep down here. Too far from the sun. When we take over the world, we'll need special crews, fed on hardfood like factory livestock, to scour the subways and bunkers.' They passed through a hefty metal hatch. 'One rule: close all hatches. If we get hit, and we may well, it's best if all our compartments are watertight. Here.' They passed into a small cabin: inside sat a small, plump, bald-headed man. 'This is Drago, our medic. He will do some tests.'

Without a word, Drago stood, touched the back of Issa's hand with a wand. Then he sat down.

'A shorthair, you'll notice,' said Li. 'We're not automatically prejudiced against shorthairs, you see.'

'What about the raft?'

'The raft?'

'Shouldn't we do something with it?'

Li was looking at Drago as she spoke. 'The best thing we can do with the raft is leave it floating about the Med. It will be almost entirely ignored, but there may be one or two wealthy people who see it, or hear of it, and are moved by the fact that these were human beings, once. Perhaps they'll become aware that the rich are perpetrating a crime against humanity.'

Drago cleared his throat: 'Yes,' he said.

'Not that I doubted it,' said Li.

'Did you test for gWhites?' asked Issa. 'Of course you did. I don't need to ask that. Answer me this question instead: why shave your head?'

Drago put his hand to his scalp, as if surprised by the question. 'What makes you think I shave it?'

'Perhaps you don't want to take the Bug,' Issa said. 'But why not just let your hair grow? That way at least you'd look like your comrades, even if you weren't.' She looked from Li to Drago. 'I don't see the strategy here.'

'I am naturally bald,' said Drago.

Issa thought about this. 'What is that? A sickness?'

'Not at all. A hundred years ago most men were bald. Or they *went* bald, eventually. Now, of course, there are treatments to cover the fact. I prefer not to take treatments.'

'Gracious,' said Issa.

'Come along,' said Li, taking gentle hold of Issa's elbow. 'Let's be going.'

'We have organized a massive overrunning of the US coast at and around New York,' said Li, as they climbed together back to the sunlight. 'Partly the intention is the destruction of the city. But in fact that assault is a cover for a more specific task: we intend to seize an old man called Rodion.'

'I know,' said Issa. 'Sudhir told us.'

'You discussed it with her?'

'She told the whole raft.'

'Really?' Li was frowning, or else screwing up her eyes against the light, because they were stepping back outside again. 'She wasn't supposed to do that until after you got across the Atlantic. Assuming you ever did. Still, no matter.'

They went to the prow of the ship. Issa was struck by the way the prow cut so sharply through the water. 'The invasion will be a long-drawn-out process. We can't coordinate for all our people to arrive at the same time. But that doesn't matter. We'll gather as many as we can. It's a way of applying pressure.'

'Lots will die,' said Issa. It was one of those statements she made that struck her as true only as she uttered it. She didn't know where the sentiment came from, or why she voiced it;

but once it was out she understood it touched on something centrally important.

Li nodded, slowly. 'Quite right. Many *will* die. We're fighting a war, my dear, you realize that, I hope.' She watched Issa's face, and seeing her unconvinced, added: 'More will die if we don't make this sacrifice. Believe me. Your friends on the raft are only the start. We'll be exterminated like weeds by the end of the decade, unless we act.'

Issa took a deep breath in. 'Oh,' she said. 'Well isn't it hopeless then?'

'Defeatism!' chided Li. But she kept her keen eye on Issa.

'We can send a million people into the USA. They'll just infect us with that horrible disease and we'll all die.'

Li said: 'You are a canny child. But you mustn't give up hope. The Shackle Virus was developed, we think, in a lab in Abkhazia.'

'Where's that?'

'Between Georgia and Dagestan. But they haven't used it. Human rights, they say, which is bang-on. Ironic, actually. But there you are. Anyhow, a few countries with what they call "serious indigent problems" have used it. Stanbul is one. Kirim another. But not the US.'

'Not yet.'

'Exactly! But if they use it – when, I should say – then they will kill millions, and they will make heaps of corpses upon their own land to poison their landscape and put Attila to shame. And many of their own people will die, for the virus is not as discriminating as its inventors hoped. And anyway by then we will have moved on. You can help.'

Issa nodded. 'What shall I do?'

'You know Rodion, you say. You say it so casually, as if it's nothing at all! But he is the last living member of the Redeemer's own inner circle.'

'I find it odd, all that Redeemer stuff,' said Issa, walking a little way down the side of the boat to watch the wake drawn, like a comet trail, through the dark blue of the ocean. 'He was only a man, after all.'

'True,' said Li, coming after her.

'All those shrines to him. He was a man, not a god.'

'It doesn't matter. What matters is that he unifies our people.'

Issa found it beautiful, the way the water, cut and forced apart at the front, simply joined together again at the rear, in blithe forgiveness of the violence performed upon it.

'You can help us liberate Rodion,' Li said. 'You can perform a great duty.'

'Duty,' said Issa, absently.

The ship moved much more quickly than the raft had done, of course; but timing was more important than brute speed. It was a question of arriving at the *right* moment. An armada of rafts of every kind, small and large, well-organized and shabby, was converging on the American city. From the south and across the Great Atlantic from the east, bringing a huge number of longhairs towards one point. It was impossible that they would all get there exactly at the same time, of course. Rather the strategy was that they apply a crescendo of human pressure, bodies pouring into the lands north and south of the city, and culminating in a fully armed military assault on New York's Manhattan citadel.

'Li doesn't *know* if you're really an old pal of Rodion's,' said Christophe, a muscular longhair who liked to walk about holding a gun, and who took an avuncular interest in Issa. 'But she loses nothing by bringing you along, and may gain something important. It's not going to be easy, kidnapping him.'

'Liberating him from the prison of New York, you mean?' Issa said, slyly, having picked up the idiom.

'Sure! That! Yeah!' Christophe's laughter was not kind.

Quite apart from the speed, being on the barge was very different to being on the raft. The crew, for one thing, was a disciplined unit. They were kind to her, in a distant sort of way, but there were no spaces in the social knit to let her in for conversation or companionship. She didn't mind. She got to spend every night in a bed, in a room of her own – the first time since the village. She slept very long and very deep. Each morning, woken almost invariably by the clump of booted feet marching in unison on the deck overhead, she felt she had made up a little more of some profound spiritual debt. She felt, day by day, wholer.

They passed Gibraltar, sticking out of the sea like a stegosaurus' spine. Issa expected trouble, but there was none. Soon she felt a difference in the rhythm of the thud and slap of the boat's passage: an Atlantic rather than a Mediterranean resistance to their motion. On deck, where she spent most of her time gazing at the seascape, the fluid plateau had a new quality to it: the dints were deeper, darker grey, the peaks rawer and more liable to snap off into dusty-looking sprays of bright white. The wind was colder, and Issa was given a lined jacket and new boots, for which she was very grateful.

Some days she sat on the shifting deck and watched the surface of the sea so intently that she almost saw through it, to the substructure of struts and wires and spars, the endlessly moving pistons and cogwheels that maintained the incessant rise and fall of the surface cloth. But then a wave would hit the flank of the barge and a cloud's worth of spray would rain horizontally, drenching her with chill and salt and wet, and she'd be forcefully aware of the material reality of the medium.

Only once did they see a raft – toiling awkwardly through

waves the sizes of house-roofs, up and down, its exposed longhair passengers clinging on desperately. It looked on the very threshold of capsizing; and the weather wasn't even especially severe. Issa found Li belowdecks, going over something with the doctor on a tablet. Li listened patiently to Issa's pleas that they rescue the rafters, and then told her that they would not, that there was no question of anything like that. 'If we stopped for every raft, we'd fill up with useless bodies before the week was out. They'll be fine. You'd be surprised how resilient these craft are.' Issa went back on deck to see how they were getting on, but the raft could no longer be seen.

They had three days of relatively calm weather, and then a storm: vertical seas, black as night at three in the afternoon, rain flying in all directions, the cones of the decklights buzzy with furious atoms. Issa got her arm through a supporting strap and held on as the floor imitated the wall and the wall the ceiling. She felt the heave of the sea inside her bones. Where the raft had slid up and down waves, the barge plunged directly through. The sound of the prow colliding with repeated cliffs of water, the horrible down-up bucking that followed, and the insane flood of water pouring down from the deck to gush along the floor was the worst of it. Otherwise it was all just shaking and rocking, and she didn't mind that so much. But every cascade of water pouring past her into the bottom of the keel filled her with dread. Didn't that mean that the barge was filling up with water? Wouldn't it reach a certain point of saturation, and sink? She hung, pivoting on the strap, for half an hour in a state of horrible, acidic dread at this prospect, before her conscious brain reacted against it. The passivity of her situation disagreed with her. If the boat started to go down (she told herself), she would pull herself up the ladder and out. Then she would find whatever floating debris it had left behind and hold on to that. She could live off the sunlight, she reminded herself, and drink rainwater, and she would be fine. She knew, really, that this was nothing but a comforting lie, but it was good to construct a narrative that demonstrated there was nothing circumstance could do to defeat her. It made her feel better.

Two hours later the storm calmed. An hour after that, things were steady enough for Issa to release the strap. A bruise, shaped like a snake, reached from armpit round to elbow.

Christophe told her that the storm had pushed the barge back off course, and had damaged the engine. So they spent another day in open water, bobbing like a cork, as the engine was repaired. A plane overflew them, but so high it might as well have been a spaceship – except only that its passage drew a great cowl of noise after it.

The engine repaired, they set off again. The sea was flat and as dark as a bed of silt. The clouds had been dabbled together by toddlers' fingers playing with some white putty, and the sky was cold dark grey. The barge moved as smoothly as a skater over this new substance. Issa went fore and peered over the edge to where the keel cut into the ocean like a plough into soil. 'Issa?' somebody said, behind her. Christophe. 'Could you come below.'

Issa went, giving her hands alternately a rub and a squeeze. The innards of the barge smelt of coffee and something savoury, which meant that Drago was cooking. He needed to eat, of course; and some of Li's women and men ate hardfood with him, to maintain their muscular development. It meant that twice a day there was a little dinner get-together below-decks. Issa passed the open door in which the meal was being eaten. A semicircle of happy faces.

Down the corridor, round a dogleg and into Li's cabin.

'Good,' said Li, looking up. 'We need to start thinking practically. Sit down.'

Issa sat, and so did Christophe. Li slid a tab over to her. It struck the lip of the table and stopped. On it were some images: an old man, seated, in an open space, a park. He had his head on one side, as if listening to somebody speaking. 'That's Rodion,' Issa said.

'That doesn't prove you knew him,' Christophe observed. 'It's not exactly hard, finding out what Rodion *looks* like.'

Issa looked him straight in the face. 'Do you think I'm lying to you?'

'I wasn't saying that,' said Christophe, not meeting her gaze.

'This was taken earlier in the year,' said Li.

'The Park, in New York,' said Issa.

'Just so. He often goes there. We also have some footage from his house.' She reached across to tap the tab, but Issa intercepted her hand. 'Wait.' Three more figures had come into frame: a stout, baby-faced middle-aged man, a young lad and an older girl. Issa was conscious of a peculiar sensation of simultaneous expansion and shrinkage within herself. Perhaps you've had that sensation yourself. She felt an intense stillness in her soul; and at the same time she felt a vertiginous sense of tumbling.

Li asked: 'Do you know him, the man, there?'

'Yes,' said Issa, her windpipe suddenly smaller than it needed to be.

'He's one of Rodion's friends,' said Christophe, 'and his kids, his daughter there – she's especially friendly with the old boy too.'

Issa felt something build inside her, and wondered what it was. Then her face clenched, and she sneezed. She rubbed the knuckles of both thumbs into her eyes. She felt very peculiar. She felt very jangled, and yet none of that janglement seemed to affect her behaviour or voice or breathing. 'When did you say this was from?' she asked.

'Earlier this year,' said Li.

Issa looked at the girl, at the young boy, at the man. 'That's George,' she said, feeling the oddity of calling him by his first name.

Christophe stretched out in his chair. From the corner of her eye, Issa could tell that he was smiling a big beamy smile. 'Maybe you *do* know Rodion!' he said. 'So you recognize young George, do you? What about the girl?'

'The girl is his daughter,' said Issa, the words bouncing through immense empty chambers located somewhere inside her body. But they came out sounding normal: 'She's called Leah.'

'Very good,' said Christophe. 'I am impressed!'

'Is that right?' Li asked. 'About the name of the daughter?'

'How would I know? But that man is definitely called George. How did you know them, anyway, my sweet?'

Li reached out a forefinger and moved the image on to one of Rodion's house.

'I lived there,' said Issa. 'Thereabouts.' She could hear what Christophe was asking her, and was aware of those other people, in that place. But her attention was somewhere else. A great, sudden tide of thought was filling her up. 'I played with – that girl.'

'So how did you end up . . .' Li asked, distractedly, pulling out her Fwn and fiddling with the screen.

'My family went on holiday. The next thing I knew I wasn't in the hotel any more, I was in the back of an antique van, and it was driving on and on. For a very long time. Then I was with this woman, but she died. I don't know what she died of, she was pretty feverish by the end. Then I was with another woman, and she sold me to . . .' But Li was murmuring something to Christophe, and it was clear enough that neither was interested in the whole story. Nor did Issa want to go through it all. She tapped the image and it went into run-mode. Another one taken in the park. What sort of a feeling was this, watching the images of George putting his hand, affectionately, on the top of Leah's short-cropped head? Watching the synchronies of their smiles? Well, it was a clear emotion, even a pure one. It was not a disagreeable or confusing emotion. It was anger, that was what it was called. Issa thought to herself: I am not *caught out* by this. She thought: I have already disengaged from all this. The image run came to its end, and looped back to the beginning again. There was old Rodion, and there he sat, and now into frame came the other man and the girl. Really, though, *anger* wasn't the right word. It wasn't a thorny or aggrieved thing she was feeling. It was a feeling with a similar forcefulness but with a completely different trajectory. It was as if these images disproved her own existence. It was that the young girl in the images genuinely *was* Leah, and that her dad's little affectionate gestures were directed towards their proper focus. And who else was there on the whole rainy stony Earth to whom they ought to be directed? This sequence of images simply emptied her out, left her a void consciousness. Liberty. So her anger was not resentment at being replaced. It was more like the happy fury of a genie, released finally after a lifetime's confinement in the bottle, into the endless freedom of the open air. He has forgotten me, he has erased me, he has put somebody else in my place – all that. None of that. Instead: the thrust and the roar and a cloud of fire and then the cloud was below her, roiling on the ground, and she was above it and clear in frictionless rocketing spaceflight.

Free of her past. How many people get to say that?

'Hey,' said Li. 'You hear about that. It happens a lot, though, doesn't it?'

'You do hear about it,' agreed Christophe. 'It's – a thing.'

'What?' she said.

'The snatching – what's the word?'

'Kidnapping,' said Christophe.

'Kid-kidnapping,' said Li. 'Sure.'

'Can I go now?' she said, watching her father come into the frame for a third time, and watching him half-turn his face to smile at old Rodion, and watching the little girl who looked like her – although, truthfully, not *very* like her – press the ice cream to her lips, and watching her dad lay his hand tenderly on the top of her head. Erasing the file of her life. Returning her life to factory settings. It was a kind of birth, and only painful in the way that birth is for the squeezed, forced-down-the-pipe infant. Inside her heart there was a clear flame burning, almost invisible, except for the slight tremor it imparted to the objects seen through it.

'Sure.'

She got up, disgusted with herself for the way her legs trembled as she walked away. It was the sort of muscle-shimmer dogs get, sometimes. It was a kind of horse-flank twitch. But she could still walk, and she walked out of the cabin and past the disgusting fleshly smells of Drago's hard-food cooking, and she got herself up on deck. Breathing very deeply. She laid herself out in the thin, late fall sunshine, and made the most of it. The sunlight may have been stronger than she realized, because she could feel it burning on her face.

When she fell asleep, there, it was like a shutter clanging down inside her head. When she woke a cold drizzle had started falling, and she was wet through. She went belowdecks.

*

The barge pulled into an island bay – not Triunion, according to the crew, but not so very far from it. Li threw a rope around the roof of a four-fifths submerged building to anchor them. Issa stood on the deck and surveyed the island. The slope of the shore was stacked with shanty roofs and plastic-board shacks: longhairs, most wrapped about with blankets for the colder weather, filled all available horizontal spaces.

They moored there a week. A dozen or so people went ashore on the second day, and Issa was offered the chance to go along. She refused. She preferred to spend her days on deck, watching the mix of clouds and blue in the sky. Always changing, and always the same.

When Li returned, Issa caught her elbow. 'We're going to grab Rodion, and then use him to unite longhairs all across the world behind our cause,' she said.

'Soon,' said Li, surprised.

'And what about New York?'

'We're going to smash the city,' said Christophe, coming over to see what the business was.

Issa looked from her to him, and back again. She released Li's arm.

On the fifth day a raft came into the bay: a vast undulating platform carrying perhaps a hundred longhairs. There was no sign of disease in this crew. Li went aboard the raft and talked with the cadre leaders. 'Come up from Argentina,' said somebody, leaning on the rail and watching the crowd. 'Eager to get on. Eager to pitch in to the fight!'

The raft didn't stay at the island, passing with painful slowness past the barge and out to sea. Issa watched it until it slipped into the long narrow slot between sea and sky. It was gone.

People on the boat were talking about timing. It was all about coordination, they said. About hitting the sweet spot of getting as many people as possible behind the first assault.

When Issa slept she dreamt of smashing the city. She saw the sky descending as a white-hot solid plane, burning the towertops, sparking and crumbling them, pressing them flat against the earth. She saw it all squished out of being with a horizontal blast of light, like a ripple spreading on a pool. Everything was a perfection of compression. Then the lit sky lifted away to reveal not a polished glass desert but, counter-intuitively, a pleasant landscape, a table of green fields and a set of cushiony hills. Trees cast their shadows distinctly upon the ground.

Sometimes, when she woke, Issa would experience a moment of pure contentment, such that registering her sur-roundings and shaking the last of the sleep out of her head would feel like a dip down into gloom. But it was OK. She needed to think practically. She needed to think what she would do, once the city was gone. She was a dizzily un-constrained person. She could go anywhere. The only con-tamination that remained was the urge to return to New York; and once the city was gone, she would be free of that weakness too. Where should she go? The world would be all before her.

At the end of the week, suddenly, the mood on the barge changed. Although Li issued no direct orders, it somehow became generally known that they were heading off, that the time for the attack was upon them. The engines were warmed up, and the barge pulled away into open water.

That evening Christophe found Issa at the prow, watching the ceaselessly fascinating way the boat in motion cleaved the waves. 'Have you ever been to war before, Issa?' he asked.

She looked at him, and it was obvious the answer he was expecting. She shook her head.

So he put an arm about her shoulder. 'You might think there'd be no need to ask that question, since you're so very young. But you'd be surprised! I've met veterans of Florida who were younger than you.'

'I don't suppose,' said Issa, still looking out to sea, 'that war is so *very* different from peace.'

'Spoken like a true Spartacist! Always the struggle, eh?'

'What will you need me to do?'

'You come along with us. We're going to steal a flitter – we have a number earmarked by people on the inside – and we're going to go collect Rodion. You'll accompany us. He may be less than pleased about coming along. We'll restrain him if necessary, but he's very old, and it would go better all round if he could stay calm. Talk to him, get him to remember you, chat about old times. That kind of thing. OK?'

'OK,' said Issa. 'And afterwards—'

'Afterwards we get out.'

'I mean . . . the city?'

'We'll destroy it,' said Christophe. 'To begin the action of revenge for Triunion and for Florida.'

The day passed, and another one did. Then, after the long voyage, events came to a head with anticlimactic rapidity. In the morning they came to a coast marked by a long dyke. The barge made its way through the channels formed by a number of mostly submerged rectangular buildings: the waves were small and numerous and little blots and blurs of snow were swizzling down from the dark morning sky. One of the buildings had once had giant letters arranged along its flat roof, displaying the name of whatever corporate or governmental business had been conducted within. Now only a five-metre A remained, the waves splashing around its spread legs. Li brought the barge in and threw a rope around the shoreward limb of this huge letter.

They waited for an hour or so. Issa watched the dyke, expecting – she didn't know what. Longhairs to come swarming over the top of it? The dyke itself to crumble and fall? The US Army? But nothing happened. Black clouds threatened a heavier snowfall, but it did not quite come. Only a few flakes moved in the sky, cold and grey as old ashes. Thunder groaned wearily away to the south, but there was no lightning. Issa had a hat, shoes, a cotton jacket, but she still felt the cold. She walked around the deck to get a better view of that way, pulling her blanket closer around her, and watched the landscape. The dyke ran a long way north and south, but in the latter distance there was a white bar between sea and sky, like a giant's rib laid upon the ocean, water become a bone. The thunder came from that direction, but there was no lightning. Then she did see some flickers of light, but they were coming up from behind the white bar, not down from the sky. She understood then: that white line was the Hough Wall, and that behind it was Manhattan. The word 'home' came to life inside her, she couldn't stop herself. But at least she had the discipline to remind herself that (the hand tenderly patting the crown of the other girl's head) it wasn't home, any more.

She almost expected to see Rageh, standing behind her, but when she turned about the deck was empty. It was horribly cold, and there was hardly any sunshine. The weariness was gritty inside her muscles. But then a deep, resonant boom echoed over the water, and she looked back to the south with a little chirrup in her heart.

There was some sort of midge-like activity over the Hough Wall, but they were too far away properly to see it. A little later she saw a bird approaching them, and a moment later she could see that it wasn't a bird after all. Li and Christophe came bustling up onto the deck. Issa looked again away to the south, and she could see that it was a flitter. Then everything happened very quickly. It grew larger and larger, and then it suddenly reached them. A domestic machine, it touched down on the deck of the barge. Li bundled Issa up inside it, and Christophe and another man came after. Issa recognized the man from the barge, but couldn't think of his name. Then without any ceremony, or introductions, the driver took the flitter up again, and in moments they were swooping low over the water towards Manhattan itself.

After so many months of slow, antique travel it was momentarily disorienting to be moving with such rapidity. But Issa adjusted her mind, and peered through the window. The Hough Wall swept beneath her, and there were the towers of the city. Memory surged inside her. *Home*, said the voice. *Home!* She shut her eyes, but of course she had to open them again. The towers, the towers, palaces of kings and princes! The flitter nipped past one monolith, a thousand metres high, and swam into the chasm of air. Looking down, Issa could see the streets swarming with people. Longhairs, longhairs, and in amongst the profusion of motion and bustle she could see the writhe and tumble of individuals falling, collapsing, tumbling. There were a great many shorthairs too, some armed, some not, either fleeing or resisting. A police flitter schwomped past, no more than ten metres below Issa and going in the opposite direction. 'There,' Li shouted to the pilot. They banked, turned up a different street, and this one was even more crowded with people: longhairs swarming like ants. And further in, two police walkers wading through this sea of people. And the crickle crackle of continuous gunfire. That background noise was not the ocean, behind the Hough Wall. It was the sound of so many thousands of people yelling with one yell.

Issa's stomach clenched and heaved, but it was only the flitter swooping down. A moment later they were on a roof, and they stumbled out, and she was breathing actual New York air. But the air was filled with roars and yells and the battering noises of weapons being discharged. Snow was trying to fall, butterfly flakes falling sluggishly through the cold, but then there was a deafening clatter. Away to the side Issa caught a glimpse of a door dancing and bouncing into the breeze like a thrown playing card. 'Come on,' cried Christophe, and the four of them bundled inside the building. It had the inevitability of a dream. She knew this stairway. She knew this room: and there was Rodion – standing, looking with dismay at the strangers inside his house. She didn't remember him looking *quite* so old, but it was certainly him. It was him in the flesh, live and breathing and real. In her head with vivid, winter clarity she thought: *Now we can take him and finish this place for ever*. It was a giant thought, the kind of thought a god might have.

Rodion had opened his mouth.

Issa took one step towards him before she saw the other person in the room, and then, as it were, her consciousness tumbled down the spiral staircase inside her head. 'Daddy!' she screeched. Never before in the long history of humankind had a man looked so startled. She ran and grabbed him about the waist. Everything else just fell away. It all vanished. 'Daddy!'

'No!' he cried, in terror. 'No!'

'There's no time for this,' said Li. Christophe and one of the other men were behind Rodion, one at each shoulder, and the astonished old boy was propelled from the room and up the stairway. The stairs had been programmed to respond to his presence (Issa remembered this!) with gentle undulations of individual steps so as to facilitate his passage upwards. The unexpected motion of the steps threw Christophe, and he almost stumbled. Issa was right behind. 'He comes too!' she called to Li. He was her daddy after all. 'He comes too!'

'Don't be stupid,' snapped Li, pushing past her. 'We're not here to collect all the random strangers of—'

'Watch out!' bellowed Christophe.

There was a knot of people coming up the stairwell from below. Li dashed upstairs; moaning, Rodion was dragged behind her. Issa was not far behind. Yelling below them. But, between the undulating stairs and the impediment of having to drag the reluctant old man, Li's foot slipped. She fell forward and banged her knee. 'Oh!' she cried, in pain.

As she began to pick herself up again Issa ran against her. It was not precisely a conscious decision. But neither was it entirely a surprise to her as she did it. She felt her shoulder connect forcefully with Li's stomach; she put as much of her energy and weight into the tackle as she could. Li was jarred sideways on the step, knocked against the wall and started to fall. Her mouth made an out-puffing 'o' and then she was tumbling downstairs. The people coming up yelled with surprise and alarm, and a high-pitched voice called 'Arto, watch out!'

Issa herself rebound from her collision, and her back hit the other wall. She steadied herself. 'Come on,' she told her father. He was staring at her with the look of a man trying to process a blit. 'Come!' She heaved on his wrist, and he began bumbling up the stairs.

There was a loud commotion below them.

It went something like this. A man was ascending. His chunky, handsome head, shortcropped dark hair and a fierce expression, was on a level with Issa's feet. He was lifting something up towards her, except that it wasn't towards her, it was a gun and it was aimed further up the stairs. Somebody cried 'Arto!' and then the whole space was filled to bursting with *noise*, horrid deafening *noise*. It was so insanely noisy that Issa screwed her eyes tight, and the noise tripped over itself, like the devil's drumfill, and extended. It was guns being fired, of course, she knew that. But she had no idea guns could be so loud! Somebody punched her in the chest – right in the middle of the chest! – and, shocked, she opened her eyes to see that it hadn't been a punch. Rather, Christophe had knocked into her as he tumbled down. He was kneeling, strangely, and descending at the same time. She looked again and saw that he was sort of rattling down the stairs on his knees. That must be painful! But he had his arm out, too, and an antique pistol was in his hand, and it was chimneying smoke, and his eyes were shut, and then his gun fired again. She saw the momentary horizontal white stalactite of flame at its tip, and then saw its retinal afterghost printed upon the back of her eye. But she could also see hidden somewhere behind that jagged glare inside her eyeball, Christophe falling forward and continuing to tumble, face down now. His legs came up, bizarrely, and his feet wiggled. Then his whole head-down body rotated and he collapsed down the stairwell. Issa looked about her. The chunky, fierce-faced man had gone, and Issa looked again and she saw him pressed backward against the wall, with his head at a curious angle, and his arm straight up, like he was trying to catch a waiter's attention. She couldn't see his gun. But she could see that his shirt was soaked with black fluid. Then she saw that he wasn't breathing.

After all the great press of noise, it was ringingly quiet. Inside Issa's ears an angel was singing. The angel's song was one, pure, seamless, celestial note; but she understood what it was. It was: *home*. Rodion was three steps above her, sitting down, his mouth still open – but breathing, living, alive.

She pulled her father's wrist. 'Up,' she told him.

He did not have the power to resist.

There were more people downstairs, and at first she thought they would be armed, just as the fierce-faced man had been. But then a young lad came up the stairs, looking scared, and he seemed familiar to Issa, although she couldn't immediately place how she knew him or put a name to him. It would come to her. But he had no weapon. It was clear that he had no weapon. 'Come up,' she called to him, feeling that she had to take him with her as well. So he came up, looking at her with an astonished face. And behind him came a plump woman, and she knew who *that* was. And finally up the stairs, with the perfect mirror-logic of the grown-up world, came she herself, Leah, the real and consummate Leah.

'There is,' Issa cried, very loud, her heart full of happiness and weeping at the same time, 'no time! Upstairs! Upstairs!'

By sheer force of her will, she moved all these individuals to the top of the stairs and out on the roof. They were out. Issa was in charge now. They all rushed to the waiting flitter, and Issa pushed all the others in through the door before climbing in herself. The driver was protesting, and waving a pistol, but when she got in at last he put away his weapon. 'Li is dead,' she told him, with uncontradictable forcefulness. 'We have to go *right now.*'

'Do we have him?' the driver asked, gape-eyed.

'That,' said Issa, grabbing the pilot by the chin and directing his gaze towards where Rodion was tremblingly sitting, 'is Rodion. Now *go.*'

The driver looked at the whole cabinful of shorthairs who were now inside his flitter, but if he thought about arguing with Issa he immediately thought better of it. The door shimmered shut and the flitter lifted into the sky. It was five metres above the roof. It was ten metres up, and fifteen metres. The top of the Hough Wall was visible through the grid of the taller buildings.

'Wait,' said the driver, looking down. 'Isn't *that* Li?'

It was. She was there, emerging from the top of the stairs and through the frame where the roof door had once stood. It was unmistakably her, looking up at them. The flitter wobbled in its ascent, and stopped. It hovered.

Li on the roof was staring in rage, or bafflement, up at them. She had a weapon in her hand.

'We do not go back for her,' Issa told the driver.

'What do you mean?' he replied. 'Don't be crazy! What do you mean?'

'She is about to fire at the flitter,' said Issa, with total focus. 'See?'

'She thinks we're abandoning her!' said the driver, and Issa could see that her spell was broken. 'She won't fire if we go back down.'

The gong chimed. Or whatever it was. A proud, profound sound. A sort of deep-clipped, giant's cough, like a vast door being slammed a long way off. 'Look,' said Issa, her composure returning to her. She was in charge. She had never stopped being in charge. 'Look.' The driver followed the line of her arm. In between the buildings, the vertical line of puffing-out dust was clearly visible in the very middle of the Hough Wall.

You might have counted off the silent seconds, had you been there. One, two, three, four, five. 'That's not supposed to happen yet,' said the driver, in a low voice.

'We can't go *back*,' urged Issa.

Everything depended upon this. Everything came down to convincing the driver of this one thing: persuading him not to land the flitter back on the roof, but rather to take it higher and to fly away. Issa had never met him before that day. She did not know his name.

Then the wall broke in a thin vertical line, with a thunder-clap. Water came through in a great pillar that broke into two, like the pages of a white book being opened.

The flitter wobbled, and then began rising. The driver's eyes were on the wall. In moments they were far enough above the roofs to get a good view of the splinter that had appeared from top to base in the structure, and the blank pages of Atlantic water that were waiting to be written upon.

Issa went back into the cabin. 'Dad!' she cried, grabbing her father's two hands in her own. 'Daddy, it's me.'

He looked into her eyes. She saw what happened. She saw him understand her, not only her words but the wholeness of her. And then he pulled that understanding back into the shell of his head, as a snail withdraws itself. His eyes looked at her, but his soul did not. 'Who are you?'

'It's me, Daddy!' she said. 'You remember!'

'No,' he said, not loudly, but with great force. She saw right through the moment. There was a crystallized future, right there. He was going to have to choose between the changeling daughter who had his heart, who had brought him all the happiness of recovery and renewal, and the real daughter whose loss had caused him such pain. He could not choose them both, that was clear enough. It would become clear to him too, in time. He would have to choose the one or the other. Of course, the changeling had spent years growing herself like a bush of strawberry-red roses, all softness and thorn, about his heart. And of course, the real girl had spent years growing into something perfectly alien. But as she looked at her daddy, all her anger sublimed away, she thought to herself: I do not know which he will choose.

It all trembled. Her heart was the point around which the world pivoted.

Then his eyes opened wide, and water came out of them. 'Leah?' he cried, unable to hold back his love for her. 'Is it you? Is it? Is it you?' And he came over to her, and said; 'Oh my beautiful girl!'

Everything else fell away into the void. Nothing else mattered. She was weeping, and she called out, 'Daddy, my daddy' and embraced him. It was wonderful and terrible to feel his torso shudder with tears as she held him. He felt smaller, inside her hug; more frail. 'It's alright,' she told him. And the *all* and the *right* were equally balanced. 'It's alright,' she said.

'My beautiful girl!'

'It's alright.'

At that moment the whole flitter rang like a bell: a hole popped into existence on the floor, and a bigger one clicked open in the roof. Boom, boom. The noise levels suddenly increased, and air blew through loud as a snake's hiss. 'Come *on*,' yelled Issa, her face still wet, though she was no longer crying. She moved herself back over to the driver. Bundled by circumstance, and propelled only by her willpower, he zipped the craft forward. They flew in the direction of the Hough Wall. He had been told, Issa thought, that he was to fly back to the barge. Thinking quickly, she ran through possibilities. They would have to try and dissuade him of that. But that would come later. It was clear that she was in charge now, clear that her whole life had shaped her for this role. Right now, though, everybody was at a window, and looking down. The white foam was filling the bay like a latte, and as they flew over the last of the buildings they saw the advance line of the onrushing bulge break, with a great arc of lace and frill, upon the old docks of the city. The Hough Wall groaned like a living thing, and there was another gunshot crack. The pages of the book became a curved screen, and the story of turmoil and foam was visible upon it. Issa watched the mass of water fall through the air. And at the back of the flitter, Leah, her better half, her other self, her real being, her authentic copy, the *actual* her who did not (now that she came to look more closely) really look that much like her, spoke, her voice breathy and amazed and teenage in a way that Issa had long since lost the ability to parse, and which she would never recover: 'Oh,' she said, 'my,' she said, '*God*,' she said.

Water was pouring over the white wall now. It sparkled in the winter sunlight as if, oh my *God*, it was full of stars.